THE RAY OF
HOPE

JANET JOHNSON ANDERSON

Archway Publishing books may be ordered through booksellers or by contacting:

Archway Publishing
1663 Liberty Drive
Bloomington, IN 47403
www.archwaypublishing.com
1 (888) 242-5904

ISBN: 978-1-4808-9263-7 (sc)
ISBN: 978-1-4808-9264-4 (hc)
ISBN: 978-1-4808-9265-1 (e)

Library of Congress Control Number: 2020913380

Print information available on the last page.

Archway Publishing rev. date: 09/14/2020

Also by Janet Johnson Anderson

Avhi's Flight
After the Tornadoes, Reflections for Recovery

We must accept finite disappointment but never lose infinite hope.

—Martin Luther King Jr.

INTRODUCTION

Sometimes sorrow is obvious: rescuers finding drowned bodies, residents of the Lower Ninth Ward returning like refugees, the teary-eyed woman in a mud-stained housecoat standing painfully alone knee-deep in water.

Sometimes sorrow stays hidden and snakes its way into our hearts and thoughts when we least expect it: the high red line marking floodwater levels on empty buildings for example. This is subtle and not too alarming until you realize that if the people living there didn't leave before the storm, they probably perished.

On August 29, 2005, Hurricane Katrina unleashed its fury along the Gulf Coast, causing unprecedented death and destruction. Flooding of nearly two-thirds of the City of New Orleans multiplied the disaster, destroying homes and neighborhoods, and forever changing the lives of its citizens.

Despite the malaise of tragedy, each sunrise and sunset brought beauty to a landscape of devastation and debris. The Second Line of people following jazz bands breathed life back into the city's soul and brought jubilation to the suffering. The outstretched arms and hands of neighbors—first consoling one another and then working together, clearing a path for relief and renewal—reminded a nation that even amid fragility, there was hope.

Hope may not rise quickly, but it will also never completely fade away. Even without a clear vision for recovery, there is hope. When courage for the moment can't be found, there is hope. When the slightest glimmer of light and goodness pierces darkness and everything that is corrupt and evil, there is hope. When a voice can be lifted, there is hope. Despite tragedy and trials, and the unrelenting, insurmountable odds that many of us might face in the making of our life stories, if there is a spirit of community and love, there is hope.

This is such a story.

CHAPTER 1

PORT OF CAUTION

"I don't wanna lose this baby," she cried, and she squeezed his hand as she clenched her teeth, trying not to bear down. There was a wave of pressure, pain, a moment of relief, and then the wave again. His shirt was soaked in sweat. She feared a complication. He knew they needed to get to that hospital.

"I'm here, I'm here," Wynton reassured her. But he was anxious. He did not want to deliver his child like this. He didn't want to have to deliver his child at all. They were so close, within a mile of the hospital, when the engine stalled. But this early in the morning, who could expect more than a squad car on routine patrol? It had been thirty minutes since he stepped into the street waving his arms at an approaching van and it swerved to avoid him and sped away.

He was realizing that the vow of parenthood was quite different from the condition of parenthood, the latter of which required mental awareness to override emotional rawness. It seemed the whole world was drumming down on him as this drama unfolded within the confines of a car. It was not at all a matter of applying textbook learning, drawing on safe ideas, or cleverly exerting practiced techniques they had learned in classes. They were in the thick and thorny complications of childbirth.

He met Belinda's eyes in such a way that nothing needed to be said. The panic and emotional struggle of an all-too-real human condition had suddenly sent them into a clouded fall, reeling and tumbling head over heels. He prayed his soul would swell and for a moment take over his literal and practical life, rise from his chest, and inspire him to carve a way out of this dead end. His mind swam. The enormity of life and death without disguise permeated everything. The whole universe, perhaps, was participating in this whirlwind moment.

He glanced at the empty street behind them, then looked at his watch; the numbers on the dial ran circles around each other. Belinda moaned and clamped down on his hand. What could he do? If he ran, he could make it to Mercy in eight to ten minutes. He cringed, knowing they had left the house in a panic, with no regard whatsoever to what had been discussed and practiced. They had just fled without her bag or a cell phone. He had grabbed the car keys and they had taken off, certain they'd be at the hospital within minutes. All he had was his wallet from the hall table.

There were no homes, no front doors to knock on this close to the medical district; there was only the occasional office that wouldn't open till eight.

"I gotta get to a busier street," he told her.

"Don't leave me!" Belinda wailed as she fought another strong contraction. The baby's head had lowered, and she knew it would not be long before it crowned and she would have to push.

"Bae, I gotta get around a corner, and ..."

He hated leaving her, but if he had stayed, he wouldn't have found help. Fortunately, Keisha was born safely just moments after entering the emergency room. Her body, less than eight pounds, was strong, and he recalled how he felt when he first cradled her in his arms early that morning. Every trial, mistake, and joy crystalized in her fresh, bright, mesmerizing eyes; he was renewed.

Today was her birthday, and he missed her as he reminisced about her birth. It had been a harrowing night of confusion and helplessness, followed by sheer elation. Nothing brought him happiness like Belinda and Keisha. He savored the thoughts and let the vision of them linger and warm him. It felt like before, when he was with them—when he was complete and lived in a world surrounded by love.

Wynton paused, shook off the momentary memory and began surveying the throngs of people lumbering past his station, assessing who was returning home or just passing through. He thought New Orleans residents had a keen interest in the way others perceived them—a strange attribute from a people who defend and embrace traditions regardless of how odd or seemingly archaic.

Working in security for Customs, he knew the Port of New Orleans gave rise to unlikely forms of life: crazy vendors who curse at those who pass by declining to purchase their wares, old men with knee-length gray beards and dreadlocks, and cooks who carry lemons and spices in their pockets.

This, after all, was the place of grunge and ghosts, drawn carriages and cobblestones, nudity and rooftop parties—the place of Blue Dog art, drive-through daiquiris, streetcars, and go-cups. It was a place where humidity swathed the body in slow-melting ham fat, where Mardi Gras was a lifestyle, and where tawdry behavior burst along the seams of Bourbon Street. Unlike any other American city, New Orleans oozed with daring mysticism and outrageous whimsy.

It is never routine, he reflected as his eyes rifled through the crowd. New Orleans portrayed everything in life as fragile and precarious, and as though nothing should be taken for granted. He glanced at his wristwatch. 2:58. He'd take another welcome coffee break soon. That was when he spotted Eric and Sara Doussaint. They were grappling for their things after an overstuffed canvas bag had been searched and was spilling out onto the floor. They were too distracted by the disarray to notice anything else. Wynton, however, had a keen eye for trouble lurking among the mundane.

They have lost their edge, he thought, as he watched them gather their things. He spied out the station window at all the tourists shuffling down the gangway like sheep mindlessly clamoring along in a flock. He considered that perhaps after a few days at sea, the ocean waves had lulled and dulled their senses, quieted their instincts that could serve them well.

Louisiana's occasional backup in dry dock, and recent cruise scandals of illnesses and inept personnel, had slowed ticket purchases. Despite profit risk, companies were lowering costs, hoping to lure travelers back and gain an uptick in sales. Lowered prices attracted more people, and as far as Wynton was concerned, more people meant more criminal elements. Today was no different.

He spotted the ragged rail of a man with the Doussaints. He squatted alongside Sara to help her collect clothing and placed a small semitransparent cylinder in among the fabric. She had been played without knowing it—or she was part of the game. When Wynton approached them with his hand atop his sidearm, Sara looked up at his tall, statuesque figure with fear. Eric was already standing with his hands raised, asserting there had been a mistake, though he didn't know what the mistake could be since they had just arrived and had been cleared. Wynton motioned for Humberto Alvarez, a nearby guard, to assist him, and the two agents escorted the three of them to a small concrete room to the right of the escalators. Wynton's muscular frame made the room even smaller when he entered and stood beside Alvarez.

Wynton had seen enough innocent bystanders to know the Doussaints' confusion was genuine. He held them there nonetheless, to elicit whatever marvelous story this man, Marco Palerno, would concoct with them present. Palerno did a fair job of spilling the beans of their so-called mutual plan, his small part, and the fact that the vial, of course, remained in the Doussaints' possession. He did his best to sell the suspecting guards on his innocence.

But Wynton was keenly aware of the murky and quick-breeding efforts of criminals. The Doussaints were pale, and their mouths were open slightly; they were breathing too heavily, like fish out of water. Wynton was sure their heart rates had jumped ship altogether. He winked at them as he circled around the back of Palerno's chair, and leaning forward, slapped his hand on the laminate table in front of Palerno and told them that they'd all be taking a trip downtown.

Alvarez grabbed Palerno's thin frame under the arm and jerked him upward, cuffing his hands to lead him out the door. The Doussaints, fearing the same looming fate, stood up slowly. Wynton smiled and told them they were free to go. It had all happened so quickly; they were dumbfounded by the outcome. Wynton nodded and said again, "Free to go." A flush of relief washed over them, calming them, and they thanked him. Eric extended his hand, and the two men clasped a firm but friendly handshake as they moved toward the door.

Sara read the badge hanging low from his neck and spoke softly as she tenderly touched his forearm, "Thank you Mr. Ellery. Thank God you were here."

Wynton had honed his skills early in life amid large family gatherings along the Mississippi coast. Instead of basking in the rounds of applause or laughter like other relatives who had mastered the art of storytelling, he spent his childhood listening and observing. It seemed like a stream of conversations from aunts, uncles, and grandparents, all mingling in a living river of familiar voices. His people used stories to free their imaginations from life's dead ends, and in doing so, freed their listeners as well. It became normal to hear the same stories about kin over and over. He had come to expect that the moment a silent gap opened, someone would rush in to fill it up with words.

Wynton realized that when talking happened, other things did not. So he concentrated on how to be attentive and how to be present, never wanting to be anywhere else. Most people, Wynton speculated, believed they understood their lives, who they were, and their place in the sweep of things. They presumed they lived in a world that made sense. He knew all too vividly, though, that the rug gets pulled out from under long-held assumptions, that maps get misplaced, and that the narrative they've made about their lives can lose meaning.

Beyond intuition, Wynton had been grounded in his faith. He grew up lending credence to that still, small voice in his head that interrupted the rant of a fractured world. It was his belief that provided him a bit of serenity within the shock of life's chaos.

He was glad he had deduced the one-sidedness of the incident with Palerno, and he was happy to send the Doussaints on their way. Each day, he hoped he could live his faith. Today's test was just another small indication of how positive energy could affect others. He watched the Doussaints leave, completely at ease.

As Eric had expected, Sara was on her cell phone during most of the ride home. When they arrived, she tossed the driver two twenties, continuing her conversation, not waiting to receive change.

"Of course not," she said in a dramatic, breathy voice. "Who would suspect someone helping you." She then turned to Eric. "Honey, get the change, will you?"

"It's what I do," Eric replied, and he shrugged as he moved to the back of the cab to claim their money and luggage while Sara slowly walked ahead of him.

"Can you imagine?" she exclaimed, laughing as she cut across the lawn.

"It was no laughing matter," Eric chimed in as he swiftly came up alongside her, loaded down with suitcases, the canvas bag, his laptop, and her toiletry and cosmetic carrier. "Hey," he continued, "it could have been serious—dangerous if we'd been entering another country instead of our own."

"Eric!" Sara scolded. She stopped and then put her hand over the phone and gave Eric that look—the look that said, "I'm on the phone, and haven't we talked about this before?"

Eric pulled his bundle away from her and resumed his path straight for the door. As he was fumbling for the keys, he dropped everything in a heap and stood quietly at the door for a moment. Sara ended her conversation and came up behind him.

"Eric, are you okay?" she asked. There was no answer. She realized she had snapped at him and slipped an arm around his waist. "Honey, I'm sorry; what's going on?" she asked in a softer tone as she pivoted to face him. With her other hand, she tucked her phone inside her shoulder bag and reached forward to brush Eric's brown locks off of his face. She stared at him for a moment, still infatuated by his wholesome good looks and boyish charms. She recalled seeing Eric like this one time before, the morning after he had returned from his deep-sea fishing trip. Eric had said he'd been seasick, but clearly he had been emotionally shaken from that trip, not physically ill.

She caressed his cheek with her fingers and leaned forward to kiss him.

He embraced her, and they shared a long, passionate kiss. She shook her head, her red hair falling a bit from its pins, and pushed away from him as she spoke. "Now *that* is the way to end a vacation, Mr. Doussaint." Her smile was infectious. It spread from ear to ear above her thin chin, and her dimples and twinkling green eyes sent signals to Eric. He loved the way she could change him in an instant. Eric smirked back, pulling at his lower lip with his two front teeth as he paused to unlock and open the door. Raising a suggestive eyebrow, he motioned her in.

"Welcome home, Mrs. Doussaint," he said, humming as he followed her into the foyer.

CHAPTER 2

BACK HOME

"So what really happened down there, Eric?" Sara asked. He didn't want to talk about it at the time, but she knew going fishing with Jimmy in Mexico on the eve of an election had not been a good idea. Surely Eric had not actually thought it through.

He began by telling her they had not done any fishing. She reassured him, fishing or not, trying to understand Eric's need to get away that night. Jack was on the brink of winning the state senate seat for a third term, barely but decidedly squeezing out his opponent. It had been another bloodbath of showing no mercy to his rival, who stood his ground, refusing to buckle under the pressure of the press. Eric had been placed in charge of his father's campaign as a stepping-stone to get his name circulating among the state's movers and shakers. Only Eric was not comfortable with the dirty tricks and, most often, was clueless to the kind of influence his father used behind Eric's back. "Christ, if anyone deserved a break, it was you; Jimmy can get anyone into trouble without even trying," she said, consoling him.

Carlton James Guillot, Jimmy, was Jack Doussaint's senior bodyguard. Sara was certain he had a military background—Special Forces, perhaps. His muscular arms, rivered with popping blue veins, hung out and away from his body. He walked with a confident, rolling gait, and his crew cut drew attention to his squared, rock-solid face. He still addressed Jack and his business associates as "sir" and never seemed preoccupied, always ready to jump on the next task when asked. She didn't like him; he came off as being ruthlessly gritty and unfeeling, and wherever he went, trouble usually ensued.

"The men who travel and drink with him on these so-called fishing trips call him Mr. Clean," Eric stated. "Jimmy has embraced the name like a code of honor signaling he is a man that gets the job done and can come out of an unpleasant situation smelling clean—an underlying threat that he will carry out his mission without loose ends." He looked at her. "I really thought we were going fishing to get away from everything."

"I know," Sara said, nodding in agreement.

"But some matters of crime and punishment fall to the judgment of the streets," he continued.

"What is that supposed to mean?" she asked.

"Well, evidently keeping a lid on the cauldron of crime and commerce of sin means piecing together all the elements beyond Louisiana that influence New Orleans."

"I don't understand; what are you saying, Eric?"

"I'm saying the mob, the Mafia, Mexican warlords, and the cartel get away with murder. Literally." Sara watched Eric as he retrieved an envelope from the nightstand drawer. He opened the envelope, genuinely uncomfortable, and pulled out a dog-eared photo. She shot him a stare that demanded an explanation. It was a picture of a beautiful Hispanic woman. Her hair was coiffed to one side, and her bare shoulders modeled elegance.

"She's gorgeous; who is she?"

"She was part of the Mexican tour of my father's infidelities," he replied, wincing with awkwardness. "God, nothing has consequences, and every little thing has consequences." He turned to her. "As it turns out, she belonged to a partner of sorts down there, but she had an affair with Dad that was unsustainable. The distance, the clever games, whatever romance was there—it started to collapse. The partnership dissolved at the same time, and she got caught in the middle."

"Jack had a mistress in Mexico?" She didn't really focus on any partnership, but only that Jack had an affair in Mexico.

"I met her, Sara. We went to her home; she was charming." He swallowed his disdain and continued. "They used her to get back at Dad's connection down there. I had nowhere to go, and didn't know where we were except that it was out away from everything." He paused. Looking back on that dark day made him feel lifeless. He paled as he began an unnatural story.

"They took her into another room. I could hear the slaps, the thumps of punches, the birdlike sobs. I could imagine her broken nose, a blackened eye, her lips bleeding, the bruises she would have around her abdomen and back. It was as if time slowed and I was no longer a sensible being in a sensible world."

In fact, he had wished time itself had ceased. He remembered the dense knot tightening in his stomach, wondering whether there was a way back from this inner tumult of pain, confusion, and foolishness after having been in the midst of it all.

He began again, overwhelmed by his own weakness as he was by the unfolding violence and cruelty of that night. "I could see her, Sara, when they came out. She was hunched over, breathing sporadically … I … I could see her afterward balled up like a small girl without a defense. She needed tending to—sutures, ice, help of some kind. Jimmy and his henchmen came out and shoved me out the front door into the car before I could say anything."

"My God." Sara passed her hand through the thickness of her long, wavy hair. Her lean limbs braced her as she reared up in bed. Eric was nearing the end of his horrific story.

"As soon as we came back into the city, I jumped out of the car the moment I saw the police. Jimmy stopped the car with a screech, but I was already talking to an officer, so they sped off. I kept trying to tell the officer that a woman in a mansion along the coast needed help. Instead he spun me around, cuffed me and threw me in the backseat of his squad car. He said I should leave things alone and leave town as he drove me farther into the city. He stopped, yanked me out of the patrol car and took the handcuffs off. I stood there rubbing my wrists from the pinch, trying to absorb what was happening. The cop told me I didn't belong and said he was going to look the other way." Eric turned to Sara. "I … I was dumbfounded. Then he yelled at me to beat it. My head was spinning, but at least I had enough sense to take off. I jogged until I got back to the center of town. The bright lights made me feel safe again as I walked to the hotel." He looked at Sara to see whether she understood.

She rolled over onto his chest, adjusted the sheet-twisting blankets, and asked, "Is that when you called Jack?" Her body pasted itself to his skin, and she drifted into the familiar smell of him.

Eric nodded. She knew it would have been the last thing he'd have wanted to do—have his daddy save him. "Yeah," he said calmly. "they sent a car for me, and I was home the next afternoon." They both sat in silence for a moment.

"How'd you get the photograph?"

"Oh, Jimmy threw it at me in the backseat as we were leaving. He was angry at me because he was angry at Dad. I've never seen him frustrated with Dad before, but he said this was not what he signed up for. I assume he meant harming women."

Sara rolled back onto her back, and the two of them floated for a few minutes in the numbing pool of life and love, of business and its cold, un-earthly impulse. Sara sensed Eric's wounding from having experienced such desperation and his own unheroic role. She finally understood the passive disconnection that washed over him those few days after his trip. Sometimes there was conversation, sometimes silence, often a dark pit close to depression, with restless nights and pointless days.

They stared silently at the ceiling above them, a linen of paint and pine passively engaging their thoughts, gathering all the light and air of the room, calm and composed even as the roof overhead bellowed in the wind.

Sara rolled back up on Eric's chest and reached beyond him, fingering at the pack of cigarettes on the nightstand, pulling them closer to her grasp. After tapping the pack, she pulled a Newport out and rested it between her lips as she looked for the lighter. Eric caught the tip of it and pulled it out of her mouth and sent it sailing across the bed. "You need to stop smoking."

"I'm going to; you know I am as soon as I am pregnant."

Eric seemed relieved now that he had finally opened up to Sara. He had held his story in for so long that now he not only felt the weight of his burden lighten but also felt closer to Sara, having shared his experience with her.

"Well, we'd better get busy then," he said as he sat forward to meet her chest-to-chest. She grinned as his hands closed in around her back. Her mouth opened and moistened as she leaned in to kiss him, when the phone rang.

"Don't," she said, climbing onto his thighs, scooting to straddle his hips.

"Have to," he replied. "He knows we're back." She tried to kiss him and arouse him, distract him from the ringing, but he pushed her aside and leapt toward the corner chair and the small table nearby to pick up the phone.

"Yeah, not bad," he replied, turning to see Sara had found the lighter and had retrieved a new cigarette she was about to light. Eric cupped the phone and whispered, "Not in bed, Sara; c'mon." She gestured, raising her shoulders and open palms as if to imply she didn't know what he was talking about. He shook his head and turned away from her, fingering the shade along the bay windows. He could see a portion of the neighborhood, the typical upper middle class subdivision of homes built high off the ground along the lakefront, with live oaks and trimmed boxed hedges as boundary lines.

"Yeah I know," he said into the phone as he eyed a neighbor trying to kick-start his old Harley. "Piece of junk," he muttered. "What? No, no, the neighbor," he assured the party on the other end.

Sara knew it was Jack. Eric could never get a word in edgewise as his dad rambled on and on about one venue or another.

"Yes, fine, we'll be there." He stood upright, bolstering his confidence as he said goodbye and hung up the phone. He looked at Sara.

"No, not on our lovely day off," Sara quipped.

"It's important, and we can be there and back within a few hours," Eric replied.

"Where's there? And don't you mean we'll be there most of the day?" Sara sighed. "Why don't you ever say no, Eric?" she asked, though she knew exactly why. Eric was in the last semester of law school and received a hefty monthly income as heir to his majesty.

"Look," he pressed on, "he bankrolls everything we have, everything we are. If we have to show up here and there, so be it."

"Yes, I know." Sara shrugged as she lay back down, inhaling a smooth, white stream of smoke.

"C'mon," he said as he darted back under the sheets to her, "we have time before the game; let's just start our day right here."

Eric was a creature of finely tuned routines and stayed in check between watches and calendars. He had a need for schedules. He believed that by following a precise regimen, one could somehow keep the disorder of life at bay. Everything about him was planned for except the occasions when his dad would call to request his appearance at social engagements.

Sara was romantic and impulsive. She would be the first to admit she broke composure more easily and didn't always maintain a cool head. But the two not only complemented each other; there was an unseen gravitational force that allowed them to easily slip into each other for comfort and emotional truth. They awakened in one another, and there they saw the illuminating semblance of something greater than themselves because of who they were when they were together.

Still, Sara never misread the innuendos, the coordination and coincidence of a nod and someone ending up in the hospital. She wondered how Eric could be blind to so much of what ensured his dad's movement through power. There was, after all, a considerable amount of hand-wringing around Jack Doussaint. He allowed very little latitude and was mindful of vetting who was and who was not ready to get in bed with the combustive elements of politics. *Eric must attribute it all to his wealth*, she thought. After all, Eric himself was under pressure to perform because of the money. He never really tried to see what the money actually did, who it went to, and why it went there. She didn't believe Eric actually knew and looked away; rather, she believed he was aloof to his father's political scheming.

Sara thought that Jack, like many, eager to unlock the door of power for his own gain, was born first with luck, and then with the willingness to listen to the animal within and know when to show its teeth. Sara could only guess for herself. The clues were there, but Jack's entourage was too slick to ever connect him directly to any foul play. Someone was always set up, duped to take the fall, and she hoped it would never end up being Eric.

She squashed the little bit of cigarette remaining into the metal ashtray. Laying her head back down onto the pillows and rolling her eyes over to Eric, who had been watching her, she grinned. They would go, but they would make love first.

CHAPTER 3

WHO DAT

Wynton fingered the frame that circled his wife and young daughter; the pewter was wearing from his regular caress. He missed them so much. It had been three years, but the pain had not lessened with time as everyone had told him it would.

"Wish you was here with me," he said aloud. His mind puckered with visions of them burying themselves into his open arms, his own edges dissolving into the wings and wind and astounding light he imagined them now to be. He wished he could break free and empty himself of this life to join them.

He drew a deep breath and replaced the photo onto the small table in the hall next to the wire basket filled with mail. "Miss you, bae," he said as he let go, and then searched the drawer tangled with keys, rubber bands, pens, and stray nails, to retrieve the spare house key.

The lighting in the hall was dim, hushed by the brightness of the adjacent dining room to the left and living room to the right, where books filled white shelves to the ceiling and glass cabinets reflected the white lights like a summer sun shimmering atop water. This morning, like most, the yellow glow from the east windows and skylight spread out and filled the corners of the house, which helped to lift his spirit each day.

Raymond could never know the extent of Wynton's pain, but he would be the closest to understanding it. He was more than a brother and friend; Raymond had saved Wynton that tragic night three years ago when he could no longer bear the darkness that so easily sank into these same rooms.

Raymond knocked two times on the door and called out, "Up, ole man?" Wynton answered the door as he was placing the key deep into his front pocket. He was up, but he was groggy.

"Ray, we need to stop for coffee on the way."

"No. No way you making us late, E," Raymond replied. Between the two, Raymond felt Wynton was more of a man that he could ever be. Wynton had the stature and the deep tone of what Raymond thought was a real man, so Raymond had nicknamed his brother "Mr. E," a takeoff of "Mr. T," which had ultimately been whittled down to "E." Raymond took after his mother, pencil thin. "C'mon," he continued, "a big guy like you? We gotta roll in early nufh to squeeze you in your seat." Then he brought out a Starbucks cup from behind his back and held it up to Wynton. "'Sides, dogg, I got you covered."

Wynton pushed him backward playfully and closed the door behind him. "You're a mess," he said as they cut across the grass to the car.

The drive would be congested, as it always was on a football Sunday to Who Dat Nation.

"Man, E, done had me a sick time couple nights ago!"

"Really?" Wynton responded, completely unimpressed. "Who with?"

"Ah, dogg, you know I don't kiss 'n' tell. But you know," he tapped his brother in the side as he drove, "she liked her shots, and lemme tell you, before we finished them drinks, her blonde hair was across my lap."

"You didn't do nothing," Wynton chuckled as he raised the still steaming thick brown paper cup to his lips.

"Yeah, well I wudda, except her ole man done shut the place down. She was willing, brutha man. Ooh, she was a dime," he swooned. "Like a white Kelly Rowland."

"Rowland, huh? I thought you was loving Keri Hilson."

"Sheeiit yeah, who ain' wanna bone that Hannah. Just saying who she be like, dogg."

"Dream on, Ray," Wynton chimed in.

"Nah man, she was all mine." He grinned. His thumb was tapping out nervous energy on the steering wheel.

Wynton situated himself into the old Cougar. It was a bit small for him, but it had a V-8 under the hood, and he enjoyed riding as he had in the old days. Half his coffee gone, he wondered whether it was the six-year difference or whether Raymond was just hell bent on never growing up. "So are you going to see her again?" he probed.

"E, we meeting today at the game," Raymond replied.

"What? No. No we not," Wynton snapped. "I'm not busting someone's butt because you can't keep your pants zipped," he vowed in a labored tone.

"Look, E, would I do that?" Raymond asked, trying to sound sincere.

"Yes, have," Wynton said.

"Cold," Raymond quipped. "You and me, we seeing the game alone—the bruthas, 'kay? Then at half-time, I is gonna be off for a little intamission fun." Raymond positioned himself in his seat, thrusting his pelvis and looking at Wynton for approval.

"Boy, you don't never stop." Wynton smiled back. "One of these days, it's gonna catch up to you." Wynton thought Raymond was scrawny and immature, but he'd always had a way with the ladies. "Just drive, Ray; just drive," he cackled as he pushed a disc into the car's CD player. "Seven Steps to Heaven" came on. Wynton settled back, letting Miles Davis seep into his bones.

"A'ight, E, see? That's what I is talking 'bouts; relax and have a good time." Raymond made a hip-hop motion with his arm and hand, knowing he could easily make his big brother laugh.

"Yeah, Ray, it'll feel good to be off duty and just kick back," Wynton agreed as he closed his eyes, focusing on the music.

"And Mikey's gonna do right by us too." Mikeal Shelton had been a long shot, but he had found a place on the team. He hadn't played in a game yet, but he was suited up each week. He was a star to his family and friends, who had watched him rush for the all-time record at Baymont High and play special teams with the Alabama Crimson Tide until his junior year. That year his collarbone wouldn't set right. They had to break it twice more, and he missed all his senior year. It was a miracle anyone picked him at all after not playing an entire season. But Mikeal looked good at the professional tryouts. He was fast, just like his younger teammate at Alabama, Mark Ingram, only Ingram had managed to stay healthy all four years, and this year he was on his way to the Heisman if the Crimson Tide could continue to surge ahead. "Look; Mikey done bin a great plug. Maybe we can meet up with him after the game," Raymond remarked with enthusiasm.

"You're right, Ray; it's going to be an easy day." Wynton nodded, his eyes still cinched tight. He knew Raymond was concocting something, but he conceded to the thought of a day off, a football game, and some time with his brother. "You'll grow out of it one day, Ray," he mumbled as he rested his head back against the seat. The sun was shining on him, the motion of the car starting to lull him as they rolled east on Interstate 10 to New Orleans. Donaldsonville was only forty minutes out from New Orleans, but with game traffic, the trip would take them twice as long. He wouldn't miss anything by dozing off. I-10 was a raised, lonesome highway over swampland punctuated with few exits and a nondescript view. Raymond glanced over at his brother settling into a nap, glad to see him letting go.

"That's right, you sleep." He quickly punched the radio buttons, turning on WYLD. "Transform Ya" by Chris Brown was playing. "Cool," he whispered to himself. As he drove, Raymond thought about his big brother.

Wynton coveted the photos he had of his wife and daughter. But there were only a handful which included him, as he always managed to avert his eyes or turn his head altogether as a camera snapped, not wanting to be captured on any day at any place in time. Raymond loved the photo he kept folded inside his own billfold: his favorite shot—the one where Wynton was stooped slightly, speaking with some unknown woman. The camera had caught that fleeting moment each caught the other's eyes. He had not bent his head to one side to avoid being photographed. Instead, his posture, face, and hands were all telling of the brother he knew well as a compassionate, honorable, faith-filled man.

Wynton did not like being examined too closely by a lens, which he felt only challenged the appearance of who people were. He cared more about what the lens did not capture—the inner workings of who people really were. Still, Raymond thought the picture he kept of Wynton was priceless. At thirty-four, Wynton looked ageless. The photo of him could have been taken during any era. His naturalness in uncomplicated white clothing; the smooth, dark caramel cast of his skin; and his face, which absorbed all light and made him look luminous, as he looked now, asleep in the sun—golden. He was classically handsome and revealed an inner glow, a peek into his heart and mind, a glimpse into the kingdom he served. His calming presence, Raymond thought, could take one's breath away.

Wynton was entrenched in a vision of the waterfront, where he felt so at home. Raymond looked again at Wynton, studying him. Where others seemed broken and barren inside, or without defense or desire, he saw in his brother a pure and wondrous temple of faith, a splendid heart, and a sound and humble mind. He could have been jealous or dismissive toward his big brother, whom he could never emulate, but he wasn't. He saw Wynton's goodness better than anyone, and he loved and cherished him all the more because of it. He himself was a gangly tumult of emotions and was quite certain that when heaven rooted in a particular person like his brother, it could not possibly be successfully transferred to someone else, certainly not to him. Wynton had a vision of hope, and Raymond wondered what comforting meditations, if any, could possibly find their way to him. Would they come to him? Could they whisper something beautiful to reassure him as they did to Wynton? The two were so different but were so aligned with one another because of blood.

Today, Raymond thought as he drove, *is going to be a great day*.

CHAPTER 4

LEVERAGE

"I know you, Eric," Sara said. "Once you're there, you can't back out."

"Honey," Eric beckoned her, "these are important men for my father and for me. Congressmen, the senator. You know I hope to work with Senator Avery someday soon. We can't fend off Dad's money if I don't have a job," he reminded her. "C'mon; it's the skybox, free food. We'll leave after half-time; I promise. I just need to be present. The path is set for me; I just need to complete the steps."

"And where do we fit in, Eric? Huh?" Sara asked, agitated at his father's control over him.

"Baby, we are in this together, carving out our life together, planning a family." He did a little bump and grind to break the tension.

Sara smirked and headed to the bedroom. "All right then," she called back down to the living room, "I'm not pregnant yet, so I'm drinking."

Eric wondered for a moment what their lives would be like once Sara got pregnant and had to quit smoking and drinking.

"I'll be eating more," she called out. "I know what you're thinking, Eric Doussaint." She did. It always amazed him that she could tell during a long pause what idea was running through his head.

"God," he exclaimed, climbing the stairs, "I wish I could put that sixth sense of yours to work for us."

"You can't afford me," she teased.

He didn't really want to afford her. Eric thought her abstract photography was invariably boring. He thought photography was by nature an abstract of reality, always of something, so attempts to make it appear to be of nothing seemed silly. Photography as an art meant one had to have the eye to see it, the yearning to create it, and a body of work with personal spin. Sara, at her best, was only chronicling her life at ground level.

Yet Eric knew that photographers, unlike photographs, benefitted from great age. He supported her efforts with patience—perhaps more patience with her than she had for herself. She was feisty and too eager to make a statement. Eric thought that if she settled into the flow of this art, she might end up like Imogene Cunningham. Cunningham, who was never much better than just all right, had covered so much time and territory that the sheer volume of her work had helped her to become the art photography world's unofficial mascot. His mother and her sister, Aunt Isabel, were fans of Cunningham. Although she didn't pursue her interest, his Aunt Isabel had an excellent eye for photography. She was, Eric thought, the only person on earth who could take Eric's picture without causing his soul to vanish.

Sara appeared in the doorframe dressed to impress.

"Wow, when you give in, you give in all the way," he said, gawking as if he'd seen her beauty for the first time.

"Will Daddy approve?" she sneered, not really wanting the adulation.

"Just a minute," Eric said as he rushed by her to change into something more appropriate for business. Hopping on one foot while pulling up a sock at the foot of the bed, he noticed Sara's birth control pills atop the dresser. With both socks on and his pants up, and swinging his arms through his striped button-down shirt, he reached for the oval yellow container. Half the month's pills had been punched out. He paused, wondering if Sara could read his mind now, with him having just discovered she wasn't trying to get pregnant at all. He placed the package back on the dresser, scooped up the brush, and ran it through his hair a couple of times. He looked at himself in the mirror. The image seemed to mock him. Who was this man his father was refining? Who was this husband now filling with questions? His thoughts dimmed as Sara called out.

"Eric!" Her singsong voice rang clear. He appeared in the hallway, not sure of what to say. "It's going to be hell after Lake Pontchartrain," she said, and she was right. On game days when the Saints were in town, traffic was backed up in every direction. The bridge from Mandeville into the city was a forty-minute drive without problematic traffic. Today, emptying into I-10 would be a parking lot, and it would be quite a haul driving into the sun. Ever since Katrina, nothing generated quite the masses as the rallying of Saints fans; the Who Dat Nation had come alive to rescue the souls of survivors who had lost so much.

They took the silver BMW. The X5's lighter interior would make the drive more comfortable. It was mid-October, but the weather was still in the upper eighties. A bright sun could make it feel like summer again. Eric liked the elevated feel of the SUV. He didn't often drive the X5, but it felt right for a Sunday game. He had a new polished blue Z4 cooling its wheels back in the garage. This was Sara's bimmer, and it smelled like her, lightly fragrant. He drew a deep breath in, enjoying her scent.

He thought back to the image of her pale yellow plastic pill container and visualized the display of half the package of small white pills and the empty, punched-open silver foil slots. He didn't know what to make of it. He couldn't clearly calculate or restrain the questions running through his head. He felt as though he had been struck blind, suddenly groping and stumbling where he had been confidently standing a moment before.

He wondered how this God of Sara's would interpret the situation. He didn't believe that God tested people with things like diabetes or the seeding of tumor cells any more than jimmying floodwaters or pitching hurricanes at the coast. He didn't believe God planned AIDS or heart disease. God didn't trigger rock slides or volcanos. But he wondered, *If God does not cause everything to happen, does he cause anything to happen?* Did God stick a finger in now and then? Did he budge, nudge, hear, help? Was God out of the loop completely?

Sara was an avid reader and had read him excerpts from Annie Dillard about how she thought God was oddly personal and that sometimes, dazzlingly or dimly, God showed an edge of himself to souls who sought him. Ms. Dillard suggested that God suffered the world's necessities along with followers, suffered their turning away, and joined them in exile. Eric believed that everyone lived in what they sought. So what hidden part of Sara had shown up in plain sight in the form of birth control pills?

He had so many questions for her, but he figured they'd discuss it another time—not now, while he was forcing her to accompany him to another one of his father's events. Sara was staring at him when he shook off his reflections and focused back on driving.

"Where've you been?" she asked.

"Huh? What?"

"You were somewhere else just now," she remarked.

"No, just this monotonous traffic," he replied.

"Hmm," she said, and she turned to look out her window at the water as they passed by. It was a boring drive, with the same elevated four-lane concrete road going on for miles and miles across the same brackish brown water with small, rolling whitecaps. The cars jockeyed for place among each other until the end of the bridge. And there was no conversation for the ride. Sara knew that from time to time she said too much about Jack, took too many negative shots, goaded Eric on. She realized this was mostly due to her own insecurity, but the tenor of their marriage had seemed to change in the last year. She would say something, and Eric would distance himself. She hoped they would never become like other couples they knew who seemed to be living in a steady state of gentle decline. She observed that the day was clear, free of clouds, and she supposed not much would dampen their Sunday together, even if it was by command of the great Senator Jack Doussaint.

CHAPTER 5

GAME ON

"Fifty-yard-line seats!" Raymond exclaimed. Then he paused. "Damn, we behind the wrong team. The Buffalo Bills! Man, c'mon!" He shoved his hands into his front pants pockets like a pouting child.

"Hey, it's the middle of the field, so what?" Wynton remarked. "It's not like New Yorkers are going to come down here to witness their own ass-whooping, Ray. Saints fans are everywhere."

"Uh huh," he conceded, "guess you right." Wynton never argued. He wasn't competitive with anyone that way. But neither did he require much time between hearing an opposing point and refuting it. Raymond turned to the field with his arms spread wide open in agreement with his brother. "This like being on the field, only better. We not gonna be knocked round like them cameramen." He smiled that wicked "got this" smile that was so fashionably Raymond.

The Mercedes-Benz Superdome had been repaired and renovated, and everything around them was shining like new. The Saints' fight song was blaring, and people were filing in and filling seats here and there. Raymond liked to watch people and guess what their occupations were, whether they were married or not, whether they had kids or not, and what motivated their presence or attention. Even waiting with nothing to do was fun for Raymond. The same was not true for Wynton. He didn't like to observe people for fun; that was what he did for a living.

"Ready for a beer?" Wynton asked. He pulled out some cash and waved it at Raymond.

"I is always up for something if you paying," Raymond answered.

"Abita?"

"Yeah, fine. You finna swing by King's Table too?"

Wynton crossed in front of him, understanding Raymond's request for shrimp as he started down the row toward the aisle of stairs. He nodded and waved his left hand with the money up in the air as an answer. Turning around to sit down, Raymond caught the eye of a woman with two small children behind them.

"How you doing?" He smiled at her, assessing that she was way too put together for a mother of young children—certainly too pretty for the likes of the guy next to her, who was adjusting the bulge of his belly over his lap. "Uh huh," he mumbled to himself, his back to them now. *They're always ready*, he thought. Society's image of motherhood had extracted sex completely from the picture, but he knew better. He knew women and the fire that burned in layers deep beneath their skin, the flame beneath nightgowns, and the heart's begging for permission.

Raymond thought Wynton didn't notice women because he was too immersed in his own genius. He was, for the most part, self-educated; but having been born a genius, he was always trying to drag Raymond into a conversation about physics, Shakespeare, or the Bible. He didn't agree with Wynton that everyone was on his or her best path to wisdom. Of course, Raymond himself would be the first to admit he was not on any path to wisdom, but only women for now. He quickly switched the focus of his thoughts to his rendezvous at half-time.

Wynton returned carrying a container holding two beer cups and sandwiches.

"Gonna need two dome foams to wash this down, dogg," Raymond quipped.

Wynton handed the container to his brother, and then, looking past the family behind them, he spotted the vendors filing into the stadium with beer or boiled peanuts strapped to their chests. He smiled as he mimicked his brother. "Got you covered, dogg." He pointed to the aisle closest to them as he reached into his pocket for his money clip.

"A'ight, my man," Raymond responded. Wynton stood waiting until a beer vendor was nearby; he motioned with his arm and hand with money in it. Two beers were sent down the row, and Wynton's money passed on up the row to the vendor. He turned around and sat down with a beer cup in each hand. Raymond set one sandwich on Wynton's lap and grabbed a beer. They both took an exuberant swig from their cups, then placed their second beers down on the concrete beneath their seats. When they looked at each other upon rising back up, Raymond raised an eyebrow and nodded ever so slightly backward, over his shoulder between them.

Wynton bent his head down, shaking it while laughing. He knew what Raymond was referring to and what his inference meant. "C'mon, Ray; the game is in front of you, there on the field, okay?"

They both laughed. The Bills were taking the field. Soon the fanfare and fireworks would start and the Saints would come running into the stadium.

CHAPTER 6

SETTING THE PLAY

A quarter mile down the street at Geaux Saints Bar, three grim figures discussed their plans and chanted their mantras of revenge. The older, heavyset man raised his bourbon for another gulp. Slamming his empty glass back on the bar, he motioned to the bartender for another as he sneered at his two less-sophisticated colleagues. "This time Doussaint pays." The two men nodded. "He doesn't send his crew down to sniff around my backyard," he scoffed, "without paying a price."

Imon Durrell was not cartel, but he was also not too distant from the Mexican Familia and had prowess in the underworld. He was a scuttling toad of a man. His salt-and-pepper hair was slicked back and hung in a wave at his collar. Though he was overweight, he never perspired in the heat. His face was heavily lined from years in the sun, and his dark eyes were slight, hooded by heavy, draping lids. He had safely, quietly smuggled in the drugs and front money Jack Doussaint used to set up his political opponent. Doussaint, however, had seemed to misplace his loyalty when Durrell moved in to set up shop. It seemed to him that Doussaint's memory shortened as his line of bodyguards grew.

"So do you have your stories straight?" Durrell asked with guttural authority as to their murky conspiracy. The two lanky Cajuns answered in their southern French drawl that they did and that they were prepared. Durrell looked them over. Their faces were ruddy, wooden, snake-eyed. They were in jeans, black Saints jerseys, Saints caps, and even black Air Jordans. "That's the look; when you get inside the gates, one of you pick up a beer and get a souvenir or a flag—something to stick out of your back pocket," he ordered.

"Goddat," Lester Clay replied. He then asked, "boss, why we not goin' fer he's famile?"

Durrell lapped at the last few drops and darted a look at him. "This hit is better than family," he said.

"Dis gon hurt 'im?"

"Yes, in a very big way." Durrell smiled.

Clay and Trice LeMonde gathered their money and sunglasses, adjusted their scraggly hair and caps, and then swaggered from the bar to the entryway and slipped out into the shock of sunlight. Durrell was on his phone, cautioning his driver to pick him up in the alley behind Geaux's kitchen. He left a couple of crisp Franklins on the grease-slick counter as he bolstered himself. He then glanced around the dimly lit vacant joint for anything out of the ordinary and eased through the swinging door out the back.

Sealed inside the rented black limo, behind darkened glass, Durrell nestled into the smell of leather and money. It wrapped around him like a fur. His driver waited, facing forward, as Durrell called his standby. He tapped the glass in front of him twice and the driver shifted and moved the car into a line of traffic.

Durrell spoke harshly. "I don't care; you stay on them ... make sure the job is done." He reached into a side pocket for his vial of coke and, with his index finger, rubbed a small amount of cocaine across the gums of his upper teeth. "Listen," he snarled, "you take them out or I will send someone to take you out." He listened to all the reasons it would not be easy to find a clear shot at both men among the crowds of people, but he didn't care. "Stick 'em, then. Do whatever it takes as long as they've done the job and the kill points back to them." After an exaggerated sigh, realizing the beefed-up security the Saints had demanded as of late, he conceded begrudgingly, "Look; I know this Brees guy is suddenly the big star, but you're an expert. You can do this." Summarizing the final details with his co-conspirator, he then said, "This is our last conversation."

Durrell closed his sleek platinum flip phone and tucked it into an inside breast pocket of his suit coat. The roads were clogged in all directions. "Back to the penthouse!" he shouted to his chauffeur. The driver nodded once and veered into the next open left lane as they neared the interstate ramp. Durrell reached for the mobile oxygen mask and tank that remained on the backseat floor for moments like this, when he felt his lungs squeezing to catch air.

CHAPTER 7

ENTERING

It was complicated, VIP parking, but it was worth bypassing the ridiculously long lines of people entering the gates. Isolated parking had its rewards, one of which was an elevator up to the skyboxes. Eric pulled in between the white lines and cut the engine, closing his eyes for a second as he listened to the ticking sounds the engine made as it began to cool. First out, he came around the back of the vehicle to open Sara's door. She stepped elegantly out onto the pavement. *Chic*, he thought. She was simple and elegant.

"Wondering why you married me?" she asked sarcastically as she took Eric's hand to stand up.

"Well, just wondering," he said.

"Something's on your mind you're not telling me," she remarked, pursing her lips.

"Let's get up there," Eric responded. He shut the door and pressed his key to lock it. The lights flashed, and the bleep of the alarm echoed as the two walked hand in hand to the elevator.

Upon entering his father's skybox, Eric was first greeted by his mother, who hugged him and, smiling, commented on how handsome he looked. His dad jumped in. "You're late, son; the game's already into the second quarter. Come on in." He ushered Eric away from Sara to the front of the room along the windows.

"Don't mind him, dear," Eric's mother said in a pacifying tone to Sara.

"Oh, I'm getting used to it, Renee," she replied. "Which way to the bar?"

"Dear, let me tell you, if you're trying to get pregnant, you need to stop drinking soon," she said discreetly as she put her arm around Sara's shoulder and led her to the bar anyway.

"Yes, I know," Sara said, "but I'm not pregnant today, and, well, here I am on our day off," indicating her preference to be somewhere else of her choosing.

"Yes, dear, I'm not too keen on the drive down from Baton Rouge for a ball game either," her mother-in-law stated in a cutting tone. "It is not always easy to be Mrs. Doussaint, is it?" That was not a question that needed affirmation, but a statement—a life sentence Renee herself was now serving. Though she did seem to assume her role with ease, Sara wondered how much of her lifestyle was by choice and how much had been heaved upon her simply for marrying Jack Doussaint.

Renee had the flamboyance and charm of a southern woman, but she was like a fine wine. Just the taste of wine can reveal where it was grown. She was no different. A tasty conversation with Renee easily revealed her rearing amid highbrow society. And just as wine aficionados learn to detect the enrichment of body, aroma, and technique, peeling away the layers of who Renee was, was a delicious complexity. Sara liked her and knew she had much to learn from her.

"Ramos gin fizz," Renee told the bartender.

"And a Creole Bloody Mary," Sara added

"Yes ma'am," he said, and he quickly served them.

Sara and Renee took their drinks and moved aside the crowd to the far corner. Once anesthetized, Sara could shift into neutral and let the chatter of the room waft over her. There was a sheer cloud of noisy narcissism circulating around Jack and his henchmen. She was unimpressed with the extravagant expenditure of hosting skybox parties to begin with, but the profitability of power represented today seemed over the top.

"Is she here?" Sara asked.

"Of course," Renee replied, and she pointed to the blonde woman in the gold lamé dress next to Senator Avery by the window. Her face held no trace of self-consciousness.

"God, how do you stand it?" Sara asked as she took a sip of her drink. She was referring to Maddie, Madeleine Breen, Jack Doussaint's mistress. She couldn't fathom the mettle it took to include his wife and his mistress in his affairs.

"Well, I just pretend she's not here, darling," Renee replied. "She's just for show, a sign of real power for all the big shots in the room." Her words seemed ordained. Reasoning flowed like a ribbon of truth, streaming out of her like delicate, courageous strands of silver.

Maddie made Eric uncomfortable too. He had lost respect for his father and felt sorry for his mother. Jack Doussaint was rude and brash, an ass most of the time who had not become successful by accident. He knew how to play the game. He knew whom to connect with and whom to trust—no one. That's where he thought others failed; they trusted someone close to them. Not Jack. He was a one-man show, a self-made billionaire who owned the highest seats in local government.

If you weren't a player wanting to join his troupe, Jack was awkward to be around with his drive to prove something all the time. For him, competitiveness was just a civil means of channeling his natural aggression. There were constant implications and secrets, and the dreadful convenience of vengeance. Jack was absolutely drenched in self-importance and abhorred the mediocrity he felt surrounded him. Eric knew he didn't want to be like his dad, but he was going to need his help to start to open doors. So he went along with his father's deals, made sure to be present, to be visible, so they would know who he was. Simply being Jack's son would alter every businessman's attitude toward him.

Eric gazed past the buzzing crowd of senate supporters to catch Sara's eye, and he winked. He held up his whiskey glass as if to say "cheers" and, smiling, downed the rest of his drink. Sara pursed her lips again, this time to gesture a kiss. Eric was raising his eyebrows up and down as he stared at her when he was interrupted.

Jack barged in. "You remember my son, Eric, Don?"

Senator Avery replied, "Yes, of course. Good to see you, Eric." He extended his hand. Eric shook his hand firmly, attesting to the strength of his character with his grip, and both men smiled. Don Avery was aging, but he wore his age well. His hair, which had a distinguished salt-and-pepper look, as well as his sideburns and moustache, more salt than pepper, softened his look around the edges. He was tan and impeccably dressed, and there was always a shine on his shoes. He was a born salesman, a hawker, weaving his tales greasy and thick for the ripened, affirming applause. Every bit the politician or the televangelist, Eric amused himself by thinking the two were essentially the same. One solicited money promising people of the state glorious outcomes down the road for their well-being during the next four years. The other solicited money while promising the masses glorious outcomes for their well-being too, down the road in an afterlife. Neither had the power to promise anything, and both were exhibitionists full of themselves more than they were filled with hope and desire to do something good or make a real difference for the people who funded their platforms.

If Eric was going to take office and become one of the rare candidates who really did desire to make positive changes, he would need to get on the good side of Don Avery. Senator Avery was the Ted Kennedy of the Louisiana legislature. He had been elected over and over and boasted of his compassion for the people of his state. They believed him, and why not? He was, Eric thought, a walking billboard for winning candidates. He indulged the senator by listening to his self-proclamations and his keen advice toward Eric's efforts upon graduation.

Sara and Renee remained tucked away in their corner, undetected in their conversations about the guests that surrounded them. Renee was a woman of integrity, so conversations were sensitive but probing. She had her own swamp-land language and accent, her own speed of speech; it was rich. Tense and tone shifted constantly as she shared her unique tidbits of wit and wisdom. She did not, however, have the fertile imagination Sara had. When Sara saw Maddie on the move, she poked Renee's arm. "It's almost half-time," Sara said. "Wonder where she is going?"

"Don't, dear," Renee swooned.

"Oh, I bet she's off to the ladies' room before the room clears. Think I need a visit myself." Sara smiled as she cast her gaze forward.

"Sara, don't play with fire, dear," she warned.

"Just a bathroom break, dear," Sara replied in a singsong voice without addressing Renee directly. She was already on the prowl, just a few feet behind Maddie as she headed for the door.

CHAPTER 8

HALF-TIME

The crowd cheered as the two teams jogged off the field still displaying enthusiasm for the game. Both teams had played well, and as the score suggested, this was a battle between the defensive lines. Brees hadn't been able to clinch a drive with a touchdown; neither team had. The Saints and the Bills had been held to field goals the entire first half.

"Mikey done did good, E," Raymond exclaimed. Wynton had been right; they were behind the visiting team, but everyone in the stadium was cheering for the Who Dat Nation.

"Yeah," Wynton agreed, "but I've downed enough beer to send me traveling, Ray."

"Hey, I told you the game was just you and me, brutha, but it be half-time, I is off to make a different kinda score."

"For real? I thought you were just playing me," Wynton responded with surprise.

"Do I kid 'bouts the ladies? E, man, I is kissing gold today." He pulled out a single gold-toned key on a chain and held it up for his brother to see. "Mikey done score big time for me!" Raymond flashed that boyish grin from ear to ear that so many women were drawn to. *He's got something*, Wynton thought. *He's small, but he has a dangerously beautiful smile and sincere eyes.* Raymond had no educational degree, but he was street smart and had the gift of conversation, including small talk and comedic interludes. He knew just what to say, and to whom, at just the right time.

Wynton reached out across his chest to tap the top of Raymond's head. "Guess you know what you're doing."

Raymond replied, "Truth. I ain' gonna be sitting up in here saving your seat for you to be releasing some beer, hear? See you when the second half start." With that he climbed over the backs of their seats and headed out and up the aisle the way they had come in.

"Oh, fifteen minutes is all it takes huh?" Wynton yelled to his brother's back. Raymond extended the universal middle finger signal for "not listening," and Wynton cackled a deep, resounding laugh as he watched Raymond blend into the sea of people streaming out into the pavilions.

A man's voice came over the loudspeaker, introducing the act that was about to take the field. A small percentage of fans remained in the stands and gave a half-hearted attempt to applaud whatever and whoever was about to entertain them.

Wynton grabbed his cap and headed the opposite way to find the nearest bathroom. He realized it *did* feel good, after all, to kick back with his little brother and enjoy a ball game. He hardly ever thought about his wife, Belinda, and his daughter, Keisha, when he was with Raymond. Raymond was either too amusing or too annoying for Wynton to think long and hard about himself. But they crossed his mind. For a moment he paused and thought how wonderful it would have been if they were with him today, here at the game, relaxing on a Sunday afternoon.

Belinda was a beautiful, tender woman with the same majestic strength he had seen in his mother and grandmother—a strength that spoke of the heroic survival of a lineage of African women who were stolen and placed into subjugation. These were women who had to reinvent themselves, find safety within themselves; otherwise, they would not have been able to endure their tortuous lives. One of Belinda's heroines was Eva Jessye, the first black woman to win international distinction as the director of a professional choral group, and the choral director who authenticated the sound of Broadway's American classic *Porgy and Bess*. Ms. Jessye said, "You should not suffer through the past. You should be able to wear it like a loose garment, take it off, and let it drop." Belinda often recalled and tried to embody that statement of freedom.

Though she worked for a small marketing firm, Belinda was a writer at heart. She struggled to bloom beyond the boundaries of feminism and color, and yet not completely erase her voice as a black woman—not an easy task. Wynton loved her for staying true to her convictions and moving forward toward her desires.

He paused, recalling the sensation of her fingers softly curled into his, the pulp of her kiss, and he bowed his head, trying to suppress feelings of loss. She would have enjoyed sitting here in the Superdome, exposing Keisha to another venue and culture.

Keisha would have resisted coming. Keisha liked dolls and dance, not sports and boys, but he felt sure she would have enjoyed the sights and sounds at the game. He could picture her in her cotton print with bluebells, her hair swept off her face by one of her favorite brightly-colored velveteen headbands. He smiled, reminiscing about how she liked to reach up and feel the velvet from time to time.

He took a deep breath, recalling how her skin smelled of peaches. He missed bouncing her on his knees and flying her around in the air. She was lanky, just like her "Uncle Ray-Ray," as she called him—all arms and legs. She was always hungry like "Uncle Ray-Ray" too. He thought about how she couldn't wait to help her mommy batter and fry catfish to eat them afloat in ketchup.

He missed her sweet energy and laughter and wished he had been given more time with them. Belinda and Keisha were dead to his touch, and he was lonely without them, but he clung to his memories of them, keeping them alive and near to him whenever possible.

Raymond, meanwhile, neared his rendezvous point, and felt strangely nervous. He had the key, so no one else was going to be there. Still, he was watching the corridors and those people who were stationary along the walls as he walked toward the door. She was, after all, a beautiful woman, and she obviously belonged to someone important who supplied her all those jewels. Maybe she had everything but excitement in her life. He supposed it could be a drag to be taken care of all the time. He thought maybe she just had jungle fever and was looking to switch from uptown to downtown long enough to feel alive. The more he thought about her, imagining her undressing and holding on to him, the more aroused he became and the quicker he walked.

There it was—for all practical purposes a dead end down the corridor. Raymond looked sheepishly around him as he approached the door. No one was paying attention to him at all. Women were streaming in and out of a restroom, but it was far enough away that they were easy to dismiss. There was a portly, bald Hispanic man about to lose his lunch near the trash can; but beyond that, no one else headed his way or seemed to pay attention to him. After a last glance, he unlocked the door and slipped in.

CHAPTER 9

WATCHING

The lines were swollen, ramps were thick with people, and there was a mixed smell of heating gumbo and jambalaya, and beer.

"It be hafh-time," LeMonde said to Clay.

"Just drank yo' Bud; we wun fid in," Clay mumbled under his breath as he and LeMonde strolled toward the exit to the skyboxes. They had been told their target would be meeting someone, and Clay wondered if any of the wealthy ever came out to be a part of the lowly crowd for just a bit before returning to their highfalutin airs. Clay and LeMonde watched the fans come and go, in and out of bathrooms, up and down the ramps with food and souvenirs.

"Oh dagumit," LeMonde muttered, "fogot de souvenir."

"Fogit it and pay 'tension 'ere," Clay snapped. He drank from his paper tumbler a couple of times and wondered how this was going to unfold.

"Jes like he ord'd." LeMonde smiled a distrustful smile. "We still fid in good," he added. The two were a bit anxious because of the uncertainty of their situation. "She bound to com 'roun, soon," Clay pressed. "We 'bout to git a move o'; you reedy, man?" LeMonde nodded. They were both ready, but the notion of how was rising fast. How were they going to take her down here in this crowd? They could move in alongside her and tighten into a mass of people and stick her. Or they could approach her and move her off into a remote area. Clay had pointed out a door ajar across from ramp 24 near the ladies' room—a supply closet, perhaps. It was obviously unimportant if left unattended. Maybe a mop or a pump was kept there for overflow. They weren't sure of its purpose, but they knew an opportunity when they saw one. For now they were content to wait.

Across the concourse, beyond their train of thought, a sharply dressed man in a charcoal suit and Windsor hat moved closer, keeping Clay and LeMonde in view. He didn't worry about fitting in. He was not going to be any of the players that would be fixed in the minds of any witnesses. He would never be near her. As he strolled, he twirled a toothpick around in his mouth—a habit he had engaged in since his teens, giving him something to gnaw on other than his thoughts. He had worked diligently on clearing and controlling his thoughts to focus on the job at hand—delivering the package of goods and nothing else. No mini dramas or hard-luck stories were going to sway him from his cold and calculated objective.

Behind the water fountain across from gate 28 was one of the three pieces he would retrieve. He came to find it empty. "Doesn't work," someone called out as he was about to lean down and push the knob for a drink. He turned around, facing the rush of people back and forth; pushed his hat up from his brow a bit; and nodded as if to thank whoever had spoken out. While he gazed out, looking for recognition of his acknowledgment, his left hand was busy behind the fountain, feeling its way toward the back of the porcelain bowl. There, taped along its smooth surface, was the thin, cylindrical silencer. He quickly recovered it and placed his hand, now cupping the piece, into his pants pocket.

He was on to the next stop, gate 26, where the men's room sprawled out across from the beer vendors. There he waited for the third stall to open up, entered, searched behind the flusher, and found a small, crumpled brown bag on the floor. He scooped it up off the floor and emptied it into his hands. The sleek black Glock 22 reflected the overhead florescent lights. He jammed the weapon into the back of his pants, flushed, and moved on.

At gate 24 he asked for a small box of popcorn. It came to him with a full magazine just beneath the layer of freshly popped kernels. He winked at the attendant as he gave up several dollars. The attendant took the money nodding, knowing fully what his part had been and whom this man, still rolling a toothpick around in his mouth, represented.

CHAPTER 10

THE DOOR

Sara was smiling as she filed in line behind Madeleine, her red hair tossing and bouncing with every determined step. She had a little spring in her swagger when she thought she was onto something. Right now she was full of herself, and her stature resembled a playful know-it-all with an air of sophisticated danger.

"Who does she think she is?" she said to herself as she squeezed past the remaining guests to clear the doorway from Jack's show-and-tell. Eric saw her pass and kept a watchful eye until she slipped past the kiosk and turned left. "Poor Renee," she told herself as she thought of the terrible price Renee paid for being the wife of a successful ass. To her surprise, Maddie quickened the pace and did not go toward the restrooms but turned toward the exit and headed down the stairs toward the ramps of vendors.

Now she was skirting past the throng of people without caution. Sara had been the one who bumped into the others as she kept her eyes focused ahead on Maddie's blonde hair instead of watching carefully for those around her. They were down one ramp and nearing the food pavilions by gate 24 before she knew it. There was a thinning line of women waiting for the public bathrooms. Sara wondered what she was up to—why she had chosen to leave the skybox and come down here to this bathroom. But Maddie slowed and moved past the restroom altogether, heading for a door at the end of the concourse.

Sara was astonished that the tables had turned and that Maddie knew exactly what she was doing and now Sara hadn't a clue. She decided to fall into line among the other women awaiting entry into the poorly ventilated bathrooms. She could keep an eye on Maddie without being conspicuous and just keep backing up, letting other women slip into line before her. She watched as Maddie looked left and then right, depressed the door handle, and cautiously stepped in.

Clay and LeMonde had her in view as well and thought she had practically come to them gift-wrapped, isolated from the crowds at her own whim. The two were relieved by the circumstances as they moved in. "She a looker," LeMonde remarked softly, glancing toward the women's restroom to notice anything peculiar.

"She dead," Clay rebuked. He was reaching down into his boot for his blade.

Sara had turned from her gaze for the moment, eyeing instead the number of women in front of her. Now standing in line, she suddenly felt the need to stay in line and use the facility too. When she turned back to look down the corridor, she saw the two men approaching the door. "Idiots," she said to herself. "They think that's the men's room." She then wondered what area lay beyond that pivotal door. Maybe they knew its purpose; Maddie obviously did. Where did that door take someone? She was curious, but her urge to use the facility kept her moving forward in line. She'd head over that way after her bathroom break.

For Clay and LeMonde, what seemed like easy pickings soon presented a problem. As LeMonde touched the handle, they heard more than one voice. The sounds were muffled but distinct enough to let them know one of them was the person she had planned to meet, as they had been told. LeMonde looked to Clay for reassurance. Clay said softly, "We own need her," determined to do the job right. The door opened slowly and silently as the two figures stepped inside the darkness of the room. Clay put his finger to his lips and motioned for LeMonde to fall in behind him. They stopped and listened to a swirl of sounds, breathing, groaning, the rustle of clothing. Clay whispered, "They fuckin'," and both men puffed up their chests with confidence. This distraction would make their job even easier. They carefully, quietly stepped past stacks of clean towels folded neatly on shelving toward a turn in the wall that led to a slightly brighter open area. Clay peered around the corner to find Madeleine bent over a laundry counter, her hair falling down around her bare breasts. Her gold dress was lowered down to her waist, and behind her, rooted deep inside her, was a young black man giving it his all. Clay moistened his lips and turned back to LeMonde. "She fuckin' nigre," he whispered in disbelief. LeMond wanted to see. He inched himself forward to lean around Clay.

"They goin' addit a'ight. He workin' her, and whoo, she startin' to sing."

The confusing mixture of murder and erotica suddenly excited Clay. Lust slipped down into his pants, and he cupped his crotch with his free hand. He moistened his lips and turned to Lester, whispering, "Keepa watch out." Then, quickly, without consultation, he changed their plans. He moved out from the shadows, catching the couple by surprise. Raymond, caught off-guard, had no time to defend himself as Clay leapt toward him and struck him with the handle of his knife, whipping him across the temple. Raymond was knocked unconscious and collapsed on the floor near the dryers, hitting the right side of his head on the concrete with a thud. Madeleine, trying to scream and kicking wildly, had been dragged back off the counter, her mouth cupped by Clay's thick, smoke-scented fingers. He dropped his jeans and moved into her from behind. He thrust and grunted faster and faster as she tried to straddle the counter and pull herself away. Just as he was about to peak, with a cruel jerk, Clay pulled her tight against his body and reached around her, stabbing the steel tip of his knife into the soft flesh of her abdomen. He jabbed and jerked from one side to the other, gutting her open, forcing a weak scream in a last airless gasp.

He quickly pushed her away, letting the blood burst shoot forward. It jetted down from the deep, gaping gash, saturating her as blackness rolled in and she slumped and folded into her pooling blood on the floor by the counter's edge. Hardly a drop splattered backward onto him; no killing had ever been as sweet. LeMonde, who had been keeping a watch for intruders, motioned for Clay to hurry along. It had been an easy and, for Clay, delightful job. Content they had done well, they emerged from the laundry room door. Clay tucked his shirt in and put his Saints cap back on. Just as he adjusted his hair beneath the cap, they each felt a pop, and their heads and shoulders were thrown back. Clay's hands were still up around his hairline as they hit the door and slid down to the concrete.

CHAPTER 11

IN AN INSTANT

Sara dried her hands as quickly as she could, hurrying to catch up with Maddie, who had slipped out of sight. She emerged from the damp and stuffy enclosure refreshed by the cooler air. She adjusted her waistband and turned toward the door to see the same two men she had seen earlier lying on the ground at the doorway she thought they had entered.

Completely taken back, she sensed deep in her bones that they were not hurt but dead. What should she do? Had Maddie done this? What *was* beyond that door? Any fear of the unknown situation gave way to her curiosity, and though she knew she should retreat, she moved forward toward the bodies. *Must have just happened just this minute*, she thought, because no one had taken notice just yet. Or maybe someone had noticed but had assumed the two men were drunk. She kept walking toward them.

Wynton was wondering whether Raymond had planned to return at all. It was already several minutes into the third quarter. Little mister rendezvous had obviously cooked up more than he had told Wynton about. Still, if this mystery woman was with someone else, she'd have to return to him shortly to stay above suspicion. He wondered what Raymond had gotten himself into. He was capable of loving and leaving, so where was he?

Sara eased up on the men, not sure what to expect. She gasped and covered her mouth with one hand when she saw the bullet holes in their heads. "My G-God," she stuttered, turning to see that no one was looking in her direction. In fact, no one was left in the corridors at all, and across the pavilion the beer vendors were cleaning up their mess from the onslaught of half-time fans.

She carefully pushed the door with her two forefingers, suddenly aware of leaving fingerprints. She felt she should turn and run, but where was Maddie? Where did this door lead to? It opened easily, and as it did, the two men's heads rolled down to the pavement, keeping the door ajar. Sara squeezed inside. Fear was starting to edge out her curious nature, but she inched her way carefully forward. She heard a soft groan from around the wall of towels and stepped into the light to see a crumpled body, lifeless and bloodied on the floor by the folding counter. It was Maddie. "What?" she whispered. What was going on here? She had gone to the bathroom, and Maddie was dead.

A thin-framed young man was coming to his senses, holding his head and positioning himself as he scooted upward. "Oh!" Sara exclaimed as she turned to run.

"Don't! Don't leave!" the man called out. "Help!"

Sara stopped and looked back at him. He looked confused, and there was no weapon near him that she could see.

"Wait," he pleaded with one hand and arm outstretched toward her. She could see one side of his head had some blood on it and his cheekbone was swelling, but other than that, he really wasn't hurt.

"Did you do this?" Sara asked anxiously, exasperated.

"No, no," he answered quickly. He was pulling himself up and looking at Maddie's body on the floor. His pants were fully unzipped, and he awkwardly covered himself as he stood up.

"Who are you?" Sara inquired urgently. Just then there was a scream and a clamor of feet just outside the door. "My God … what happened here?" Her heart was pounding and her vision blurred as she panicked. A pocket of air rose in her lungs, expanding with pressure, making it difficult to breathe. She didn't understand anything that was unfolding before her. Raymond had dressed, and nearing her, he told her they needed to leave.

A moment later, the entire room's overhead light flashed on and a clear, deep voice yelled out for them to freeze. "Hands up!" an abrupt voice bellowed as a robust man in a dark security uniform turned the corner with his gun drawn. Another man jumped forward and shoved Sara and Raymond face-down on the stainless-steel laundry counter.

Sara and Raymond knew better than to say anything just yet. "What have we here?" a third, surlier, man exclaimed as he moved into the light. "Messy," he said with a wince as he squatted down to lift Maddie's arm away from her face with his pen. "Three dead, two unharmed … what the hell," he said as he stood up facing Sara and Raymond.

Raymond reared his head and uttered softly, "We didn't do nothing." The first officer slammed his head back down with excessive force and told him to shut it. The third man, in street clothes, moved the hair from Sara's face with the same pen and asked if she'd had a good time this afternoon.

"This isn't as it seems; I just happened by," she said. Just as quickly, the same first officer shoved her head back down on the counter.

"You too, missy—shut it!"

CHAPTER 12

POINTS

Word was getting out, and a small crowd was beginning to fill the hallway. Two more policemen were there, ushering people back away from the scene. A patrol car with its lights flashing was coming up the ramp to shut off the only way in and out of the end of the concourse. Three ambulances were tightly wedged in a corner near the crime scene, the EMTs readying their gurneys to be extended and rolled toward the bodies.

Criminalists were already on the scene, deciphering physical evidence, and the coroner's office of forensic medicine was gathering clues that presented themselves near Clay and LeMonde. There was no powder on the bodies, so it hadn't been a face-to-face killing. They scoured the floor and walls for any extra shots to determine how many rounds, if any, the shooter fired beyond the two bullets that hit the victims. Once the bullets had speared neat, round holes through each man's forehead, they had pushed fragments deep into the brain, forcing blood and a watery mash of gray brain matter out the back side. First the men had hit the door; then they slid down onto the pavement. Using the path of coagulated blood, the criminalists were able to trace the trajectories of the rounds, and they then handed off the mechanics of the crime to investigators.

Yellow tape was extended around them as Sara and Raymond emerged from the door, their hands behind them in handcuffs. They were led to two black-and-whites, and each one was pushed down and into a squad car's backseat. A maintenance man had just shown up, and a couple more detectives were aligning the bodies from across the pavilion, trying to find the angle of fire.

The game, still close in score, had just entered the fourth quarter when

Eric and Jack walked into the clamoring of investigators and thrill-seekers. A rookie cop held his hand up. "Can't pass," he said as he prepared to fend off the two men who approached with certainty.

"I'm Jack Doussaint," Jack piped up, expecting to be let in immediately. He scrunched his face in frustration, as if he had just smelled something foul, when he was kept waiting. Eric's thoughts were scattered; he was clearly jolted by the bits of information they had received. Where was the mop of flaming red hair? He was looking in every direction except right in front of him, in the backseat of the car just feet away. Sara could see over her shoulder that Eric was searching for her and that he was noticeably shaken.

"Senator Doussaint"—the gruff, overweight detective moved forward and extended his heavy hand for a quick handshake—"I'm Jamison, chief detective. We've got a real problem here, sir." He lifted up the line of tape that cordoned off the area, allowing Jack and Eric to pass through underneath. "We've got three dead bodies and your daughter-in-law on the scene unscathed. Doesn't look good." Jamison turned to face them. "She says she knows one of the victims and that you know her too." He motioned for them to follow him past a large plastic barrier that had been set up to hide the bodies from public view.

Eric followed Jack as they turned and entered the area, still in shock that there had been a murder and somehow Sara was involved. He felt dizzy and looked pale. Jack seemed unbothered by everything except that he had been kept waiting. Jack stepped boldly forward as the coroner's assistant unzipped a full brown body bag to display Madeleine's face. Her features seemed distorted and were bluing from the loss of blood, but Jack could clearly recognize it was her. "She bled out," Jamison pointed out. "Gutted from side to side." He let the silence that followed hang in the air for a moment.

"How?" asked Jack.

"Don't know," he replied. "That's something maybe your daughter-in-law can tell us."

"Sara, Sara … Is she here?" Eric's senses sharpened.

"Come with me, young man," Jamison said belligerently, irritated that only someone with Doussaint's political clout could gain access to detained suspects. They walked back out the way they had come in, near the squad cars. Jamison motioned for the officer standing nearby to open a door.

Eric saw her. "Sara!" he called as he ran the last few feet to her side. She scooted forward and put her left foot out.

"No, no. Uh-uh, girlie!" Jamison called out. Sara was not to get out of the car.

Eric fell to his knees beside her and grabbed round her with all his energy. "Baby," he whispered through her thick locks. Sara began to cry.

"I don't understand any of this," she said, sounding desperate for him to shed some clarity on what had unfolded. "Take me home," she begged.

"I don't think I can yet," Eric said softly, and he kissed her cheek. "Dad's going to take care of everything. Don't worry, baby." His presence calmed her, and she guessed she could get through the uncertainty. As Eric held on to her momentarily, she reflected back on everything that had attracted her to him to begin with. Eric was a sensible man, and his stability made her feel safe, assured her that everything would be all right. "If only we hadn't come," he said softly.

"Shh," Sara said, quieting him. She knew he would blame himself. She took a steadying breath and said, "Eric, this is not your doing; just get me home."

Eric was moved back away from the car, and Sara's door was closed. "Look," Jamison stated, "you're gonna have to follow us downtown and fill out some paperwork. Better get your attorney down there with you too."

Jack nodded and then turned to Eric, telling him to head back up to the skybox, and as discreetly as possible, let his attorney, Ed Kapinsky, know he was needed. Eric didn't want to leave Sara, but he understood he'd just be in the way. Jack had his pull, and Eric knew he'd take care of Sara. "Sure, Dad, and I'll keep the rest of the guests occupied with food and drink," Eric said. He then started on his way back up the ramp. The crowd out along the field was cheering. Eric made a subconscious note that the Saints may have finally made that touchdown the fans had long awaited.

CHAPTER 13

GOING DOWN

He was just about to turn toward the elevator when Eric saw Wynton Ellery jogging with a security guard in his direction, toward the car he had just left. Their eyes met momentarily, each recognizing the other. Time and space crawled and blurred as they passed one another in what seemed to be slow motion. There were no words spoken, but the question on their faces was the same; raised eyebrows and forehead lines gathered together as they tried to reflect on the swell of too much information too quickly, and the odd chance of crossing paths again.

Why in the world was a port of call security officer called in? Eric pondered nervously as the elevator doors closed. Wynton's presence upset Eric's determination to remain focused and confident. Wynton had been good to them, but why was he here now, with Sara in trouble?

Wynton thought it odd to see Eric coming from the same place he was going to, but he shrugged it off, concerned now only about Raymond. When he came up to the police tape, the security guard called out to his chief. Jamison strolled over.

Wynton's deep voice spoke out as his hand extended. "Hey, how you doing?"

Jamison did not shake his hand but simply asked, "You the brother?"

"Yes," Wynton replied.

"This way!" Jamison barked, and he took the lead. Wynton followed, uncertain of what he was about to see, turning past the barrier and past coroners scraping at concrete, and approaching two squad cars. The right rear door of one car opened, and he could see Raymond in the backseat.

"Ray!" he called out, his entire upper body trying to lean past the shoulders of another cop standing guard. "Raymond!" he called again, extending his muscular arm out to his little brother.

"Sorry, man," the cop said. "Can't get any closer."

Raymond was watching but didn't say anything. He had gotten himself into a real jam this time. He figured Wynton would do what he could, but he knew it didn't look good, being the only black in the bunch; cops weren't going to overlook that. Instead he just nodded at his brother, who was stretching to get as close as he possibly could.

Wynton backed off from the guard and side-stepped away to a different viewpoint. The new angle revealed someone in the back of another car near Raymond. He couldn't make out the figure until she turned toward him. Sara? Sara Doussaint! What was Sara Doussaint doing in the back of a squad car like Raymond? Was she the mystery lady he'd been meeting? No, she couldn't be; she was not blonde, and she seemed too happily married to Eric. Still, Sara Doussaint! Wynton was astounded, stunned, and confused by both the presence of Sara with his brother and the allegations he was hearing fly out of Jamison's mouth.

"Know what I mean?" Jamison asked.

"What?" Wynton asked, not entirely following what had been said.

"I said it's a peculiar bit of information, these three dead bodies and your brother unharmed but in the middle of it all; know what I mean?" Jamison repeated loudly.

"Uh, yeah," Wynton asserted, thinking every bit of it was peculiar. How in the world was Raymond caught up with the Doussaints?

"You said you're in security?" Jamison asked.

"Yes."

"What do you carry?"

"Glock 22, .40 caliber."

"Did you bring it today?"

"No, it's at home with my uniform. What kinda rounds did you find here?"

"Don't know yet. Here's your brother's car keys though." He dangled the silver key ring for a moment before handing it off. Wynton bent down, gave a thumbs-up to the back window of the squad car in case Raymond was looking, and headed out to the parking lot to get the car.

Jamison looked around, watching law enforcement do its various jobs, glancing at the enlarging crowd of spectators that had been cordoned off. *What a mess*, he thought to himself. Sergeant Matthews approached him.

"Did you get a look at the shots, Mick?"

"Yeah, I did. If they're measuring correctly for the shooter's angle and the shot impact, that's a hell of a hit."

"Nine millimeter?" Matthews inquired.

"Ha. I've seen a nine mil bounce off foreheads. Small and fast, but can't do much damage."

"A .223 or .308 rifle? One shot and you're finished."

"There's no way the shooter stood over there with a rifle and no one noticed."

"A .40 or .45 can cause that kind of damage."

"Yeah, we'll see. As soon as the black-and-whites leave, call Port Authority and check on Wynton Ellery's work history. He's the brother of our male suspect and has a sidearm."

"Got it, Mick."

Jamison watched him walk away. *It is what it is*, he thought. *You climb one hill and there's another hill. The wounds, the fears, habits that cripple, tangles they long to escape ... everyone wants a taste—a sense of something more.* But even he knew it is the unremarkable, everyday, ordinary stream of things that suspends the quality of life. He tapped the roof of the squad car to indicate that he was finished and that the officer inside could leave the scene when he was ready.

———————— • ————————

Sara felt the blood rushing to her head as if she stood up too quickly. Her hands and feet were tingling, and she had a sensation like vertigo except that she was sitting down in the back of a police car, wearing handcuffs where there was little to do other than observe. The car itself smelled vile—a saturation of cigarettes, leather, sweat, and odd smells that must be endemic to police cars. Policemen standing alongside the car were talking to onlookers who were trying to press past the yellow tape. *Everyone has deduced we are criminals*, she thought as she watched the crowds trying to peer into the car windows. Smelling a good story and never underestimating the awfulness of people involved, reporters from the *Times-Picayune* and three TV news channels were already present to extract what juicy, scandalous bits of details they could find for their headlines.

The cage-like metal grid that separated the front of the squad car from the back reminded passengers emphatically that chaos happened without prediction and that cause and effect were inescapable. This was not at all like any recurring bad dream she could awaken from; this was real and devastating, and it made her feel helpless.

Of course there were compelling clues: a dead body, a table smeared with blood, and a man regaining consciousness. There was a fleeting whim of time in a world that plunged her into peril, and now, with lights flashing, they were off. Policemen glanced at the cars as they passed by toward the stadium exit. She noted there was a heavy, unspeakable suffering that rode along with them.

At the station, she thought about how it had started out as a routine October day, sunny and crisp. But now she'd been ushered into a small, windowless room—clammy, without air-conditioning. Here on the second floor, it felt surreal to be mixed into the disturbing, seedy world of criminals and the police, whose stout, heavy-handed military-style presence seemed to be bulging with power. She winced from the glare of the ceiling light but found the blinking camera in the corner reading every move she made and deduced it was there to make anyone feel guilty. She sat down near the pale wall and waited, just as she was told to do.

Her personality was guarded at times; she thought that was good. Unfortunately, she had a persevering belief in seeing things through that put her at a disadvantage. She had the ability to listen, learn, and change, but as had occurred numerous times before, her curiosity and temperament could take her to places she was not able to handle emotionally. This was about to override all those previous errors.

In a separate interrogation room, Raymond's stomach lurched as he sat staring into the depths of his own soul. He was reeling in an unexplainable loss, descending into a mix of images of Belinda and Keisha at their funeral. He flashed back to the funeral home engulfed in roses, Belinda herself bearing the likeness of a rose, laid out in a wine-colored velveteen dress. The pearls around her neck were like small stringed lights that softened her face. Keisha in white was beautifully angelic, serene, cushioned among tufted silk pillows. There with her, all life was captured and timeless. Images of his mother's funeral flashed intermittently with the images of Wynton's family. He was emotionally and physically exhausted but somehow critically awake, attuned to life's frailty.

He felt a layer of sweat shimmer at the surface of his skin. He was inhaling short, heavy breaths, as if he were suffocating. His game plan had been sabotaged, and though he was no killer, his presence with Maddie was a conspiracy of sorts, just like the time he had been caught, as a teenager, sneaking into the basement of his girlfriend's house to make out while she was grounded. He was trying to grapple with the aftermath of the last couple of hours. Loss trumped his anger at the unfairness of life, situated on the awful things people do to themselves and to each other. Railing in his head was a voice that insidiously whispered, "You to blame."

He imagined Wynton's voice lobbying for his freedom and felt fairly confident that Sara's corroboration would mean something, giving him some consolation that he would not wake up under an unfamiliar ceiling. Still, he was keenly aware of the flow of injustice and how police coerce confessions. A kaleidoscope of incoherent thoughts swirled in and out of his head. He felt like a bee caught in the wrong hive, with everything circling, buzzing around his head, and with panic and dread stinging his skin.

Jamison was talking. He could see his mouth moving, but Raymond wasn't listening well. Finally Raymond slumped into the back of his chair as if retelling his story had drained him of all his vigor.

CHAPTER 14

WHEN ALL IS SAID AND DONE

"Good, good." Durrell sighed upon hearing from his shooter. "We're heading home." Durrell did not wait for a response but shut his flip phone with a decisive snap and stuffed it back into his coat pocket, content his jobs had been carried out without a hitch. He tapped his driver. "To the airport," he said abruptly. He then slid back into the oversize leather seat, grabbing the hand and arm of the shapely young woman beside him. "Demelo querido mio," he whispered to her. She smiled and loosened the buttons of her blouse.

——————•◦•——————

Wynton put the key in the lock and slowly opened the car door. He slid into the driver's seat and readjusted the seat height and leg room. He looked around; nothing seemed out of place or unusual—nothing that would predict such an explosive end to their day. He sighed. Raymond was constantly in trouble, but he knew he was not capable of killing anyone.

Wynton threw the keys up on the dashboard and rubbed his forehead and eyes. He leaned his head against the wheel for a minute. He didn't know what to think. He was to drive down to the station and wait for Raymond there. He couldn't wrap his brain around it—the murders, Raymond's meeting for sex, Sara Doussaint. He felt sad, and that opened the floodgates to immediate and vivid memories of the accident that came rushing back to him now. That other time, he was surrounded by police cars, ambulances, and body bags. He didn't want to remember that day, but his emotions were raw and he had little control over the images that welled up inside him.

"Raymond," he uttered, and his mind took him to that day. It had been a pleasant evening; they were supposed to pick him up. He was waiting street-side for them when he caught a glimpse of the car. He watched it grow closer as it traveled toward his block. Just across the median, about to turn toward him, they were close enough for him to see Keisha in the backseat when they were struck, blindsided by a speeding van from a side street. The dirty, old blue van barreled into them from out of nowhere, slamming into the back door, where Keisha sat, and pushing their car into oncoming traffic, where they were hit head-on. He stood there frozen in his stance for a moment, stunned, not sure of what he had seen.

The crashing, crunching sounds of metal tearing and bending, glass breaking, hinges groaning, and tires squealing brought him back to his senses and the horror of the scene. He rushed across the pavement to their car, unable to get to Keisha. The van had folded right into their backseat. He strained to find Keisha and called out to her, not able to see her at all, hoping the hit had moved her over but knowing she lay crushed beneath the side of their vehicle and the tons of weight smashed on top of her.

Wynton's mind spun as he stroked his head, scanning images around him to see whether anyone was coming to his aid. Suddenly he didn't know anything. Panic rose like a flock of birds and scattered through him. A shock of pain tunneled into his chest as the world jolted to a stop, the sky darkened, and everything human shut down. His breath thickened, but his bones gave way and he stumbled. He was sure he was going mad as he continued to scream for Keisha from the depths of his lungs. He cried dry, rasping sobs so deep from within his body that his head shook and tears rolled in streaks across his cheeks.

He paid no attention to the driver of the van who was collapsing in on his daughter, or to the driver of the car crumpled into the front, where Belinda was. He spun around to run to the front to see about Belinda. The corner of her door was jammed into the ground, and he could see where she had smashed headlong into the windshield. He saw her move and softly groan, and with the adrenaline pumping in him, he didn't think but quickly swept broken glass pieces out from the driver's window, unaware he was slicing his own hand. Once the glass fragments were free and the door frame smooth, he pulled his wife from the wreck.

He was terrified. Keisha was likely dead, he couldn't see past the smashed car bodies to find her, and Belinda didn't respond as she should. He glanced along the length of her body, assuming she had just unfastened her seatbelt as she was about to hop out and let him drive. He guessed she had suffered internal damage as he scooped her limp body into his arms; except for her head, there were no gaping bodily wounds. "Belinda," he whispered as he choked back tears. "Belinda." He sat down, rocking with her in his arms, looking up at the moonlight, and thought for a moment that everything seemed like a dream. Bystanders had by then crowded around the vehicles, assisting the other drivers. Belinda drew a short, shallow breath. "You just go ahead and sleep, sugar," he said. "Best thing for you." Then, soft and clear in her sweet voice, she whispered a short prayer and drifted off, never to wake again.

He held her, bent over her, kissed her face, and took her lifeless hand and kissed it as well. Again he began to cry. He wept for a long time, his whole world dissolving into tears, and his tears flooding down his face like a swollen river. He was unsure at that moment if he could ever recover.

Like a blessing somehow, for a moment, he was able to focus on their love and how Belinda was so love-filled. She had a radiant aura, and he swore that he could feel the warmth of her skin beneath any article of clothing she wore. He hoped she knew how good she felt to him when she was completely relaxed in his arms. The images swirled in his head, vague and scattered, vivid and intense. He was kissing her in the dark night air beneath a single streetlamp, hugging her at the bottom of her stoop, cradling her in the front seat of his car, stroking the smoothness of her hair alongside her in bed, admiring her glistening belly when she was pregnant with Keisha.

He wiped his eyes and pictured her again. He saw the two of them together, saw himself fingering the small of her back in the shower, saw her hand on his shoulder as she nuzzled into his neck while slow dancing. He saw her legs, her breasts … saw her straddling and facing him while making love. He thought about the gleam in her eyes just as her breath began to shorten and quicken; the way she quietly, gently owned him afterward; the way she slipped inside of him when they collapsed onto one another bathed in sweat.

Her body was becoming heavier, her skin paling, as he gently cradled her. He heard her whispering in his ear and felt her shaking him. He felt sure it was her shaking him, shaking his shoulder, but it was not. It was one of the paramedics that had arrived. He resisted them, but there was nothing else he could do but release her to them. He offered her up, moved out of their way, and sat on the curb, shocked to see his precious, beautiful, innocent wife and daughter carted off into the cold, sterile vault of an ambulance.

In his mind, he could hear the well-intentioned wishes that would greet him and tell him this was God's will, hoping for his swift acceptance. He rejected the notion that God willed disease, accidents, and war, or that evil drifted into the hearts of men. God, he thought, did not give people what they could handle. God helped them handle what they had been given by a wayward world. Now Belinda and Keisha had been taken, and he was left wondering about painfully honest questions deep in the core of his being. He believed brokenness and wounding did not occur in order to break the human spirit but to open hearts so God could act. Still, he wondered what God could do with his hopelessly homeless spirit now, as he mulled over and over the scenes of his loss.

It was a bleak, cutting, tumultuous time. If it hadn't been for Raymond, who had pulled so much together, he could never have had a funeral three days later—not in the midnight of his suffering. He had spent every waking moment those days considering all the ways the accident might never have happened. Any change in detail might have altered the horrible outcome. He couldn't shut it out. He wouldn't even be alive if Raymond hadn't stopped by—if he hadn't talked through the long hours of that night with him after all the friends and relatives had headed back home, leaving him so utterly alone. That awful night, he had been caught on the jagged hook of those dark, bleating, suicidal thoughts. Unbearable misery swept through every thought, word, movement, and memory, leaving him in a dulled, bloodless state. He kept revisiting the scene of the accident, the hideous screeching of twisting steel, the last smooth touch, the body bags, the sirens. It was intolerable. Raymond could not feel the devastation and despair that flew through Wynton with hurricane force, but Raymond knew he was weary to the bone despite the heavy-fisted grip he had on his gun. The groaning of his heart led him to cling to the notion that one shot could remove the pain.

Raymond's compassion and optimism had kept Wynton alive. They both were well aware of the notion that life without storms didn't exist; but that night they shared the bits and pieces of life that offered incredible, beautiful, limitless views. Months later, Wynton sifted and sorted his feelings, sought counseling, prayed, and rested in the unknown. He came to accept that dark night, accepting himself in his humanness. He hoped to find a shred of holiness, a bridge between where he was and what he used to be—a bridge to where and what he would become.

Raymond didn't comprehend the deep spiritual and psychological change Wynton went through because of loss, but he adapted to Wynton's slower, more reflective healing rhythm as he hung out with his older brother. Together they unearthed the notion that survival as a family comes only when members are willing, one by one, to become the place of nourishment for each other.

"Raymond," Wynton uttered again, and he grabbed the keys off the dashboard to start the engine and go find his brother.

CHAPTER 15

PARTY OF FIVE

Chief Detective Jamison held up two photos and then pinned them to the whiteboard. "We've got Sara Doussaint, white female, age twenty-seven, well-to-do. And Raymond Ellery, black male, age twenty-eight, blue-collar, street-smart." Then he held up a picture of the blood-soaked victim. "And this is Madeleine Breen, white female, also age twenty-eight, living well off the higher-ups. So let's start with her." Jamison taped the body shot on the board. "We haven't identified the two white males found outside the door, but assume they killed her. They were intent on killing her. Why? Because of a black lover?" Jamison spoke as he thought the strategy through amid a team of investigators.

"Really, you gonna go there?" Jamison's senior detective said, himself a black man. Calvin Johnson was a longtime friend and a valued member of the squad. He had a broad brow and finely molded chin for an older man. He had a small afro with a side part, left over from the seventies. He could have been the brunt of jokes, but he was blunt by nature, so none thought to ridicule him.

"Screw you, Johnson," Jamison responded to his friend, not angry but annoyed. "I'm not in the business of being PC; I'm trying to figure out what is going on in some lunatic's head. Anyone want to add something?" Johnson backed off, not conceding, not because he felt diminished but because he believed Mick Jamison was the only person he knew that never discriminated. He truly dismissed judgment based on skin; he never saw people as their color, didn't like labels, and instead saw everyone as being equally capable of crime or violence.

"They looked like typical fans," Captain Leland Hughes noted, leaning against a filing cabinet across the room. The captain had walked a beat and risen through the ranks the hard way and was now in the evening of his career.

Sergeant Toni Raskins, the first black female detective in their ward, spoke up. "But surely they didn't just happen along."

"Maybe they dared each other to kill someone randomly," Davies suggested. Joseph Davies was the only Yankee on the team, a Chicago boy who had decided to return to his roots. He had a helmet of black hair and olive skin, indicative of his Chickasaw and Caribbean background. He was a damn good detective who was unafraid to tackle challenges and thorough in his investigations.

"Come on." Jamison was growing impatient. "That's all you can come up with? We've got the postmortem report from the lab, still waiting for forensics and pathology. But c'mon, what developed here? Were there any others who were missed in the fire and took off running?"

"If they didn't approve of Ellery, why kill her and not him?" Johnson injected.

"That's a good point, Johnson," Jamison responded. "And why would you leave someone alive who could ID you later?"

"Since they didn't do that, we can leave race out of it, can't we?" Detective Gordon Webb pressed. He had no patience for half-assed investigations or wild goose chases.

"What if they wanted to teach him a lesson to take back to the black community?" Jamison pushed.

Raskins snarled, "Yeah, as if the black community really wanted their young black men to date white women to begin with."

"Maybe they left him alive to take the fall for the murder," Detective Dan Gandy offered. He was not overly assertive in his work, not aggressive. He didn't try to outshine anyone, but he was reliable and was often the glue that kept the group together.

"What if they were after her all along?" Jamison offered. "She *is* a pretty big player—mistress of Senator Jack Doussaint. I mean, someone had to know what they were up to in order to follow the two guys and kill them after Madeleine Breen's death. So it had to be preplanned, and if so, she was targeted specifically."

"Then how does this Raymond Ellery guy fit in?" Gandy asked, his thin frame leaning in and his slender finger pointing to the picture of Raymond that Jamison had just placed on the board. Sara's photo was next to his, and below them were the pictures of the two thirty-something white male Cajuns. A close-up of the bloody knife was on the board as well, the only murder weapon found on the scene. "Chance? Poor choice?"

"Well, as soon as we get forensics back, we'll see," Jamison replied. "Meanwhile, once we get DNA, check to see if these two have any priors, and then check with parole and nearby halfway houses to see whether they were reentering society by roaming the streets. And contact toxicology to see if any of the three victims had anything in their system."

"Right," Gandy replied, and he turned from the meeting to use his phone. Gandy was also not the usual high-strung detective. He would be content to do nothing. In fact, he'd sleep all day if he could.

"Remember: there is no insignificant detail," Jamison offered as he searched through the nearest desk drawers for a light.

"Yeah, well, you'd better find someone else's nose to bloody in this besides the senator's. I mean it," Captain Hughes said as he strolled over to join the group of detectives. With a hint of menace in his voice, he did mean it. Jack Doussaint was a force to be reckoned with. Everyone knew his name, his family, his business, and his power.

"How and why have all these paths intersected here?" Jamison growled. He tapped at Sara's photo. "She says she was just following Maddie to see what she was up to." Then he moved his finger to Raymond's mug shot. "This guy says he'd made plans to meet her there for sex at half-time, and the brother confirmed his talking about meeting some mystery woman on the drive in for the game." Jamison paused and sat down on the corner of the desk. "That takes care of these three being on the scene, but why these two characters?" He gestured to them with his thumb over his shoulder as he reached to pull the lone cigarette from behind his ear. He fingered it for a while, contemplating.

"Boss, maybe it's like you said; maybe they were racist pricks and she was targeted for her relationship with a black guy," Nolan, the youngest detective, stated as he looked sheepishly over at Johnson for approval. He took his cue at how to react from the others around him. He was shy, and his full mop of hair was messy. His wrinkled clothes screamed "desperately single." Still, he was rather gallant and loyal to the heart and soul of good police work.

"Nope. Ellery said it was their first time," Jamison stated, "and according to the timeline from Sara Doussaint, he would have already been in the door before they could have ever eyeballed Breen. They wouldn't have seen them together until they were inside the laundry facility." He added quickly, "But why not kill them both? Why just her, and why that way? This death was personal, vindictive." Jamison, now rolling the cigarette back and forth between his thumb and middle finger, was ready for a smoke. "Davies," he continued, "call Criminology and have them send someone over here to explain to us the sociological meaning of gutting her; then get a hold of something, anything—footprints, handprints, hairs, any kind of trace evidence—that will help add to DNA findings."

Davies nodded and went to his desk.

"Maybe it wasn't personal; maybe they just liked killing," Donald Matthews said.

Jamison reproached his good friend. "Wha?"

"Maybe it was sexual—you know, uncontrollable ecstasy," Matthews suggested.

"You been reading *Cosmo* again, Donna?" Jamison jabbed at him.

"Chief, just saying, maybe we'd better check for more than one sample of semen."

No one had any answers yet. No one knew why the two white men had been shot; they knew only that it was a professional hit from across the pavilion. They were without a motive to begin the intricate process of unraveling the mystery of these three murders.

"Matthews, take a couple of uniforms and get back to those vendors to help jog their memories about what they saw." Jamison spoke quickly and moved on. "Johnson, check into more than one offender's semen, and check with records to see what was catalogued as their pockets and her purse were emptied. Webb, take Reynolds and go meet with stadium security and find out who sat in front or behind the Ellery brothers, and see if they noticed anything or can vouch for their whereabouts."

Webb nodded in agreement. Richard Webb was a stocky, clean-cut man who kept his blonde hair in a military cut. He was acutely athletic and conditioned, ran the city marathon each year, and was attempting to train for his first Ironman triathlon. He was well read and a bit of an intellect. He would do a good job finding the details of that day.

"Rass, get in touch with Ballistics and see how the hardware is matching up; then check with Criminalistics to see if they were able to lift any prints besides our party of five."

"On it," Raskins replied as she grabbed her notepad from the desk next to her and hurried to catch up with the men who were in search of further evidence. It was difficult to be the single woman among male cops. So much of the trust issue relied on being one of the boys in this man's world. She hadn't tired of being a woman, but she had tired of the women who conjured their existence with cosmetics and silks, and the men who hovered like flies after their scent. So at least it was easy for her to escape the dog-and-pony show between the sexes and become part of the team. So far, Raskins was more subtle than threatening to the male egos or style of investigation. She had the credentials to keep up with every one of the men and the confidence to lie low. There wasn't one detective that couldn't get along with her; she had a personality everyone liked and a character everyone respected.

Captain Hughes took Raskins's seat and put his feet up on an empty chair. "The rest of y'all get to work," he announced, sending the lingering detectives back to their desks. "Whatever we find, we've got to keep the senator out of this," he said in a calm, matter-of-fact manner to his chief detective.

"I know," Jamison replied, but at fifty-four he felt he was already too old for this. "But she started out at his party," he continued, "and his daughter-in-law was at the crime scene. We all know who Maddie is. Hell, the only one who should've wanted to kill her is Renee. Do you think she hired the two to take her out?"

"Nah, Renee was always the better woman, the bigger person, as long as Maddie was alive," the captain reasoned.

"Maybe she snapped," Jamison asserted, running his stubby fingers through his slightly graying thinning hair. "Maybe she finally got tired of it all."

"No, not Renee, she's too smart. She has never given much credit to Jack and Maddie in the first place. It's all for show; you know that, Mick."

"Maybe someone wanted to get at Jack," Jamison stated.

"That is pretty likely," Hughes replied, "Jack Doussaint is a cold and clever strategist, and he has his share of enemies. But listen; we have to distance him from this case—got me?"

Jamison didn't like it, but he understood his captain. Captain Hughes always looked crisp and composed as the Watch Commander who oversaw the station. But his face, a road map with contours and fissures that stretched across his brow and fell into his sunken cheeks, told the story of a career man involved in a lifetime of police work. Where he needed to, he could push his advantage.

CHAPTER 16

RIGHT AT HOME

"Look, just come stay with me a while," Wynton told his little brother, "until all this clears up."

"I dunno." Raymond hesitated. He was not himself; all his confidence was gone.

"Ray, they're not hunting for you, 'kay? The prints on the knife weren't yours, and they believed you when Sara confirmed you'd been knocked out. Everything else is circumstantial evidence; let it go."

Raymond was a wisecracker, a real smartass at times, fueled by an array of deeply held resentments toward authority, but he had never been involved in violence—not even a bar brawl over a girl, which one might assume would happen more often than not. Raymond claimed he was a lover, not a fighter. Wynton knew, however, that his choices against fighting reflected his rather small stature—not exactly the brawling type.

"E, I ain' never been near no murder, and now this—her. Why her? She was fine-ass delicious, and probably a bitch to someone, but dead? Cut up and left to bleed out? That's brutal, you know?"

"Yeah, Ray, I know. I see trouble all the time on the job, but give it up or it'll eat away at you."

Raymond knew Wynton was right. They had believed him—reluctantly, but they had believed him. His story matched up with the evidence. Sara had credited him as a victim, not a perpetrator. Left to his own memories, all he could picture was a white man in a cap before he was struck—nothing more specific. He didn't have any alibi going for him at all, not without Sara. She was the key to his freedom, and he was feeling embarrassed that he had been involved in this mess.

"C'mon, Eric and Sara are cool, a'ight? They're not like his pops. Just be glad you're not in bed with Daddy Doussaint." Wynton hugged his brother and shook him just a bit, trying to rattle some sense into him.

"Right, you right, E," Raymond responded. "I'ma hang here with you a couple days and see where this thing go." The truth was that he was in no hurry to get back. His small, hopeless apartment offered hand-me-down furniture and the constant low chattering of televisions from up and down the hall. The place was as plain as the inside of a box: a bed, a small table, two chairs, and empty walls. In one corner there was a pile of clothes, a small single kitchen counter, a sink, and a stove. Even with the blinds open, no amount of light or paint could offer optimism. The room itself was drawn, sullen, and mute. Raymond, like so many, was forced to swallow the depressing day each morning just as one would swallow morning vitamins—a simple, rote, rehearsed dismissal of the day.

He had thought more than a few times how easy it would be to disappear in the shadows of that dilapidated tenant building. He could open the latch of a window and feel the wind tugging at it like a creature with a will. His own desires were so small inside him; his body would act like a brittle casing against the stronger will outside. It was depressing. The morning sun did not splash softly through any dappled trees in scintillating gold like it did at Wynton's. It slammed into his windows with a growl. There was no comparison; of course he'd rather be at Wynton's, where there was time to think and settle into the day.

"A'ight then, brutha-man," Wynton pronounced in a victorious tone. He would be glad to have Raymond nearby instead of worrying about him without knowing where he was. It would also be the first time Wynton would have an overnight guest since the accident. It was time to let some of that go too. How he missed and loved his family, but a broken heart would never bring them back. It seemed maybe he himself had to man up, not just Raymond. Wynton followed Raymond out to the car to help retrieve his bags. He had brought one gym bag of clothing and two grocery bags full of alcohol and snacks. "Ray, this not a retreat." Wynton smirked as he looked over the assortment.

"I'm just hanging, bruh; ain' not all for me—some for you too," Raymond quipped.

"I gotta be at work early in the mornings," Wynton replied as he brought the bags inside.

"Lightweight," Raymond scoffed. He closed the door behind them and tossed the gym bag on the floor.

"Anyway," Wynton said, ignoring the name-calling as he set the groceries on the kitchen countertop, "you'll be sleeping cozy tonight." He picked up the gym bag, opened a closet door to grab a pillow, and placed both in the master bedroom, which was just left of the great room.

"Nah, bruh, I ain' taking your bed. I'ma sleep upstairs," Raymond insisted.

"I don't sleep there anymore," Wynton replied. "Not since ..." He slapped the couch with his large hand. "This is my bed, Ole Reliable." Wynton grinned at his brother as he turned to head into the kitchen. "What you hungry for tonight?" he called as he pulled a rickety drawer out from under the counter.

"Food," Raymond replied, and he flopped down on the couch.

Wynton never quite grasped how Raymond, an endless eating machine, never put on weight. He decided to fix something easy. When he finished scraping the last morsel out from the frying pan, he entered the living room with two plates of steaming rice and chicken legs. He handed one to Raymond and sat down on the couch next to him as he swiped the remote from the coffee table and changed the station.

"Discovery? Really, E? C'mon, this is punk. Turn on BET or sports or something fresh."

"Nope," Wynton replied, happy to be king and commander of the remote. "There's always a chance to learn, little man."

Wynton didn't necessarily excel in math and science, but he had a great appreciation for them, aware of how everything in life was mathematically and scientifically connected. He was continually telling Raymond how math and science fed the brain. They helped one think precisely, decisively, and creatively, and to look at the world from multiple perspectives.

Though he acknowledged that the brain was easily the most powerful machine in the world, he professed that the traditional thought that the brain is fully formed by adulthood was wrong. He was of the opinion that life experiences constantly shape and mold the brain in fascinating ways. He believed there is an art to effective reasoning and critical decision making—an art available to everyone if they'd open the door to math.

Wynton's big brother's words of wisdom often reflected thought processing. Perhaps he clearly saw Raymond's impromptu and immature behavior. Today was no different. "Look, Ray; whether you're the head of a Fortune 500 company, work for a government agency like I do, or are just running a household, you are constantly making decisions important to you and those immediately around you. Reasoning—we do it, hear it, judge it every day. Conflict is everywhere. Handled badly, it can do real harm. Handled well, it can be useful to build better relationships and life situations." He paused to eat the last couple of scoops of rice. "You have to decide your path, and the best way to decide involves accurately defining problems and framing your decision on what may be lost or pose a risk. Making a good decision"—he turned to face Raymond—"or choice, and avoiding a horrible one is not a chance act, Ray. It's a skill; it can be learned, seasoned."

"Yeah, yeah, I know, E. I done bin letting my social and emotional side influence the rest of me," he said with sarcasm and a bit of disdain, repeating what he had heard so many times before.

"Brutha, look; you need to learn how to sidestep potential mistakes."

"'Fine, I will; just don't be getting started on one of your mental math lectures," Raymond quipped jokingly, though he was dead serious about not wanting another lecture.

"Just study; study things around you." Wynton patted his brother's shoulder as he rose and headed into the kitchen. Raymond was relieved. Wynton could easily begin talking about one subject and then slide right into another topic with lengthy ramifications, reflecting on faith, pain, and grief, or love and prophecy. It was just a week ago when he got a sermon on how people need to become more aware of their shared humanity, and the wisdom and vision of others; how music and art transcend language and allow people to perceive things that are not associated with language; and that great works teach something universal and central about the human condition.

Raymond had quickly tuned him out and wondered if his big brother would ever offer a lecture on apologetics for exploring these large ideas at the expense of his younger brother's sanity. There weren't many times Raymond did not want to be around Wynton, but the times when he was reeled into a lecture or sermon were the exceptions. Wynton was a remarkable man, but his insights felt more like punishment than wisdom. "E, you a trip, man," he mumbled to himself as he cleared his plate and utensils from the couch and followed Wynton into the kitchen.

As they were scraping and rinsing their plates, Raymond told Wynton the thoughts he'd had while at the police station.

"I kept seeing flashes of funerals, of Belinda and Keisha, and of Momma."

"Well, one traumatic event can conjure up memories of other traumatic events."

"Yeah, but Momma's death wasn't nearly unsettling as her end days." Raymond regretted how the cancer treatments had corroded her body and destroyed her will to survive, yet, still hadn't saved her. He sadly remembered how the nursing staff took turns spooning vanilla pudding into her slack mouth like a mother bird tending to the runt in the nest—spoon, swallow, spoon, swallow, rest—with the narrow line of her lips trying to move in sync with her animated tongue.

Wynton and Raymond both felt that palliative care had ruined their chance for a real goodbye, with the steady drip of morphine keeping her drifting in and out of a chemical stupor. They had watched her eyes grow large, the veins along her hands and wrists tangle, the folds of her skin decay, and her breath come and go. She had ended up breathing in loops like a child lost in dust. They had been by her side, slipping through the blue haze of hospital halls, past the smells of dying, and snores from sour, gaping mouths, to watch her nerves, like wires, snap from the legs to the rib when she was rolled over to change the dressing of a bedsore. It had seemed to them that her skull flattened on the pillow—just flattened like a frog, the brain docked and riding out the waves of pain.

Wynton thought back to the ward. Some lay beneath crucifixes with Jesus frozen to the bones, nailed to his vertical and horizontal axes like a chunk of beef. Others waited for their visions of starchy ghosts, and still others wailed for Lucifer. All were lifted into the mechanics of each day amid the odor of orange and jam, with curtains wormed back in bunches, and no-frills slippers placed on their feet as a hopeful display that they might be going somewhere. "She was never lucid enough to have any meaningful closure." Wynton said. "And Belinda and Keisha was ripped from us too quickly,"

"Well, at least we gots each other," Raymond replied. They gave each other a hug and then opened the refrigerator door to find the beers they would share back on the couch in the great room.

Raymond headed back immediately for his few moments as ruler of the remote control. Wynton paused by the kitchen window and looked outside. He knew too well how it felt to be faint of heart. He had fallen on hungry days, grieving a stone-cold world. He had been wild-eyed at the ruin. He had dared at first to outlive the anguish but was now afraid the dare might come true. How many times had he leaned into the window, near to the big, sure sky, and asked for just one word—a whisper? So often he had asked for a quiet prayer and a hand to cool his brow, a soft kiss miles and miles beyond this life. He would still gladly die—offer up his last breath—to have them back.

But Wynton had also known the face of worship that thirsts and speaks, calls to God and angels, hears and sees the blessings, and teaches endurance and the wonder of love. Every day, he could choose to defy compromise, choose to cling to the healing power of hope.

CHAPTER 17

ONTO SOMETHING

"I just don't know why you did it, darling," Renee stated as she poured her martini and reached for an olive. "Honestly, this whole mess could have been avoided."

"Except for the actual murder, don't you mean?" Sara replied.

"Yes, dear, I simply mean that if you weren't there, this mess would be Jack's to deal with, alone, away from the family."

"Mom," Eric jumped in, "that's enough for now, all right?" He was on his way upstairs to the study to talk with Jack and Ed.

"Yes, yes. Go on, dear. Shoo! We'll be fine," his mother assured him. Eric shot a glance over to Sara to see whether she was content. She nodded and watched him as he passed through the french doors to the stairwell.

"Martini, dear?" asked Renee.

"Sure," Sara replied.

She handed the glass to Sara. Sara held its stem and drank half of it all at once, feeling it burn. The taste was bitter and clung to the back of her throat. She contemplated the bitterness of their pending small talk.

She liked Renee, but Renee was not much help for chitchatting, and it made Sara uncomfortable to have to discover things they could talk about. Anything that was off the subject they had been discussing upstairs would be a relief. Still, she'd try; it was her mess, after all.

Jack was upstairs, pacing back and forth on his expensive Persian rug, a cigar in hand. "Ed, as long as we know Sara is in the clear and out of this matter, that's the important part. I won't have family dragged into this," he directed.

"It'll be done, Jack," Ed reassured him. "Police records will be buried, and the media will have nothing to sniff after 'cept the two did the killing." Ed Kapinsky was a reliable old friend and an impressive attorney as well. He'd seen Jack through a number of scandals before; this would be no different.

"But Dad, who'd want to kill Maddie?" Eric asked as he entered and closed the large mahogany door discreetly behind him.

"They didn't just kill Maddie, boy," Jack hammered back. "They wanted to get to me. She's a part of who I am in the business world. This was a message son, loud and clear."

"Kill someone to cause you trouble? I don't get it; who is that callous? I mean, Dad, that's a pretty big risk to take just to dig at you," Eric suggested. It tired him to say it, and he couldn't imagine the foolishness or fearlessness it would take to pull this off just to rattle someone.

"That's just it, son; who could pull this off without risking anything?" Jack snapped his fingers as if he had just had an epiphany. "Ed," he continued, "call up that dick of yours and see what he can find out about those two shot in the head. If we can learn more about them, we'll find the link to the one who has nothing to risk."

Ed replied he would and thumbed through the papers in his briefcase for the detective, whom he'd last used in Tijuana. "Could be," Ed stated, "this might be payback for a certain visit south."

"You mean Mexico, Ed? That trip with Jimmy?" Eric asked as he looked over to his dad for the real answer.

"Maybe." Jack hummed as he spoke, avoiding eye contact with his son. "Durrell's been known to travel."

Eric was desperate for answers. "Sara's involved in a murder because of your escapades in Mexico?" Eric asked indignantly. "That woman hurt and Maddie dead because of some game over territory?" He spoke louder, angry that he had unwittingly been part of one of his dad's power plays. "That's why they let me go. It was you all along, wasn't it? *Wasn't it?*" he was furious and standing face-to-face with Jack.

"Eric," Jack said slowly trying to pacify him, "business is complicated. There are simply things you don't know ... that you don't need to know about ... but things that get done nonetheless."

His tone and his words did not console Eric in the least, and he turned on his heels to head back down to his wife.

Sara put her drink down, stood up, and walked to the bay windows. She folded her arms across her chest and appeared to contemplate the southern exposure for some time. Then, with a sigh of resignation, she began to share her hurt. She was embarrassed at how sorry she felt for herself. She was also tired of the same issue repeatedly shaking her confidence. She was, after all, an adult. She understood life was a series of tragedies sprinkled with occasional joy. Still, her emotions took control so often she could not always suppress her personal rage or sadness that reflected how deeply and early she had been wounded.

She did not possess extraordinary reserves of patience—not like Eric. Worse, her sarcasm held a condescending tone, and her complicated mixture of regret and defensiveness was becoming brutally difficult to control. "We have periods of coming together and breaking apart," she whispered, barely audibly. "Like waves." She wanted refuge from the continual crashing waves and imagined life in winter somewhere, snowed over, confined and hidden.

"What?" Eric asked as he entered the room. "What about waves?" Eric was stern in his inquiry, angry that his dad had so easily used him and recalling the image of Sara's birth control pills.

"A drink, dear?" Renee asked him as she held up her martini glass.

"No, Mom, not now." He turned from his mother to Sara. "You're not even trying to get pregnant, are you?" His tone had become caustic and indignant.

CHAPTER 18

DEATHS

Eric's eyes were staring right through her. Her first instinct was to avert her eyes, and she struggled to look back at him, his dark eyes curious and intense. Her heart was crashing, and she felt as though her life had suddenly been blown open. Sara realized she was making a mistake as she spoke, though she continued to speak; it was similar to taking a wrong exit off the highway but barreling ahead at full speed, keenly aware of being lost and without an on-ramp in sight. When she finished, the truth was out; Sara had hesitated to get pregnant because of the loss several years earlier.

She told Eric and Renee both that she remembered sitting on the examining table, swinging her legs while waiting, trying to keep the green paper gown from falling off her shoulders. She recalled the conducting jelly over her abdomen and watching excitedly with Eric for the show—for the image of their anticipated child wrapped into a ball. They'd planned to frame the ultrasound.

Eric had pointed to the dark oval shape in the middle of what looked like a satellite picture of a weather storm. "Remember what you said, Eric? You said, 'Is that it? Is that the baby?' But the technician was silent. She left for a moment, though it seemed like hours, and returned with the obstetrician. He put his stethoscope on and began to press here and there through the gel. We knew something was wrong before the doctor ever spoke.

"'I'm sorry; your baby is dead,' he said. 'Baby dead, baby dead, baby dead.' That's all I heard and replayed in my mind over and over the next few days." In fact, the words chugged inside her like a train starting to roll—a train that would speed up and course through her uncontrollably for several days. Sara looked at her family with such sadness. She paused from speaking, thinking

Eric must have grieved quietly and alone because he had never shed a tear with her. Sara, on the other hand, had cried and cried, amazed that one person could cry as much as she did.

"The thought of being pregnant again scared me," she said. "There, it's out. That's the truth." The real truth was that insecurity and discontent had grown in her as simply as a child would grow, fattening in the spread of her shelter when the body is dumb, when death, too, is in the egg. She had memorized the feelings: the umbilical cord curling, tied where it was torn, sent nerves, pulled like wires, rushing back into her skin. There the saddle of motherhood was dying with the crowning head, the flattened skull creeping from its harness, flopping in the rush of water. She felt the sterile ghosts hover over her as she prayed for the cushion of lies she ought to hear instead of the stirrups, allowing the glove its oily rape, and the hard tablet of death. They said she'd be better, but they refused to hear that she, too, was dying.

She wondered whether they could understand that it was fear filled with a sadness that permeated every pore of her being with darkness. In retrospect, Eric had made allowances for her emotional needs. This is what made him a godsend—a warming in the polar cap of men who cooled their heels, waiting for wives to outgrow their chrysalides, where grief had swaddled them in their darkness.

Was there really anyone to blame for somebody who should have been born? Even the earth puckers when buds are plucked from its dark sockets of soil. How could anyone expect her fragile, bristling soul to surface and exist alongside the blood of this baby?

"After all," she insisted, "I was the one who found Mother." Sara was now referring to her mother's death when she was five. Eric was intrigued and positioned himself on the overstuffed arm of the sofa next to his mom. He'd been trying to get Sara to open up to him about her mother for years. She continued. "The blood just left her head, and she collapsed. It struck me that she paled so abruptly and fell like a building imploding … a natural-looking fall, like a folding with the knees buckling … the torso moving down, the arms fluttering gracefully sideways as if she could fly. It was only once she hit the floor that I was able to move toward her. I raised her head up, trying to bring her back to consciousness. Of course, that never happened. God"—she moved her hair back off her shoulders—"I kept practicing what to say to her. I wanted to comfort her; I wanted her to wake up and comfort me. I wanted to choose the right words, somehow—what I could not articulate—so I wouldn't make things worse." She paused for a moment, reflecting. There was pain in her voice, and not a hint of joy. She wasn't just telling her story but was reliving the agony as so many trauma victims do until they finally speak out.

It was odd at five for her to be thinking of her mom in a paralyzing state of unconsciousness. She looked at Eric and then at Renee for understanding. She wondered whether they were listening. Their somber facial expressions seemed to say they were. "It would have been so easy at the hospital to simply put my arms around her and sob at my loss. Instead I remained frozen and smiling, unable to utter anything except the word "Mommy." I saw my dad standing beside her, in the space between me and her, but he did not say a word. It was an unpleasant confrontation of fear and sorrow, and when he stared at me with a look so fixed and knowing, I could not move." She slowed in her speech. "Though the expression on his face seemed to dare me to speak, I could not. I was uncomfortable under his gaze. Honestly, I could think of nothing I could say that could improve the situation. Dad smiled slowly as he approached me, and as he scooped me up in his arms to leave, I saw her face—the lifeless, beautiful face of my mother prepared for passage. Then, just as quickly as the door with opportunity had opened, because we had taken her to the hospital where there was medical equipment and doctors, the door closed, permanently.

"I don't remember any music at the funeral, only the intense silence. The sun drenched us with heat as we stood around her open, dark grave. The silence down there was as deep and dark as night." A shaft of terror had shot through her as she felt the future of blackness and ruin closing in on her. Even the earth itself, shoveled into a nearby pile, seemed filthy and abandoned. "After the funeral, everyone came back to the house, and with all the food, it seemed like Thanksgiving, except everyone was somber and in dark clothing. I felt hollow, lighter than air, and probably ill and faint. No one talked about what had happened, and I all I could do was wait—outlast the crowd or wait for someone to interrupt the shuffling motions and guttural sounds of eating. I wanted to lunge past our guests, past all the wine glasses and candlelight, into the night air and scream. Instead I clutched my throat at the inability to act upon my urge."

She turned again to the windows, her arms straight down beside her. "And now here's another death, multiple murders!" she exclaimed. Every defense she'd ever consciously or unconsciously taken refuge behind suddenly dropped. It was like a total eclipse, where the eyes dry, the heart drains, and the lungs hush as the disk of night slides over daylight like a lid.

Eric and Renee were quiet. Eric was absorbing the significance of the story he had suspected for years. Renee, who watched Sara deep in thought at the window, was glad she was opening up but didn't want to push her.

No one knows before they are devastated, Sara thought, *that the world holds such suffering.* It could smack of noise, the bleating cries of anguish, or it could be numbing without a motion or utterance—the stench of silence that hardly a mind or soul can bear. Couldn't they understand her torment?

"I feel helpless, Eric," she stated softly, diminished by her own words and feelings.

"Baby," Eric reassured her as he crossed the room to reach her. "I thought you were deceiving me, trying to control our relationship. I had no idea what was bothering you." Eric put his arms around her and smiled as her head rested on his chest. Sara grasped him tightly and wept.

"Well, darling, if anyone deserves a good cry, it's you," Renee said sympathetically. "No one expects a five-year-old girl to ever really get over that kind of loss. Darling, we certainly can see how terribly harsh this whole situation has been. But dear, women have miscarriages and stillborn babies and get pregnant again all the time. And my goodness, you had nothing to do with the stadium murders." Renee was sincere. Sara felt some solace at having given voice to her fears as she relaxed in Eric's arms. He caressed her head, hair, and shoulders.

"It's okay," he asserted softly. "We'll take it slow. You do not have to go through any of this alone." She reached up around his neck and pulled herself toward his lips and kissed him. There it seemed the fear, resentment, and cover-up fell away from her in the warm wash of his mouth.

CHAPTER 19

THE STUDY

"The police already identified the two at the door," Ed informed his private detective by phone. "No family, a few misdemeanors and felonies. One's handprint was on the blade, and traces of his semen were inside Maddie."

"Shit, why did you tell him that!" Jack scolded him as he threw his hands in the air.

"It's the other shooter. He's a pro; did it nice and clean," Ed continued. As he listened, he removed his sport coat and fitted it along the top of the burgundy-tufted leather desk chair, and rolled up his sleeves. He sat back down. "Uh huh." He pulled a pen from his square black briefcase's pocket.

Jack had finished his drink and walked his empty over to the bar, and he was putting fresh ice in his glass. He cut at the massive ham and swiss on rye, pulling it apart and taking a third into his first two fingers, eating as he strolled back over to the matching overstuffed burgundy leather sofa across from Ed. "All right then, report to me every day," Ed dictated. He then placed Jack's desk phone back onto its cradle to charge.

A bottle of amber-colored bourbon sat on a table next to his chair, as did a clear tumbler that always had an inch or two of Jack's finest in it. "Shall I pour?" Ed asked, looking at Jack seated across from him.

"It's what I'm waiting for," Jack replied, and he handed Ed his glass, which contained three small ice cubes. Ed was a rather quiet man. Being around Jack made him all the more low-key. Jack's words often grew heavy and gritty, and there came to be a thickness in the air about him wherever he was present. Ed knew that if one was on Jack's team, it would be overpowering, like someone who rinsed in too much aftershave. If one was not in Jack's camp, however, his attitude and insinuations could be quite bruising.

Ed poured Jack his bourbon and reached for another old fashioned glass for himself from the shelf below the tabletop. "You're starting to run low," he commented as he emptied the decanter.

Jack took a deep breath as he sat back and glanced around the spacious and tastefully decorated study. It looked like a gentlemen's club with its heavy mahogany, massive hearth, and large nineteenth century globe, and it was cloaked a bit in amorality. "I can still visualize so much of my grandfather," he said. Jack had patterned his study after his grandfather's study. He often talked about his grandfather when he ran out of things to do. It was his grandfather, not his father, who had set him on his path to power and wealth. There was a picture of Jack as a boy holding a large fish with his grandfather out at sea, on his grandfather's yacht. "He just smelled of his study. The leather, the alcohol, cigars, and books," he commented, content he had recreated a bit of him here in his own room.

Jack's grandfather was a big man, tall and square, stalwart, with dark hair pressed down to one side with Vitalis, a squared jaw, and large hands. His father, on the other hand, had looked more like a boy, diminished, overshadowed, and frozen in posture looking for his place in the world. No one would remember better than Jack sitting in that drab room with a single bed and a dresser, with no pictures on the wall, spoon-feeding rice pudding to his father at the end. Like a pigeon with a message coming home, Jack would sweep through the air and land the spoon on his father's tongue. His father had been placed on morphine and a feeding tube, but he craved rice pudding every now and then.

The undusted table and chairs, the wheelchair, and the smell of rank perspiration and chemicals were all painfully vivid. It was easier to draw on the robust nature of his grandfather than to recall the long, sterile corridor of a mental institution and the lingering images he had of his father. He had detached himself from the drawn, graying face, eyes in a blank gaze, his body slumping dejectedly in bed when he was finally moved to the infirmary where he died. He had kept his distance, afraid of catching his father's poor prognosis, as if his dying could transfer, as if death could eat inside him and drain him to the parched man he saw that day. At the funeral, his grandfather had dressed his dead son in a black suit left over from his college graduation. He looked better. Cushioned in the coffin, well dressed in black, peacefully asleep, he looked better than when alive and empty. Jack sipped at his drink, and his thoughts returned to his problems. "So what's the best plan, Ed?"

"Well, of course you'll need some account made by a witness—one who was there and is still alive," Ed claimed. Jack was not pleased at his sarcasm. "I don't know if he can get any details of any event leading up to this," Ed said sharply of his detective.

"Indeed," Jack replied sternly. "You can start by checking out Durrell and see if he has connections here in New Orleans besides drug running."

"Blood evidence will not link him to anyone, Jack."

"Just look into Durrell. We'll link the pieces together."

"Fine, we'll get on it, but if he has to go into Mexico again, the cost is double."

"I don't give a damn about the cost; just get the results." Jack had no patience for anyone on his team who did not understand the priorities. They didn't have to pin anything on him just yet; they had only to find the areas of his weakness—find where his guard would lower, and let the lucrative moment show itself. The timing would make him culpable. Ed loosened his collar. "So," Jack said, "are we good?"

"We're good," Ed replied. "My guy can burrow into anything. We'll hear from him at the end of each day."

Jack rubbed at his sore knee joints as he rose. "Very well, we wait. How 'bout nine holes?" Ed nodded, and the two filed down the stairs, out the door, and into Jack's black Jag parked at the front of the home.

CHAPTER 20

SCANDAL

Jason Broussard was almost finished. He was the last of the detectives who offered up details of their interviews, but it appeared that despite their having questioned many individuals, they still had only a sketchy notion of the killer—nothing tangible. "It's just guesswork," he concluded. Broussard was the only local. He had grown up in Treme, graduated from LSU, and moved to Metairie. His wife worked at University Hospital and gave the team insider information on perps in surgery from time to time.

"Okay." Jamison scooted in as Broussard sat down. "Clay has a sheet for stolen goods and got six months for acting as a fence. There were no IDs or wallets on them, and their pockets were empty. Everything we've extracted from DNA is running through the database for any sort of match to give us more information. Neither one of 'em has family. Perfect if you want to waste 'em after a job."

"Semen from Ellery and this one here." Johnson pointed to Lester Clay. "So he fucked her and killed her." He raised the notion again. "Why sex up the target?"

"Because he's fucking low-life scum. He saw the opportunity!" Jamison bellowed as he spit out the last bite of his prepackaged sandwich from the vending machine down the hall. "God, these things are awful," he said as he wiped his mouth and walked toward the trash can, glad to see the last few bites thrown away. It was a horrible choice for breakfast. "Right," he started, wiping his mouth again with the back of his hand, "we've accounted for the two slobs for hire being at our party. One of the two of them killed Maddie, got his prints on the knife, and left knife residue in his boot, where we assume it was concealed. And we know they were hit professionally but don't know by whom or how." He moved over to the nearby table and held up the baggie containing the murder weapon. "This is a twenty-five-centimeter single-edge-grind serrated utility knife. It's made to cut through crustaceans. If residue confirms the murder weapon was at some point tucked into the right boot of our buddy here, he either stupidly left it on the floor of the crime scene or it was taken from his boot and placed on the floor. It was smeared with blood and body matter. This was not a flesh wound; he gutted her. Now, wouldn't you wipe this shit off on your pant leg and take the knife with you? But there was nothing on his clothing."

"You think someone planted it there to frame him?" Raskins asked.

"I don't know; do you?" he motioned to her and then to the others. "Left to try to frame Ellery? No one's prints on it but Clay's. Why would he leave it?" No one had an answer.

Matthews moved on. "Chief, think the shooter was just backup?"

"I do," Jamison replied. "Whoever ordered the hit didn't want to rely solely on those two." He poked his first two thick fingers on the close-up of the dead men Durrell had hired. "This guy, the unknown shooter, was clean—in and out without anyone detecting him, especially not his prey. He was goddamn invisible!" Jamison was clearly irritated that there was no evidence and no leads for this shooter. "A small number of assassins are delusional or impulsive killers; most stalk their target, planning every detail of the crime. They know the habits, schedule, nuances, and security details. The killer had to successfully execute his plan, and more importantly, get away from the scene of the murder. He followed our boys here. He familiarized himself with the area, knew his weapon, and was damn good. One bullet each, no spares, no miscalculation. We can all agree he had a silencer, since he was able to pull off two shots across a mob of people and no one heard or saw a thing. Without a silencer, the sound of gunfire would have ricocheted all over that pavilion." Jamison was starting to get hot under the collar. "Nolan, talk to security and see if they noticed anyone out of the ordinary in there the week beforehand."

"Sure thing," Nolan said, and he went back to his desk to grab his keys and wallet.

"So he's so good he could have taken her out on his own. Why hire the other two first?" Matthews asked as he moved closer to Jamison. "A stepping-stone?"

"Yeah, one more link further away from the guy who gave the order."

"This is all so perfect," Raskins thought out loud. "Every detail accounted for to lay the blame. Open and shut; there's no other evidence of a third connection."

"Except we know someone had to give the order," Jamison replied.

"We're never going to catch the shooter," Matthews admitted. "Too clean—nothing left behind."

"That we know of," Jamison interrupted.

"Crazy?" Raskins asked.

"No," Jamison said. "I think it is someone quite sane and calculating."

"Maybe a spook?" Raskins was hunting to uncover any possibility.

"Uh, you mean 'operative'? And no, I don't think so."

"So we're looking for someone big that wanted Madeleine dead for a reason that moves beyond our party?" Matthews inquired. He circled the whiteboard with his finger, making larger and larger circles. "To include who?"

"Wait; let's back up," Jamison interrupted. "If a contract had been put out on Maddie, why New Orleans? Why not up at the Capital? Why at this time, in this public place, of all places? A pro could have caught up with her anywhere, anytime. It could have been done quietly, discreetly."

"Easy access in and out? Easier to get lost in a crowd?" Raskins offered.

"Maybe," Jamison replied.

"Maybe they wanted the hit to be public—you know, a scandal," Webb offered. "Maddie was killed because she was the senator's mistress. The hit was specifically public to expose Senator Doussaint's dirty little secret and send the media nipping at his heels."

Jamison rubbed at his chin as if he were caressing a beard. He stood facing the whiteboard for a moment as his team watched, waiting for his response. They were already nodding and nudging one another, confident in Webb's revelation. "I think you're right." Jamison stated tapping at the photo of the murder weapon. He spun around to face them. "I think you're right, Webb."

"This is going to put a dent in the captain's desire to keep Senator Doussaint clear of this case," Matthews acknowledged as he sat back down.

"Just because it's his mistress doesn't imply he's involved," newcomer Gene Reynolds added.

"Sure it does," Raskins immediately interjected to the recent recruit. "It doesn't implicate him in the murders, but he becomes a primary player."

"So you want to get back at the senator for something? Why this way, and why Maddie? Why not his wife or his son?" Gandy asked.

"A blood relative makes it deeply personal," Jamison claimed, "but Maddie was part of his presence in business. Everyone knows that. Maybe the hit was somewhat personal but it was by someone who got burned in his business affairs."

"Agreed," Raskins stated.

"Yup, right on the money," Davies remarked.

"Exactly … the money!" Webb proclaimed as he stood up. "It's the business of money. Doussaint burned someone in the wallet. It's classic—textbook. Murder over money and a business deal gone wrong."

"Maybe the competition," Davies added. The detectives were buzzing with innuendos and conversations among themselves. Webb had offered the best motive so far.

"All right," Jamison interrupted, raising his arms and hands to quiet everyone. "Let me remind you of the sensitivity required in this case. Webb, look into Doussaint's business deals and bank accounts over the last year or two. Find out if he paid out or received large amounts of cash at any time. Also look into his travels over the last couple of years. See what he's been up to."

"Right, on it," Webb responded, and he grabbed his sport coat from the back of his flimsy desk chair to head out.

"Rass, check into his son's travel. His wife said they had just gotten back from a cruise; find out where they went, who he met, and if he had any substantial trips, income, or expenses over the last two years."

"Gotcha," she replied, and she gathered her things from her desktop. She gulped down the rest of her morning coffee, throwing the empty white styrofoam cup in the trash beside Jamison.

"Good," Jamison exclaimed, pleased that they had substantial focus.

"Do you think the senator's camp had anything to do with this?" Matthews asked awkwardly.

"That's what you're supposed to be finding out!" Jamison snapped. "Get busy."

"Yeah, boss, got it," he said as he moved toward the double doors. Jamison scanned the room. Webb and Raskins had just left the squad; the double doors were still swinging. A few groggy officers were waking up with coffee at their desks. Others were busy filing, on the phones, or glued to their computers. He noticed through the double-door windows that uniformed patrolmen out by the entrance were arguing with a higher officer—*shift assignments*, he thought. He had just turned to walk back to his office, content that a few pieces of the puzzle might be coming together, when Captain Hughes turned the corner.

"Putting the pieces together, Mick?" Hughes asked.

"Yeah—well, sort of," Jamison stammered as he averted his eyes from his captain's view. "This has the potential to blow open, Cap'n. It's going to fucking blow up in our faces, and you know who is going to play a part whether we want him to or not," Jamison stated.

"Well, you have to make sure it doesn't," Hughes replied, wincing as if to say, "That's the way it goes."

Jamison's frustration was starting to well up. "Am I supposed to solve murders or protect dickheads in power?" It was a rhetorical question, but the captain answered anyway.

"Both," he said, and he slapped his chief on the shoulder as he brushed by on his way out to his own office. "And can we please get all our evidence in to prove our theories?" Jamison scowled at the implication that he was to jump through all the hoops and cover everyone's interests at the same time.

CHAPTER 21

POWER OF WATER

Wynton washed his hands and broke two eggs into a bowl. He drew small handfuls of chopped white onions, green pepper, and diced ham from a worn cutting board and threw the ingredients into a sizzling skillet. Raymond watched the onions soften as Wynton poured the frothy beaten eggs over the ham and vegetables. He added salt and cayenne pepper and winked at Raymond. When he slid the finished omelet onto a plate, Raymond bent over it as if her were inspecting the paint job on a used car. He straightened up. "You make it look so easy, E."

"It just takes practice. It's good for breakfast, lunch, or dinner." He paused. "Especially good late at night when you can't sleep." He gave the plate to Raymond and stepped behind him, opened the refrigerator door and reached in, and pulled out some encased sausage. "Look what else I got at the market this morning ... andouille," he announced. "Tonight you get to practice with this," he stated as he held up the meat for Raymond to see. Raymond rubbed his sore shoulder. "Oh no. No you don't," Wynton chastised him. "You don't get outta this one."

Raymond took a breath of sweet onion-scented air and smirked at his brother. "A'ight," he replied, and he smiled that milk-white smile. "I watched Momma and ate that nufh to know what to do with it." Periodically, Raymond set the dial on the coffee maker, and he knew how to use the microwave, but that was the extent of his cooking skills.

Wynton grabbed the folded *Times-Picayune* off the counter and slapped Raymond's abdomen with it. "Know what to do with this?" he asked snidely. "You can look for a job."

"Ah, man, you know ain' nobody hiring."

"You love food so much; why not connect with a restaurant, Ray? Ladies like to dine together in groups; it's the exact place for both your loves." Raymond smiled; he hadn't thought about looking into the food industry. He was pushing his food around with his fork as he pondered the idea. Maybe a restaurant and bar would be a good match. He had been let go four months earlier, when the hospital supply company, HCA Delta Division on Park and Canal, was absorbed by Ochsner Medical Center.

"Is not going be much different," Raymond said, changing the subject, commenting on their morning plans. "They's still abandoned and full of vagrants." He was talking about the trip they'd make to the old house.

"Yeah, but this is the last time; the city's bulldozing before Christmas." They had gone every year on their mother's birthday, but finally, four years later, it would be the last chance to survey the house before the city gutted the street as part of the lingering cleanup from Katrina. He got up to retrieve flashlights from his toolbox. "C'mon, Ray, eat up; let's get moving," he said as he left the room, went down the hall, and exited into the garage.

Moments later they were on their way. Raymond slipped a pair of sunglasses onto the bridge of his nose. They'd be driving through areas hit hardest by Hurricane Katrina—areas still devastated and painful to see. They drove through Meraux, looming with smokestacks and vast crude oil storage tanks. "Who know how much gallons of toxic crude gush outta there unchecked," Raymond commented.

"Mmm hmm," Wynton agreed. "It's a shame." They were headed deep into fishing communities where residents lived in a handful of hamlets nestled on the vast apron of a marsh, Lake Borgne, a sprawling brackish bay, and the Gulf of Mexico. It had a history rich with rum runners and gun smugglers, swashbucklers, and mercenaries—a fascinating mix of Acadian immigrants, Creoles, and Cajuns; but it was now overrun with trailer parks and oil refineries.

Through the long, seedy grass of the levee north of town, clamshell roads skirted the neighborhoods. There were a few shotgun houses on stilts, sunken trawlers, long-legged chicken coops, and camp boats. Beyond it, the Intracoastal Waterway stretched out, with the banks on each side carpeted with low willows. The steamy scent of slow-moving water filtered through the leaves of cypresses and cottonwoods, and one could scoop up a mess of soft-shelled blue crabs from the lake's shallow grass beds.

Below, the area was bustling with shipping lanes of the Mississippi, with thousands of workers coming and going, servicing oil and gas wells and processing facilities in the deep-water canyons of the Gulf. There was a railroad trestle where a daily steam engine brought supplies and hauled away the bounty of area fishermen to the New Orleans markets. It was fish-rich and fertile, but beyond it, St. Bernard's estuary was like an uncharted wilderness with its labyrinth of barrier islands, bayous, and sprawling marshes, all ringed by a moss-draped cypress swamp full of alligators and venomous snakes.

Here, self-reliant families scratched out a meager living by virtue of knowing how to handle a boat, weave and set a trawl, use a cast net, cook gumbo, and handle themselves in a fight or a squall at sea, none of which were trivial skills. But among the metal-skinned double-wides, where others might ask, "Why would anyone settle in a floodplain?" bayou people, whose lives and work were intricately woven, would reply, "How could we live anywhere else?" Many were relieved that the initial storm surge had veered off course and headed east to Mississippi, but all around were signs of the height and intensity of flooding. The watery devastation and disappearance of whole communities was stunning.

The French Quarter had been virtually unscathed, save for some downed trees in Pirate's Alley and Jackson Square. The adjacent Central Business District along Canal Street likewise had suffered only moderate damage. St. Charles Avenue and the Garden District had been spared. But for Chalmette and St. Bernard Parish, there was only wreckage.

A few leftover trailers and newly constructed prefab houses edged some of the area: a declaration that life rebounds—a counterpunch of sorts to the nearby empty lots housing old, rusty chairs, and to the crushed, silent churchyard that now filled only on Saturday mornings with farmers selling fresh vegetables and cornbread. It was a place still ripe for the occasional politician to tromp through before an election, wearing a banner for the poor, defending some retrospective or prophetic testimony of service. This was a place where locals returned, considered their dark fate, and wept even as the years rolled on. It was a lot to take in on their way to Delacroix each year.

They arrived in an area that had changed little since they were last there to clean and gather up salvageable items. The shrubs and trees remaining from the storm were larger, but everything looked as if both the water and character of the neighborhood had been squeezed dry. The blistering paint on the small homes that were still standing needed sanding and a new coat. Some doors didn't close completely, warped from the weight of water. Yards were overgrown and dry, and weeds were browning amid sun-bleached bark chips.

Upon getting out and standing, it was also apparent to Raymond and

Wynton that there wasn't even the slightest breeze to skim across their skin. The entire aura of the neighborhood was wrought with desolation. Wynton paused and looked up and down the street, pondering the impossible images on TV: people baking on rooftops while waiting for rescue, and others wading through sewage, carrying a few meager possessions. The recovery had been slow. Streets had been caked with sludge, and everything remaining was dead or encrusted with shades of brown mud like a sepia-toned photo. It stung the imagination. Approximately eighty percent of the city had flooded; fifteen hundred people had died; and four years later, only half of the displaced population had returned.

They came up to the house and peered in through one small mud-soaked window. The walls were dingy, with the same wash of color from years before. Everything was marbled with brown tones of deluge. They walked around the entire house before pushing their way through the front door. There were patches of earth here and there, as if mercy and grace had tiptoed between everything obscene.

"First time we come here, this looked like it done bin picked up and shook real hard before setting back down."

"Cinder block frames are easily shifted by water."

"Is just all tore up." Wires hung low from what was left of the roof like snakes in trees.

"We should go by the cemetery while we're here."

"I ain' going over to that pauper's field when most the stones missing. Didn't Auntie Dee tell us we should let the dead rest?" Wynton shook his head.

Raymond felt as though they had just pried open a path to the dregs of society. There was nothing more worth salvaging: a worn sofa with springs cutting up through the foam, a dingy mattress and box springs barely attached to a fraying faux-wood headboard. The paisley spreads were soaked and ruined, and the hollowed nightstand that had been toppled and battered was missing a leg. There were a couple of large black leaf bags filled with odds and ends they had packed on their last visit that would go to charity.

Raymond scowled, his lips tightening. Wynton felt a chill despite the stifling, suffocating heat of a small enclosure with most of its windows boarded up. There was still the muggy, pungent scent from waters that previously rolled through these streets. To the left were two doors. One led to a filthy bathroom where the cracked sink and tub had been pulled from the wall, and its toilet was missing. Down a dark hallway was the other door, which led up to a small one-room bedroom.

The house looked so small to them, and the farther they moved in, the darker it became. The musty rooms seemed to drag the breath from their lungs. Wynton led the way upstairs with the beam of his flashlight. Raymond tensed as he pushed open the door to see a stained mattress hanging off a rotting frame. Beside it was a worn chaise with foam stuffing exploding in small pockets where the fabric had frayed. Beneath it was broken glass from the window that had been blown out and recently boarded shut.

A portion of a small, withered chest of drawers remained in the corner. Wynton fingered the sides and corners of each remaining drawer. Empty. They were all empty except for a tiny, tangled chain along the groove of the lowest drawer. Wynton pulled on it in a zigzag motion, freeing it from the jagged wood filament. "The last bit of Momma," he said sadly, and he placed the tightly knotted chain in Raymond's hand. At one time it was a thin gold chain, but its sheen was now marred with mud and soot. It had a toxic smell; Raymond cupped it, coveting it anyway.

Raymond let out a sigh, stretched his neck, and rotated his shoulders in an attempt to dispel some of the tension mounting in his upper back. "Man, hate to see what it musta looked like from inside a home in the Ninth Ward."

"No one would know; none were left standing," Wynton replied. "Those homes were literally blown away … only concrete pilings left behind." The image of people sloshing through a fetid stew, hunting possessions, bothered them each time they came. With vacant lots materializing where homes had been, they were sure the area looked like a cemetery, which it was, in a sense—a graveyard of hopes and a certain way of life.

"Let's go down to the kitchen," Wynton said, slapping Raymond's stomach as he passed by on his way to the stairs. It was a poorly constructed kitchen with one counter, a two-burner stove, and absolutely not enough space for more than one person. When they got there, Wynton said, "Close your eyes, Ray. What do you see and feel?"

"I can hear Momma's deep laugh," Raymond answered.

"Yes," said Wynton, "and I can almost smell the collard greens boiling on the stove." Their mother's heart condition had worsened amid the deluge. She never got past the ruin and how salt-crusted puddles left in her home caused such uprooting, just when she had organized her life and arranged her house the way she liked. Neither could she move beyond the notion of how many neighbors were gone: gone without plans to return, without plans of revival— just gone. It was pure dread that killed her—dread of suffering that wrapped her in the paramedic-orange shock blankets that ultimately could not save her.

"She just give up," Raymond recalled, opening a cupboard.

"Well, I don't think giving up as much as being overwhelmed," Wynton replied. "It was too much for her." He glared at all the cupboards. "I think we got all the plates and cups last time." Raymond closed the door and didn't bother to open another one.

"'Member how she say the sea sang out through lips of mud?" He turned to his brother.

"Uh-huh. How it rolled and swept out bloated corpses like driftwood," Wynton said, continuing Raymond's thoughts.

"She was pretty deep for an uneducated woman," Raymond replied, stammering a bit. "You and her got the same way of thinking."

"I'm thinking how she used to throw her arms up in the air and call out, 'Black Jesus, hep my boys.' She prayed a lot for you. You always found trouble, always throwing people the middle finger."

"Lawd, Black Jesus, there go my baby 'gain," Raymond said, squeezing out his best Momma voice.

Wynton snickered. "C'mon; let's get going."

Wynton called to mind a story written by James Lee Burke, "Jesus Out to Sea," that was in a 2006 issue of *Esquire*. Two New Orleans ne'er-do-wells sat on a rooftop, waiting to be rescued from floodwaters. They summed up their pitiful lives and the music they played. As they talked, a large wood carving with Jesus on the cross floated by them, and one remarked how New Orleans was a song in your heart that never died. Wynton thought that song grew stronger in chords and stanzas every year her birthday came around.

They both had quieted as they collected their things, seeming to reflect on the lost lives of the Ninth Ward that had swirled beneath the surface of water that fateful day—the lives of those who might have collided into bricks, trucks, or branches, or that could not swim or stand against the rogue flow that had sucked them deep into the surge. There was no theory or theology that could explain why some remained safe and others got swept away. "The hand of God some shamelessly bragged," Wynton said aloud as he thought about it all, as if God chose certain folks to flourish and others to die.

"What?"

"Oh, just thinking this all was not so much fate but more likely human futility and man-made structures that weren't strong enough."

CHAPTER 22

POWER OF A PEOPLE

They had known hurricanes before. Most of them broke past bulkheads, covered lawns, flooded woods, crept up stairwells, and raised surf that beat at night against their door, but they had emerged unfettered. Still, in light of a slow recovery, life went on. Around the bend of the Mississippi, in the Market Café, a small band would be playing Louis Armstrong, hornbills would be stalking the evening ferry from a safe height, and sparkling trinkets would be on display on vendors' stands in the French Quarter. Palmists would foretell futures in the gaslight, there would be rappers performing behind St. Louis Church, and prostitutes would be wrapped in leather, awaiting their clients like night goddesses. Far off on a city podium, Tulane students would perform some Greek tragedy, the women of the St. Thomas inner-city housing project would be reeling in bright clothing off clotheslines, and along the city shores, fishermen would cast their nets as they have for hundreds of years. Not much remained, but no one could question the resilience of the New Orleans people.

Outside, Wynton and Raymond felt the incessant heat of the day, and it was barely noon. They each opened a car door and threw a bag of items for charity in the backseat. Before sliding into the hot interior of the Cougar, they were greeted by Earline Monnaie, who came back to the neighborhood frequently with her nurse aide. Miss Monnaie was in her nineties, a thin and frail widow who opened every conversation with "My huzbin, God res' his soul." She was a storyteller who had made and sold fruitcakes on the streets in her midlife years.

"Morning, Miss Monnaie," Wynton greeted her. Raymond nodded.

"Aftahnoon i'n't it, boys?" she replied. "Look it, look it, tha' flood done made the bottom of a gumbo pot look like a fingabowl compare to dis." She chuckled a little at her own indication as to how things still appeared. "Rubbish everwere, and our ald'men talk. All they squawkin' runs like water down a road, leavin' mud in its trail."

"Yes ma'am," Wynton concurred. Raymond nodded again.

"Wha' you boys doin' here t'day?"

"Just looking round the ole house, ma'am," Raymond stated. "Got the last of Momma's things to take to charity."

"But you leavin' empfty handed," she remarked.

"Just put a couple of bags in the car," Wynton interjected. "The rest is—"

"Junk!" Earline said, finishing his sentence. She began telling some of her same stories, and her nurse put the brake on her wheelchair, realizing they'd be there a while. She talked about traveling around the Old South by rail. On one hand, her stories evoked a time without haste and too much worrying—one filled with simple pleasures and a kind of hunger that meeting folks could perfectly fulfill. But the reality for blacks was racial prejudice, and she told them how awful it was and how they had no idea. First she told them the folk cures for syphilis that were practiced in her youth, encouraged by the whites, with appalling effects. Then she told them the harrowing story of her mother witnessing a lynching in Georgia. "And she tol' me they brought they chil'en 'long to see," she piped. "They chil'en!" She shook her head sadly. "Long as I live, I wilt nevah undastand them things of our past." She paused and looked at the brothers from their feet up to their heads. "Hate an' crulty ... how it root an grow, then root deeper." This was simply stated, as if all of humanity had betrayed her.

"Yes ma'am," Wynton replied. The Ellerys smiled and listened to her intently, though much of what she said they had heard before. They had realized some time ago that she was a living cultural treasure. She wiped at tears from her nut-brown eyes beneath her thick, bottle-like glasses—the sentimental tears of a woman in her tenth decade whose past was more vivid to her than her present.

"So many colors of peoples here long time 'go. Like a field of flowers. But no one meaned to keep it nice." She was right. New Orleans had a bizarre history as thick as the humidity. It was the largest slave market in North America, and yet it was the only southern city with free men and women of color. It was the first city to build an opera house and the last to install a sewer system. Much of the architecture was rotting or in dusty process of preservation; it was largely of Spanish influence, since all the wooden French buildings had burned in the 1700s. It had elephant-ear greenery and bougainvillea blossoms, which Tennessee Williams likened to bloodshot eyes.

"Nowadays peoples come here for they first feast of oysters or a glimpse of a nekked woman with the lights on." She was right about that too. "Used t'be peoples was all out everwere t'gether." She stretched her hands out, pointing to the area before her. Her arthritic fingers swinging out from long, boney arms looked like hooks. "Lawd, use t'be you could smell this city: chicory coffee an' spilt beer, sloshed hot sauce, an yesterday's fish, garlic chik'n an mule dung."

Unfortunately, after Katrina, the city smelled once more. Raw sewage, industrial chemicals, and a nauseating odor of decomposition permeated everything. Bodies of animals and humans had rolled and bobbed in the wake of rescue boats, surfacing with the froth of floating trash. Gas mains burned underwater or burst, filling the sky with flames. Anyone who lived in lower Louisiana was affected forever by Monday, August 29, 2005, when the center of Hurricane Katrina passed through.

Miss Monnaie still had all her faculties, including her boisterous opinion. It was hard to ignore what living might have been like for her. She still had bright, scouring eyes, and Raymond and Wynton assumed she still had the same menacing dreams. But cruelty never laced her voice. She had not let fear turn sour, and she had learned to remedy her disdain for growing up with rough black skin in a lily-white world.

She had sized them up, wondering what they might be thinking. "Oh, I knows is toufh. Each season, each day come, not too simply, but no one undastands. We go through creation too fas'. Seeds pushin' through decay, fragrance soft and purty, gulpin' fo' air. We don' notice like someone drownin' or suffocatin' less time scream at us. We don' notice the threat streamin' in, gettin' heavier than whatere emptiness is lef' behind. Is not a nice worlt. Songs of freedom come 'roun' once in a blue moon, an' then the hands of God lay 'side you still an cold. No pity stirrin', you jus' gone." She paused. "I feel like an ol' woman. Ain' nuthin' green an fresh in me, but I done ain' got no heavy stone weighin' me down neither. An till tha' happen, ever'day we still human, we keep climbin', seekin', huh? Huh?"

"Yes ma'am, you is right 'bouts that," Raymond chimed in, pointing at the senior, who understood how to walk the road. In fact, she sailed headlong into the gale force of life knowing that one day she would wash in that wondrous, anchoring love of her God.

"I miss yo' momma." She paused. "Ain' she got a sista here in the area?"

"Auntie Lucille? Ah, no ma'am, she moved north to Jackson, Mississippi,"

Wynton responded. Their Aunt Lucille, who rode out the storm in her home near Folsom, in the rural countryside about fifty miles north of New Orleans, had endured a harrowing night of tornadoes, and intense heat while going without electricity for days. "After neighbors cut a narrow path through hundreds of downed trees, her nephews on the other side of the family came to get her and drove her to Jackson to stay."

"Everbody's done gone," she lamented.

The Ellerys were saddened for her losses, but they were glad to bump into Miss Monnaie on occasion; she made them smile.

"You're so special, Miss Monnaie. So glad we saw you today, but we'd better head back," Wynton said as he reached out his hand to her. Raymond nodded and waited for his turn. It was a sort of anointing as she clasped a hand between both her aging hands and said, "Bless you son," to each of them.

The Ellerys made a U-turn and waved as they passed by, heading back to Wynton's home. "She something," Raymond commented.

"Yeah, too bad she feels so alone and out of place now. She's a smart ole bird," Wynton said. It had been a worthwhile visit.

CHAPTER 23

HENRY

"Before we leave the area, let's grab some good old fashioned soul food over at Li'l Dizzy's." Li'l Dizzy's Café was a no-frills joint first opened as "Eddies" in 1947 for soul-food breakfasts, lunches, and a buffet option in the Seventh Ward. Located in Faubourg Tremé on a portion of the Morand-Moreau plantation, it was sold by Claude Tremé in 1810 to the City of New Orleans, and it is considered to be the oldest existing African-American neighborhood.

"Aw man, we too late for breakfast. They got the best grits and pork patties," Raymond lamented.

"But we're not too late for lunch. Gumbo, catfish po'boys, homemade hot sausage, and the best fried chicken anywhere. Mr. Baquet is serious 'bouts doing the Creole-soul tradition proud."

Raymond smiled. "Yeah! Hell yeah!"

The crowd was thinning when they arrived. It was one o'clock, and the café closed at two. They grabbed a center aisle table and noticed the man sitting next to them. "Ain' that Mr. Rochon, Momma's neighbor?" Raymond whispered to Wynton just before sitting down.

Wynton nodded and leaned toward the man sitting alone. "Mr. Rochon?" he asked. The man looked up, hesitated for a moment, and then smiled and extended his hand.

"The Ellery boys! How y'all?" he asked. "And call me Henry. Join me?" Wynton gazed toward Raymond, waiting for approval.

Raymond shrugged and replied, "Guess so, but we just starting to eat; look like you done bin finished a while."

"Yes, have, but sure would be nice to sit with you boys a spell. How's yo' momma doin'?"

"Mr. Rochon ... ah, Henry ... she passed not too long ago." Wynton informed him as he signaled to a waitress. The Ellerys ordered and pushed their table flush with Henry's.

"Tha's a shame," he replied. "Sure is a shame."

"How you doing?" Wynton asked.

"Same. Ain' changed much. Miss my wife, the neighborhood, yo' momma, an' nem good neighbors."

The Ellerys began eating, lending an attentive ear to a pleasant old man that still needed to share the stories they'd heard before.

"My wife, Tinlo, she was from Bhutan, you know—a beautiful place teemin' with life. Why I needed to come back an' bring her here, I dunno." He paused, somber in his reflection. "She just stopped touchin' me that day, you know? She always hooked her elbow up under my arm. Then she wa'nt touchin' me no mo. That day her body done got bent back and tore at the neck and shoulder. I couldn't stand to look at her body no mo. I lifted her up outta the water and laid her 'tween some outstretched branches. They held on to her like hands. Divine hands, I thought. Who else could cradle deafh so gently?"

"That was a dreadful day," Wynton consoled him.

"A man passed by pullin' a child behind him on a dirty mattress. Another with a horn strapped across his back. I didn't see any other women. I could hear 'em. I could hear the pitch of names bein' called out; some hollerin' fo' lost ones; some callin' out they prayers, aksin' God to save 'em from dis hell." He shook his head, displaying disappointment at things not mentioned. Raymond rolled his eyes, having heard this saga the last time they met up with him.

"They were ol' men and strong-bodied young men holdin' onto somethin'—a cooler, a bulgin' backpack. But they looked the same: dingy, war-torn, an holdin' firm to the weight of what they was carryin'. It don't matter, you know, if you gots money or not when you lose everythin'." He looked at Wynton and Raymond to see whether they understood—whether they could understand a bit more about their mother from the conditions of that fateful day.

"My neighbor, Willie, said he was out collectin' his children, but I hadn't seen no child go by. The heat of the day seemed to wear off too quickly, 'cause ain' no one want to be there in the water, huntin' loved ones at night. All we heard were cries of disbelief and fear. Don't nobody want that goin' on all night long while you tryin' to find yo' way outta the water. You know, no electricity—that means no light. They was no lights nowhere, an' who know what is in the water witchu." He shrugged, returned his gaze to his cup, and sipped at the last bit of his drink. Something defenseless in the way he held himself, his rounded back and shoulder, seemed to divert attention away from his dark, pinched face.

"I 'member next day when we saw reporters. They was pepperin' folk with questions, but they ain' sharin' no news. No one knew to what extent the storm had done hit, if others lost so much or just folk in our area. We guessed it was over for the most part or reporters wudda nevah bin there yet. Some of 'em just stared at us as if they had forgotten how to speak. Others seemed heartsick to give us any mo' bad news."

Indeed, as Wynton recalled, when the rains first started, meteorologists reported incessantly about updraft, atmospheric pressure, and air mass. There was no real explanation beyond rain about the water that jumped the levies. Folks stood knee-deep on street corners, ignorant of the havoc wreaked, aware only of the smell of gasoline and how quickly things change. Soon came swollen floating bodies, submerged cars, children wet and shivering, mass evacuation, looting, and the shock. The shock. Wood pallets and sandbags became irrelevant small bridges. Rooftops became islands, and wailing from behind guardrails amplified the drumming doom.

"One told me, 'whatever prayers you been sayin', keep on sayin' 'em.' His words cut me to pieces, so I couldn't move. I seen women pull they children, huggin' 'em tightly. They was sayin' God had done spared 'em, yet I had lost my wife." He sighed. "There was a row of corpses, cover'd, but a carpet of flies hoverin' about 'em nonetheless. An ol' man was shooin' dogs away with a stick. I was just thinkin' somewhere in that rottin' pit of bodies might have been my Tinlo." He paused, tearing up. "They told me we'd have to leave the area and might never get to come back. I said a silent prayer for all nem peoples and walked away. Found Mavis, then yo' momma later on." A light was returning to his eyes.

"Momma always spoke kindly about you, Henry. I hope we're not upsetting you." Wynton stated, hoping in part to get him off topic.

"No, no, you know Mavis lost her husband and a son. I wondered if her tears would ever stop. Our bodies were wet, covered with insect bites. We had bruises and open sores, cuts that was sure to be infected, but we didn't see nuthin' but the primitive looks around us from the disaster. We was taken to a refuge place and squeezed in between bunches of folk, where we could stay on cots. I never allowed myself to dwell on the details."

"Yes," Wynton said, engaging him.

He smiled at the Ellerys. "Yo' momma was a great hep. Her and Mavis got to work right away, found some packaged cheese and crackers, and canned fruit. Had some Co-Colas and settled in a'ight. Aftawards, they had areas with some hot food, and a area fo' medicines. We was feelin' lost with family could never be replaced, but we was also 'live an' safe, you know?"

Wynton saw Raymond unusually pushing and jabbing at the food on his plate like a sulking child. He made a mental note that his brother felt deprived, poor, or rootless. For all the folks Wynton had to pull aside, criminal or not, he could see in Raymond the same running, falling fear that dragged others into darkness. Their mother had lost everything. This man speaking with them had lost everything, as he expressed in his tale of the violent choreography that washed away the lives of so many. Raymond was safe but sad—angry too. Despite Wynton's cautioning, Raymond was angry most of the time.

For a moment, Wynton was lost by Henry's exchange, not hearing him well. As he reflected on what Henry was saying, he was struck by the notion that it was the same thing Raymond had been whispering in his ears over the past several years. "... the choice white men get that others ain' nevah got—choose where to work, where to live, but mostly choose for blacks too. They determine where we oudda live, who we should be scared of. Our losses ain' nevah quite big nufh to matter like they own loss." He glanced back at Raymond, uncertain whether he was listening to Henry or whether he was listless from hearing something he felt he knew all too well.

Like his stories, Henry was unforgettable. Even the wrinkles in his skin looked waterlogged and pruney, as if he were frozen in time, forever entwined with Katrina. He had woven love and ruin into transforming recollections that reflected a myriad of messages, absolutely none of which resembled reason.

The Ellerys thanked Henry as dishes were cleared. It had been fitting to run into him on their last trip to their mother's house. His eyes were sullen and bloodshot as he talked about those first few days. Now, as Li'l Dizzy's was closing and they'd all soon be departing, he returned his stare far off into space. He was breathing deeply, slow in his mannerisms, seemingly half-conscious; he looked as he had when they first entered.

Looking them over, a thirty-something waitress asked, "Any thang else I can git you boys befo' we close? We finna close in jus' a few minutes." They shook their heads as they returned her gaze. Her silver hoop earrings flashed like fishing lures. Raymond nodded, momentarily interested. She refilled their sweet tea anyway and then slapped a check on the table and headed back to the amber light filtering through the kitchen's swing doors.

"I got this, Henry," Wynton said quickly as he pulled out nearly a dozen ones and a couple of tens and walked the amount to the register. Copper and cast-iron pots and pans dangled overhead from a makeshift rack. Wynton ran his hand along the terra cotta countertop inset with painted ceramic tiles.

Raymond picked at a small blister on his hand as his eyes followed Wynton's every step. He noticed the botanical prints and bright turquoise and yellow glass paperweights that cluttered the counter's surface. Then he noticed the shape of the cashier, who was wearing a long print halter dress in African colors of green, yellow, and black. He made a mental note as to her bare mahogany shoulders, which were as smooth as bedposts. For a moment, he lingered at the wide-toothed tortoiseshell comb tucked into the soft part of her hair. Its reflective shine signaled to him like a lighthouse beacon, and he thought about what she might know about men.

Wynton returned with a free neighborhood newspaper beneath one arm, his dark forearms flickering with light looping from behind the metallic fan above. He threw Henry and Raymond a quick smile and spread out his large hand to thank Henry for his time and stories. Raymond stood up in the gap of conversation and thanked Henry for sharing the painful ruin of his life, and he then wiped at his nose on the short sleeve of his T-shirt, clearly moved.

CHAPTER 24

KEISHA

The hot air wafted around Wynton and Raymond upon opening the door and stepping out onto the streets. An unusual October felt like full-on summer, and it fell like an anvil. By midmorning, the dread of heat shuffling in without a cooling breeze to smooth away the flesh's beading sweat made it a psychological and mental challenge to simply push forward into midday. Those who worked outdoors started early, prayed to the cloud gods, and dreamt of air-conditioning and shuttered windows. The walkway between the restaurant and the parking lot was full of people. They slowly waded back into normalcy, weaving their way in and around the lunch crowds, trying not to stick to those they bumped into or collided with. They walked and dodged the others silently, reverently walking through the area after the storm cleanup. Then, the area was bare and as fine as a scar, smoothed over where trees and homes had been ripped from their roots. The frames that remained were skeletal, with interior furnishings soaked in rank refuge. Some with heavy banisters and carved newel posts gleamed in the new day's sun. Others with solitary posts stood amid leveled debris. There was a constant sound of hammering, chainsaws buzzing, and bulldozers cutting new paths farther down the street. Their hearts sank at the overwhelming images that flashed and ran like a slideshow in their thoughts.

Wynton palmed Raymond's shoulder. "Can you think back to the first time we were here?"

Raymond thought for a moment. "When we saw them fishermen drag a shark up to weigh?"

"Uh huh. That monstrous head seemed as wide as we was tall."

They recalled the battalion of teeth protruding from what looked like a toxic grin. So frightening, they thought, it was the one species among many that rightly belonged to the sea.

Wynton thought about the devastation of a shark powering up through the blue to surface amid bones and blood, churning in the frothy surf. It sickened him as a boy, and now, again, he felt the same nagging angst in the pit of his stomach while considering the monstrous power of wind and water.

Once back in the car, Raymond weighed whether or not to say anything, and he then spoke up.

"You ain' said nothing 'bouts Keisha. Was her birthday this month. You good?"

"Yeah. Lots of memories about loss these past couple of weeks. It's okay." He turned on the radio, letting the music take him back through the years. He recalled them sleeping all tangled together on special birthday nights, the three of them snuggling, waking, turning, flipping, tugging at sheets. He recalled her little hands across his chest in the early hours before daylight as he lay there with the two people he loved most. His emotions ran from calmness to euphoria. As he felt her little heart serenely beating, he was completely at ease. Then, in a split second, he felt so elated, as if he could jump up and run out into the night air, invincible.

She had been a baby who slept and woke with a smile and raised her arms eagerly to be held. She grew into a beautiful child. She had a full, round face framed by bouncing black curls, and her lashes were long and dense. She was her mother's daughter in looks and temperament, with a calm and deep wellspring of love. Her little girl world resurrected blue skies and opened doorways to wonder with a magic-tapping wand. Her whole world meditated on "once upon a time," waking and slipping into lush green "happily ever after" days.

He recalled Keisha padding across the room with daffodils to welcome him home as soon as she heard the click of the front latch—how she found her place at a table, not shy in the least about showing her appetite. Just like her Uncle Ray-Ray, she ate as if she might not eat the next day. She smiled, slowly pushing too large a spoonful of food to handle in her mouth. Then she covered her mouth with her hand while she chewed, with her cheeks puffed out dramatically, her eyes locked on her daddy all the while.

She had a guileless pose in the beginning hours. With her arms thrown up above her head, she looked exposed and vulnerable, fragile and content, innocent in a dreamy state, pure and magical. She was awake, and the future beamed brightly in her eyes. Wynton's heart overflowed with love and happiness when he was with her. While raising Keisha, holding on to her had been easy. It was not done in the way the sky holds a cloud or a dancer flies his partner. It was not as simple as the islander with his shop upon his back. It was not like those who carry everything or those who let everything fall. It was not even done with patience or courage. Nurturing Keisha was as simple as breathing.

He thought about past birthdays—how she cupped her hands around her mouth as she blew, enthralled by the flickering flames that sputtered to hold their own atop her favorite whipped-cream cake. Blowing exhausted her, made her feel lightheaded. Ultimately, she'd clasp his hand and pull him closer to center stage. In a muffled voice, she'd nudge him: "Bwo, Daddy."

He missed the tiaras, walking on tiptoes, and the endless card games of go fish. He missed making Cream of Wheat with brown sugar, the surprise cat attacks on the couch, and those dear baby eyes peering into his, searching to become full-grown. He thought back to the sick feeling that rose up in his stomach that crisp morning when they walked her to her first day of school. They had been oblivious to traffic and the other students passing by. Keisha hummed most of the way, slightly nervous. Wynton felt helpless against the pain of letting go. Her hand released. Leaves tapped lightly as a breeze picked up. Wynton felt it had been an undercurrent to the feelings swirling inside him that day—a continual undercurrent for the feelings he had trouble dealing with ever since.

CHAPTER 25

THE CITY

Wynton changed his thoughts as he drove. This time he was reflecting on the Crescent City he had loved for so long. Just driving could be a crazy challenge. The bend in the Mississippi River dealt a kind of directional wild card. Approaching the West Bank, you'd really be going east, not west. Add pea soup fog, the fact that New Orleans was built on swampland that lies below sea level, is bordered by water and crisscrossed with bayous and canals, and you have the makings of a disorienting, eccentric outpost.

The city's personality spilled out amid encounters with alligators in the drainage system, the Krewe of Crawfish parades, The Second Line in the middle of St. Charles Avenue, the melee of Mardi Gras, and heads of cabbage thrown like volleyballs from floats on St. Patrick's Day.

Wynton smiled on recalling the French Quarter's heady aroma of open-air breakfasts like café au lait and sugar-dusted beignets at Café Du Monde on Decatur. He and Belinda went there some Sunday mornings to skim through the newspaper and watch passersby as they sipped their steaming coffees from an outdoor table. Jambalaya, nectar cream, and the best turtle soup with its shot of sherry were found here. He thought about all the legendary Dixieland musicians playing to the souls of Congo Square. Whether at the Saturn Bar, which showcased a psychedelic dragon, several pairs of panties, and a bumper sticker that said "I'd Rather Be at the Opera," or at the Napoleon House, which was more than two hundred years old; where there were people, there'd be music and food. He thought about the slave trade and how every brick in the French Quarter had a story to tell. Now the Ninth Ward would bear witness to another big part of New Orleans history.

He thought about the superdome amassed and the collapse of vital functions that made a nation shudder. He recalled the sheer weight of days without rescue and the images of people wading, shoes in hand above water. He considered folks still waiting for that steady, streaming, flow of change and the illusion of fair play. It was a grave situation, but they kept hoping and dreaming despite feeling forgotten and unimportant. They had remained grounded in their simple yearning for freedom from menacing skies and political storms that followed.

"Ray, did you know there's a picture in Dooky Chase taken late last year of Obama when he was a senator, about to dine on some of our fine local soul food?"

"Uh, no."

"The president looks happy, the staff looks happy, but it stands in direct contrast to another N'awlins image taken three years earlier. That one is a photo of a family stranded atop the roof of a flooded home. The word "help" has been written out several times, all misspelled."

"Yeah, so?"

"One image speaks to the institutional failure that makes the city susceptible to disaster—not just that of levees that break, but also of the poorly educated underclass that waited days for rescue. The Obama image suggests something different. Man, Dooky Chase was a hangout for leaders of the civil rights movement in the sixties. The restaurant was devastated by the storm, but here it is now, rebuilt and thriving, and last year hosting the nation's soon-to-be first black president." Ray was hesitant to comment and sat upright in his seat, wondering where this conversation was going. "Pundits, geophysicists, and Congress seriously debated writing off N'awlins as a lost cause, that rebuilding a drainage swamp that lies below sea level was not worthwhile." It was true. native wags writing for the *Times-Picayune* suggested the United States had always distrusted this strange city with the habit of marching to the beat of its own drummer and were anxious to use this tragedy as an excuse to do the city in. Yet thousands of Americans in and beyond New Orleans rose to the challenge. They waded into basements in one-hundred-plus-degree heat and slopped out trash, rubble, and corpses. They fixed each other's roofs, planted gardens, and reconstructed homes as well as the cultural climate, with a stunning statement of hope to those who had written the city's hasty obituary.

"So don't nobody done write us off," Raymond scoffed.

"No, don't you get it? The incredible history here ... what was and is now amazing history ... and we're a part of it," Wynton rebuked.

"C'mon, bruh, don't play me; we got nothing but bruthas drumming on buckets, and po'boys."

"Nah, man, we got alligator sausage, grilled baby drums, cannibal salad, oyster lugers, Cajuns paddling pirogues up the slough, Creolized bayou accents, pecan trees, Basin Street jazz, and zydeco."

"You making me hungry."

"You're always hungry." He paused. "This city is where Walt Whitman first tasted sin, where Abraham Lincoln gained his sense of the shame of the nation, where Samuel Clemons ended his riverboat career an' took up writing. Don't you get it?"

"No, I don't; ain' no sense to it."

"This is the original melting pot, where Africa and Europe coerced southern charm."

"You mean where folk shuck oysters and suck crawfish heads."

"No, this is home of the free lunch and lagniappe."

Wynton laughed at his brother's persisting pessimism. "You mean where mask and bead turn into gossip and voodoo."

"Ray, this is the city of a unique history of collision, absorption, corruption, and freedom, and it has always been larger than its stereotype."

"So what's your point?"

"All these places we're driving by—for miles buildings were stripped of their shingles, and their windows caved in. Streets were awash in trash; live oaks punched through roofs."

"Don't forget looters taking everything not bin bolt' down, and nem cops who head for higher ground, driving off with new Caddies from the dealers," Raymond chimed in.

"Yes, yes, bad choices made."

"Bad choices? Bruh, how 'bouts murder and rape? How 'bouts that a third of the po-lice ditch they duty for they own selves?"

"Okay, add the evil element; that just helps magnify how fragile life is and how nothing should be taken for granted. Did you realize what we did and saw today, who we spoke to, where we live—what N'awlins means to this world? It's magical, it's spiritual, it's heartache and heroes. How people can keep on going in an inhospitable place never intended for humans is beyond words. No one with good sense should live here, but we do. We're living it, Ray; that's cool as hell."

Raymond gave thought to what his brother was saying but realized the day's trip was special because he was with his big brother. "Yeah, E, is pretty cool."

"It *is* cool, Ray. While politicians and Army Corps of Engineers officials still squabble over who was at fault for the collapse of canal floodwalls, writers, artists, sculptors, and musicians have come to life. This is the place they are now compelled to document: the catastrophe, the recovery, the plight of our people, even their own fears for what has been lost. The people have become as vital to the recovery as any federal relief aid. It is cool, brutha; it is very cool to be living now—living here."

"He coming next week, you know," Raymond added.

"Who?"

"The president. Coming on the seventeenth. Gonna tour MLK charter school in the Ninth Ward and giving N'awlins more than a billion dollars."

"Yeah, part of the stimulus package. But the Army Corps of Engineers is only a third of the way through the fifteen-billion-dollar system that's supposed to provide a hundred-year flood protection. Wonder what an extra billion will do."

"Nothing. The president ain' gone be doing nothing for us here."

"Hey, he promised he'd come back as president, and look; he's coming down here in his first year." He paused. "I read there's going to be a town hall meeting at UNO Recreation & Fitness over on Lakeshore."

"Only ticket holders admitted. How's come you didn't apply for a ticket?"

"What about you, with all your free time?"

"Ah, man, I don't see no change happening anyway just because a brutha's in the White House."

"C'mon; he already signed legislation to expand publicly funded insurance for children, and he's working on a health care program that can insure millions currently not eligible."

"Let's not forget he sent more troops to Afghanistan already."

"Ray, not everything can be done in a short period of time. He's only been in office ten months and he's got a lot on his plate—major screwups that have to be remedied. This visit is significant."

"He only coming back as president for like three to four hours. Just for show. Blackness done bin systematically devalued for generations; nothing new gonna happen here."

"Hey, he's coming. And he's trying to get things done the way they were supposed to have been done in the first place. Going with Nagin to break ground at Cooper Public Housing."

"They rebuilding the projects?"

"No, developing a new mixed-income community where the projects used to be."

"Uh huh, just displacing more poor folk for the mix, and probably 'nother kickback for our lucky mayor who keep making trips to Jamaica. Wassup with that!"

"Oh, Nagin, they'll catch onto him soon enough, just like the city council members who went to jail in 2007 for bribery. Fraud at all levels, brutha. He is lucky to be doing the rounds with Obama now as president."

But Raymond argued his point again. "His trip here is for show, just like everyone else who done bin down here from Washington." Wynton shook his head and scoffed at Raymond's negativity.

"Ray, did you know that after Katrina hit there were more than nine thousand people living in temporary housing, and that number's down now to about fifteen hundred?"

"If FEMA wasn't so screwed up, that number be down to zero right now."

"All I know is Obama's visit right now as president is going to help focus our country's eyes once again on N'awlins and the aftermath of the most devastating natural disaster in American history. It's decidedly significant; we're witnessing more and more history from right here in our backyard!"

CHAPTER 26

LOST CHILD

When Sara showed up at the Children's Advocacy Center, she was disgusted that Tyler was missing and everyone seemed dismissive. Sara was growing bolder in her anger. "You must have some idea where he is."

"Why? Because he comes and goes here? That doesn't give me much information as to where he is coming from or where he'll head next. I haven't seen him today."

The center was like some place underground, she thought, *just short of serving time.* Here, young children and preteens filled rooms that echoed noise like a subway. There was arguing, crying, and ceaseless, mindless television. The walls in the hallway were a color of light brown that blended into the heavy-hanging odor of cooking, urine, and pine cleaner. There was not much glass, which limited the view beyond what center officials wanted visitors to see. Sara knew living here was a sort of hell. Pounding voices, bureaucratic mismanagement, sleeping on plastic sheets, and eating watered-down, meatless stew on cracked, dingy old plates meant each child here was at risk of falling through some sort of trapdoor and falling into the cracks, where they could easily become lost and forgotten forever.

"God," Sara said, dejected at her dead end, "what kind of mother dumps her kid!" She was not expecting an answer; she was simply befuddled by the notion of a mother abandoning her young son like a broken part thrown into a junk heap. Still, the social worker offered some food for thought.

"Oh," she said in a knowing way, "only a petrified heart coaxes a mother to leave her child to face fate alone."

"Wha? Huh?" Sara had moved past her own expression and was trying to think of where Tyler Kessler was. "She just left him."

The social worker continued. "If you're unable to stand on your own, there are little choices to help you with further mounting anguish. Exhaustion and desperation override everything else."

"How can you be so compassionate to people who abandon their children?" Sara truly could not fathom her patience and complicity.

"Mrs. Doussaint, I know you've helped Tyler, but you don't know his world. There is a consequence in being here like this. You can't possibly understand the underbelly of society, where poverty and loneliness linger and filter into these young children. These are exactly the circumstances where a foster kid's sudden disappearance can go unnoticed."

Sara was shocked at her frankness and her cruel outlook. Maybe it was a clearer perspective of the real world than Sara could ever imagine. "Hey," she replied, "I may not be poor, but I'm not stupid. He said to meet him here today at five just before dinner was served. I know he's not playing me. Come on; I'm paying him good money to help me. He'd be here if he could."

Tyler had happened along while she was doing a shoot and was intrigued enough to stick around a bit when they first met. Sara talked with him and let him help her with her equipment. He was uncommonly bright and had an old soul for a seven-year-old boy. They had hit it off, and within a few weeks' time, he was meeting her regularly.

"Well, maybe so, but he's not here. Do you want to leave a message?"

"Yes, tell him I was here." She began writing on a torn piece of paper. "And give him this note with my number." She looked to the front door. Eric was sitting in the car parallel to the entrance, looking at her. "All right, just give this to him. Thank you." Sara quickly scooted down the hall to the entryway. Outside, she opened the car's front door and fell into her seat, frustrated.

"So?" Eric asked as she put her seatbelt on and adjusted her clothing to sit comfortably.

"Oh," she answered, fingering her hair off her face. "He's not here. She said she hasn't seen him today." She sighed and turned the radio on. "It's ten after six; let's go," she directed reluctantly.

Eric put the car in drive and looked over his left shoulder before accelerating. "Well, you never know with these kids," he said. "They do what they want."

"No, he would have been here, Eric. I've really gotten through to him. We have a friendship—a bond."

"Yeah, well, something came up. Forget about it; he'll call." Eric was certain it was no big deal, nothing worth worrying about. Sara, however, felt ill at ease.

"I just know something is wrong."

"You really don't know him or anything about his life or his world," Eric said.

"That's just what the social worker said," Sara interrupted in a dry and unimpressed voice, surprised at their similar wordings.

"Well, maybe it's true. Either way, there's nothing you can do." He leaned toward her and patted her knee, letting her know he cared and wasn't trying to simply pacify her.

Sara pulled the visor down to see herself in the mirror. She was flushed, and her hair needed brushing. She stared at herself for a moment. Maybe the social worker was right; she knew all too well that fear had its hiding place amid radiance and longing; that a heart might hold on to a place to be afraid in. She snapped the mirror closed and returned the visor to an upright position. Her mind was racing. What had she and Tyler last talked about? She tried to quell her uncertainty as she stared out the window, watching all the images go by.

Tyler was a confident little boy despite his living circumstances, and he was eager—certainly eager to help Sara with her photography. He had a keen eye and caught on quickly about how to operate the camera, what the lens options were, and which choices produced the desired results. He was a superb young fledgling, and Sara thought he just might grow up to be a good photographer one day. Sara enjoyed his company. She felt he was charming and adorable when he was with her.

She recalled that first morning running across him when she was shooting in City Park. He was unafraid and just came up to her and asked what she was doing, showed an interest, and then stayed with her through most of the afternoon. It nearly broke her heart when she learned he didn't have a family or a home but stayed downtown at the center. She wanted desperately to give him something substantive to make up for so much of what he lost out on.

"Eric, you know, he's just a few years older than our little boy would have been."

"I know, honey; I know you care about him, but his whereabouts and his interests and instincts are beyond your control."

"I know," Sara agreed half-heartedly. "He's so, so precious. He's just this sweet little helpless boy with such maturity. He takes every single calamity, every hurdle and trouble, so nonchalantly. He is fearless and so agreeable. I worry about him ... that something will happen to really harden him, you know?" She turned to see Eric's face. He knew Tyler filled a spot in Sara's heart. He had met him, and he liked him too.

"Maybe when he calls we can arrange for him to stay with us for a while. I don't know ... a visit, or maybe foster care."

"Really, Eric?" She sat upright, pleased with her husband's supportive response.

"We'll see," he said. "We'll see."

Dusk was approaching—the time when ordinary objects took on a different appearance before dark. She was watching the shapes and shadows blur in the lavender haze as they drove past areas that had been hit by the storm so many years ago. She recalled the birds during Katrina. She and Eric had bailed some from the surge of water in Mandeville. Amphibians simply submerged, but there was a dreadful feathered downpour, like a false migration, as birds who had not escaped were frayed, driven by the winds onto gutters, reduced to straw as they splintered through the trees in their fall. The looming human desolation amid mud was awful, but those were not the images she witnessed firsthand. What struck her was seeing the peeling, rotting wings—such lifelessness delicately pinned between branches. There was an unforgettable silence amid the sights and sounds from the crippling tentacles of wind and water. Like machinery, it came thinning the sky-blue, grass-green fields of life, reducing sprouts and ribs to a jagged, reprehensible black-brown vault.

She had wondered in the aftermath of such somber and swollen devastation whether mankind was meant to suffer in order to learn to dig deep past the pain to find shelter and fortify. It was a cruel and sad lesson to bear, she supposed, but without endurance, what was the point of nature's alarms? If decency and conviction did not survive beyond the mildew and decay, where was life's compensation? She was wondering now whether Tyler could be compensated for the wreckage he had faced from a broken heart.

CHAPTER 27

THE STRAIN

"I just read a good article by Dr. Robert Sapolsky, a professor at Stanford, about how stress affects your body."

"You too, Matthews?" Jamison squinted his eyes. "Jeez, my ex ragged on me enough about this job and stress to last me a while, okay?"

"Hey, just sayin', boss. Most of the diseases we get are worsened by stress. Once you understand the intricacies—"

"Dammit, Matthews," Jamison interrupted. "Can we leave neurobiology to the scientists and get back to this case?" It was, of course, a rhetorical question, and Matthews knew better than to answer or prolong the subject.

"All right, now, we think we're moving in the right direction, but what do we know for certain?" Jamison was calming down. "Like Donna here"— he gestured to Matthews—"let's understand our own physiology. We live in our bodies; ours is the only one we'll ever get. But do we really know it—its complexities?" He sneered at Matthews, who was sliding downward in his chair, clearly aware of how he had annoyed his friend. "Look; we think we know ourselves, but we don't—not really. So let's not also assume that we are thinking through every aspect about this murder case, okay? You guys check the hot sheets?"

"Yeah, eighth district and also Saint Bernard Parish have a similar MO," Gandy offered, "except that it's black on black."

"Just a bunch of thefts in the French Quarter and Downtown Development District," Webb added.

Davies chimed in, saying, "Nothing satisfying. An elderly man was killed during a robbery gone sour in the four thousand block of Gen. Ogden Street.

The killer was tracked down by surveillance within thirty hours. Turned out to be a teenage boy angry at his foster parents because he could not have a dog."

"A couple multiple shootings over near the B. W. Cooper housing complex, but no witnesses to substantiate any information," Matthews stated.

"Reynolds, Nolan, wad'd ya get?"

"A could be," Reynolds reported. "Paco Jimenez, Hispanic male, age twenty-nine, and Perry Traisance, white male, age twenty-five, at West Bank Expressway Barber Shop and Tattoo Parlor. A lone shooter entered the building and deliberately shot and killed both victims in the parlor while they were working on tattoos. The initial motive was alleged to have stemmed from a conflict between Paco and a female who had recently received a tattoo. The male friend of the female allegedly returned and shot both vics, but the case is without witnesses. No one saw a thing."

"Yeah, well I vote for the original motive—not likely our guy."

"I got something," Nolan said. "Tamara Cole, white female, age twenty-six, in the abandoned City Hall Annex Building on Canal Street. The victim was located in a stairwell on the third floor. She suffered deep lacerations to her throat and abdomen and subsequently bled to death. Follow-up investigation revealed Ms. Cole, a local entertainer, came to New Orleans from Pine Bluff, Arkansas, with her boyfriend and two small children. It was ruled a homicide by the Orleans Parish Coroner's Office. Never found a motive or suspects."

"Okay, good; thanks, Nolan. Could be the same two killed Maddie; we don't know their motive in the case either, and slashing the abdomen—that's coincidental."

"Or maybe not," Matthews insisted. "We've got a third killer linked to someone who knew where these two would be, and that they'd be killing Maddie."

Raskins was tapping her fingers, waiting for an opening. She figured that if gender and race can work against you, she knew deep down there could also be a heavy price for being wrong. She had a cool head and good intuition and tried to make sure she was right before she offered her opinion. "I went back to the crime scene last night," she said. "Everything is taped off. Pictures were taken of where the bodies were found and all the background—every foot, at every angle. I glanced around to the adjoining vendor areas and ducked through the boarded doorway to the laundry room. I was assessing details. There was white tape where Ellery had fallen, and numbered tags here and there where prints were taken. I went across the ramp to the indicated trajectory point." She paused for emphasis. "Did you know no cartridges were found? Who would stop and pick up the shells?" Jamison seemed dismissive as he asked whether there were any more reports.

"Maybe the Annex Building was the first job to see if they'd go through with it before they moved on to this job," Webb offered.

"Either way, we've got to find that link," Jamison stated. He asked Gandy, "What did our shrink say? Offer anything?"

Gandy responded, "A no-brainer. Said our killer has no feelings of moral responsibility and will be hard to find because he's practiced hiding or blending in full sight."

"Anything else?"

"Oh yeah." He glanced down at his notebook. "He takes taking the law into his own hands quite seriously."

"Well that doesn't seem to help us much."

"She's a counselor, not a psychic, sir."

"Okay, moving on, let's talk ballistics. We're looking for a .40 caliber pistol; could be a Beretta, Smith & Wesson, or a Sig."

"Or a Glock 22," Davies said of the standard issue .40 and .45 caliber sidearm.

"Don't go there," Jamison scolded. "That'll open it up to everyone: patrolmen, you and me, the FBI, and the DEA."

"Or a Glock 44," Johnson added to the conversation. "Old, but a nice weapon—.22LR, barrel recoil, spring assembly, speedloader. Could be the newer model with optic, and mount with lights and lasers. Either way, expensive—not what typical street thugs are using."

"Broussard, call the crime lab and see if they lifted any trace materials, and put a rush on it!" Jamison stood up and dismissed his detectives for the evening, except Donald Matthews. He was told to get to Jamison's office.

As the room cleared, Matthews entered Jamison's small, unkempt office, closed the door, and rested his arm atop a file cabinet. Jamison's pinstriped shirt had pulled up out of his wrinkled khaki pants as he bent over to reach down to the bottom right drawer of his desk. He grabbed the bottle and two small glasses and swung his body around to flop into his broken down, rickety desk chair.

"Jeez, Don, why do you insist on trying to humanize me in front of my crew?" He poured two whiskeys and handed one of the two glasses to Matthews. "I'm not a human—not to them. I'm supposed to be the heartless machine that nips at their heels and bites their butts to keep 'em going."

"I know, Mick, but look; you're stressing out in front of everyone out there!"

"This is a damned stressful case," he replied defensively. "How can I gather evidence for a DA to prosecute someone if I have to stay clear of a primary player?"

"We're already scouring for all the details about him anyway; just don't tell the cap'n," Matthews suggested. "He's got to know more than he's telling."

"We don't know that for sure," Jamison replied. "Evidence, man, evidence. And meantime, Hughes will cut me loose on this one. He's only got four more months until retirement, and he does not want anyone bloodied on his watch." Jamison felt exhausted. "It's not how I do my job. It means something, all right?" He swallowed his glassful like a shot. "With all the low-life crap we put up with day in and day out, it has to mean something. It has to mean we make a difference—maybe even make a better place of this shithole, you know?"

"Yeah," Matthews said, consoling his friend. "You do; you make a difference, Mick. You're damned good at what you do." Don Matthews, who previously worked vice on the streets with hookers, lacked some of the appropriate respect and manners other detectives inside the squad might expect. He was loyal, though, and strangely lighthearted given his background. He and Jamison were in the academy together, so he knew what buttons to push to rile up his friend and boss.

"All right, all right, cut the touchy-feely shit, okay? We've got to find a way around Doussaint unless it's the only way we solve this case. And if it's the only way, then we damn well better have a tight case with every little bit of evidence and wrongdoing accounted for."

"Mick, you got to look at Cap'n too. He's high up there; might be dirty himself, or in bed with 'em."

"Don't you think I've already thought about that?" Jamison answered indignantly. "Christ, I don't know where this case is leading, and that's not something I'm at all comfortable with." He slammed his bottom drawer shut. "And another drink's not going to make it any easier."

With just a moment's pause, Captain Hughes knocked on the door as he was opening it into Jamison's office. "How's your triple murder coming along, Mick?"

Matthews tucked his glass behind him, gesturing for the captain to take the extra chair.

"All right, I'm on it, Mick. Night." He motioned with his head toward Hughes as he passed behind him.

Jamison nodded and then turned to his captain. "It's going in circles."

"Well, I stopped by to tell you I think that Ellery kid is not as innocent as he seems. There's something else there, Mick. We're just not getting it. I tell you this punk's guilty of something." Hughes tapped on a file with his long, narrow, waxy finger. "You look back into his file and give him another going over; you'll see."

Jamison knew Ellery was not a murderer, but he nodded. "Yeah, Cap'n, I'm going to have to look harder, deeper, into quite a lot."

The captain smiled, assured that his chief of detectives was going to play by his rules. "Say, you know," Hughes suggested, "the commissioner wondered about this Ellery punk's brother. Might look in his direction too."

Jamison held his tongue and did not look at Hughes, keeping his gaze down on the top of his desk. "Actually, sir, this thing is such a mess, anything is possible." He knew Wynton Ellery did not merit further scrutiny; nor should he be an actual suspect. But he was referring to the powers that be.

Hughes quickly swiped, "Not quite anything, Mick—got it?" The slim silhouette of the captain slowly went by, his head up, smug in his power. Jamison leaned back in his chair. He was tired, strained from the case, distressed by the freely given authorization to pin a murder on an innocent man in order to cover up the trouble of the higher-ups. He wished for a moment that he was still married, just long enough to think about someone rubbing his neck and shoulders and back to relieve tension. Then the moment was gone. What paired with willing hands was his ex-wife's mouth—a constant, discouraging, chiding mouth that pointed out all his errors and flaws. "Nah," he said aloud to himself, "I just need to get laid." He rummaged through the disarray of papers to find his lighter and then reached to pull his suit jacket off the coat tree in the corner. He was going for a drink, and if he spent his money wisely, he was going to take someone home with him tonight.

CHAPTER 28

FLOODGATES

They drove over to Clio Street near the exchange before heading back across the lake to Mandeville. Eric turned onto the now darkened side street, just past the swarm of mimosa trees in the park, toward the dead end where much had been abandoned and run down. The streetlights remained broken, and kudzu, whose mammoth blades strangled everything green, climbed the palmetto thickets and the wood planks along a few of the empty plantation homes jacked up on stilts. He slowed as he reached the street's end and parked in front of a tan, weather-worn slatted building that needed scouring. It was next to the church Sara had grown up in and was so fond of. Saint Paul's, her old Methodist church, was the last flicker of life to the otherwise dismal and forgotten area. The dark red brick church was not large by most standards, but it was dignified and elegant, with five long, multipaned stained-glass windows at the front.

Sara was first to get out of the car. She spied the heavy oversize doors that opened into the vestibule. Her thoughts flowed through those doors, and her mind's eye took her beyond, into the narthex, with its wide-open wooden archways. On one wall there hung a watercolor of a dark-haired, dark-bearded, tender-eyed savior in white; on another, a painting of a contorted, bloodied Christ in the ecstasy of suffering. There, more searching and more daring than the silent, peace-filled savior, it seemed to be the cruelty of the crucifixion itself that fascinated her. *A different Jesus, however humanized, however modernized,* she thought. *There is a Jesus who knowingly still suffers in order for us to endure.* Jesus, Mary, angels as good as the good fairy, and a personal, fatherly God to love and forgive her had become ever more prominent as she relentlessly explored the eternal themes that obsessed her: love, loss, the nature of relation-ships, and death—the death she had carried with her since childhood.

There in the narthex was a large, gold-plated wood cross that drew con-gregants' attention to the main doorway to the sanctuary. She followed her drifting thoughts through those doors and into the sanctuary, visualizing how the sun shone bountifully through those stained-glass windows on Sunday mornings as though the architect had commissioned the light and air of Protestantism into the design. Everything came into vivid focus. There was an aisle where a scalloped shell of water awaited baptisms, and oil was nestled in bronzed inkwells. Rows of smooth, weathered oak pews flanked the aisle right and left, looking like a net of amber light caught by a fisherman's cast. The cast, of course, would be made by the minister from the larger of two altars, as prominent as a stage. Sara whispered sullenly, "Oh forgive us, Lord." The day was slipping away, and she wondered what she was doing there. She considered that, left to her own lips, her own eyes, and the progression of her heart, she would still be climbing her own pain. Mountains of change that rose and fell like ghosts had thwarted her growth. Not until the Carpenter and this place had she learned to pick the lock of her bones and peel back the wall of flesh that separated her from God.

Sara smiled and shook her head a little as if to clear it. The old church hit her with a pang of sentimental affection. For a moment, she saw herself—that tall, lanky, bony, lonely girl with pale skin and hair streaming down her back. This had been her real home—the place that had offered her validity after her mother passed away.

She never tired of visiting adaptations of transformation. Her photographic interest in the abstract was, in fact, a logical extension of the genre that evolved in her collective unconscious because of her faith. She had a dogged conviction to remove sentimentality and trite images. She seemed grim about her sense of loss but, quite innocently, captured whatever came to mind—whatever was at hand that enticed her own independent and incisive judgments. The results seemed more ambivalent than her subject matter. The more she suffered and grieved like some confessional poet flung into the abyss, the more impactful the final framed image.

Sara had a slumbering intelligence with hiding places where impatience and anger sulked. It was here at this church, carefully coiffed with flowers and stained glass, where she could release some of her troubles, where she could cry aloud to God publicly about so many private details. Here, in the stimulus of a good sermon, she could dwell in the cerebral, spiritual, and bodily experience, restoring life to the silent, symbolic taboo of irreversible loss and the ache that lingered and fattened through the years.

Eric got out of the car; his shirt stuck to his back with perspiration. Even though the sun had set, the humidity remained. He flapped his arms and pulled at the front of his shirt, sending fluttering puffs of air through the fabric—a momentary delight before the shirt was clinging again to his skin. He came around and stood behind Sara, hugging her closely. How large she felt here this night, grown beyond the young lungs and nervous fingers of the girl who had searched the sanctuary for the warm, ample face of God and the arms and skin that smelled of a mother. She felt so far from that childhood now. In his arms, she wondered if Eric had any idea of the happiness and contentment that had taken possession of her.

"We have a good marriage, don't we?" she asked as she placed her hands over the top of his.

"I think we've been in love a long time," Eric responded. "Longer than most couples." He reached up to tuck a stray lock of hair behind her ear. The touch sent a shiver through her neck and back.

"I learned about love here," she told Eric. "I drank it up in morning worship and on Sunday nights with the youth group." He began to caress her. "The church was my summer—my greening season of expression. I loved every brick, every hinge, every pew and hymnal, the light of God that shone down on me like the sun."

"Mmm," Eric hummed as he focused on the vacant, unlit street and the hushed, darkening evening.

"Hopeless," she said to him, knowing his methodical movements, long practiced and long rehearsed. He tilted his head, considering her attractiveness.

"You intrigue me," he whispered in the same ear that he had tucked hair behind, and he then kissed the nape of her neck. She turned toward him, placed her mouth on his lips, and kissed him sensuously.

It was beginning to mist, and Sara noticed the lone, flickering streetlight a half block down. He was running a finger around the inside of her waistband. A force of warm languor whirled through her, but she was pretending to be indifferent, noticing how the sky's low clouds formed around the two of them, encasing them. It was hard to resist Eric; she felt reborn with every lingering sensual moment.

"Eric." She breathed his name.

"Mmm," he hummed again. A fleeting thought swept through her to strip off all her clothing and expose every inch of who she was to the misting rain and this sweet man. Instead, she kissed him long and passionately, clinging to the moment. They were buoyed there arm in arm, a lost weight, their bodies lifting, reaching for each other. A beautiful notion was nodding in her mind. She sensed the way they belonged, moving, as if nested in each other's touch. It was important for her to hold still, fold into him, sink into his eyes and not talk, gathering in the essence of everything: the mist, nightfall creeping in, the warmth and smell of Eric, and her own freeing thoughts. She embraced him harder but then quickly pushed away. There was a sound—an unnatural sound. "It's a cat," Eric said without knowing or caring. A shadow passed by, darting through the undergrowth.

"It's there," Sara pointed to what seemed to be a rustling near a bush by the entryway.

"Sara, it's a cat," Eric said again, and he moved toward her mouth to help her refocus. There was another rustle, and a shadow flickered along the doors. She looked to see a bird lifting up to fly away, spreading its wings and flapping once before stiffening its wingspan to soar upward. She watched the small body until the bird was blocked from view. She herself felt drawn up. She was under his spell.

Then came a cough.

"My God, Eric," she said as she pulled away from his grasp. "We came here hoping … Tyler!" she called out. Her hand pressed to her forehead, shielding her vision from the misting rain to see a child starting to stand up from a crouched position by the entrance. "Tyler!" she called again, excited. "We came here to find you, but we didn't see anyone when we pulled up. I—I didn't think you were here," she explained as she was running to him. On reaching him, she wrapped both her arms around him and pulled him close.

"This is where you told me to meet you if ever—"

Sara cut him off. "Yes, yes, dear, I knew you hadn't forgotten we'd meet. I'm so glad to see you, but you're supposed to call me before coming here. I don't want you on this deserted street alone." She gave him an affectionate hug and squatted down to him so he could see her eyes. "Are you all right?" she asked, considering his young age and the variety of crime available in the city. "Sweetie, you need to stay at the center, go to school, and call me before you scamper off to God knows where in this city. It's not safe, Tyler." He bowed his head, feeling scolded instead of welcomed. "Oh, but honey, I am so glad to see you." He looked into her green eyes and grinned.

Eric was soon behind her, slightly embarrassed. "I suppose you noticed I like to kiss my wife, even in the rain," he said jokingly to break the ice. Tyler laughed. They each took him by the hand, heading back to the car.

"Come on," Sara said. "Would you like to go to our place?"

"Yay!" Tyler answered without hesitation. Though he didn't know where that that place might be, he was giddy at the prospect.

"Yay!" Eric mimicked as he opened the back door for Tyler and buckled him in.

CHAPTER 29

MOTHERS

After arriving home and getting some food into him, Tyler and Sara slipped away to the guest bedroom. "This would have been my son's room," she said, opening up to Tyler. "You lost a mom, and I lost a son … I think we're good for each other." Tyler agreed, shaking his head but not speaking. He was eyeballing the room's size and the decor, which would have been for a little boy. He sat down on the bed; the mattress lay atop a shelving unit. Tyler thought about all the books and toys he would have lodged there if he had grown up in this room. Sara moved to sit next to him after observing his watchful eye.

"Know what?" she asked. Tyler shook his head a little. "I've discovered that it is not always up to us to understand death and rage and goodness—not really." She knew he must be remorseful about being left, about not having a stable household to grow up in, and about not having the kind of room he was in right now. "But sweetie," she continued, "I do believe that in the darkest hour, God can restore us. We can't determine the nature of God, but we can know he's there. He's close, Tyler, and I'm here. I know you have doubts about everything around you, but it's going to be okay."

Sara pulled off Tyler's shoes and kicked off her own and then crossed her legs underneath her on the end of the bed. Tyler turned and folded his legs up underneath him as well. She touched his knee and smiled. "When my mom died and I was lonely, I thought I wouldn't be able to stand it."

"You lost your mom too?" Tyler asked. "How old were you?"

"I was five. I was very young like you and didn't really understand why or what would happen with the rest of my life." Tyler nodded in agreement again.

"I really thought my sadness would well up in me and I would burst, literally. The pain was terrible."

Tyler scooted over next to Sara, and she put her arm around his back and waist. "That year, after my mother died, others told me that she died because God wanted her. I didn't understand, because I thought God would know I wanted her too. As time went on, I just dragged my anger around with me and never told anyone how I felt." Tyler chuckled nervously. "Instead I saved up money."

"What for?" Tyler asked.

"I was always looking for loose change that no one would miss."

"I do that too," Tyler said.

"I did it because I wanted part of my brain removed." Tyler squirmed a bit and scrunched his face as he looked up at her, thinking she was a little bit crazy. "I figured all the bad memories must be in one place in my brain, so I was saving up for an operation that could take it all out of me." She gave Tyler a big squeeze. "In our storms, we struggle with our views of who we are. Unfortunately, we usually need help from our parents, and you and I missed out, kiddo. You got left completely, and I was left with a father so stricken by grief it consumed him completely. It was like a black cloud came over our home, and I didn't have anyone to explain to me precisely what had happened. Consequently"—she patted his side—"I blamed myself. I knew I must have done something horrible if God didn't want me to have my mother."

Sara paused to see Tyler's eyes growing wider and moistening as he looked up into her face. "Sweetie, sometimes there's just not a logical explanation available to us for all the unhappiness." Tyler hugged Sara's waist hard and began to cry. Sara assumed no one had taken the time to talk to him about his loss as he got moved from place to place. She imagined he was simply told what was his and what the rules were. She knew he felt empty, and she wished he could give up the feelings of rejection. She wished she could soften the blows for him as he was hurt or overwhelmed. She had spent years falsely learning to see and think of herself based on how others treated her or what they told her when they misspoke. *What an awful, awkward time of growing,* she thought as she comforted him, *this age of developing self-concepts, while constantly searching for surrogate parents.*

Tyler wriggled loose and, turning his body, lay down, putting his head in her lap. She stroked his blonde-flecked, soft brown hair. "Your mom did not let go of you easily," she insisted. "It was never because she had to love you or care for you. That was the easiest thing she could do. That was the great reward to her—getting to love you and care for you." She paused, remembering what the social worker had told her. She reflected on how desperate life would have to be to let go of a child. "Sweetie, her life had gotten horribly uneasy, dangerous, and careless. I can't imagine how bad her life was that it forced her to make such harsh choices." She stroked his hair again and saw that he had surrendered to sleep. *Poor, exhausted thing*, she thought. "She loved you enough to let you go," she whispered.

Her own head felt heavy, and her heart ached for this young boy. She knew there'd be plenty more days like this one. And then there were images that would never leave. She carried images of a mother with limp arms, palms open, waiting for something more than air to fill them. Sometimes she could not stop the flow of details. What were the images that were haunting Tyler? She couldn't imagine living on the street at such a young age. There was a hard edge to his life that she had never had to face, and she wondered if she could even bear the intrusion of that world in her life.

Sara reflected on her mother's beauty. She was a natural, with luminous skin and deep green jewels for eyes. Her disposition matched her appearance: calm, inviting, accepting. She couldn't think of a time her mother was ever angry or disapproving. Of course, a five-year-old can't remember much of his or her early life at all. Still, Sara liked that she could hold on to such a positive, happy view of her mother. She had a warm memory of a mother's sweet embrace, and the affectionate, devoted smile that encouraged her. If there was a side she'd never seen, she didn't want to know about it. Poor Tyler didn't have these memories.

Sara assumed her mother had been an amazing woman to have affected her father so. He shut down when she died. He was a besieged father with cold hands and cheeks that had given up, as if he could not fully engage the world without her, as if he were lost without her by his side, and as if the only thing he loved in all the world disappeared forever, which it did.

Sara favored her and thought as she grew older that her looks could help create a bond with her father, but they never did. She thought about his pain too. Perhaps it had been difficult for him to have lost a wife but to have continued to see so much of her there in the face of his daughter. He went through the motions of fatherhood but shut down like a morgue emotionally. She wouldn't have experienced any normality at all if it hadn't been for her father's sister, Louise. She was patient and kind—a big woman who had devoted herself to being fully present in Sara's life, much like a mother. She had never moved in, but she was always there.

Sara didn't think often about her Aunt Louise. This was out of guilt, she now suspected. It dawned on her while dating Eric that her aunt had given up much of her life to look after her. Sara had never appreciated or fully understood the sacrifice she had made. In fact—too often, she recalled—she had resented the intimacy between them and had accused her aunt of trying to be her mother. As a teenager, she made sure to remind her that she was not.

After her father died, she didn't keep in touch. It was too much work for a young adult focused completely on herself. She now regretted her abstinence and self-absorption. She wished she knew how to reconnect and thank her aunt, but for the most part, she kept those notions on a back burner. Maybe one day she could give something of herself back.

Eric tiptoed into the room and motioned to her about putting Tyler into bed. Sara nodded, and Eric scooped Tyler up and held him while Sara folded down the blanket and sheets. She watched Eric lower him into the soft blue cotton and glanced all around at the blues and yellows that would have welcomed their own son. She noted the blue-ribbon baby hangers were still in a row in the closet. She also wondered how long Eric had been there in the doorway and whether he had overheard her talking with Tyler.

"Oh, let me take his jeans off before we cover him," Sara whispered quickly to Eric. Tyler's jeans were old, faded in the knees, heavy, and damp, with fraying hems. She inched the jeans off and laid them across the bedpost, and she helped Eric tuck him in. As the back pocket hit the post, the sound of change shifting ended abruptly as items fell out onto the carpeted floor. Sara stepped aside, noticing warmly the slightly curved, compacted shape in the bed as she squatted down to pick up his loose change.

Her instinct was to clear out all his pockets and wash his jeans overnight, but she knew better than to take control over the little he had to claim. She scooped up the handful and laid it out atop the dresser. It was mostly change, plus a tiny lightbulb and a metal shell of something—maybe part of a bottle cap. She thought it odd, but he was a boy, and she was not familiar with gadgets and things little boys collected. She left it there for him to find the next morning.

Eric left the room and returned quickly with a small covered night light and plugged it in at the other end of the bedroom. She glanced back at Tyler, who looked to be all elbows, knees, and dreams. The two quietly stepped out and closed the door. Sara stopped Eric in the hall and put her arms up around his neck, "I'm so happy we could keep him safe and comfortable tonight; he has missed out on so much love," she said with a smile. "You're a kind man, Eric Doussaint." She kissed him.

"Hey," he prompted, "wasn't there something we started this evening in the rain that could be finished in a shower?"

"Why yes, I believe so," she sassed as her mouth, ever so slowly, curled up into a delightful, delicious, sultry smile.

CHAPTER 30

THE HARD LINE

"Okay, what do we have?" Jamison opened the morning briefing just as the two youngest detectives bounced into the squad room, pushing and shoving each other like playful little boys.

"You did."

"No, you did!"

"Hey, go lubricate yourself."

"You wish, you fag."

"Hey, don't fuckin' call me queer!"

Agent Raskin jumped in. "You're both pricks, okay? So go play with yourselves somewhere away from where we're working!"

"Reynolds, Nolan!" Jamison bellowed as he left the incident board, heading to his office. The two young men appeared at their chief's door immediately. Jamison motioned them into his office with the folding and opening of his right hand. "Fellas," he calmly started, "you do know we're beyond the dark ages, right?" He didn't wait for an answer. "Your banter about homosexuality ..." He closed his eyes, shutting out the stupidity of his detectives for a moment. "You *do* know that the force today is quite diverse, don't you?" The two looked confused at what he was getting at. Jamison's volume increased, "Do I look like I need a damned sexual harassment case in this squad?" He then said, louder, "Are you itching to attend sensitivity training?"

"Sorry, boss; got it," Reynolds remarked. They both slinked back to their desks as the rest of the detectives snickered and then turned back to the whiteboard, where Jamison had returned.

Johnson was talking about Maddie's things. "Not only that, Maddie's pocketbook had been swept clean. Not a thing left in her purse, and nuthin' that might have been hers found on Ellery or the two bozos outside."

"Ahem." The captain cleared his throat as he strolled from the double doors toward the group of detectives. "Mind if I butt in?" Without waiting for an answer, Captain Hughes addressed Jamison's team. "We need to check out these Ellery characters thoroughly. The brother could have been involved all along. Maybe he was present—a lookout. Maybe he knew his little brother couldn't control his sexual urges. Maybe he tends to rage uncontrollably during sex acts. Maybe it was meant to be a three-way; we don't know."

"Yeah," Johnson said, "but Cap'n—"

"They said they'd been drinking; blood tests show it," the captain continued. "Maybe the brother panicked and cleared out Maddie's purse in an effort to retrieve Raymond's contact number." He glared at Johnson. "I'm just saying we can't trust these two brothers."

Jamison glanced at Johnson, noticing his disapproval and defensive posture. Then, with a grimace, he turned his head back to the captain, whose two cents, he thought, was unnecessary and sent his detectives in the wrong direction, considering the sense of urgency the team was working under.

The last twenty-four hours had proved to be fruitless—one dead end after another. But police work had changed since the debacle of post-Katrina chaos. The department was riding a tide of political correctness and had become community relations specialists sensitive to the slightest complaints from its citizens and criminal elements as well. It was obvious to him that the captain was not adhering to the new role of the force.

Crime was running rampant, city leaders were focused on tourism, and judges were on the take. Government actions seemed more like one publicity stunt after another to allay criticism, to appear to be proactive, and to signal, above all else, care for the safety of its residents and guests. The reality was that the NOPD took care of its own. Street thugs were dragged into alleys by authorities and beaten, patrons in the French Quarter were rousted, dope and weapons were seized, and those blowing their FEMA money on chemical adulterants were heaved out the door, where other officers encouraged them at gunpoint to stay the hell away.

Johnson was handling the morning briefing well. Jamison reached across the Coffee-Mate to grab one of the six danish rolls. "Ew, Danish; is there any food more depressing than Danish?" he asked rhetorically, not expecting an answer. "These things are stale upon arrival." He paused and turned toward Hughes. "May I see you in my office?"

Both men moved to Jamison's workspace. As he closed the door and put his hand down on the desk to balance himself, breathing hard, trying to catch his breath, Jamison stood up across from Hughes. Their faces were a foot apart as Jamison aired his scorn.

"What the hell was that?" He wiped his forefingers across his brow. "Christ, Cap'n, don't you think you were out of line?"

Hughes smiled thinly. "I happened by and offered a viable source to check out."

"How 'bout checking it out with me first? Me—the one in charge of this investigation!"

"Now, Mick, don't get bent out of shape over a suggestion."

"A suggestion! You told my crew to go hassle a guy who is clean because you think blacks can't be trusted."

"I was just saying maybe we overlooked something."

"Look; I am either in charge of this case or I am not."

"Well, friend, if you don't steer clear of Jack, you might not be on board much longer."

"What! What does that mean?"

"Do I have to spell it out, Mick? You know how the higher-ups play. You'd better focus the search on someone other than Jack. Besides, I believe you might find evidence you first skimmed over."

"You mean find something you or your buddies planted, don't you?"

"What's fair is fair. That big brute of a brother cannot possibly be that squeaky clean."

"He is, dammit!" Jamison spewed as he slammed his desk and then the file cabinet with his fist. "I didn't work my ass off to get here just to be used as a puppet by a bunch of big shots."

"Well, Mick, we never really know why we end up where we are and what purpose we are to fulfill."

"Dammit," Jamison said again, only calmer. "You're telling me to overlook the evidence? You're telling me not to follow a prime player?" He was clearly irritated.

"I'm telling you to concentrate on Ellery and wrap this case up. Check your transcripts; maybe you missed a call."

"Cap'n, it's got to be obvious to you that this case is opening up. It's not just about Maddie; there's a real shooter here."

"Mick, don't be a loose cannon. You've got a good career; don't blow it."

"What are you insinuating? I'm not going to be the scapegoat."

"Just charge Ellery. Case dismissed."

"What!"

"I want a copy of the full report on this case in my office the day after tomorrow, Chief!"

"I don't want any part of this—certainly not any part of persecuting a framed man. How high up does this go?"

Hughes straightened his jacket and stood completely upright. He then tapped Jamison's shoulder as he passed by, heading for the door. "Charge him," he said as Jamison exited, and he pulled the door behind him.

Jamison, exasperated, screamed at the door, "Yeah, well good morning to you too!"

CHAPTER 31

MATCHBOXES

Eric and Sara were busy in the kitchen when Tyler woke up and scampered in. With terra cotta accents, the essence of earth escaping from the potato bin, and the musk of the forest from the hanging basket of mushrooms just above the chili peppers, with one look it was easy to visualize everything red simmering here: a brisket with onions in red wine, cinnamon-bathed apple tarts, dark damson plums steaming on the burner. It was welcoming; it felt like home.

"Morning," he said with excitement.

Sara stopped her mixing and turned to face him. "Good morning, sweetie."

Eric was pouring juice and held up the carton, pointing to it, gesturing to Tyler to see whether he wanted some. Tyler nodded, and Eric reached back into the cupboard for a second glass.

"I'm guessing you might have had a good night's sleep," Sara said.

Tyler beamed. "I sure did."

"Well, I'm glad. Now what do you think of some homemade blueberry waffles?" She grinned at his eyes peering over the granite countertop to see what she had been working at. She had her hair pulled back in a ponytail. Tyler had never seen her with her hair pulled tight, and he reached forward to flip his hand back and forth through the ends, intrigued by the way her hair hung loose from the yellow band.

"So would you like some yummy, delicious blueberry waffles?" she asked again.

Tyler scrunched up his face when he looked up at Sara. "Waffles, yes; blueberries, no," he stated. "With lots and lots of syrup."

"Coming up." She gave him a thumbs-up and then grabbed the silver mixing bowl and a worn red spatula, and she opened the hot waffle iron. Sara didn't just feel relaxed and rested; she felt newly energized. So much of the normal burden she was used to carrying was gone, and now this young boy who warmed her heart was in her home, sharing a slice of her life. She was truly happy, glad Eric had stayed home with them.

"Okay, champ," Eric said as he folded his paper and laid it down atop the large, oval oak table. "Come sit by me." He scooted out the chair next to him. Tyler hurried past Sara to the chair and glared with glee at Eric's offer. Eric winked at Tyler and then, in an overly dramatic voice with an exaggerated deep tone, stated, "We men folk would like our manly bacon as well." Tyler glanced at Sara and nodded, licking his lips in agreement with Eric's order.

"That's coming up too," Sara told them as she pried the encrusted waffle off its griddle and poured another smooth cupful of batter onto the heated grid. Sara watched Tyler observe his new surroundings. His eyes touched on everything in the room. She brought the plates of steaming waffles and bacon to the table and went back to pour the shallow pan of heated syrup into a warmer. She returned with the warmer and some napkins, placed them in the table's center, and then scooted herself into place.

Tyler ate voraciously, squeezing oversize bites into his small mouth. Sara and Eric looked at each other, both wondering about the last time Tyler might have had home cooking.

"It's so bright in here," Tyler remarked with his mouth full and smacking with syrup. The venetian blinds were pulled up and tied off, and the natural sunlight poured into their east-facing bay windows. The walls were a soft yellow, a color of butter that came to life with the rising sun, and the appliances, chrome, reflected and expanded the light, filling the entire room. "What are we going to do?" Tyler asked.

Sara dabbed a napkin at her mouth and then at Tyler's mouth. "What would you like to do?"

"We could take in a ball game in a few days, maybe go to a movie today," Eric suggested.

"Or work on photography," Sara added. Tyler was content to stay put.

"Do you have any Matchbox cars?" Tyler asked.

Eric chuckled. "No, none here, but I bet my mom still has some of the cars I collected. We'll have to ask her and get her to look up in her attic."

"You have a whole stockpile?" Tyler asked in amazement.

"No, not a stockpile … but some. It's worth looking into anyway."

"Hooray! Can we go see them now?"

"Well, I have to call and see if we can come by … and make sure my mom knows where she put them."

"Call, call," Tyler begged him. "I've seen enough games and stuff."

"Oh really," Eric teased him. "And just when was the last time you went to a Saints game?" Eric was certain that the surprise of treating Tyler to a pro game on Sunday would excite him.

He smirked. "About two weeks ago." His grin led Eric and Sara to believe he was putting one over on them.

"Two weeks ago?" Eric asked him.

"Yep. Let's call about your cars," Tyler said, beginning to whine a bit.

"How did you pay for your ticket? Did a friend take you?" Sara asked.

"Saints tickets are pretty expensive," Eric noted.

"I know," Tyler said looking down at his lap. His expression had changed; he looked sad. Eric and Sara thought the expression confirmed their suspicion that he couldn't have paid to see the game. But his expression was one of shame, not sadness. "I didn't exactly pay," he added, lowering his voice.

"So you really weren't at the game?" asked Sara.

"No, I was." He hesitated. "I just didn't pay."

"What do you mean?" Eric asked.

"Well, an older kid at the center told me if you want to get in, you look for a man with lots of kids and go get in line with them. You know, just go up and start talking with the kids. Usually they have a family pass, so it doesn't matter if five or six kids go through the gates. And most dads assume you're a kid in line behind them and are just talking to his own kids. Anyway, you just slip through with them, then go the other way. The dad never knows."

"Wow, that's thought through," Sara said, amazed at the intricate understanding of authority and distraction at pivotal moments.

"So you were really there?" Eric asked.

"Uh huh."

"What was the score at half-time?" he asked him.

"I can't remember," Tyler said as he polished off the last of his orange juice. Eric grinned at Sara, figuring he had just pinned Tyler into the corner and that they would establish the truth in a moment.

"You can't remember the score? It was pretty amazing, considering the score at the end of the game," Eric pointed out.

"Well, the Saints were losing, I remember that, but I don't know by how much. I wasn't paying attention."

Eric leaned over to grab Tyler in a playful stranglehold. "You sneaked into an expensive game and didn't pay attention to the score?"

"I was watching this weird guy," Tyler said as he broke free of Eric. "And I saw you," he said, pointing to Sara. Sara was not smiling; she was astonished and intrigued.

"Me?" she asked simply.

"Yeah, you went from the bathroom into another door, and then you went into a police car." Sara and Eric sat straight up, a little shaken, a bit in awe of Tyler's accounting. "Mostly I was watching that weird guy," he finished.

"What weird guy?" Sara probed.

"He shot two guys right in the head," Tyler answered nonchalantly.

"What!" Eric exclaimed.

"What?" Tyler asked, now a little nervous and teary-eyed.

"Oh sweetie," Sara said, consoling him, "you didn't do anything wrong. We just can't believe you saw someone shoot two people."

"I did," he assured them. "He had a toothpick in his mouth, and it looked funny 'cause he was making it move around all wiggly."

"Did you say anything to anyone? The police?" She was eager to understand the whole of his story.

"No way. If I talk to the police, I go back to the center, and that place is stinky."

"Oh my God, Eric," Sara stated, rattled at the revelation that Tyler could probably identify the murderer.

"I know," Eric said, trying to appease her. "Listen; I'm going to call the station chief. His name was Jamison, right?" Sara nodded, confirming the name.

"No, don't tell on me!" Tyler wailed. "I'm sorry."

Sara moved next to him and put her arms around his shoulders. "It's okay, Tyler," she said. "We are going to keep you safe."

"He's going to tell on me that I sneaked in," he said in desperation.

"No," she assured him, "he's going to tell the police that you saw the bad guy who shot those two people. The police would like to know because they never saw him, so they don't know who to look for. You'll actually be helping the police find their suspect."

"I will?" He smiled. "I'll be just like the go-gos."

"The what? The go-gos?"

"Yep, they're those guys in camouflaged jeeps that say 'Go, go!' … and then run fast and shoot. Have you ever seen those kind of army guys?"

"Uh, I don't know if I have," Sara replied, still uncertain about the go-go part.

"They shoot up all the bad guys. Hey, did you ever see Turboman?"

"I'm not sure."

"He shoots right from his fist, and then he has a motor, and he can fly ... and ..."

Eric slid back into the kitchen like a child sliding in his socks across the slick ceramic tiles to Sara and Tyler. "Couldn't reach Chief Jamison; left a message for him. So we'll wait to hear and then go talk to him about the guy you saw, all right, buddy?"

"Yeah," Tyler said, now folding his napkin to make a pretend gun. Sara rolled her eyes at the notion that Tyler had no clue how important this man was. Tyler lifted his head. "Let's go call your mom and see if she can find your cars." Tyler pulled at Eric's arms until he got up. Sara cleared the dishes from the table, rinsing and placing them in the sink as she watched the two run and slide, making their way across the kitchen floor and down the hardwood to the study.

CHAPTER 32

BODY FOUND

Jamison was somber when he entered the pine-and-brass corner of Mimi's restaurant for lunch. He squeezed in at the bar between Raskins and Matthews. Matthews passed him a Budweiser, and he washed down some of his anger with a couple of swigs from the cold bottle. He glanced at his team. They looked like prophets pinned to the counter, talking in tongues. "Look," he spoke up, "you've all been told to look the other way. I'm telling you we're staying on track and sniffing for the facts." He called out down to the end of the bar counter, "Johnson." Detective Johnson was between bites of an overstuffed sandwich and leaned in to hear his chief. "When you finish, call and get those Ellery brothers back in for questioning. Take a couple of boys and go get them if you have to."

"Wha'?" Johnson replied, indignant about what he was being told to do. "You kiddin' me?"

"Do I look like I'm kidding? I want them in here tomorrow morning, period."

Johnson threw the rest of his sandwich on his plate, causing it to rattle. "Damn," he exclaimed as he pushed himself away from the bar, brushed the crumbs off the front of his slacks, and stormed out.

Matthews turned to his boss and softly, without moving, asked, "Mick, what are you doing?"

"Relax," Jamison replied. "the cap'n wants them in, we'll bring them in, no harm done; it's all for show to keep Hughes off our back."

"Why not let Johnson know? It's a sore spot."

"I want Johnson's anger in that interrogation room. If he's not pissed off, the cap'n will know something's up." He leaned forward to include all the officers around him. "If you're worried about your jobs, don't be; I'll take the fall. I will gladly be the fall guy for what is right; no way I'm going down for a dirty high-ranking official."

"Captain's just trying to keep things tidy before he retires," Raskins suggested.

"No, he's covering and wants us to do the same."

"Look," Matthews interjected, "we can just keep him out of it."

"Yeah, well, if we open this big damn can of worms, we'd better have the evidence to back it up."

"We could put surveillance on the captain as well, boss," Raskins whispered to Jamison.

"I want immediate surveillance on everything we've targeted." He paused and then leaned into the bar and looked left. "Gandy, Davies," he called, "pull some of the boys from the Fourth Precinct!"

"Got it, boss," Richard Gandy replied. "First stop after lunch."

"No! Now, dammit. Retrace your steps and take everything apart."

"Right," Davies answered, and he pulled at his partner, who was quickly slurping down all the rest of his beer.

"Hey," Jamison said, addressing the bartender, "you gonna feed me sometime today?"

"Sure, Mick," he replied. "The usual, coming up."

"Don, get a team and go back to the stadium and blanket the area. No leaks or I'll close ranks!"

"No problem, Mick," Matthews assured him.

"I want the pieces pulled together, *stat*."

Jamison received his sandwich and quickly removed the limp pickle slice from his plate. He wolfed it down as he had done with all his meals as of late. "God, I hope this is over soon," he remarked casually, unaware of whether anyone was listening. He felt unsettled when he got a call.

"Yeah, hey, Chief, it's Webb. We got a tip there's a dead woman in Algiers Point we'll be interested in."

"Not our jurisdiction," Jamison replied on his cell.

"I'm pretty sure it's connected to our case. Park ranger on the scene said the vic's throat's been sliced. She's also been posed postmortem, and he's the only one seen her. Says she's a part of Senator Jack Doussaint's team."

"What! Shit. Call the crime scene techs to get out there before anybody screws up the site. For now, make sure they've sealed off the area and get back to me."

"Yeah, will do. We're going out there now."

———————•●•———————

Webb and Broussard pulled up to the entrance of Algiers Point wondering in advance whether the victim had been killed here or killed and placed here. A couple hundred yards ahead, two sheriff patrol cars were parked on each side of the graveled path leading to the rest of the park. A uniformed deputy stood guard at the head of the trail and motioned them through.

Webb opened his trunk, removed a pair of army-green rubber boots, and slipped them on. He had learned long ago boots saved him from ruining three or four replacement pair of shoes each year. Broussard waved him off and went immediately to the first car. The deputy had a country boy's raw-boned strength beneath mirrored sunglasses. "I'm with homicide," Broussard said. "You have a body for us?"

"Sure do," he responded. "This way." He gestured beyond him and began to walk toward the woods. Webb caught up. They removed the covering and looked at the body. She looked a bit green, pinned to the earth, sinking into the grassy reeds like an alligator taking cover out of water. Her thick black hair fanned out from her head, awash in weeds and bugs, and blood from her throat had matted, pressing the skin flat, and it was bubbling over with maggots—a gruesome discovery.

"Hmm, not just posed, but staged with a Mardi Gras mask," Webb commented.

"Different, that's for sure," Broussard said. He then asked, "anyone else been here, driven here?" He looked at the fading tire marks and footprints.

"No," the deputy assured him.

Broussard thought they'd lucked out. "Well, when the crime scene boys get here, tell them we want photographs and casts of these tracks and shoe prints. Anyone else, keep to the side of the trail. No smoking, no food, no anything that'll screw up the crime scene, got it?"

"Got it, sir," the young man replied.

"All right, deputy. Thanks—you did a good job." The two turned and walked the trail toward the wooded area beyond the body, waiting for the deputy to return to his car. In the fall, the trees, creeping and crouching on their wooden legs, seemed suspicious, with twisted roots and wood berry bins where leaves wept and sank to a pit of pine needles. It was not a safe place. Even the sky sagged and wheezed bells of mildew. In the shadows beyond the pines and cypress, leaves, ferns, moss, and ivy turned the ground cover blackened green like some captive, dense undergrowth. It was like staring into a mud-soaked terrarium; like peering into a living museum of the underworld—a place where ears remain as alert as canines, and eyes widened by paranoia become wary of everything suddenly still.

They turned back to the field, not noticing anything wrong or out of place near the woods. They began looking for any discarded items. Broussard plucked surgical gloves from his pocket, handed a pair to Webb, and put his own pair on his hands. Webb bent down to scoop up a couple of cigarette butts. Farther down near the embankment, he found a torn piece of an empty matchbook.

"It's advertising a topless bar in Old Algiers," he said. He pulled out a baggie from his pocket and placed the items inside. This was only a preliminary effort; the crime scene techs would comb the entire area in great depth, carefully looking for hair, clothing fibers, and other small and indiscriminate items that might be linked to the murder. Broussard saw that the deputy was not in sight and motioned to Webb as he turned and walked up slope on the wild, spongy grass and moss to return to the body.

He uncovered the body of the black female lying on a darkened bed of rotting vegetation. Her dress had been sliced open, exposing her full and rigid breasts.

"Implants," Webb stated flippantly as he filed in behind Broussard.

"Hey, some respect!"

"What, I'm just making an objective observation."

"Yeah, that's why you're still single."

Webb took two pictures of their find and then looked around the seemingly peaceful environment. There were a couple of live oaks, their boughs heavy with Spanish moss, and small cypress trees with butterfly orchids attached to their trunks. The park and swampland to the north, with mosquitoes the size of bats, was a popular place for dumping bodies and dealing drugs.

"The killer not only posed her postmortem; he was either strong or angry, because the cut is deep," Broussard said. His jaw tightened as he bent down to remove the mask. "Okay, let's see who we've got." He gingerly lifted the mask with his thumb and forefinger in the eye area and laid it on her abdomen. Webb craned forward to view her face from over his partner. Broussard drew a long breath. "Christ, we've seen her before." Webb took another picture. It was Senator Doussaint's press secretary—a public figure who had stood beside him through his various trials and campaigns.

"Shit, what is her body doing down here?" Webb stated. "She's been dolled up to look like a whore. I'll call the chief, and he'll have to contact the senator. Damn." He pulled out his cell to dial Jamison.

Forensics and pathology were working hard to finish quickly as several men scanned the grounds around the body. Sex crimes had come and gone; there was no sign of struggle, no bruises, no semen, and no sign of penetration trauma. The first news helicopter appeared overhead as Jamison, Raskins, and Matthews appeared on the scene.

"Jesus! Nikea Chandres," Jamison blurted out. "Rass, you're going to have to go up to Baton Rouge and sift through her place, talk to her neighbors." Raskins turned and headed back to her car, talking on her cell. "Webb, check with the park ranger as to how we get a list of the park rangers who rotate working here, then go to the city office and get a list of every possible worker that could have been here this past year: groundskeepers, botanists, gravel company workers, sanitation—everyone. Somebody knew the patrol routine, when they could drive in here and not be seen."

"Yes, got it," Webb responded as he left.

"Broussard, that leaves you to get over to the Old Algiers area and—"

"To check on the empty book of matches we found earlier."

"Exactly. I'll call the superintendent and Hughes; they'll want to get over to the senator's home to speak with him.

"Got it," Broussard said as he departed.

Later, back at the squad room, Jamison had Raskins on a speaker phone, asking what she had found. "The landlord, Philipe Vasquez, is a short, stocky Latino, about forty-five, and has a ragged goatee and disposition," she began. "Said the owner's going to want it rented … Didn't seem all that concerned about her death. I searched her apartment. Not a thing out of place—not even a dirty dish in the sink. Everything looked scrubbed clean except for closets bulging with clothes and shoes." She cleared her throat before she spoke. "She was not attacked sexually, but she was killed elsewhere and dropped off at the crime scene, because I checked her car in the adjacent garage. Navy four-door Nissan Altima. Found drops of blood, most likely hers. Her family was notified. Sister Darlene said she never complained about anyone threatening or confronting her and that she was not involved in any conflict at work. She has no idea why someone wanted her dead."

"The news is already on top of it; we might gain a bit of information from whatever they can dig up," Gandy proposed.

"Ha! Media supposition teasers; tha's all they'll provide," Johnson scoffed.

"Well, maybe it will lead to someone calling in to the TV stations with real information," Gandy refuted.

"Surely somebody saw something," Webb added.

"TV …" Jamison was cracking his neck. "What's that crime spot on the CBS station?" he asked.

"*Crime Line*," Gandy answered.

"Let's do it. Gandy, call over there; it's time to open this to the public. We've got no real motive, they're not going to find any trace items from Algiers Point—there's nothing to build a case on." He turned. "Matthews, you're going to need to go on tonight. Since she was a rather public figure, they'll want the publicity and connection to the police as an advocate partner." Jamison was running his thick hand back and forth over a tension knot on the back of his neck. It was another loop in a plot that went nowhere. "So now we know this is not random; Maddie and Nickea are both connected to Jack Doussaint. Anyone have any insights as to why she, they, were the chosen vics? And why here in New Orleans instead of Doussaint's Oak Hills?"

"Has to be the senator's business transactions or partners," Davies mentioned.

"I agree," Raskins chimed in from the speaker phone. "According to Vasquez, Chandres was the ideal renter."

Broussard came in late. "Need any help with further interrogations?" Gandy asked jokingly. The detectives laughed.

"All right," Jamison snapped. "Can we get back to work?" He paused. "Rass, we'll see you in the morning. Thanks." He hung up the phone. "Now, who's gonna run the gauntlet of reporters and cameras?"

"I will," Johnson said begrudgingly.

"This is going to be a high-profile case, so choose your words wisely," Jamison warned his friend. He then turned to Broussard. "Mister topless bar, find out anything?"

"A seedy place—the usual afternoon drunks staring blindly into their drinks. The place smelled of sweat and piss, sex and booze. Talked to some dancers … useless."

Nolan piped up. "Yeah but the view was decent, wasn't it?"

"Shut it, rookie," Broussard said in a curt tone. "Showed pics of our two boys to the bartender. He said he had seen them there a few times but they hadn't been in recently."

"How could they be connected to Chandres if they were already dead?" Davies argued.

"They couldn't," Johnson explained, "but maybe this place is an ideal spot to pick an' choose who'll kill for you."

"Webb, who bailed Clay and LeMonde out?" Jamison inquired.

"No name, but the clerk said he had a heavy Hispanic accent. An older guy, looked Mexican, well dressed, pulled out a hefty wad of money."

"Mexican ..." Jamison pondered. "Doussaint has some sort of tie to Mexico we're not picking up on." It was obvious it was going to be grunt work for now, much of it going over ground already covered. "We've got to be sure we don't miss anything. Call your families and tell them your weekend will be spent here with me. Everyone will be on overtime if need be. I want this case worked raw! We've got an autopsy scheduled in the morning at nine with the assistant ME. Then we'll call Doussaint's lawyer and get him down here. We can't lean on Doussaint yet, but we can damn well have a chat with his adviser!"

As the squad room was emptying out, Jamison sat in his office contemplating the next morning's autopsy. He gazed out his window into the murky glow of the streetlight. He watched as the light was consumed by a fluttering wave of vagrant moths, and he pondered who would kill two of the people closest to Senator Doussaint. He poured himself a drink, slid back into the comfort of his broken-down chair, and wondered whether there ever really was a chance to be safe. How did evil develop? Where could it be found—in the eyes? In the heart of a man? Did it slip into a soul or a mind gone mad? His experience with the job led him to struggle with the illusions of goodness. He thought only children had the ability to respond to kindness so well in the midst of bleak living. It warmed him to hear children laugh, knowing at that moment that, despite the harsh world, they could feel safe and free. He thought about so many who went unnoticed, unloved, uncared for—too many poor and hungry, too many homeless, too many abducted and trafficked, facing cruelty and sickness, abandonment and powerlessness. When he heard a child laugh, he heard the laughter of all children, as it should be. He hoped the many who suffered would soon become the very few. His ideas exhausted, he headed home, hoping for a decent night's sleep for a change—hoping to be fresh enough to handle an autopsy first thing the next morning.

CHAPTER 33

AUDACITY OF HOPE

Raymond cleared the table and put the dinner dishes in the sink. Wynton went to the hall and pulled the newspaper out from beneath the pile of mail. Upon returning to the kitchen, he slapped the paper on the counter next to Raymond. "Did you see the headlines today?" Raymond hadn't, and he never would, left to his own devices; he didn't read the newspaper. "There's another murder linked to Jack Doussaint."

Raymond suddenly became interested, took the paper, and sat back down at the kitchen table. "Can't accuse me of this one. I wasn't nowheres near that lady."

"Of course not."

"Still, I *am* black, and the only black man in a murder case." Wynton sighed. "Hell," Raymond continued, "folk see a brutha in his twenties, and what does they think of? Crime! They sees my sable skin and broad nose, my tight-coil' hair, and I ain' seen as an adult human being with any kinda character. They sees me as a hoodlum with animal instincts."

"Things are changing."

"C'mon, man; no one done bin trying to help poor black folk. Black men like me be filling prisons, black kids not able to read, and images whites see of us on they TV are either violent or looters. Things ain' changing. We our circumstances, and black communities still waiting on this country to come and change them circumstances. But they ain' coming; they afraid of us. And meantime, we tired—tired of teaching our kids that 'merica see us as less."

Wynton left momentarily and came back with a book in his hand. Wynton was never quick to anger, and his feelings were never easily bruised. Raymond figured everyone was meant to go through some internal awakening if they were to grow up. Wynton surely had. His faith in goodness never tarnished or wore thin.

He showed the cover to Raymond. It was titled *The Audacity of Hope* and had a picture of the president on it. "Let me read you something he wrote," Wynton said, and he opened the book to a section midway through. "No one is exempt from the call to find common ground. We have communal values, mutual responsibility that should be expressed beyond our church, mosque, synagogue, and beyond neighborhoods or workplaces. We must work as social cohesion." He closed the book. "We all have to work to find common ground. Don't just aks white folks to come to you."

"I aks you, hadn't them rungs on that ladder of opportunity done bin greased and made slippery for us? Ain' it the white man laws that be stacked against us?"

"Our rights and how we live is universal, Ray. We spend most of our time arguing about how to argue—about how to use the law. All our rules tell us how to think, not what to think. That's why it gets complicated. For the most part, we are on our own and have only our own reason and judgment to rely on. People think laws are perfectly clear and can be strictly applied to all of us, but there is always room for interpretation because nothing is static in an ever-changing world. Obama as president is trying to show white and black America how those interpretations affect us all."

"You believe that?"

"I do, but not as simply as you'd think. I think white America believes our government provides us with a fixed blueprint with rules. I agree with the president that it is not a fixed blueprint but a framework. The government is not always right, so government should be more than enforcing rules; government should regularly challenge our motives and interests, individually and collectively. There has to be a fundamental humility, flexibility, and curiosity in the way society sets its structure, because nothing is absolute, and we must allow for God's grace to shine upon us."

"Those your words or the president?"

"A little of both. It's in here."

"How you remember all you read 'bouts what he say 'bouts the government?"

"Well, it's not verbatim, and it's a summary of some of what he states. It's easy to cite information when someone speaks out on what you already believe."

"Yeah, but all this talk 'bouts the law don't erase my blackness and how people see me."

"It's more than laws; it's about life in general. It all comes down to the quality of courage. If you have the ability and desire to live outside the boundaries of nationality, race, religion, wealth; if you have a decent work ethic—"

Raymond cut him off. "No, don't tell me we gotta work twice as hard to get half as much. Don't no one say that shit no more." He paused and lowered his head. "Even if it's true."

"Nah, I'm saying if you have respect and compassion for others, if you can remain optimistic despite societal values, and champion justice, then you have a sense of purpose. And that, Ray, means you value this brief life we've each been given. It takes courage to go through our daily living—especially when things are stacked against us. But if we can move forward, and remain faithful to our hearts, then that is the real quality of courage."

"Them your words or his?"

"A little of both."

"Ain' moving up if we kept poor."

"It's not the money; it's culture."

"Easy to say if you gots money."

"If you've been wealthy for generations and you were suddenly placed in the ghetto, you'd have problems because you wouldn't know the rules."

"You'd have problems if you was a white boy," Raymond sneered at him.

"Likewise, if you've been poor for generations and you're trying to climb that ladder, you will also have problems. What might keep you safe in the projects might get you fired from a job or kicked outta school. It's culture, not color, because if you're poor and from the Appalachians, you are going to have the same problems."

"'Cept them from the Appalachians ain' gonna be hated just looking at 'em. They might feel some class problems, but they ain' gonna be dissed for they skin color. Is different if you is poor or if you is poor and black. Grayboys tell us our culture be making us poor. Black folk don't deserve to be told that, bruh. Eating greens and listening to OutKast ain' never oppressed nobody."

"At the end of James Baldwin's book, *The Fire Next Time*, he says we must assume everything now is in our hands and we can't falter on our duty to end this country's racial nightmare. You have the passion, Ray. Harness it."

"You cudda bin a good politician."

Wynton shrugged. "Politics too infrequently depends on common sense, reason, and a vision of possibilities. The president's coming next week. You forget, though, that he's been here several times already. And he worked with the Bush family, fundraising in Houston when they were sheltering twenty-five thousand evacuees from here. He has talked about meeting those folks and listening to their stories that were most often filled with the absence of insurance or family to fall back on. He concluded that our people had been abandoned long before a hurricane struck." He paused for emphasis. Looking directly into Raymond's eyes. "That's a refreshing change of thought and attitude!"

"That's just because he be a brutha."

"Nope, don't you remember watching TV with me when we saw President Bush in the square, acknowledging the racial injustice that the tragedy of Katrina exposed, and that he proclaimed N'awlins would rise again?"

"Just words. He caused the problem by not sending help."

"And ... Obama said he sensed the nation had reached a transformative moment—that its conscious had been stirred from a long slumber and would launch a renewed war on poverty. That was also a wonderfully powerful, hopeful statement for our community."

"Yeah, you done see how quick that shit faded."

"Yes, some slipping, and Obama has had to swallow some of his anger and set aside some of his blackness in order to work to improve basic decency. But, Ray, he said he would never surrender to what has been instead of what might be. He doesn't have all the answers, but he is asking questions. He's shaping the nation's dialogue on race. His unique and pivotal position as the first black president will affect life for us, because our platform just got center stage. Obama gives hope not just to the black community but to the whole country and the world—a hope that a new racial climate has emerged in America, or that it will. I, for one, am profoundly moved by Obama's election legacy. His presidency represents where we've come from and gives our people inspiration to continue to move forward."

"You always calm me, bruh," Raymond admitted. If Wynton wasn't lecturing him too esoterically, he usually learned something or gained a little peace of mind.

"Hang in there, Ray." Wynton smiled and tapped him on the head with the book. "I'm always here for you."

CHAPTER 34

AT THE LAB

Jamison met the next morning with the assistant medical examiner as scheduled. He stared into the face of an innocent woman who had been carved up because of her associations. Gregory Ward picked up a scalpel for the initial cut, turned it to one side, and gave the date and time for the overhead microphone recording his observations. "We are about to begin the postmortem examination of Nikea Chandres, a thirty-eight-year-old black female. The body is well maintained and shows no identifying scars or tattoos. There is bruising about the arms and shoulder, indicating a struggle before death. There is one exterior wound, a deep cut that has forcibly severed the thyroid cartilage, trachea, and right carotid artery, causing a massive loss of blood. The victim would have continued bleeding until the heart stopped. The wound appears to have been administered from behind, in a left-to-right motion, indicating the killer used his or her right hand."

Ward shuffled his feet slightly, took a breath, and continued. "The wound goes back to the spine and has caused a nick in the third vertebra, indicating a heavy-bladed knife—possibly a hunting knife." Then he began the Y-shaped incision that went from each shoulder to the sternum and ran in a straight line to the pubis. Jamison handled the autopsy well. Opening the body cavity did not bother him, but he dabbed some Vicks into each nostril to avoid the putrid smell of inner organs as they were exposed and removed. Most autopsies took ninety minutes to complete. Nikea Chandres's was no different. There would still be microscopic analyses of various organs, and subsequent toxicology reports, but the initial evidence was clear. There was nothing abnormal; she had died because her throat had been slit open.

"Where you from, Doc?" Jamison asked as he removed his latex gloves and wiped his nostrils to remove the ointment.

"Upstate New York," the young examiner answered.

"What're you doing down here?" Jamison responded, curious about this Yankee.

"Are you kidding? New Orleans, murder capital of America? My job is guaranteed," Ward joked. Jamison did not look amused. "No, really, I don't like snow and don't mind humidity, so here I am."

Jamison was not impressed.

Back at headquarters, a briefing was underway when Jamison walked in, sorting through his messages. "Good job last night on TV, Don. Anyone gather any new information?" he asked.

Matthews stood and spoke. "Our canvass of the park area pretty much drew a blank. No one paid much attention to that area."

"Same with her neighbors," Raskins cut in. "They didn't hear or see anything unusual in the days leading up to her death. Oh, except one woman." She paused to consult her notebook, thumbing back a page or two. "A Mrs. Gladsden. She said the vic commented to her a couple of times that she felt like she was being watched and seemed slightly edgy."

"She probably *was* being watched," Jamison said. "What about the parents?"

"Blue-collar types from Mississippi. No connections here 'cept their daughter."

"Boyfriend?" Jamison urged on.

"Ex ... a kickboxer. Hadn't been in contact with Chandres since they parted three months ago," Raskins answered.

"I've got a message from Eric Doussaint here ... says it's important. Let's see what he has to say." With that, Jamison left for his office.

CHAPTER 35

LOOKING

Wynton unlocked the door and entered, tossing his keys on the hall table. He unfolded the office fax he'd tucked under his arm. He read it again, still uncertain of its meaning. Raymond was in the next room with headphones on, his back to Wynton. He was singing along loudly to "Blame It."

"Blame it on the vodka, blame it on the Henny. Blame it on the blue top, got you feeling dizzy. Blame it on the a-a-a-a-a-a alcohol." Wynton, chuckling at the spectacle before him, tapped Raymond's shoulder. Raymond spun around and pulled the headphones from his head. "Wassup?" Raymond greeted his brother, smiling.

"You're in a good mood; did you find a job?"

"Nah, ain' bin looking," Raymond responded in a deflated tone.

Wynton read the fax again. "Damn, I'll have to take off," he muttered in a low, soft tone. Speaking up, he said, "I should probably call someone to find out about this."

"What, brutha, find out 'bouts what?" Raymond was trying to peer over Wynton's large arms to see what he was reading.

"They want us back in N'awlins," he said, slightly irritated.

"What? You kidding, right? E?" Raymond probed seriously. "Who want us, and who is the 'us' part?"

"The police want us, you and me, back in for questioning first thing in the morning. We can call and tell them we're coming voluntarily, or they will send a squad car to pick us up." Both men were silent.

"What for?" Raymond demanded in a rather frantic voice.

"Don't say," Wynton replied.

"Why, why ..." Raymond was starting into a childish fit.

"It's normal," Wynton guessed, trying to calm his younger, nervous brother. "It's absolutely normal. They gather information and need to bring people back in to verify similar or conflicting accounts. They're just looking around."

"No, they bringing the bruthas in to pin the crime on 'em," Raymond responded.

"Stay calm, Ray. If we were under suspicion, they wouldn't give us a choice; they'd come get us with handcuffs."

"I don't like this," Raymond said.

"Don't matter if you do or don't; we are goin' to N'awlins in the morning, little man." It was something neither of them had expected. They had thought Raymond had been cleared, their stories had been checked out, and they had been sent home for good.

"Yeah, is normal. They just trying to wrap this up," Raymond mimicked, trying to convince himself as he sat with his arms crossed in the desk chair, rolling across the dining room floor, putting a little distance between them. "You ready to go through this again?" he asked. "We not gonna remember every detail; our facts gonna be different. Is natural our recollection ain' gonna be 'xactly the same."

"Don't start worrying about something that hasn't happened yet, hear?" Wynton reminded Raymond. "Don't start looking for trouble just because it is plentiful in the world."

"What we needa look for is some hunnies and kick back with some Hennessey and weed. Wanna go to Jeff's or D'ville with me?" Raymond asked hopefully.

"No," Wynton replied definitively.

"C'mon, E; when the last time you got any?"

Wynton moved toward Raymond. "What is it with you! Don't you see the trouble here because of your playing around? What are you thinking? Do you ever just stop and think?" Wynton left Raymond and went into the kitchen, opening the refrigerator to assess what to make for dinner.

Raymond entered the kitchen, approaching Wynton slowly. "E, C'mon man. Sorry." Wynton didn't answer. He slammed the refrigerator door closed and moved to the sink to look out the kitchen window.

"You don't get it," he said sadly. "What me and Belinda had was special. I miss her."

"I ain' say replace her, E, but you gonna quit banging forever?"

"It's not about sex, but intimacy. Do you even know about intimacy, Ray?"

"Hey, I get real intimate, brutha," Raymond responded indignantly.

"What's the point!" Wynton snarled, and he started putting away the dishes left in the drainer from the night before.

"You suffocating in it," Raymond replied confidently.

"Ray, the power of intimacy is never suffocating; it's real freedom—fresh air. Moving along with the one you've chosen to be close to is not confining; it's like throwing the windows open in spring. It was the car accident that choked everything, not my deep, wonderful relationship with Belinda."

Raymond cut in. "But they's more tail out there."

"Not just hooking up, Ray. Choice. Choosing each other without settling. You just settle for whatever you can find."

"Yeah, well, settling feel awful good."

"There's a bigger picture to life than getting laid," Wynton said, shooting him down.

"Dogg, sexing is part of that big picture, and you ain' be including it at all," Raymond replied, defending his position.

"Intimacy in marriage is not just the physical act or the expression of love between two people; it is a profound and mysterious weaving together of the many different strands of the souls."

"Uh oh, here we done go."

"It marks the fundamental shift in perception of oneself and one's world, laying ourselves open to wisdom and creativity so that we are not just holding a marriage together but making something of it."

"No one done understand the soul."

"True, I don't think the soul is meant to be understood. But we know the soul is polycentric, always capable of seeing any situation from more than one point of view. If we can nourish the soul, entwine our soul with another's, then we are liberated from the tyranny of our own narrowed vision."

Raymond rolled his eyes. "What the fuck is you talking 'bouts?"

"This is intimacy, my brutha, and trust me, what you think is an intimate act between two people isn't; that's just sex."

"Hey, when we remove our clothing, we removing barriers, bruh. We expose ourselves and our inhubitions."

"What you are describing is the word 'vulnerability,' not intimacy of the soul. You're talking about breathing skin to skin, tangling in each other's dreams and needs, but passing through what is woven quickly."

"Yasss! Now you is digging me."

"I'm talking about digging deep within. I'm talking about giving into the mystery which weaves hearts together."

"That shit ain' never gonna work on a dime piece."

Wynton turned to face Raymond and edged his way into the corner of the counter, where he leaned and composed himself. "Just leave it alone, 'kay?" Then, shifting gears to lighten the conversation, he added, "Now whatchu gonna fix us for dinner?"

Raymond balked. "Me?"

"Yes, you. Gonna take some responsibility?"

"I dunno nothing 'bouts cooking."

"Hey, you're living here, and I work; step up to the plate."

"A'ight, lemme boil some hot dogs and get us some chips," Raymond responded, knowing he couldn't offer much and it wouldn't sound too appetizing.

"A'ight then, Ray. That's a start; that's a start." Wynton turned and, leaving the kitchen, said, "I'm going up to change while you get busy." He didn't wait for a response but jogged up the stairs, landing in the second-floor hallway slightly winded—not from exertion but from his conversation with Raymond.

He had kept his cool, but Raymond had touched a nerve. Wynton felt drained from the emotions welling up inside him. How he missed his family.

He carried himself gingerly down the hall, stopping outside the first room—Keisha's room. He leaned against the door frame, listening for sounds of a little girl's laughter. He stepped in, turning back to the hallway for a moment as the clanking sounds of pots and pans in the kitchen floated up the stairwell. He shook his head slightly, noting another area where Raymond could make improvements, and then fingered the pair of white satin booties Keisha kept atop her dresser. He smiled as he touched them, fondly recalling that she kept them because she couldn't believe her feet had ever been that small. How he wished he'd had more time with her.

He walked across the room to her window seat, moving the lacy white curtains aside with his first two fingers. Across the street and down a half block was St. Bernard's Catholic Church and Elementary School. On weekends it became the neighborhood park—the only playground around. It had been Keisha's favorite place to go.

There were six swings and a set of monkey bars, a baseball diamond used mostly for kickball, two four-square boxes, and three hopscotch games painted in bright yellow on that old charcoal-gray asphalt near a basketball hoop. The outfield grass was well kept, thick and green—the perfect place to play running games like red rover and dodgeball.

In the corner where the swings met the grass edge and a broken sidewalk that led away from the school's gate into the neighborhood, there was a worn tetherball where the boys hung out, pummeling the ball back and forth as they talked. At the other end, closest to the school doors, was a circle of green benches where the older girls sat together making lanyards, teaching each other how to braid long strands of plastic into necklaces, key chains, and bookmarks. Keisha had not hit this phase, though she had been attracted to the bright colors and the cool, slippery feeling the crafted items had when she was allowed to hold them and run her fingers through the strands.

Wynton let the curtains fall back, closing off the window as he left her room and headed to the guest bedroom, where he had moved his things. He sighed a deep breath as he pulled off his dirty blue security shirt and reached into the dresser drawer for a clean T-shirt and boxers. He removed his belt and pants and let them fall to the floor as he headed to the bathroom. At the shower stall, he reached in, turning the water on. Once he felt the spray of water was warm enough, he stepped in and shut the world off behind him. Wynton let the spray of warm water stream down his head and face. It was soothing. He reached up and adjusted the nozzle to pulsate and then turned and backed up into the rhythmic stream, which pulsated on his shoulders. Engulfed in the water and the steam, carried away from his burdens temporarily, he began to cry.

CHAPTER 36

OVERNIGHT

Raymond opened his eyes, closed them, and opened them again. He squinted at the glowing red numbers of the digital clock. 1:36. A single shelf lined with books sprouted from the wall next to him. He turned on the bedside lamp and scanned them. First was *The African Heritage Study Bible*, followed by a variety of paperbacks by Toni Morrison, Thich Nhat Hanh, Natasha Munson, Maya Angelou, and Henry Louis Gates Jr. He pulled out *The Two Princes of Calabar* by Randy Sparks. The binding cracked upon opening as if new, the pages inside pristine.

He flipped through the pages, not speed reading—not reading at all, in fact. He just turned the pages as his mind wandered back to the laundry room, back to Maddie … back to the horror. It seemed pointless to wonder why she had been killed. Anything reasonable would not change a thing and would never erase the vision of her dead body on the floor, soaked in blood as heavy and rigid as a pool of glue. He had made mistakes before; he admitted that. But how could he have possibly known something would go so terribly wrong?

He tapped his fingers across the top of the book, frowning. He glanced at the bookshelf and then at the door. He suspected leftovers might be in the fridge, closed the book, and pushed it back into its place against the wall.

He gently opened the door and tiptoed out, determined not to make a sound. A deep voice came from the other side of the couch.

"Can't sleep neither?"

Raymond cleared his throat. "Ah, uh … no, man, not at all."

Wynton rustled out from under his blanket and sat up, wiping at his eyes.

"There's been plenty of sleepless nights here. Hungry?" He stood, yawning, stretching his long arms over his head.

"Did you hafta aks?" Raymond responded.

"I guess it's not surprising—not even in the middle of the night." He gazed around the room and walked toward the wall to turn on some lights.

"Hadda jacked-up dream," Raymond began. "I was a lawyer and I just had me a landline and was stuck home waiting on service for damage done to my property."

"You had property?" Wynton said, egging him on.

"Ah ha ... funny. I think my subconscious be telling me to just stay put for a while."

"Well, in general that's a good idea; can't hurt to hunker down and let the world float away for a bit. But as for tomorrow, you're going into the city with me."

They walked into the kitchen. Wynton opened the refrigerator, and they exchanged glances. The light showed the shelves were lacking. There were no leftovers, just a few eggs, condiments, butter, orange juice, beer, a cut tomato on a small plate, a couple ears of corn in the vegetable bin, the remaining few hotdogs, and the package of andouille.

"We should have thought this through," Wynton said.

"Who able to think at one-thirty in the morning?" Raymond said as he opened the cupboards, revealing boxes of rice, cereal, popcorn, a third of a loaf of bread, peanut butter, and some canned peaches. "Popcorn work for me," he stated.

"Yeah, sounds good," Wynton agreed.

Raymond put the bag of popcorn in the microwave and got out two small bowls from the lower cabinets. "I gots ginger ale in with the voodoo juice I brought," he told Wynton.

"Perfect," Wynton replied, and he fished out two cans from the brown grocery bag Raymond had set next to the liquor cabinet in the dining room.

While the microwave hummed, Raymond stared out the kitchen window into the night. It seemed right to lament his decisions while searching the darkness. He peered, trying to find signs of life.

"Anything interesting?" Wynton asked as he came up behind Raymond. Raymond felt tethered to the infinite and disorienting night sky. Wynton had caught him speechless, too stumped to nod or shake his head. "C'mon then," Wynton coaxed his brother as the microwave beeped. "Popcorn's calling."

They headed toward the TV. Wynton pulled the blanket from the couch, threw it onto a nearby chair, and then tossed the remote to Raymond. "Turn on whatever you want."

"For real?"

Wynton nodded and then sighed. "I'm sorry about earlier," he said.

"You wanna talk 'bouts it some more?"

"Nah, we straight."

"A'ight, cool. I'm sorry too, E." Raymond looked briefly into Wynton's attentive eyes.

"I'm also sorry for what you're going through with these murders." Wynton knew what had happened had little to do with sex or living an unguarded life.

"I done jacked up awful this time," Raymond said regretfully. He then shrugged and looked away, embarrassed.

"No, no you didn't," Wynton said, studying Raymond's face. "Life's just complicated and full of unfortunate incidents, one after another boxing us in or out. You'll be fine; you're doing just fine." He knew there wasn't much he could say. There would still be some worrying left to do, but for now a smile, a few nice words, and some love were important.

"Thanks, bruh." It still didn't make any sense, but he was thankful for Wynton's support. That's the way it is with love; good intentions or not, you stick with each other no matter the circumstances. "So ESPN?"

"Sure. Should be some replay of a college game." Wynton was right; Notre Dame was playing Michigan. The two eased into the couch, oblivious of their burdens for the time being, letting secrets, guilt, missteps, and grief sink deep down into the overstuffed cushions.

Raymond let the cool drink pooling in his mouth calm him. "Hey, E, remember when you a freshman and date that senior? What was her name?"

"Regina."

"Right. That was impressive, bruh." He gulped down another carbonated swig.

"She was my first real girlfriend."

"See, that's just you. You done stand out more than most of the senior class. Ain' you go with her to the prom?"

"Yeah I did." Wynton threw a handful of popcorn in his mouth.

"Homeboys don't stand a chance cupcaking with bruthas like you 'round. Tall, muscles, booming voice. We just nine balls."

"I was polite; that was the essential ingredient," he replied, still chewing.

"What?"

Wynton took a sip to clear his mouth. "Ladies like guys who know how to be polite and respectful. Those guys in twelfth grade were cocky and self-absorbed. They just wanted a babe on their arm for the evening. What kind of choice was that?"

"Whatever. Your reputation was set for the next three years. Had your choice of shawties; cudda gone to prom all four years." Raymond cupped some popcorn to his mouth.

"Hey, I really liked Regina. It was hard to see her go off to college."

"Yeah, I bet it was." He smacked his lips at the last of the salty butter. "You not even fifteen yet," he snickered.

Wynton smiled, glad his story could lift his brother's spirit. He scooped up another handful and commented on the game. "C'mon, Notre Dame beat LSU last week and they're letting Michigan get so far ahead?"

Raymond looked back at the TV and propped his heels up against the coffee table. "They's gonna come back. No way they can whoop LSU and then lose to this team. LSU is strong this year, E. 'Sides, is a replay; Notre Dame wins."

Wynton glanced at his brother and grinned. They both sat transfixed by the bright screen. Neither was that interested in the game, but neither one was tired enough to call it a night quite yet. For some time, they just sat staring, without conversation, listless and reflecting.

Wynton thought about Raymond's moving from one woman to another with casual affection. He considered that maybe the absence of a father in his life was the stone in his heart. There was never an anecdote for simmering affection or anger. He had lost the ability to find himself.

Maybe it was Belinda, the love of his life, whose voice continued to speak to him—pure grace, filling him without practice or predetermination. He wished Raymond could find that special someone who could turn his outlook around.

Raymond was trying to find a reason why he resisted his brother when he was most often correct in his guidance. He pondered at how different their worldviews were and how their approaches to relationships contrasted.

He searched for an excuse as to why he simply had less structure to his day. Wynton had scheduled well his hours at work and at home with his family. He had time to get to school, time for homework, and then time for play. With Belinda's help, he had carried out food preparation, Keisha's bath, and story time before bed. Even now, alone, he still left for and arrived home from work at the same times every day, and meals were the same. *Perhaps*, Raymond thought, *with structure there is less time for loneliness.*

Raymond thought back to the reason he couldn't sleep and broke the silence. "So, where you think do evil come from, E?"

Wynton thought it was odd that Raymond would ask such a difficult question in the middle of the night. He really *had* seen the game before. He answered him nonetheless.

"Well, I think it shows up unrecognizable at first, barely breathing. Then it forms self-serving words like 'me,' 'my,' and 'mine' before it ever trumpets to the masses. We reflect each other, so have to be a place in us willing to override decency. I don't know. Some blame Satan. I think evil is the opposite of love and goodwill, where darkness has overgrown. Course, I believe people can't resist darkness on their own; it's too difficult. People give up or give in, become still or silent, don't look at the larger picture. They slip into that black hole of fear and hate, and they leave their pulse behind."

"So we all be shade?"

"No, I'm just saying the potential is there for everyone."

"So we all almost evil. Six, six, five?"

Wynton laughed. "No, we just have to adopt hope—hope in something larger, and hope in each other. You know, we lost Eden because we lost our oneness in the world. People do not like moving through uncertainty, and they don't wanna be challenged to grow. But if we are to promote truth and embody hope and love, we have to walk with unknowing and reconcile ourselves with faith. It's a choice. The sudden flooding, devouring, darkening weight of acedia is a choice. And, by the way, it's not so sudden."

"E, man, you unwavering strong. You like some wash of watercolor. You know, that faint image—life that dissolve into art and vice versa."

"So I'm a painting?"

Raymond felt as if he had been summoned into the conversation. "Nah, man, you like this spray—like a ray of, I dunno, something spiritual that fall on us whether we aware of it or not."

"Careful, Ray; I might make a believer of you yet."

Raymond sensed that threshold coming, smiled, and switched the subject back to the game.

CHAPTER 37

DIFFERENCE

The Ellerys reached the municipal building a few minutes past nine. They walked into the station house, to the front of the bulletproof glass, and told the dispatcher they had arrived for a nine o'clock meeting with detectives. The sergeant turned from them and talked into a headset as he pushed a button to his left. "Hey, your suspects are here."

Raymond and Wynton overheard him and were taken back. Wynton turned to Raymond and said softly, "I guess in their world there are only two kinds of civilians: victims and criminals." There were four uniformed men standing nearby. Some held coffee mugs, but they were all staring at the Ellery brothers.

Raymond looked to the ground as though something was atop his shoes and responded to Wynton, "Hope I is just here to look at mug shots or something." There was no island of comfort in this rather alien environment.

A man in plain clothing came through the double doors near them with a clipboard in hand. "Ellery!" he wailed.

"That's us," Wynton said.

"Which one?" the man asked.

"Both," Raymond insisted as he smiled.

"Follow me," he said in an indifferent tone, and he led them to a small cinder block room without windows. "Sit down," he said, and he left, leaving the door ajar. Raymond could see a handful of officers gathering out in the hall—he guessed for their morning assignments. Some were gesturing in a quarrelsome, agitated manner; there were a couple of female officers typing inexpertly, and an occasional goose honk came through from a two-way radio next to the dispatcher. Here in this room, they sat beneath plain fluorescent tube lighting that made small spaces seem smaller.

Then the door burst open and several men poured into the room: Jamison—the Ellerys remembered him—two other agents, one black and one white, and an old man in full dress uniform. "Mornin'," Jamison said as he grabbed a chair and bellied up to the table. He placed his file and yellow legal pad down and introduced the others. "That's Nolan and Johnson," he pointed to the two men now standing behind where Wynton and Raymond were seated. "And this is our captain," he said, briefly pointing over his shoulder to Hughes, who was leaning in the corner a couple of feet behind Jamison. "I wanted to come in and talk with you myself," Jamison continued. "You boys are in a heap of trouble." He turned on the recorder and dispensed with the preliminaries.

The captain grinned. He was elderly looking, with translucent skin that bore a creased face from a waning, habitual expression. He had thin, flinty eyes that carried with them the stern look of someone who could be neither surprised nor disappointed. He smiled, but it was not comforting. It was expansive and beaming like a man who had practiced his smile for many years, through many trials. The captain eyed Raymond suspiciously. With his slight physique and nervousness, he stood out in a room populated by large men wearing guns. Raymond felt it. Every nerve ending seemed to be pushing out against the edges of his skin. He heard the sounds out in the hall: the walkie-talkies, the heavy footsteps, and his heart beating in his ears. In this foreboding enclosure there was a cloud of suspicion looming. His stomach let out a guttural rumble like the slow approach of a storm, and Raymond felt as if he had just descended to some subterranean dungeon.

Wynton, however, was used to cops. Almost daily he was involved with arrested exchange students in possession of drugs, US businessmen soliciting underage prostitutes for sexual trafficking, tourists caught shoplifting, and destruction of property when a fight broke out in line clearing customs. He was not defiant, but he was not fazed in the least at the captain's menacing, sallow eyes studying him.

Jamison pulled out a handful of large photos from his file and tossed the first one out toward Raymond. It landed in front of him. He looked to find that it was the pallid corpse of Madeleine. When he saw the photograph, his body went rigid and he was filled with fear and regret. Even Wynton had a surge of uneasiness. The image was gruesome, and he felt sickened as he made a futile attempt to absorb the crime scene. Raymond could not help but also feel a deep sense of loss. After all, he had been drawn to her.

"Is this your girlfriend?" Jamison asked.

"No," Raymond answered. "I told you at the dome I met her a couple days before the game in a bar and we hooked up. I don't really know nothing 'bouts her."

"You don't, huh?" Jamison snapped back at him. "Well, let's see, you know she was pretty."

"Yeah."

"And she was loaded, or was one rich slob's bitch."

"Ahem." The captain cleared his throat to curb Jamison's insinuation.

"Yeah, you could tell by her clothes and jewelry she not be living paycheck to paycheck."

"So how in the hell did you think you had a chance with her?"

"I didn't. She come to me."

"Right. You expect us to believe that?" Nolan spewed as he stepped toward Raymond.

"Hey, let's just keep it cool here," Wynton interrupted. He spread his arms out, hands up, as some sort of peace offering. Jamison shot Nolan a stern look, and Nolan backed up to resume his stance alongside Johnson. Captain Hughes seemed pleased.

"Is true," Raymond insisted. "I don't know why, maybe she was looking for something different than what she was used to."

"I'll say!" Jamison chimed in, turning to see a grimacing smile on his captain's face.

"Now hold on!" Johnson piped up. Raymond nodded, noting that the only black officer present was siding with him momentarily.

Jamison spoke in an angry, accusatory manner. "Listen; I want to know what was going on. Don't screw around with me. We are conducting a three-murder investigation here. You were there, and you came out alive; that's not just a fortunate coincidence." He then pushed himself back and away from the table a bit. He paused and wiped his brow. "Now, how exactly did she approach you?"

"Me 'n' Smitty went—"

"Smitty?"

"Yeah, Kelvin Smith, he my boy."

"He's also now your corroborating witness."

"So we go into the city that night to party, just tryna find club bangers. You know, get us some hunnies and do some grinding to something swag. Then, when we comes up empty-handed, we thought, 'Let's roll to a couple of high-end places just to see what it be like.' We went to Twelve Mile Limit for a CÎROC and lime. Then to the Polo Club Lounge at the Windsor for a cognac. Very swank, you know; it look like some ole world man's club." No one made a comment. "Is way above our league, you know, but we checked it out before we headed home." He paused and then, pointing to no one in particular, said, "Tim Laughlin was playing; you can check."

"You were going to drive home drunk?" Jamison imposed.

"Nah, man, we wasn't drunk. We hadda couple drinks, but we danced 'em off with some fine sistahs in the French Quarter. And you know we ain' gonna afford more than one drink at the Polo Club. So we just up in there." Raymond turned back toward Johnson and said, "And you know, man, we was the only bruthas in that place."

Jamison urged him on. "Fine, so you're there …"

"Yeah, well we felt a little uncomfortable, so we was gonna finish our one drink and get outta there."

"And?" Jamison said, implying he had better get to Maddie sometime soon.

"Then this looker show up."

"Did you just call Maddie a hooker, boy?" Captain Hughes interjected.

"Nah, man, *looker* … look … er. She was fine—ravishing. And she made her way over to where we was."

"Just like that, she shows up and sees you, and boom, she's captivated," Jamison snarled.

"No, I think she show up and see the only two bruthas in the place," Raymond concluded. "I dunno what her story be, why she was there, but she knew what she want."

"So she just hit on you, just like that?"

"She come over and got next to me—I mean right next to me—and smile and aks me to buy her a drink. I figga she could afford it more than me, so I told her I was tapped out."

"And?"

"She pouts. You know, it was pretend—playful like. Then she wave to the bartender in the back for three shots."

"And?"

"And what? Whachu think when a snow bunny is digging smoke? I put my arm round her waist and pull her close in fronna me. She reached back for me and c'mon, you know I was ready."

"Christ!" spat Hughes with disgust at Raymond's story.

"Tell 'em about Doussaint," Wynton urged his brother.

"Oh yeah, so we getting cozy, sat down in a booth, and she was stretching all over me; then this old white man come in. I mean he old, but he styling, you know; he godda clip. He call out for her, and he be looking round. I didn't knows her name, so I didn't pay much attention to him. You know, I was playing with her blonde hair across my lap. I done damn near lost my mind. I mean, I'm tripping because she read me and wanna please me. I thought she finna run me a buff right there." Hughes's face scrunched up, and he shook his head at the story Raymond was telling.

"So this guy, he was Doussaint?" Jamison asked to get back on track.

"Yeah, I guess so. I don't keep up with news and politics; I didn't really know who he was. But she finely heard him, and she pops up, surprised. She turn to me and say she hadda go. So I figga this be her sugah daddy. Now I knows why she hitting on me. She want some youth, you know—someone who don't need Viagra. We was the afrodesiac for sure, but we was also the only two there at that time under forty."

Jamison figured by the way Raymond was so easily telling it that the story was probably true, but he noticed that the captain was a bit disgruntled. "So?" Jamison asked to keep the story moving.

"So she aks us if we gonna be back there sometime. I laugh and told her no. C'mon, we don't belong there. I says I is coming back to the Saints game, and she take a pen from her purse and scribble her number on the napkin under my drink then tell me call her—that she gonna be at the game too and we could meet. I be like, what? Did I just fall in a goldmine? I mean, hey, how offen do something like that play out? I figga it wasn't her real number; she was just a tease."

"But it was ..." Jamison pushes.

"Yeah, I call her, and she was for real. She told me where she be and 'bouts this party with this senator dude in a skybox."

"Doussaint," Wynton chimes in.

"Yeah, Doussaint," Raymond repeated.

"I hope you have a more satisfying explanation for her death," Hughes stated, moving forward and placing a bony finger on the table near Wynton. "You had contact with the Doussaint family previously, didn't you?" he asked Wynton.

"Yes, the senator's son. They were arriving home from a cruise where I work," Wynton offered.

"But you didn't just meet them; you nearly arrested them—that right?" he jabbed back.

"Well, I detained them. Someone was trying to use them, tucked something into their things."

"What do you mean … trying to smuggle something?" Hughes asked as he pulled out the other chair next to Jamison to move in on his suspects.

"Yes, I believe so."

"So you apprehended them?"

"I detained them in order to apprehend the guy who had marked them. I knew they were innocent."

"But they didn't know you knew; sort of looked like you did them a favor. Maybe you decided they owed you." Hughes rolled his tongue around in his cheek, figuring to outfox Wynton.

"What? Owed me for what?"

"Maybe you and your brother were both in on this meet with Maddie, huh?"

Wynton smirked. "You're crazy. I had no idea what was going on."

"I'm not crazy, boy!" The captain raised his finger, pointing to Wynton's face. "You're a pretty good shot too, aren't you?"

"I pass each time at the range," Wynton responded, clearly affected by the strange transition in conversation.

"Oh, you do more than pass; you excel at firing," the captain reproached. "Those two morons bled surprisingly little. The wounds left only a small pool of blackened blood; they died instantly."

"Kay," Wynton replied as he sat straight up annoyed at where this questioning was going.

"Just saying, you're a good shot. Could've been you killed those two to save your brother."

"I had no idea where Ray had gone to, and I stayed in my seat, waiting for him to return," Wynton explained.

"Well, the people behind you"—he turned to Jamison—"what was their name?" Jamison opened his file and stated it was Hendrix. "Yes, the Hendrix family said you were gone fifteen minutes. Did you go shoot those boys?" Hughes finally asked with a sharp, authoritative accusation.

The pointedness of his question rattled Wynton a bit. He hadn't thought they'd try to pin the murders on him. "Speculative," he replied. "You're just trying to find pieces that fit."

"We're attempting to solve these murders," Jamison reminded him.

"It was half-time. I went to the bathroom, bought another beer, and returned to my seat."

"Just that easy; you didn't think about your brother?" Jamison pushed.

"Look," Wynton replied, aggravated at the insinuations, "my brutha's a grown-ass man. He told me he was meeting someone and he'd be back. Period."

Nolan jumped in again, clearly agitated that his chief was letting this go on too long. "And just where did you think they were going to fuck among the populated ramps? The men's room?" Hughes looked at Nolan and nodded. Jamison ignored them both and looked to Johnson, whose body language shouted that he wanted no part of this scavenger hunt.

"I didn't know specifically where," Wynton explained, "but Ray showed me a key to wherever they were meeting."

The captain pounced once again. "A key. Well where do you think he got ahold of a key for his private time?"

"Our friend Mikeal, on the team, got it for him," Wynton replied. "Check with Mikeal."

"Yeah, Mikey hooked me up. He be our plug for seats," Raymond added. "It wasn't nothing more than a laundry room."

"And you called Maddie to tell her where to meet you?" Jamison asked, turning back to Raymond.

"Yeah, it was all cool. She was at the party and was gonna meet me at half-time," Raymond insisted.

"For sex," Jamison said.

"Yeah, for sex, what else was there 'tween us? She just want some young, raw blackness. And I was ready and willing, baby. They's nothing illegal 'bouts that." Raymond smiled and looked at all the officers as if he were Chris Rock working the room. Clearly, he was comfortable telling his story—perhaps too comfortable, too naive. These were not his friends.

CHAPTER 38

MEASURING MEN

"You're just making suggestions," Wynton determined. "It's all hearsay—a guess, a wild would-be. You don't have evidence—nothing whatsoever. We've told you all we know."

"Not quite. You passed Eric Doussaint on the way over to the crime scene," Hughes charged.

"Yeah, so?"

"Didn't you give each other a look, pass him a message—a code?"

"What? Looks? Codes? Please tell me you have some real leads to finding the person who perpetrated these murders."

"Oh, we have some leads all right, and I think you know full well who and how," Hughes sneered as he badgered his suspect.

"Look; you got nothing but an unobjective suspicion," Wynton rebuffed. "We have nothing left to tell you, so either charge us with something or let us go."

"All right," Jamison said, "how 'bout we put you in the holding tank till we get the paperwork to charge you with murder?"

"What!" Wynton boomed as he stood up. "C'mon, Raymond; we're leaving." He motioned for Raymond to rise from the table. Raymond hesitated; he was a little nervous about the two of them resisting the law in small quarters with three cops. "Come on, man," Wynton said again, encouraging Raymond to stick with him.

Jamison stood up instead. "I'm afraid we're not finished with the both of you," he said.

"We're leaving," Wynton responded.

"No, afraid not. If you want to be charged, then I'll charge you." Jamison nodded at Nolan, who stepped up behind Wynton. "Wynton Ellery, you are hereby charged with the murder of Madeleine Breen and ensuing murders of one Lester Clay and Trice LeMonde." Nolan grabbed Wynton's arm and recited the Miranda warning. Wynton swiped his arm loose, telling Nolan to let go of him. Risking retaliation, Johnson then moved in to help suppress Wynton, bend him over and lay his chest and face on the table. They each struggled to take one of Wynton's powerful arms, and they placed them close together behind his back in order to cuff him.

"If you cannot afford an attorney, the court will appoint you one. Do you understand what you've been told?" Nolan finished. Wynton did not answer. Raymond, surprised at the quick exchange and threatening outcome, jumped up, astonished that his brother, of all people—his beautiful, innocent brother—was being charged with murder.

"You can't do that! You know he have nothing to do with nothing!" Raymond offered quickly and desperately as adrenaline was coursing through his veins.

"Except most likely everything," Hughes said as he headed for the door.

"What? You can't just swoop down and pick people out that you choose, with no evidence!"

"Can and have," Hughes remarked as he tightened his tie and adjusted his uniform coat to fit him squarely on the shoulders. "Good work, Chief." He opened the door and slipped out into the throng of other uniforms that had become a sea of blue in the hallway.

"C'mon, Chief," Raymond persisted. "Don't do this; he wasn't never there."

"Know what?" Jamison motioned as the two officers pulled Wynton up off the table and stood him erect. "Why don't you join your brother in the tank and cool your heels a while." He paused and turned to Nolan. "Take this one too." Nolan and Johnson walked both the Ellerys to the door as Jamison verbally signed out for the recording. "This is Chief Detective Jamison. It is twenty-two minutes past ten o'clock. Session ending." With that the men filed out the door. Jamison, who was last, hit the light switch and closed the door behind him, heading back to his office.

Moments later, Nolan and Johnson returned to the unit. Johnson was banging drawers as he sifted through paperwork in and around his desk. He found the page he was looking for and turned back to his credenza to roll the page into a beaten-up old typewriter. As he began tapping the hard-raised keys, those nearest him turned, amazed that the old man still preferred his ancient typewriter rather than the computer. "Incredible," muttered Webb. Johnson ignored the stares and the words; he was focused on his page and typed at rapid speed. He ripped the page from its faded roller and marched off to Jamison. He knocked once and entered without hesitation.

"Well, come in," Jamison said sarcastically to Johnson. Johnson handed him the paper. "What's this?" Jamison asked.

"My resignation," he responded sternly.

Jamison stubbornly rebuked him. "I'm not going to accept this."

"You have no choice, Chief."

"Ah, I always have a choice. In fact, the one thing I do quite well is make sure I am surrounded by choices."

"Not this time, sir."

"Sir? Calvin, sit down!"

"I'd rather not, sir."

Jamison got up from behind his desk and crossed beside Johnson to close his office door. "Sit down!" he ordered as he pointed to the two chairs situated at the front of his desk. Johnson pulled one of the old metal and fabric chairs back a little and sat down. Jamison returned to his seat and opened his bottom drawer. He fingered around for the familiar feel of his whiskey bottle and pulled it out. He placed it on his desk and reached back into the drawer for two shot glasses. He poured and lifted one to Johnson and coaxed him, saying "Go on, take it. You could use a drink right now." Johnson took it and swallowed. He then set his glass back on Jamison's desk. Jamison swallowed his shot and then placed the bottle back in the drawer and closed it quietly. "Now, about this mess ... I know what you think."

"It's not what I think; it's what this squad room has done—has become."

"It's not as it seems."

"It's bullshit—perfect racist bullshit! How did you think I would react?"

"Cal, don't get ahead of yourself."

"Damn, Chief, I thought I knew you better."

"You do. It's not what you think."

"It's illegal and unethical and immoral. And it stinks to high heaven."

Frustrated that he was unable to explain, he just blurted out the truth. "We're not arresting them."

Johnson paused in his tirade. "What?" He was completely perplexed.

"It was all a show. I know they are innocent."

"What the hell?"

"It's the cap'n. I think he might be dirty. He keeps trying to steer us to anyone but Jack Doussaint."

"Why the Ellerys?"

"Because he's a racist old fart. He's getting ready to retire and doesn't want any waves, and he's linked higher up—get me?"

"Yeah. Uh … no."

"I've got Matthews checking into the cap'n to see if he's a player, but I need to keep him distracted. What better way to distract him than to keep him close by and dazzle him with his own plans."

Johnson relaxed. "Keep your friends close and your enemies closer."

"Exactly." Jamison put his hands behind his head and leaned back in his chair as if he were going to float away. "Look, Cal; I apologize for not bringing you in on this, but I needed your anger to be real. The cap'n needed to see you steamed as we manipulated the questioning his way or he would never have bought it; he'd never rely on me."

"Yeah, but …"

"The Ellerys. I know. They'll be told downstairs."

"Good news, bad news?"

"Yeah," Jamison chuckled. "'We used you and scared you to death, but the good news is you are getting out free and clear.' The older guy, the guard—he'll understand. The younger one? He's already bent out of shape."

"With good reason."

"Yes, with good reason, but it was the only way I knew how to play this.

"So waddya really know?"

"We've got an eyewitness coming in tomorrow afternoon."

"Shit, really?"

"Sounds pretty reliable. I'm trying to find some extra time to let the cap'n spin his wheels while we figure out all the details."

"What can I do?"

"Stay mad when the cap'n is around."

"Ah man, Yolanda is not going to believe I tried to quit today."

"Just don't tell her why." He paused. "Hey, it's been ages since your wife's been around here. How's she doing?"

"Better. Finished chemo months ago and has really improved. It's all good. Thanks."

"Well, glad to hear it. Tell her I said it would be nice to see her drop by. Better than looking at your mug all the time."

"Ha. I'll tell her."

Jamison began shuffling through files on his desk, searching for one in particular. When he found it, he stood up and looked at Johnson. "Listen, friend, hang in there; this is starting to come together, but I've got to get going. Want to sit in on the attorney interview. Are we good?"

Johnson nodded, committing to the plan, but he grimaced a bit, uncertain of the game's stakes and the outcomes of so many players.

CHAPTER 39

PRESSURE

Broussard and Davies had just started when Jamison entered. "How is it that as an attorney you have also become the senator's financial adviser?" Broussard asked.

"I've known Jack a long time; he trusts me."

"I'm told he's a smart man; why wouldn't he hire a top-notch financier?" Davies jumped in.

"Well, I'm not a magnate, but I am also not such a stupid man with regard to financial business, and as I said, he's known me a considerably long time and trusts me."

Jamison chimed in. "He has a complex portfolio of accounts, companies, offshore banking, and more. Did you, do you, know all about them?"

"I did, I do," Ed Kapinsky replied.

"How did your client come to be such a wealthy man?"

"Well, he received much of his money, a rather hefty sum of start-up money, from his grandfather. Jack was his only grandson among several granddaughters."

"So grandpa was a sexist," Jamison snarled.

"Yes, probably so."

"And when did you sign on? When were you retained?"

"Early on in his career. 1977."

"About twenty-eight years ago. Where was Jack in his career then?"

"He'd been married to Renee for four years and had a newborn son, and was avidly moving into politics."

"Renee came to their marriage with her own wealth. Was her money included? Did you, or do you, manage her finances?" Broussard probed.

"No, Jack and Renee have separate accounts. Her money came to her through generations of money. She was not about to hand over her legacy to Jack, who has neither been much of a philanthropist nor been terribly transparent."

"And so, her money?"

"Remains with her or has been donated to charities or used as start-up money for nonprofit organizations."

"And the senator's money from day one?"

"It was his grandfather who worked hard, turned average into a wealthy heritage."

"Has the senator set aside money for his family?"

"Yes, especially for Eric."

"Hmm, tell me how one remains a trusted financial advisor and an attorney, and just a friend at all social engagements."

"I don't. Jack rarely compartmentalizes his life. His life is his business; his business is his money. One is not apart from the other."

"So you are a primary player in the senator's life and business?" Davies asked.

"I am a close, trusted friend involved in much of the senator's life."

"What would you say your role is regarding being a close friend?"

"Protection."

"Protection of money?" Jamison's tone turned petulant.

"Yes."

"From what?"

"Taxes mostly."

"And how do you do that?"

"Ensure his monies are in the most lucrative and beneficial accounts."

"And would you say these investments are substantial?"

"I would, yes."

"And it never occurred to you to inquire where recent large funding came from?"

"That's not my job. Nothing appears to be illegal, if that's what you're getting at. I'm aware that is exactly what you are trying to imply, but that is also a mark of a good friend—not to nose into every area of legitimate business."

"And you, are you pulled into any duplicity or anything that may not be legitimate?"

"Listen; it is never in Jack's best interest to place me in jeopardy."

"Does he know that?" Davies quipped.

"Jack loves his family, but his empire of power is just as important—maybe more so. He knows if I go down, everything falls apart."

"So do you trust him to be on the up-and-up?"

"I may not fully trust his character, but I trust him with my life. As I said, I disappear and he loses all his security."

"Interesting. So if someone wanted to hurt the senator, you'd be the guy to get, wouldn't you?"

For the first time, there was a flicker of hesitation. Kapinsky shifted his weight in the hard-backed chair. "I suppose so." He calmed himself as he submitted to their questioning.

"So why do you think Ms. Breen was killed and his daughter-in-law involved?"

"That is an entirely different matter. I have no idea why Madeleine Breen was killed. I thought I heard it was a love tryst gone bad."

"Hmm, did you ever accompany the senator or his entourage abroad?"

"Yes, yes I did, several years ago, to the Caymans to set up some financial accounts."

"Anywhere else? Maybe to Mexico?"

Again he hesitated. He was uneasy and began loosening his tie. "On the contrary, I advised him not to travel to Mexico."

"Oh … and why was that, sir?" Jamison leaned in, curious about Kapinsky's replies.

"Well, first, it's certainly not the country to invest in right now. Secondly, it's not safe for Americans, especially rich or politically involved Americans."

"Why do you think that is?"

"Well, the cartel of course."

"Hmm, yeah, they're rough all right," Davies said.

"And territorial," he added.

"I don't know 'bout that," Broussard chimed. "They're all over, in and out of the States. Got accounts set up overseas too."

Ed asked for some water. Davies left to retrieve a bottle from the fridge down the hall and was back quickly.

"Here you go, Mr. Kapinsky."

Ed replied with a thank-you.

Jamison got back on subject. "So you warned Jack's people about Mexico, and yet they took several trips—regular trips. Even Jack and most recently"—he slowed as he turned over some pages on a clipboard—"Eric. What was going on in Mexico, Mr. Kapinsky?"

"Deep-sea fishing as far as I can tell."

"Hmm. Just as easy to chart something from your home town, give some badly needed work to locals here in N'awlins, don't you think?"

"I believe there was a town he frequented as a child with his grandfather, and by revisiting the area he keeps that memory alive."

"Aw, pretty sentimental for a cold-hearted, cocky son of a bitch like Jack Doussaint, don't you think?"

Ed sat up tall. "Do any of us really know each other and the memories that motivate us?" He was gaining ground.

"Mr. Kapinsky, seems there was a bit of trouble the last trip down. About a year ago, on the eve of an election."

"My goodness, I would have been at Jack's side at his political headquarters then, and as I said, I know nothing about any trips he and his family take other than that they are going." He felt relieved he was able to move on from the Mexico line of questioning. Anything further would be harassment, and Kapinsky knew the police weren't going to press an attorney.

"Okay, Mr. Kapinsky, did you advise the senator for or against withdrawing any large sums of money?"

"I have spent years building up his portfolio so he and his family could live comfortably. Unless it was a better investment, I would not advise him to withdraw any large sums of money."

"Did you know that, in fact, he took out two hundred thousand dollars and sent one hundred thousand over to the police superintendent and one hundred thousand to our state governor? Can you explain this action?"

"I cannot. First, it's not a huge amount for Jack to cover, and secondly it was probably for charity—you know, a way to be generous for work well done."

"Ah, but wouldn't you oversee such donations?"

"I would, normally ... but there's always an exception. It is, after all, his money, and he can do what he wants with it."

"Really ... despite knowing you are his security, as you say?"

"Well, Jack will get around to telling me one of these days over drinks, and I'll chastise him for the delay of information, fix the books, and move on," Kapinsky said confidently.

"You fix the books, do you?"

"You know what I mean; I'd have to go back and enter the deductions and rebalance the monies."

"Ever have to do this before?"

"I have, yes, a couple … a few times."

"Would you say that it would be in his best interest to keep his attorney and financial adviser in the dark, Mr. Kapinsky?" He paused. "What are we to think now that his secretary has been killed?"

"I don't know what you mean."

"I mean"—Jamison shot him a stern look—"what a coincidence that his mistress and secretary have both been killed by someone with a knife. A little personal, don't you think?" he asked with malice.

"You think there's a connection between the two?" Ed asked as innocently as he could.

"Come, come, Mr. Kapinsky; what has the senator been up to that he is being repaid in this way … and is Mrs. Doussaint now in danger?"

"I couldn't say."

"Think you ought to tell him to protect the Mrs.?"

"The senator has plenty of bodyguards to ensure the senator and his wife's safety."

"Don't you know more than you're letting on? Why don't you help us so we can spare the next life on the list; might even be yours!" Jamison slammed his papers as he got up. "Kapinsky, I'd come clean if I were you." He turned toward the recording button. "Boys, get the details of this one's transactions the last few months. This is Chief Detective Jamison, concluding the interview"—he checked his watch—"at 1:46 p.m."

CHAPTER 40

INFORMATION

Matthews raced through the congested squad room to Jamison's, knocked, and opened the door to find his office empty. He returned to his desk and threw the manila file folder he was holding onto his desktop. "Damn," he muttered. He then looked to find Raskins. "Rass, got a minute?" he called across the aisles of desks. Raskins motioned with her index finger that she'd be just a moment while she talked on the phone. Matthews rocked back and forth in his shoes, using his ankle strength and toes to balance his shifting weight. He was not anticipating Jamison's disappearance. He looked across the room at Raskins again, fingering and rolling the coins in his front right pants pocket. He turned his head to the desk behind him and met Johnson's eyes. "Seen the chief?" he asked.

Johnson stood up, tucking in his button-down shirt, and replied, "He took off 'bout fifteen minutes ago."

"Oh." Matthews sighed. "Know where?"

"Nope, but he was in a hurry. Got somethin' new?"

"Uh, yeah, sort of."

"What did you find out? You can tell me; Mick filled me in."

"About the cap'n?"

"Yes."

Raskins walked up to the two detectives, "Yes," she sang. "Does he know?" She nodded toward Johnson.

"Yeah."

"So tell us, what did you get?" Raskins sat on Matthew's desk corner, leaving one foot on the floor. Johnson strolled around to the space between their desks and joined Matthews leaning back against the front edge.

"What's up?" Johnson asked as he folded his arms across his chest.

"All right, got a bunch of stuff, don't know if we can use it. Is Webb back with the stats on Doussaint's accounts?"

"Not yet," Johnson commented.

"Get this: Cap'n retires in four months. Two months ago, he received a check for a hundred grand."

"What!" Raskins was astonished.

"That's not all; he just got some beach property in Antigua."

"Can't wait to see if Doussaint paid out a similar amount," Raskins said. "Got a photo of the property?"

"Yeah, right here." Matthews opened his file discreetly while looking around for unwelcome company.

"Sweet," Johnson commented as he surveyed the island layout.

"Don't know the connection," Matthews stated, "but the cap'n got his check from Doussaint."

Just then Webb moved up behind the three, startling them by shouting "Cap'n!" Matthews and Johnson turned to look behind them.

"Shit. What the hell are you doing?" Matthews demanded.

"Catching your detective butt off-guard," Webb answered.

"What did you find?" Matthews asked.

"Nah, yours first," Webb insisted.

Raskins cut in. "Cap'n has come into sizeable money, and property out of country."

"Interesting," Webb concluded.

"You?" Johnson prompted.

"Doussaint's finances are a lot healthier than we imagined. There's a maze of accounts, deposit facilities, and off-shore companies. Some investments, ownership of properties ... couldn't get a lot of specifics, but estimate him to be worth about fifty-four million. The way the money moves around, it's not going to be easy to find the origin. But get this: Doussaint has a lot of pals he takes care of. Got the super and cap'n on his payroll, plus a couple of higher-ups near the governor."

"That doesn't come from a senator's payroll ... and?" Raskins prodded.

"And," Webb continued, "it took persistent calling and cajoling to find the right person willing to dig through records."

"So what did you find?"

"He has been writing checks for and also receiving hundreds of thousands of dollars."

"Any trips to Mexico?" Matthews inquired.

"Oh yeah, a couple, and there was trouble with the trip last year," Webb informed them.

"What kind of trouble?" Johnson asked.

"Well, let's see. Mexican cartel; some coke; a woman, of course; his son detained but never arrested; a payoff; and a cover-up," Webb was clearly pleased with his discovery and implications.

"Damn," Matthews muttered again, this time out of amazement.

"Hey, where'd the chief go?" Matthews asked again.

"Oh, got a big break in the case," Raskins answered.

"Such as?"

"A real eyewitness."

"Wow!" Webb exclaimed. "Closing in on the shooter?"

"Yeah," she replied simply.

The detectives grew eager to get to work on the case. So many times, they'd get a lead and then it would flatline. The information Webb and Matthews ascertained whetted their appetite for unequivocal prosecution. The case was opening up, but they knew it also had to keep until Jamison returned. They were like children trying to keep a secret but ready to explode with excitement. They each went back to their desks and kept busy doing the small bits and pieces of a case, such as chronologically documenting paperwork, feeding transcripts into digital files, and returning phone calls.

Reynolds and Nolan had noticed the difference—a peak of information, perhaps, between their colleagues. Nolan motioned to Reynolds to head over to find out for themselves.

"Secretive?" Reynolds asked Nolan.

"It's something, whatever it is. Check 'em out, busy doing nothing at their desks." They both stood up, noticeably different. Pete Nolan was a mess to look at. Young and quirky, he looked like a geeky kid. Gene Reynolds had a tall, muscular build and wore high-end, slim-fitting suits and a hat most days. He looked like a confident, responsible adult. They were both intelligent. Nolan received the highest marks at the academy, but Reynolds carried a cocky air about him. He was, after all, with his superior shooting capabilities, the best rookie marksman in the South.

CHAPTER 41

HOLDING

The buzzer made a horrible sound as they entered. The door clanging shut behind them, even worse. Raymond and Wynton were pushed into the empty holding cell.

"Well, the ceiling's low, but I likes the paint. Whatchu think?" Raymond joked as he strolled around their eight-by-ten as if he were viewing a rental property.

"Nice," Wynton remarked sarcastically.

They both sat down, each at one end of the long, hard, uncomfortable bench. Wynton sat with his eyes closed, his head lowered, and his chin resting on top of his folded hands. To Raymond it seemed he was lulled into a mild hypnotic state. Raymond, conversely, felt sick; he felt trapped and humiliated, and his mind spun with worries. Their capture without evidence was staggering; he felt like a hostage. *No wonder testosterone levels are so high in prisons*, he thought. Raymond tried to listen for that magic voice inside of him, but his sense of discernment tended to be slightly muddled. Instead he nursed his resentments and mistakes like young plants, watering them, trimming back the dead leaves, making sure they got enough sunlight. Wynton, on the other hand, carried no bitterness or any other toxic affect from disappointment in this often dreary and humorless life. It seemed to him Wynton had a salve for every wound the world inflicted.

"Ah, man, don't you get mad 'bouts nothing?" he asked Wynton as his rage was building.

"There's no point," Wynton replied.

"Ne-gro, please. If you killed that lady, you be off to prison. But if the blue mafia kill you, ain' no big deal. The media talk 'bouts it, then they all get paid leave."

"We just need to be cool and wait."

"I can't believe you," he said aggravated at how calmly his brother was swallowing this situation. Raymond walked to the door and grabbed the bars, shouting out for anyone to hear. "That's right, here we are, muthafuckas. We guilty a'ight ... guilty of being black. Pigs!" he called out with fierce determination. He turned to see Wynton back in meditation, his mumbling offering thanks.

"Why you thanking God now, E?"

"Give thanks in all things."

"Not this, E; this is racism and injustice by Shay Whitey."

"God will bless those who appear to be outcasts. You need to find mental rest and balance."

"Are you crazy? This be some bullshiieet! We done bin arrested. Look round you; where is I gonna find balance? Next to the carjackers, drug dealers, armed robbers? Jesus, E!"

"What do you want, Ray? Am I supposed to run around screaming, threatening to slit my throat?"

"Atchully, that wudda least be a honest emotion, bruh."

"You know, I'm not in the mood for this."

Raymond clenched his teeth. He felt Wynton's response was not only dismissive but completely bleached of justice. "Not in the mood?" he asked aggressively, "Stop being so damn virtuous; we caged in a jail cell."

"Well, if you feel boxed in by the idea that your situation is unalterable, I can't help you change nothing."

"You a trip, man," Raymond scoffed, annoyed at his brother. "You think praying is gonna get us outta here?"

Wynton paused, stood up, stretching, and moved to Raymond. He thought maybe, with them being contained in a small space together, Raymond might listen to him this time. "You know, many won't pray boldly or even receive the blessing that is offered, because they can't see themselves the way God does."

"And you see yourself God's way?"

"I try to. At least I realize our flaws won't stop God from reaching for us. It's not that people aren't blessed, Ray; it's that they won't receive the blessing."

"So you want me to just chill and feel blessed right now? Hells no!"

"Wouldn't hurt. You might find some peace."

"The fuck? E, ain' you got no sense of self-presavation?" Raymond was tiring.

"More than you know. What experience and faith have taught me is that what is inaccessible now will manifest itself at some point in the near future." Ordinarily Raymond's determination kept him spinning in and out of frustration and he simply wore himself out as Wynton's preaching wore him down. Wynton, on the other hand, was slow and steady. He never had to tap into reserves. Raymond shrugged and quieted; he knew what was coming. "You think there is this great gulf fixed between ourselves and the divine—an abyss that only God can bridge. Even if that were true, Ray, don't you know most folks will do what they can to avoid crossing? The truth, though, is that for all the erosions and betrayals or whatever else is dark and tangled in the human condition, there may not be any human solutions. Listen, Ray, ever since the accident, I've been trying to get through to you. Here's as good a place as any; we certainly have time on our hands. We live in bewildering, drastic times; a little spiritual guidance never hurt anyone."

Raymond banged the back of his head against the cinder block wall. He wasn't going to convert him, but Raymond knew Wynton wanted his words to have their way with him, soften him. "Here's the thing; loving your enemies is nonnegotiable. Martin Luther King Jr. knew that."

"And look where that got him," Raymond rebuked bitterly. "And yes, Jesus ate with the sinners and forgave his enemies, who, course, end up killing him. So there's that."

"You don't understand the choice in loving; there's a risk, and both men knew that up front. But look; love is bigger than any darkness or hate or crap anyone can throw at us. There is loss and cruelty, but all we have to go on is faith that light shines in the darkness, and nothing—not death, not disease, not government, not the po-lice—can overcome it." Raymond pulled his feet up and clasped his knees, coiling himself in such a bodily position it looked as if he were protecting himself from having to take in whatever Wynton was going to say next. Grace, after all, would threaten everything Raymond knew as normal.

"Raymond, trust me; I can tell you that what you are looking for is already inside you. You have to find a way to balance the goose chase you're on, and savoring your life. Once we deeply trust that we, ourselves, are precious in God's eyes, we are able to recognize the preciousness of others and their unique place in God's heart. Ray, everything alive is a survivor; each one of us has been sickened, has wasted or fattened because of pain. We have all rowed out into the thick, brute darkness of self-pity, where the Creator's voice and thin breath of the spirit have drifted from us like floating debris. But each of us at the right moment must latch onto God's presence, recover the faith deep inside, and take a hard look at love and compassion, serving others as we settle into our skin and find our way."

"Keep hope alive!" Raymond commented cynically.

"A'ight, Jesse, don't mock me. Compassion is a wonderful way to renew hope, because compassion understands the meaning of sacrifice, knows how to come up from despair and air out, and is grateful to practice forgiveness. You look up and see the sky as a fist, closed tight and heavy. There's no rescue in that, no hope, no draft—just thick black air around you. And I have been there too, Ray. I have held my breath, hoping to collapse and fold deep down into some abyss. Love and compassion push us forward to be agents of healing, and challenge us to find our purpose so that we might see, hear, comfort, and love all those who cross our path."

Raymond let down his feet, legs, and defenses and looked at his brother. In a way it was like magic to see the Spirit at work in him.

"Look; we are all broken and grappling with illness, aching from loss, and bowed with fatigue, but we are given as a gift to one another to learn together what it means to be whole. Did I ever tell you about Mama Shekinah?"

"No. I wudda remembered a name like that."

"A white woman named Hedi and her husband, Colin, from Holland, were in ministry in the war-torn East African countries. On one of their trips from Uganda into Sudan, the LRA, the Lord's Resistance Army, ambushed them. The rebel militia has wreaked havoc on northern Uganda for more than twenty years, attacking the villages of the Acholi people, mercilessly beating, abducting, or murdering anyone who gets in the way, even in southern Sudan. They are infamous for abducting children and forcing them to be soldiers. Well, the soldiers attacked Colin and Hedi, who was three months pregnant. Though they spared her life, they brutally murdered Colin. She says she remembers holding her husband, who was bruised, bloody, barely breathing, and looking into the eyes of the soldiers. They were children—one a little girl. In that moment the life as she knew it was stripped from her, Hedi decided she must forgive them.

"Six months after Colin's death, she gave birth to Shekinah, the daughter she and Colin had named before his death. The Hebrew name means "the dwelling presence of God." She and Shekinah returned to Africa, this time dwelling in northern Uganda in a home with young girls who were former soldiers of the LRA. These girls who had been pulled from their homes and family and trained by threat to murder, affectionately call Hedi 'Mama Shekinah.' Her home had become their home."[1]

"That's unbelievable."

"That's compassion, little man; you might want to get better acquainted with it sometime. There's a woman in my church who is on a board battling human trafficking. She does her little bit, others do their part, and the organization really changes lives.

A man I know that sings in the choir has just returned from his seventh trip to Haiti to build homes. Even in the loss and despair, there is God, rinsing in the scrub grass, spilling from the edges, touching everything along our path, that we might cling to uncertain places because of our common purpose."

Raymond thought for a while. He believed Wynton was spiritual maturity, who heard and followed the Creator's birdcall, who exemplified poise under fire, who led his life by his values and offered himself as a light to others on the path. His instincts followed the lofty language of heaven. "You know, you shudda done bin a pastor. I hear what you preaching 'bouts, but here, now, them pigs don't have nothing on us." Raymond said with less enthusiasm, "Not even resisting arrest. Nothing."

"I know," Wynton said calmly. "We're pretty inept as far as criminals go," he added, hoping to cheer his brother. He did.

"You more than right, bruh. So you met this Doussaint guy. Think he killed her?"

"I met his son, Eric, not the senator. And who knows if or why somebody kills?"

"Yeah, but she be his, right?"

"You kidding me? Like property? No, she wasn't his. She was part of his money. When people have a lot of money, too much, they think about the ways they can control it and how it controls them. You know, unless you learn early on how to be frugal, you are at risk for always needing more than you have."

"We don't got no problem with that."

"That's right," Wynton chuckled. "Most people think about what they don't have, even if they have quite a bit, because they are so bound up in the desire to acquire. Patterns of behavior circle around money just like habits do around guilt."

---

[1] This is a summation of a story found in *Like Breath and Water: Praying for Africa*, by Ciona D. Ross.

"Deep. That's deep, brutha, but you think he killed her?"

"I think anything is possible, and when the world of money is involved, it is both possible and likely. But do I have any facts? Do I look like the insider po-lice would confide in?" Truthfully, he understood everyone was a prisoner of his or her own baggage, never really getting free from the malignant weight and the way in which lives are mapped out.

Raymond rested his head against the wall and, with his eyes closed, said, "No, no you does not." He began to laugh. Wynton joined his laughter, knowing full well Raymond was pretending to be relaxed. "'Kay, just one thing," Raymond said as he sat up straight and turned to look Wynton in the eye.

"What's that?" Wynton asked.

"Don't, under any circumstances, leave me to fend for myself."

Wynton laughed even harder. "Brutha, I got your back."

CHAPTER 42

AT THE STATION

Tyler was fingering at the condensation on his can of Mountain Dew as he sat with Sara on the bench outside the precinct, waiting for Eric, who was parking the car. Sara was worried for him. She gave him a once-over, mentally noting his forehead was covered with bangs that needed cutting. She picked up his hand and held it. It was small and more delicate than she remembered it being. He twined his fingers into hers, as if they had always held hands, and it melted her heart. It took her breath for a moment, like a memory that kissed her mind. He was a playful, smiling little god with dancing liquid eyes like wet stars that twinkled with innocence in the deep unknown.

"So what about love?" Tyler asked her. Sara's cheeks flushed red. She hesitated because the timing of this question seemed so absurd, and she was apprehensive that her words might be hopelessly imprecise.

"Well," she answered, trying not to fall all over herself, "love is sort of like a story."

"I don't believe in it the way people believe in God or Santa," Tyler said.

"I know," she replied. She knew he had starved, wept, and begged … exhausted his spirit in just seven years of living. "Well, like a book, the closer you get to someone you care about, the more chapters, you know? Love develops. It slips and slides a little, there's some mystery and comedy and sadness, and it grows and grows and goes on and on."

"And each person has their own story?"

"Something like that, which is why it is hard to pinpoint exactly what love is and isn't, because it comes in so many different stories."

Tyler digested her answers and said abruptly, "I don't like fall."

Sara agreed with him. Autumn was nature dying, with its remnants blowing around. She, too, knew autumn was difficult. For her it had meant sedatives and newspaper clippings—the time of year her mother left her, when the whole world had been reduced to lifeless debris and abandonment.

Eric turned the corner just a few feet away. "That took a while," Sara said as she stood up. She was glad to see him.

"Turns out there's not much parking near the police," he answered, and he looked down at Tyler. "Imagine that!" Tyler grinned. He was a little nervous, but he felt completely comfortable with Eric and Sara, and enjoyed them as a couple. "Have you checked in?" he asked Sara.

"No, we wanted to wait for you."

"You ready?" Eric asked Tyler.

"I guess," he answered somberly as he tossed his can, still full, into the nearby trash can. Eric was conscious of his nervousness and reached into his jacket breast pocket to pull out a Matchbox car.

"Maybe this can help," Eric said as he handed it to Tyler. Sara smiled at them both.

"Hey, it's the Silver Streak!" Tyler said, delighted. He carefully looked and touched every bit of the silver racing car, and he reacted happily when he discovered that not only did the doors open, but so did the hood.

Jamison came out to the lobby to meet them and personally escort them in. He stooped down and introduced himself to Tyler, which helped break the ice. The wide front hall was empty, but two wide hallways leading to offices on either side were congested with activity. Walking into the squad room, Tyler was a bit frightened by both the strangeness of cops and detainees amid the flurry of typing and the coarse, sputtering sound system that barked out police information. There in the midst of this concrete jungle, a gradual awakening touched Tyler. His memory would now be a part of all this commotion, and he was apprehensive of the expectations they might have of him.

He saw the lineup of criminals like sheep unwilling to submit to shearing. Everything around him was about custom and protocol, symbols of obedience. Tyler suddenly worried that if he misspoke, he could jeopardize something. This environment was a complicated world of tension and restraint, and few excuses. He felt a lump in his throat and clasped Sara's hand tightly.

"He'll only talk with you if Eric and I can stay in the same room," Sara said. Jamison complied but reminded them Tyler was a ward of the state and they were without authority in this matter as he led them around a corner and down another hall.

When they entered an interview room, a chill shot down Sara's spine as she bore in mind the time she was questioned just a couple of weeks before. She'd been entertaining a gentle forgetfulness about her proceedings since then, and now here in this room she felt overwhelmingly immersed in that same sense of inadequacy and dread. These were the rooms where human nature squared off. Passion, betrayal, violence, and grace became rigid, charmless, rote, and effortless. There was no safety net here as one was provoked beyond endurance, as one crossed the high-wire of reason amid the turmoil of survival.

Jamison opened up by introducing Gandy, Webb, and Matthews, who were already seated, to the Doussaints, and he asked Tyler how he felt coming upon this stranger without being scared off.

"My momma used to tell me to steel myself when something felt wrong. So that's what I did."

"What happens when you steel yourself?"

"You imagine your body is protected with armor. You know, it makes you stronger. It can also make you invisible." That's exactly how Tyler felt at times, though he couldn't quite put his feelings into words. He experienced a state of absence when he got lonely or felt he was in trouble. He would put on his protection and cease to remain in the flesh.

"You can be invisible," Jamison repeated as he looked around the room at his other officers and to Sara and Eric. This was not the eyewitness he had hoped for. Tyler's judgment would never be acceptable if he believed he could become invisible. "Like a superhero?" he asked.

"No. It's different. You know, you become so dried-up and unhappy no one sees you anymore," he answered. "Not like superheroes—like homeless people."

"So you pretend?"

Tyler's smile faltered. "Well, sometimes people don't care; they're just enjoying themselves, so they don't really see you. You don't have to pretend, because if no one really notices you, you are invisible to them, aren't you?" It was a very profound insight for a young boy. Obvious to everyone in the room, it was the exact answer someone who felt lost could give.

Sara's heart was in her throat as she listened. She wished she could hug him, console him. Tyler was describing heartache without any real emotion. Her body ached for him, and tears were welling up in her eyes for this sweet, innocent child who was unaware of how he was guarding his own heart in a cold world.

"You weren't really invisible," Jamison said.

"I was real, I was there, but I was invisible to *that* guy. He didn't see me.

I'm just a kid in the crowd, like camouflage." He blinked, trying to wink, and raised his eyebrows, clearly satisfied he had achieved go-go status. "I even told him the water fountain was broken. But he looked all around, trying to figure out who had said so, so I knew he couldn't see me."

"So you followed him?"

"Yeah, I mean, he was pretending to take a drink from a water fountain that didn't work. And he stayed bent over a long time, reaching around the back for something. But that's silly; there's nothing at a water fountain except water and a button to push. And it wasn't even working."

"Do you remember what gate that was near?" Tyler was asked.

"Twenty-eight," he answered.

Jamison motioned to Gandy. When Gandy came near and leaned down, Jamison whispered to him to go see if he could find tape residue at the fountain near gate twenty-eight. Gandy left the room, and Jamison continued.

"Where did he head next?"

"To the baffroom. He was there a long time."

"Near what gate?"

"Twenty-six. I remember 'cause that's my birthday … on the twenty-sixth."

"Why did you wait on him and follow him?"

"Because he was weird. He stopped and got popcorn after that, 'cept he didn't get a drink. How can you eat popcorn without a drink! That's like the trick where you have to eat a few crackers, then chew gum and try to blow a bubble."

Jamison brought Tyler back on topic. "So he went to the bathroom and got popcorn, right?"

"Yeah, but I don't remember him eating any of it. And besides, why would you eat popcorn right before you kill someone? See how I mean he's weird?"

"Where did he buy the popcorn? Near that same gate?"

"Oh, it was farther up, near gate twenty-four, next to that corner with the bees' nest."

"That's right near the shooting," Jamison said. "Webb, go back to the vendor area and find out who was working popcorn, new or long-term employees, and bring them in for questioning." Webb nodded and left.

"Did the popcorn man do something wrong?" Tyler asked.

"Well, no, but maybe he can ID what this guy looked like," Jamison explained.

"Oh, I know what he looks like," Tyler said. Everyone in the room grew silent. Tensions were on the edge; the only clue to the shooter was going to come from this young boy.

"Okay," Jamison said slowly. "Tell us everything you remember about this weird guy."

"Well, first, he dressed weird."

"Weird? How so?"

"He was all dressed up like he was going to a wedding—you know, in a suit and fancy shoes. You don't wear clothes like that to a football game."

"Anything else?"

"He was tall and had dark hair."

"Tall how? Like Eric? Shorter, taller?"

"He was a little taller."

"And?"

"And he wore a weird hat. It had a dent in it across the top, and it didn't match his suit."

"And?" Jamison tried to springboard Tyler onto another clue.

"Um, let's see ..." Tyler said, stretching his words out as he squirmed around in his seat. "Oh yeah." He sat up straight. "He had a toothpick in his mouth, and he was moving it around all wiggly."

"Anything else?"

"No, that's it. Oh, he had dark eyes. That's all."

"Excuse me a minute," Jamison said as he stood up and stepped outside. In the hall, Jamison called out to both Gandy and Webb as they were leaving. When they came back to him, he quietly told them to ask about a tall, well-dressed man with dark hair and a hat."

Jamison came back in. "Matthews, see if Criminalistics lifted any shoe prints that would indicate a man's dress shoe instead of all the casual shoes normally conducive with a football game."

"Will do, but Chief, all the skybox people—they're well dressed."

Jamison bent his head toward Eric, rolling his eyes, reminding Matthews that if he was trying to implicate the senator, he needed to recognize that his son was present. His lips were pressed hard together, and his face was turning red, as if he were holding back an explosion. Matthews understood the message, figured he *was* holding back an explosion, and quickly excused himself.

CHAPTER 43

THE ROAD BACK

Walking through the garage back to their car, Raymond detected Wynton's smirk and fought it. "I know you think it was your prayers back there that got us out, brutha, but five-oh was playing us long before we ever come in for questioning. God didn't have nothing to do with our being let go."

"Did I say anything?" Wynton asserted.

"I can see it, whatchu thinking."

"What I'm thinking is that things work out and maybe we're better off calming down and resting confidently in peace rather than throwing a fit because we only see parts of the whole."

Raymond didn't have a catchy comeback, because Wynton had actually been correct on that point. He was frustrated that the better part of the day had been spent at the station, wasting their time as pawns in a police game without so much as an "I'm sorry" or "thanks for coming in." The sting of this day, for Raymond, was not going to be easily dismissed.

They hurried to get out of the garage, hoping to avoid the early rush of traffic in and around the city. The square metal buildings dotting the airfield fence would soon be aflame in shiny orange, reflecting the setting sun. They jerked forward, accelerated, and stopped frequently as the bustle of cars moved, waited, and reacted in an urgency to get beyond city limits before the late afternoon rush-hour was in full swing.

"Tunnel vision, dogg; bacon get focused on one thing," Raymond pointed out.

"Maybe, Ray, but they're tryin' to solve three murders and get obstacles out of the way to do so. Everyone makes mistakes, steps on toes; it's not worth the fight. Let it go."

"If we was rich and famous, we be suing they ass."

"But we're not rich or famous, are we?"

"Nope, just black."

"You know what, Ray? I get you. Black men are incarcerated in record numbers and in off-the-chart percentages compared to the whole of a diverse society. I know you are frustrated with the unfair and inaccurate statutes set up by a white society. I am too. I feel for my bruthas who are persecuted and thrown into the hellhole of a cell, locked away, sometimes innocently, caged like animals and forgotten. No one is going to argue with you about the system being rigged. But do something.

"Ray, bigots who don't really think things through holler out like fools, "If you don't like the country, leave." But I say if you don't like the way this country operates, vote, volunteer, run for office, call your representative. You can pray for mercy, for forgiveness, for justice. You can challenge citizens to weigh in on injustices, go door-to-door and get signatures for legislators. Start community watch groups. Hell, Ray, apply for financial aid and go to law school and work within the system to improve it. If you don't want to go to college, at least find out when black scholars or activists will be speaking on campus. Attend for one evening and connect with a movement. Become a part of that movement. With our first black president, I guarantee you there will be some movement coming along that can make a positive change. Pick a vocation that is advocation. Think about it; what spark or fire did today's events ignite in you? To complain or do something?"

"Damn, E, I'm just complaining a little bit. You know the Klan is the backbone of this country."

"You want white folk to be held accountable, but all of us, each one of us, needs to be accountable. We, the citizens, to our society—we, the human beings, to our fellow man."

His convictions rang true but hit Raymond like a punch in the stomach. Raymond frowned and then offered a suggestion. "A'ight, reverend, you done saved me right here, right now. But how 'bouts we stop for a moment and wade deep into the baptism of malt liquor."

It was four o'clock. Wynton thought a while and declared, "It's happy hour somewhere, Ray."

Raymond grinned.

A three-car pile-up ahead of them had been slowing traffic. A sea of blue and red flashing police lights and sirens were snaking in and out of cars, finally reaching the scene. Wynton stopped for a red light, brooding as the engine idled. He knew the dark clouds scudding slowly across the sky overhead meant they had not left New Orleans quickly enough.

"We're gonna be stuck in rush hour after they finish up with this accident," Wynton remarked. Raymond searched the sky, the horizon, and the accident lights. The smell of the Mississippi River wafted through the open window. The air was dense and sultry. The French Quarter would soon be peppered with jazz music and the spices of Cajun cooking. Artists would have already set up along the wrought iron fence surrounding the square, and tarot readers would be laying down cards, all for the evening tourists, all for the tourists' dollars. "Let's not leave just yet," he said as they inched forward. "Let's stay and grab something to eat down here."

Raymond was surprised at his spontaneity. "Let's roll into Faubourg Marigny for some clubs after?" Raymond asked.

"No."

"A'ight, then where we going, Dickie Brennan's Steakhouse?"

"No."

"Mr. B's Bistro?"

"No."

"Red Fish Grill? You know the Brennan family do it right."

"No. You know, you don't have to pay much to eat well in N'awlins."

"I was afraid you be saying something like that. Don't want no muffuletta or po'boy sandwich, bruh."

"Let me turn off here," Wynton replied as he maneuvered across lanes to turn away from the clogged traffic. He turned off Brooks onto Canal and doubled back, heading uptown to the Central Business District. "Everybody's leaving work and heading elsewhere. I know a great little place where everything is made fresh."

"Oh yeah?" Raymond asked, figuring he got out a lot more than his brother. "Where at?"

"Kitreux's," Wynton answered.

"Kitreux's! That place is a dump."

"Maybe so, but it might just have the best food in town."

"Whatever," Raymond said with misgiving. They arrived to Baronne and Evato—no-man's-land. Raymond got out slowly, a bit disappointed in the environment. Wynton locked the car and came around the front to scoop up his little brother by the neck.

"Aargh," he said playfully. "C'mon, free food is free food, and trust me, you will like it here." Raymond shuffled into the entrance slowly, not at all surprised by the lack of atmosphere.

The owner greeted them and gave them menus and showed them to a table. He was old, pale, shapeless, and he breathed with a faint wheeze. They sat down and looked around. The air conditioner was wheezing just like the old man. Ceiling fans jerked and wobbled, and kitchen smoke drifted upward over the few center tables where patrons huddled over their drinks.

"Guess is too early to eat," Raymond quipped.

"Don't think so," Wynton said in a singsong tone. "C'mon, this is comfortable, unpretentious."

They both studied their menus, front and back. There were a few roux-based dishes, gumbo, and red beans and rice, of course. Raymond didn't think that was so bad. "Shrimp étouffée—nice," he acknowledged.

The owner came over to their table. "What can I git y'all? Eatin' or drinkin'?"

Wynton folded his menu and replied, "Both."

"Good. Chef's makin' amazin' snap beans with salt meat, and the crawfish bisque is a good choice too."

Wynton responded first, "I'll try the triggerfish, and your leeks and fried green tomatoes with remoulade sauce, and an Abita beer."

Raymond chimed in, "The chick'n and andouille gumbo for me, and prosciutto chips. Oh yeah, an Abita beer."

"Good. Be back with y'alls drinks," he said, and he disappeared behind distressed swinging shutters.

"Trying to size up a good bowl of andouille before you have to make some of your own?" Wynton asked sarcastically.

"Well, it won' hurt, E," Raymond replied, smiling a mile-wide smile. The drinks arrived, and the Ellerys clinked their bottles together. "Here's to the grayboys. Got nowhere to go without them on your back." Wynton shushed him, gave him a disapproving eye, and changed the subject.

"We'll have to have dessert; their bread pudding with bourbon sauce is amazing," Wynton said after a swig.

"A'ight, E, you the man."

CHAPTER 44

CONVERSATION

"I is just saying black folk always be wondering 'bouts fate and destiny, 'bouts justice differently than others, because is not just a question 'bouts when we die, but also the question if we might be better off dead." Raymond spoke with confidence, on his soapbox for a change. "For black communities, death is the result of being someplace they shudda never bin, in some situation they shudda never had to deal with, at the hands of someone they shudda never had bin near, and they is usually the po-lice, brutha!"

"Yes, I know, I see where you are—"

"And 'spite some good like Martin Luther King and the civil rights movement all way up to our first black president, we still be looking at death more than most folk. We done got more bruthas in jail, more on death row, more seniors hanging on by a thread, and kids joining gangs thinking they ain' gonna live past twenty-two. It ain' right."

Wynton helped with his brother's leverage. "We also have more unemployment, more violent neighborhoods, and more drug problems. Too many innocent and demoralized; there's not a lot to see except dead ends."

"That's what I is saying. Is the man's fault we dying and thinking 'bouts dying," Raymond concluded; glad Wynton seemed to agree.

"Doesn't matter whose fault; problem is we are surrounded with the disintegrating of our communities. Every time someone gets carted off to jail, we suffer the absence of lasting relationships—the slow death of a people."

"And all them crackers are so presumptuous ..."

Wynton cut him off. "Ooh, nice vocabulary." Raymond scowled at him.

"They think they know black people, what is like, for real, to be black.

Them crackers don't know; they never come in our neighborhood to grow up or raise they children with us. They don't know sheeiit, and they keeps talking, for centuries, like they do. They think everything done got fixed in the sixties, and now we acting all uppity —'cause we gots a black president."

"You disapprove of white people unless you're sleeping with them, huh?"

"Hey, what can I say if the ladies dig me?" Raymond said so naively it made Wynton break into a full, deep belly laugh. Raymond didn't get it.

"Well, it's like a disease, Ray, if you can name it and gain a little control over it, then you can compartmentalize it and ignore it. That's what white society has done with us. By not knowing exactly what to do with us, they claim to know us, claim it, own it, and move on unaffected."

"They give us Black History Month and Dr. King holiday and think that should be nufh. And now they freaking out 'cause all they teens want our music, our style, wanna be like us."

"Well, be angry at the race but not the individual, because some folks really are sincere in their efforts to understand racial differences. You know, we don't really know what it's like to grow up white."

"Yeah, that must be tough to be white in white society. I'm not feeling it."

"No, man, I mean they get lied to, they get beat up and molested by family too, but they have to keep it hidden and maintain an air of pretense. Maybe it's harder; at least we call it out. We know about each other's flaws, know each other's business in our churches and on the streets. Maybe it's harder living within the mockery pretending everything is okay."

"Well, I dunno. And see, I don't claim to know! They mommas worry 'bouts what painting can fill up a space on a wall. Our mommas worry if they kids gonna get home safe from school. We starting to dominate in a profession, the field of sports, and now, just now, everybody saying athletes making too much money. White people are paranoid, so our people live on the perimeter, fixed and territorial, immersed in blackness, suppressed by blackness."

Wynton was intrigued with Raymond's well-thought opinion. Pleased with his passion, he encouraged him. "Good point, go on."

"Guess when you in charge, don't matter any reasoning 'cept your own. They ain' got a clue. They don't know the first commonsense thing when living while black. Is 'bouts the po-lice. Standing up for yourself leave you bloody and arrested, and the other thing is white women. Being in the company of white women always attract hostility, bruh."

"Yes, yes, Raymond. Being a black man asserting some shred of dignity throughout history was to risk assault. To cops, anything beyond passivity has always been interpreted as aggression. Some have said the American imagination has never been able to fully recover from its white supremacist beginnings. Consequently, our laws and attitudes keep straining against the devaluation of blackness."

"The country's whole culture is anti-black: our laws, our advertising, our segregated communities, schools, Congress, and the justice system. We always be fighting against oppression. And still today, we not really accepted. They tell us by they actions that you can be on the right side of the color line but the wrong side of the property line. Sure, there are people who are making strides for change—heroes in our culture, but whites don't think there is a great need for change. They not been looking at the truth and the consequences."

"They recognize progress, but they see it as a movement, not the personal journey it is for each one of us. That's the problem, because that perspective dehumanizes the struggle and makes it easy to overlook progress made and progress to be made."

Wynton realized that perhaps for the first time, Raymond's pang of discontent was heartfelt, not out of bitterness or lewd antiauthoritarian angst. He wasn't just motoring fear around and letting it fade or rev up when convenient. There was purpose tugging at his core. Disgrace and disgust had been given arms and legs and were waiting on judgment to foot that old, long highway of black injustice. "All these thoughts, it's the deepest reflection I have ever heard from you, Ray. You've got potential. And by the way, you are right." Raymond's nerves were flushed. He felt every trace of flesh and bone falling away. His clear brown eyes had just watched the master concede to the pupil! He paused to relish the moment, drawing in a long breath.

"Word. Look at you, E. You part of the statistics; raised by a single mom with no pops round, but don't no one guess the depths of who you is just by looking at the surface. You done beat the odds, but don't no one see all you be offering if they just see you as black."

Wynton had a calm aura of authority that radiated out to others—simple charisma. *Some people like Wynton have it*, Raymond thought, *and the rest flock to those lucky few*. Raymond had to exert himself to keep pace with his brother. His mind was deep and wide, and even Raymond, who professed he couldn't handle one of Wynton's long-winded sermons, became smarter and more conscious of life by just being with him. There was no plateau with Wynton; each exposure pushed him toward the next level and beyond the place of the last. Wynton chastised Raymond at times, but he also made Raymond feel he had the ability to be exceptional—that he might eventually rise to Wynton's level of ease and intelligence instead of the brittle, prickly places he was accustomed to.

"That's why our peoples claim the blues and jazz, and leave rock 'n' roll for them white boys. We gots to celebrate our dis'pointmen's, let misery get colored over with music that speak to our pain—the pain of our blackness in a white world. We not only gots to endure it, but enjoy it. You know, the militants, the Black Panthers, they right. They anger keep 'em and our communities in check, in reality, where we gots awareness of worth."

"But the anger slips too easily, Ray. It falls into hatred that wakes and thirsts, and it cannot be quenched. You know the gift of God enables us to love and grow and change beyond our own ability. You talked about Martin Luther King. Well, it was not the bitterness of discord, but faith, that signed the Emancipation Proclamation. It was not hateful southern politics, but faith, that walked peacefully in Selma."

"And what community runs toward Jesus more than others?" Wynton asked rhetorically. "Black communities. Look at who God chooses, uses to bring compassion into a cold world: a stuttering, insecure Moses, who killed a man; Rahab, the prostitute; David, an adulterer. Everyone screws up and endures frustrations. I don't know why we have to become so vulnerable before we really connect with God. Maybe we can't become the compassionate, merciful people God wants us to become until we cry out for compassion and mercy ourselves." He paused, set his fork down and looked Raymond in the eye. "I can't help change a whole community or the ills of society at large, but I can help you. Let's leave race alone a moment. If you just pray from the heart, out of love, opening to love, Ray, you'll get an answer. The phone rings, that certain letter arrives by coincidence, light comes so you can see the next right thing to do. Most folks don't pray, because they don't want to find the truth. So they get more frustrated, less hopeful. Everyone needs to practice radical hope—hope in the face of not having a clue. That's where our people get raised up," he grabbed his fork and took another bite of his meal. "Eat up." He pointed to Raymond's plate.

"After I lost Belinda and Keisha, I prayed for God to soften my heart so I could forgive and love again. It's not easy, but needing to be right has a weight that tethers your thoughts and your health to a stubborn grief of wishing for what should have been but will never be." Raymond was shoveling his food in. "How's the andouille?"

Raymond nodded positively while his mouth was full and was able to sputter a few words over his mouthful. "Better than I make."

"What I'm saying, Ray, is that we have to make peace with what is and watch for God's work. We don't need to grow anxious just because we don't get our fair shake." He took a swig of his beer. "We lie awake in the dark, grinding our teeth, festering with stomach ulcers, and maybe do some desperate wailing, but it's because we want God to change things to our desires. In actuality, we need to cry out to God to change us into what God wants us to be." He motioned to Raymond with both hands open, palms up. "God is waiting to awaken and welcome us, but we have to let go of ourselves, our pride, our hatefulness, and our selfishness. Truth is, Ray, we will break under the weight of ourselves."

Raymond swallowed and spoke up in his defense. "We break from black injustice in a racist society. Going to church don't stall none of that."

Wynton refuted, "Not everything is black and white or simplified between two political parties. Whoever you think is the most downcast or the most unworthy, then that's who you should love most of all. We are not to exclude anyone; Jesus didn't, and his teachings never got lost in mankind's illusions of holiness. We watch the news and our stomachs ache from suppressing anger, but we must embrace God's will and our purpose of obedience. We can't go to church for one hour a week and squirm or yawn through the scriptures; we are to roll up our sleeves and get to work. It's not easy; that's why it's called the narrow path."

Raymond challenged him. "For the most part, life's intolerable and easy for people to be mean-spirited or look the other way so they not bothered. Life is punishing for most folk, and mostly black folk."

Wynton's eyes grew larger, and he smiled with enthusiasm. "Even if we are called to have extraordinary empathy, you're right. We can't do it alone; we are too weak. That's where grace rolls in—what helps us see the unseen, the flickers of the divine to stir us further along."

"You ain' never bin stuck nowheres, wide boy," Raymond commented.

"Yeah, well you neither, string bean," Wynton replied. "But you know what I mean, what I'm saying, don't you?"

"Guess so, sort of ..." Raymond paused. "Nah, not really."

"Let me put this into a familiar perspective. Grandmother Lyle died of cancer, as so many eventually do. She never bemoaned her fate but wanted to join her siblings who went on before her. Her shrinking body did not shrink her heart. She still aksed for her fake fur and her Sunday hat when she rolled out in her wheelchair in pursuit of a bit of sun. She was still collecting acorns amid fall's first leaves, her hands were out skimming the green, grassy blades of summer, and she scouted for crocuses when spring was in the air. Remember how she would hand us each one piece of candy from her special dish? How she would let us play marbles on her floors?" Raymond nodded as he cleaned his plate. "She grinned through her wrinkles, delighted in watching life go on. She had a ragged, toothy smile, and red hair from bad color jobs, but she understood. What did she use to say?"

"She told us to speak louder to the near dead," Raymond answered.

"Exactly!" Wynton replied. He wiped his mouth and pushed his plate aside. "See, it's not fair; life may not be fair to us, but we can't be distracted. Our people have stood beside so many graves ... too many. Black lives are the people before us and the people after us. All of us must fully live, or none of us live."

"But we not that far from the 1960s, and that 1600 slave-ship mentality parading round as democracy. C'mon, you know is true. Just like them whites that watched after the po-lice released dogs on our people in Selma. Just like slave owners used to do; they still onlookers today. They not chanting 'Niggas go home' no more, but they not be doing the best they can for us neither."

"Ray, prejudice is going to be with us for a long time to come. And not just against us. Black folks are prejudiced too. People are prejudiced against Asians, and gays, and people with disabilities; everyone is judging someone."

"But our peoples gots a history of abuse that go along with the judgment. And still be happening today by them people paid to serve and protect, dogg. Serve and protect everyone, not just some. You know they finna protect they-selves. Eighty percent of N'awlins went under water, but every time we turned on TV to see the devastation, all we saw was black people. Hundreds of thousands of black folk displaced and cut off from help. Why is that? What does that say about race in 'merica?"

"You're right, Ray, and I don't have the answers for you. America has feasted on black suffering, but we're changing. That's why we see some angry white folks right now that we didn't see a few years ago. Things are starting to change, and with Obama as president, we can appreciate all we're accomplishing and understand where we've fallen short. The voice to do more is now front and center. They see it, and they're pushing back. Most people don't like change, and most communities, black and white together, should be having the kind of conversation you and I are having. There's a lot to do, a ways to go, but no one can hold back progress of a people. Faith, brutha, faith and hope are alive and well. We have to choose the joyful path and make a difference. Be the harmony we seek in the world. You know, you too can open your eyes and touch the lives of those around you. Inspire someone, Ray; make a difference. There are survivors bulging with life out there. We have to choose hope instead of anger if we are to declare ourselves a place—if we are to declare ourselves."

"Hmm, but we needs a voice to stand on. Words, you know."

"Well, we have our first black president; he's bound to lend a voice."

"Long as the country don't become tone deaf."

"I'll drink to that." The two tapped their beer bottles together and took a swig.

Wynton took a deep breath and glanced out of a nearby window. The moon was sitting low along the horizon, ready to ascend as the sun took a final bow. It was a crescent moon, its thin outline around darkening obscurity, about to shine down on the crescent city he loved like a longing, final syllable, inaudible in space. He turned back to Raymond. "Ready for some dessert?"

Raymond smiled. "Did you haffta aks?"

CHAPTER 45

LINING UP

Tyler shook his head. There was nothing more he could say.

"All right then," Jamison said. "Would you mind looking through a book of pictures before you go?" Tyler shook his head again, except this time to agree that he wouldn't mind looking at pictures of people. "Matthews, go get the mug shots." He turned to Tyler and the Doussaints. "You folks can stay in here." Eric and Sara nodded and moved their chairs up alongside Tyler.

Matthews returned with an armful of books the size of large throw pillows.

"There's so many," Sara said. "Do you want to look, Tyler?" He nodded and took hold of the first thick binder, flipping through the pages of faces.

As it neared six, he was still looking. The level of voices outside had increased. Nolan had brought in vendor employees to question. Jamison stopped to check with Webb and Gandy before returning to Tyler. "Anything?" he asked.

"Yeah, Chief," Gandy answered. "We got one guy here on a green card who is pretty nervous. Said he didn't want any trouble, which of course—"

"Means he knows something. All right." Jamison turned to both his detectives. "get these guys into a lineup. I got a feeling our observant little tyke might remember the popcorn man."

"Gotcha," Gandy replied.

Jamison entered the small room to find Tyler finished and looking bored. "Already?" he said.

"Well, it was easy to pass over the ones who didn't have dark hair," Tyler informed him.

"Indeed," Jamison said matter-of-factly. "I have some men I'd like you to look at." Jamison spoke to the Doussaints: "It's officially after hours; do you mind staying just a bit longer?" They nodded in approval.

"Huh? Uh, no," Tyler remarked, scared of what that meant.

"Oh, hey," Jamison explained, "they won't see you; only you can see them. And Eric and Sara can be there with you."

"You mean I can be invisible?"

"Ah, yeah … invisible, exactly. Does that sound cool?"

Tyler was grinning from ear to ear. "Is one of them the bad guy?"

"Don't know; only you can tell."

Jamison led Tyler and the Doussaints out, past the throng of policemen and detectives. Many smoked cigarettes, and the spewed smoke hung in the air like a lilting, filmy veil beneath the lights just over their heads. Some men were clearing their desks to leave, some of them had their arms crossed and seemed angry. Tyler was nervous. He wasn't a tall child, and from his viewpoint the massive room was hard to ignore. The lineup room was just off the booking area. Along the way, Tyler noticed that a lot of the people looked dirty. Most of the ones with ties on looked sweaty and had stubble on their faces. He wondered if he needed to steel away. Sara put her arms around him, almost straddling him as he walked, and then Eric swooped in and picked him up, carrying him, letting him hide his face in Eric's shoulder.

"Here we are," Jamison said as he opened a door off to the side. There were two rooms separated by a viewing window made of one-way glass. One room was dimly lit with a row of chairs for witnesses. The other was long and narrow, with bright lights centered on the wall opposite the viewing window. That wall was marked with feet and inches for suspects to stand beside. Tyler hesitated to go in.

"We'll be right beside you buddy," Eric said as he put Tyler down and took hold of his hand.

"That's right, sweetie," Sara added, taking his other hand, "we'll all be invisible together."

"Really?" Tyler asked excitedly. Sara nodded and smiled. The three moved close to the window. Ahead of them, six men were walking in. They stopped and turned, squinting into the iridescent lights that shone on them. Tyler flinched when he saw them face him.

"It's okay, buddy," Eric said, consoling him.

"Do any of these men look familiar to you son?" Jamison asked. Tyler pointed to the third man. Jamison got on the microphone and with great authority said, "Number three, step forward." The man stepped forward as he had been told.

"Is that the bad guy, Tyler?" Sara asked.

"No," he said. Jamison sighed with disappointment. "That's the popcorn man. He knows the bad guy," Tyler reported. Jamison's eyes grew wide, and he could hardly contain his enthusiasm.

He cleared his throat and said, "Number three, step back." When he did, Jamison dismissed them. He turned to Tyler, smiling. "You did good, son. Thank you." When they came out from the darkened room, Jamison gave his crew a thumbs-up, and they shared their enthusiasm for a break in the case.

"All right, way to go," Tyler heard one say. Tyler felt proud that he had chosen someone. They turned to go into Jamison's office.

"Sit right there," Jamison said, pointing to the two old chairs in front of his desk. "Uh, um, sorry about the mess; you'll be out of here in a jiffy," he said. He then stepped into the hall. "Webb, Gandy," he bellowed. His detectives were front and center immediately. "Listen; we're going into overtime. Get that scumbag into room one. Tell him he's been identified by an eyewitness as a connection to the killer and that makes him an accomplice. Tell him if he doesn't want to be deported tonight, he had better tell us something."

"Right," Webb replied.

"Don't come out of there without the goods," Jamison snapped. He meant it. It was late in the day, but he was close to seeing this case take an important turn, and he was going to ensure they got results from Tyler's leads. His detectives took off. Jamison wiped his brow and tucked his shirt in, calming down, and then walked back into his office.

"Sorry," he said as he approached his chair. He sat down to see Tyler in Sara's lap. He didn't just look nervous again; he looked petrified. "What's the matter?" he asked.

"Go ahead," Sara said to Tyler. Eric and Sara both looked concerned.

"I saw the bad guy," Tyler said.

"I know, and we're getting closer to finding him," Jamison replied without thinking too much about it.

"No, no," Eric moved forward to the edge of his seat. He tapped his fingers atop the edge of Jamison's desk. "He means now." Jamison froze for a moment, digesting what he thought he was hearing.

"Out there? You saw him just now out there?" he boomed.

Tyler startled and then nodded. His fingers were under Sara's arms, and

The Ray of Hope | 199

he was biting at his lower lip. Jamison blew past them to his door and opened it, gasping from the rush.

"Rass, Nolan!" he screamed. Raskins and Nolan came running.

"What's wrong, Chief?" Raskins asked urgently.

Matthews was with them. "What's up, Mick?"

"Lock down." He couldn't get it out of his mouth fast enough. "Lock down!" he said again with greater volume.

"Christ," Matthews said as he spun on his heels and headed for the doors.

"Call downstairs!" Jamison sounded desperate.

"Already on it," Raskins remarked as she began to report to the front desk. A high-pitched alarm went off three times, and then a voice on the PA stated, "Lock down, lock down," with a great, calming voice; there was no rush or urgency like what Jamison displayed. This was a calm emergency—one that the bureau had practiced before. Then came the voice again: "Lock down; lock down. This is not a test." The three high-pitched tones rang out again. Doors slammed shut. No one was getting in or out. Metal bars rolled down across the double doors, as they did downstairs by the entrance.

"Stay here," Jamison said harshly to the Doussaints. He went out to face his frustrated detectives. A handful were standing with their hands on their hips, feeling displaced. Others sat at their desks, looking as though they had given up.

"What's up, Chief?" Webb asked. "We're getting our information," he said, referring to the popcorn vendor.

"Good. Okay, I want my team to circle up," he said with emphasis. "Now!" Reynolds, Johnson, Nolan, Webb, Raskins, Davies, Broussard, and Matthews surrounded him.

"Where's Gandy?" he asked them.

"Downstairs." Raskins answered.

"The shooter is here … was here," Jamison said calmly. "No one needs to know but us, got it?" They nodded in affirmation. "We don't know who he is; all we know is he's here or was here. Where's the rest of the guys in the lineup?"

"We let 'em go," Webb replied.

"Dammit, he could have been in there, or recently brought in by another unit. Rass, go check with the other detective teams and see whether they had anyone in here within the last thirty minutes as a suspect for anything."

"On it," Raskins replied, and he bolted for the stairwell.

"How can you be certain, Chief?" Reynolds probed.

"Just trust me; we have a solid lead," Jamison replied. "I want you to be alert; let's keep this quiet, but look around," he told them. "Webb, or Nolan, go relieve Gandy and tell him to report to me immediately." Webb and Nolan retreated to the back halls. "Reynolds and Johnson, go help Rass skim from unit to unit and find a tall, dark-haired man."

Jamison returned to his office, and Gandy followed shortly afterward. "Sir?" Nolan said as he entered.

"Come in," Jamison told him. "Close the door. What did you get?" Gandy lit up in the same way Tyler had beamed at the chance to be invisible. "You can speak in front of the Doussaints."

"He talked," Gandy said. "He's real nervous at the thought of being sent back across the border."

Jamison smiled. "What did he give you?"

"He admitted he met the shooter—that he slipped him the magazine. But he claims that's all he did; he took an order for popcorn, put the magazine in the bottom of the box, and handed it off."

"And who gave him the order?"

"Some guy named Durrell."

"Do you have anything on him yet?"

"None whatsoever. Seems pretty elusive, keeps the links working, distances himself from them."

"What about the shooter? What did he say about the shooter?"

"He said he never met him before or after the drop and that he was a tall, lean dresser with a badge."

"A badge? You mean a cop?"

"Guess so ... but it could be a security guard."

"Or a customs inspector."

"Yeah, anything with a badge."

"And just what did our popcorn man get out of this?"

"He gets to stay alive, and his family remains safe."

"Great, so he's in under a continual contract to keep working this side of the border. Dammit. I'm sure our dragging his butt in here is not going to help him in the least."

"Might be able to turn him."

"Yeah, yeah that's right." Jamison was surprised he hadn't thought of it first. "Get the Feds in here to talk to him and find out where he thinks his family is right now."

"Got it," Gandy said, and he left.

"You guys think the murderer is a cop?" Eric asked.

"Don't know," Jamison answered. He got up and went to his window, where he fingered a peek through his semiclosed blinds. He stood for a minute, thinking, and then went to his door and yelled out again. "Rass!"

Raskins showed up to his office promptly. "Chief?"

"Come in, Rass; close the door." Raskins came in sheepishly, feeling she was interrupting a private conversation. "These are the Doussaints," he said as he pointed to Sara and Eric. "Oh yeah, and Tyler ... and this is Sergeant Raskins." Raskins smiled, greeted them, and waved to Tyler. "You come across anything?" Raskins looked at her boss in a strange way, thinking maybe they should not be saying all this in front of the Doussaints. "It's okay, this little guy here can ID the shooter. What'd you find?"

"Yeah, the vendors all said he flashed a badge and cleared a small area, carved out his shooting nest separate from the crowds."

"Christ, this guy is incredible." He stopped midthought. "Could very well be a cop."

"Someone on the take for the senator, sir? Oh, sorry, Mr. Doussaint," she said. Eric nodded, but he was on edge.

"No, I don't think so," Jamison replied. "Maybe someone's being paid by this Durrell to set the senator up."

Eric piped up. "Imon Durrell. My father talked about him." Jamison and Raskins were both stunned and listened attentively. "My father told our attorney that maybe this was a hit by Durrell as payback for a trip south that didn't go so well for him."

"You were there, weren't you, Eric?" Jamison inquired. This is why he had allowed the Doussaints to stay—to see if they could offer anything tangible as information came in.

"I was, but I didn't realize the team was screwing with this Imon Durrell guy until after Sara spoke to you about the murders."

"Chief," Raskins interrupted, "word is there is a Mexican godfather of sorts who is in and out of Old Algiers."

"Jesus, Old Algiers is such a cesspool it makes New Orleans look like some sweet small town in Iowa. It's steeped in violence, smugglers, drug dealers, and other illicit operatives; I don't know about stepping into the ..." Jamison paused. "Well, tell you what, first you contact the commander of the Fourth District over there and ask him about the Mexican and nefarious activity in his neck of the woods. Then call the NOPD Criminal Intelligence Bureau and see what they have going on in Algiers, and find out about any infiltration from south of the border."

Matthews knocked and waited for Jamison's permission to enter. "Nothing, boss. No persons of suspect left in the building."

"All right, sergeant, get the station squared away, and call everyone together; let's call it a day," he told Matthews. Seeing the adrenaline settle down, he turned to Eric and Sara. "Guess that's all the excitement we can muster up for you folks. I want you to go home and stay put. I don't think the shooter knows Tyler has seen him, but I don't want to chance anything. I'll put a uniform outside your door, but for all intents and purposes, Tyler is in your protective custody."

"Thank you, Chief Detective," Eric said as he reached out his hand. Jamison shook his hand and made sure to do the same with Tyler.

"We'll contact you if we find something more," Jamison said as they parted. "Broussard, in here!" He then barked out to the squad room. Broussard entered his office. "Got any plans this evening?" Jamison asked in a sincere tone.

"Not really; what's up?" Broussard answered inquisitively.

"You used to work Old Algiers. I'd like you to head over there tonight and sniff around; see if you can find out any information on some Mexican influence."

CHAPTER 46

THE LIFE

As the Doussaints left, Jamison gathered the rest of his team near the whiteboard.

"Vendors claimed a badge showed up near our gate," he blurted.

"We wondered how someone could remain inconspicuous," Webb stated. "He was hiding in plain sight."

"He was a cop or impersonated a cop," Matthews said.

"Either way, he could partition off an area by flashing a badge," Jamison said.

"Well, that would certainly steer people away," Raskins added.

"Yeah, you could set up shop, do your business, and leave, and no one would question it or notice when you arrived or left," Webb pointed out.

"So how do we determine if it was a legit cop or not?" Davies asked.

Jamison paused and thought a moment. "Matthews, what did Criminalistics say about a shoe print?"

"Inconclusive."

Jamison rehashed the image of the perimeter in his head, going over and over the crime scene, the gate, and ramp, trying to discern how a cop or would-be cop could set up and kill two men without bringing attention to himself. "Rass, didn't you say something the other day about revisiting the sight?"

"I did," Raskins answered. "There were no spent shells opposite the targeted trajectory."

"So he kills two people and then stops to pick up his shells and move his barricade out of the way, clearing a path for everyone under the sun to walk and leave footprints over his own."

"Yeah," Matthews added, "if he took his time to clean up, he did so because he was confident that as a real cop, he would not be interrupted."

"Someone impersonatin' a cop would bolt from the scene, 'fraid of bein' caught," Johnson added. The detectives were nodding and buzzing with small comments.

"Okay, first thing in the morning, go back and talk to the vendors again," Jamison directed. "Find out if they noticed a policeman or any partitions set out the day before the game." Davies nodded and leaned toward Raskins.

"Nice, Rass! Hey, you drive tomorrow, I've gotta make some calls on the way." Raskins nodded and gathered her things, and the two headed out of the station for the night.

"Gandy, I want you to get up to Baton Rouge in the morning," Jamison said. "Get a court order to examine the senator's records, and get a warrant and search his home; then get to the registrar to see who's been in and out of the senator's office. But look"—he paused—"we've got to present the prosecution real evidence that won't get thrown out on some technicality. That goes for everyone. Don't screw this up." He paused, realizing it had been a long day. "All right, the rest of you get out of here; find me something solid on this Imon Durrell guy tomorrow. And where are Reynolds and Nolan?" No one answered. "Rookies!" he exclaimed as he left the team, heading back to his office. His newfound optimism about leads in this case was filtering down into the ranks. He could tell his team was regaining a breath of confidence. He was glad for them.

When he got to his office, he closed the blinds completely and poured himself a drink. He reflected back three decades, when he was green and police work seemed so easy and promising. Of course, the inevitable fall came, when he felt the change come over him and his ideals darkened. Day by day, crisis by crisis, the lows overshadowed the highlights. His attitude slighted, he found that his mentality opened his physical and emotional rawness, allowing him to become part of the sinking failures within the unfolding dramas of law enforcement. It was not at all a matter of applying textbook analogies; his work was far more complex than that. He carried it deep within his bones, and it wore on him.

He thought no one could go back and pinpoint the exact moment or event that triggered the start of a downward spiral. Cops seemed to be in continual personal strife and profound struggle and drama at work. Maybe it was just magnified for cops whose work burrowed headlong into torment and suffering.

It was just the nature and condition of the beast. He drank a mouthful and poured himself another shot.

He had struggled in his marriage, struggled to love, struggled to make a living and provide for a family. His family became the retreat from work, and his work the retreat from family; both enticed him to live momentarily on one level of his multidimensional world, and both were unable to refine the living beyond the literal.

He had paid plainly and directly for moving up in position with more responsibilities. There was no purification in the process to help leave any weakness behind. As dangerous as it was to family life, to one's own personal health, he committed himself to the common good. Life for cops just seemed to be an unforeseen unfolding of weaknesses and failures through the mess and confusion and struggle of life. He realized now, painfully, that the real thrill came as one was about to close in and rein in the criminal—about to stand victoriously with the proverbial boot at someone's throat. Maybe that was why so many cops were unfaithful; maybe the only rushing thrill they could find was the climax—that volatile moment of victory, when they could scream out as life closed in and intensified.

He lamented a bit for all that had gone wrong in his life because of the force, but he never waned in his conviction. His old habits, his routines, and even his small pleasures felt dead at times, but he was never more alive than in his resolve to solve his cases.

He understood, in its simplest and deepest level, the landscape of a watchful patience and disorienting ruthlessness. The dark pit was there, close to depression, close to brokenness, and only the successful conclusion of a case could mask the pitfall.

CHAPTER 47

DURRELL

Broussard had spent time with Narcotics, sifting through all the known dealers arrested from the Old Algiers area. They were mostly teens who had a record of previous busts. He knew he would have to be careful if he had the opportunity to question them.

He wondered why someone like Durrell would be involved with small-time, low-life users and doubted someone with that kind of prowess would stay in town long enough to oversee any scores. Decades back, US Senator Huey Long made a gift of the state to Frank Costello, who subcontracted to a crime family. The NOPD and criminal elements had coexisted with legal authority and muscle, with amoral and ruthless leadership, ever since. The recent arrival of crack cocaine and the uptick in heroin use changed everything. Now kids with the IQ of Jell-O were wandering the streets with nine-millimeters. They were as likely to sell to you as rob you, or both, and then, with complete disconnect, splatter your brains where you stood, for no reason.

The crime problem in Algiers, and specifically in the Old Algiers section, had escalated for two reasons. No sooner was a drug house shut down and boarded up than another one opened. And while the police hadn't turned a blind eye, they overlooked the smaller tricks of the trade. As he began to walk through one of the darkened, run-down neighborhoods, looking for some contact, he got a call.

"Hey, this is Rass. Chief told me he sent you to Old Algiers. I have some information you might like."

"'Shoot," he answered.

"CIB says Durrell is on their radar as a co-conspirator in a number of federal offenses. He has upped his drug trafficking in the US and is stashing millions in offshore accounts … none involving the cartel. They had no sight of him recently, but they've observed him and Senator Doussaint experiencing something more than paths simply crossing."

"That's great, Rass," Broussard whispered as he picked up his pace.

"Yeah," she continued, "but they said he's hard to catch up with, not about to risk exposure for long."

"His location is probably a rat hole: some place convenient, but still a rat hole—not what he's used to. I know just the places that would suit him."

"Actually," she said, "he might be hard to follow, but they said he has a flamboyant side. Their research shows Durrell keeps a yacht in Barbados and has been residing in a penthouse here in the area."

"Jesus, why haven't they moved in on this guy?" Broussard asked with disdain.

"Haven't caught him with the goods or a direct link to any criminal activities," she replied.

Broussard thanked her for the information and shoved the phone back into his coat pocket, careful not to reveal his handgun that was beneath his coat. He thought it odd that a major player like Durrell would establish a lowered lifestyle in Old Algiers when he could be living the high life in Spain, Portugal, or the Caribbean if he wanted to stay close to the United States.

His last conversation in the area was with retired FBI special agent Bernazzani, who had led the bureau's New Orleans office after Katrina. Bernazzani had told him then that the market had been flooded with cheap, potent heroin as new dealers were trying to gain their foothold, and that now the resurgence of heroin was far worse in Old Algiers than any other area in the country. A user could get high for hours for just five dollars. The prices were low, and accessibility was high. But then, government hadn't helped any with state lawmakers reducing the sentence for possession from life to five years with the possibility of rehabilitation or probation.

Near the end of an alley, voices spiraled together in a cloud of discontent over the heads of teenage boys. He could see them in the thin light thrown from a single streetlamp. Their clustering together formed one large, dark bunch from a distance. Closer, their jarring movements in and out of conversation made it appear as though their shadows were biting at each other.

He was trying to listen to their stories as he walked toward them. They certainly looked like trouble, and if he was lucky, they would know where and when suppliers arrived. "Evening, boys," he stated as he rolled back his lapel to show his badge. They didn't respond but rolled their eyes, annoyed that a detective would harass them this late at night. "Just passing through," Broussard said. Two of them lifted their shirts to show pistols in the waistbands of their boxers, as the waistbands of their pants were down along their thighs. Broussard chuckled, "You know, if you ever have to run, that fashion style is going to slow you down."

"You the one gonna be runnin' ol' man," one sneered at him as he answered.

"Hey, speaking of old men, have you seen any of the suppliers? A Mexican in the area?" Broussard asked.

"We don' see nuthin' unless is paid fo'," another said as he stepped forward.

"Oh, I'll pay," Broussard commented as he pulled a small wad of money from his pocket. It was mostly twenties, but he fingered a crisp hundred-dollar bill out from the rest and held it up. The tallest, probably the leader, took the single bill and the wad of money it came from.

"Whachu lookin' fo?" he asked.

"A guy named Durrell. Ring a bell … anyone?"

"He don' come down here. Got him a bitch and penthouse over near Algiers Point."

"So you know him?"

"Nah, jus' heard Cedric talkin' 'bout him."

"Cedric? Is he the distributor for Durrell?"

"He work wit' the Mexicans some, but ain' nobody findin' Cedric."

"Why? Who is this Cedric?"

"He someone yo' ass don' wanna know. He run some mean-ass weapons, don' give a fuck 'bout gettin' high."

"So Cedric works for Durrell, who works for Cedric?"

"Everyone. Any profit from stash is collected on the spot."

"Yeah," another chimed in. "Is like you godda pay up fron' 'n order to sell. The little man, like us, gettin' cheated."

"You mean gets to stay alive," Broussard interjected.

"Damn straight," the first youth said, and he pulled out a baggie. "Wanna blow?"

"No, I'm trying to find a way up to Durrell," Broussard informed them. He gave them a business card. "If you hear anything or notice something big on the move, contact me. There's more money where that came from, and if we get this Durrell out of the States, you're not going to feel so pinched." Broussard gave the tallest one a fist bump and went on his way, listening to the chatter as he left. *This Cedric, and maybe even Durrell,* he thought, *would soon find out a detective was sniffing around for them.*

Broussard had a bit of heart for these juvenile delinquents. He felt they lived in the blank spaces of humanity, gradually heating up like water before it boils. Their stories were in the newspaper, or in the corpses left on side streets or near the swamp. Each shot, stabbing, or bludgeoning somehow gave them a false sense of freedom. They didn't exist with faith of any kind and stayed hidden in dingy, dilapidated buildings too narrow for comfort. They trusted no one and had no friends. A contact would stoop into a car, dispense drugs and arms, receive money, and vanish. The rest of life was strictly street rules.

He knew he should disregard them just as mainstream society so often did. Should, but he didn't—couldn't. He regarded them by their scores, their tattoos, and their isolation. They'd sniff a line of coke, smoke crack, inject heroin, and stumble their way into little broken-down bathrooms or drafty, crumbling, empty rooms to lie down on soiled and infected mattresses until their high wore off. It was dangerous to live inside the boundaries of crime with death as its penalty. These addicts promised to stop but stayed in practice with pills as good to them as a mother, junkies who wounded their own balloon skin because they could not escape the sting of life. No, he didn't hate them. He hated the fat cats who got rich off of these juvenile thugs and junkies; the manipulators in charge were the real threat to law enforcement and society at large.

Broussard walked to the nearby station so familiar to him, entered, and asked for Sergeant Coffey. Coffey barreled through the lobby door. "Jason Broussard, you old son of a gun, what are you doing here?"

"Hey, Georgie, just passing through. Good to see you."

"C'mon back to the squad room; most everyone is gone." He led Broussard up two steps and down the corridor to his office.

"I strolled by some fresh crime scene tape waving in the wind over on Ptolemy Street. What's up?"

"A twenty-seven-year-old man died of gunshot wounds in the driver's seat of a car."

"Seemed quiet over there."

"Yeah, there isn't a lot of traffic, and the area stills every now and then. Kind of creepy, as if there was never any noise made there. But then you hear a car door, a shot, and sirens in the distance, and it's back to normal."

"Ha ha, normal. Jeez George, what is that? Heard you had an uptick in gang violence."

"Oh, God yes, robberies in Westpark, Cypress Acres; murders on Homer and Nunez; batteries; burglaries; car thefts daily. And it's moving up to Vallette in Algiers Point."

"Any reason?"

"We're looking into a gang called the 3-11 Boys. Heard of 'em?"

"No. Sorry, Sarge."

"They're tough. They move these young boys up in ranks with boots and ammunition, convert rage into a full-bellied business practice." He was right; it was a constant, common insanity that leapt from the depths of despair and misplaced anger that governed the hostile streets without reason. Death was no longer a lumbering weight but a simple, unemotional tangle in the rhythm of the city's seedy backstreets and alleyways.

"Used to be these punks would run from trouble. Remember that Calvin kid?" Broussard nodded. "Oh my God, that kid was in it up to here and could hightail it up and over any obstacle."

He was always jacked up on something," Broussard agreed.

"But not today. These boys out here, their minds are poisoned. No one cares about dying, and they egg you on, not afraid of anything. They're violent and empty, skinned alive from any feelings of remorse."

"Hey, sorry to hear that, Sarge. I mean, we always hope we can help someone—save someone from sinking to those depths."

"Yeah, Jase, there's a real darkness taking over. I don't get it. It is what it is, I guess. But there's no real way to combat the disconnect. I mean, insignificance is in full bloom 'round here, and we're supposed to lend a hand—lift 'em up from the trenches somehow. It's a disaster!" He was disgusted by the landslide and undertow of senseless, callous violence, and the new shift in policing.

"What's your captain saying?"

"Hell, you know everything has to be so damned PC."

"Yeah, we all have a load to tow."

"And the local councilmen are calling for a holistic approach to fighting crime—one that includes mental health, economic and educational opportunities, and better street lighting."

"Yeah, we heard it too. Oh, and don't forget, more boots on the ground patrolling. And ah, let's encourage the community component reporting to Crime Stoppers. Christ, what a crock."

"They're rendering us incapable; there's no logic to it at all. Same bureaucratic bullshit government is spreading across the country." He paused and rubbed at his chin. "Say, Jase, what are you really doing here?" he asked.

"I'm trying to find information about a Mexican player named Imon Durrell. Your staff come across him?"

"We know he's out there, Jase, but we can't get close to him."

Broussard stretched his neck, disappointed that he would get no leads tonight.

"Hey, can you cut out, grab a drink or a cup of coffee, Sergeant Coffey?"

"Hell yes I can. Been off my shift for hours."

CHAPTER 48

DISCLOSURE

The police were methodically going through a list of his constituents, finding nothing remarkable. Gandy told him, rather cryptically, that further clues would find their way to the forefront of all the evidence in good time. It seemed as powerful as a mother's intuition or a father's suspicion. Jack knew he had not misinterpreted the implication that the investigation would lead back to him.

Jack was guarded. Louisiana had an innately corrupt political nature, so it had been easy for him to deflect insinuations and outright accusations, but there were already hushed whispers at the capital, other legislators clamming up by phone, and an unusual aura cycling with him. He couldn't stop the memories slamming into him, the brutal reports, the image of Maddie's depleted body in death, or the congressmen begging for his attention in the skybox. It made his stomach rumble with discontent.

The police's thoroughness perplexed him. What clues could possibly be in the crossbeams and braces, or turrets and buttresses? What measurements from an old, anemic blueprint would offer discovery? Hiding places to make him culpable? They were not concerned in the least about displacing objects, and it seemed nothing was left unturned. Hands slid back and forth between sweaters stacked on shelves, beneath the bed, inside drawers of the nightstand and dressers—fingers mulling though Renee's journal. What could now be misconstrued as a motive?

He heard the boards creaking in his study, and he stiffened. His pride sent him abruptly upstairs, ascending two steps at a time, to save documents and vouchers from disclosure. He knocked a chair over as he surged into his hallowed alcove. "You'll not find any architecture of murder in my study!" he protested.

"Nonsense, Senator," Gandy replied as he stood beside him. "Everything but the victims' screams for help could be in here." He was befuddled and lost a bit of his breath as he darted from artifact to artifact, trying to salvage the posterity of his precious room. He felt as if he were encased in something heavy, like a fly trapped in a spider's sticky web, the silk binding it while the spider wrapped and processed it to be eaten alive. He heard the sharp tapping of footsteps along the back, and the low drumming of another team of officers descending to the basement. *They are everywhere*, he thought, *like cockroaches scattering in the shock of light.*

He moved to the windows to ensure connection and hit the speed dial on his cell phone. Ed was always available to Jack. He paid him well, and so he had no qualms at all about springing into action as soon as Jack demanded. The voice on the other end gave Jack the greeting he sought. "Ed, I want you over here now. Police are ransacking everything in the house." He was trying to quell his anger. "Yes, they showed it to me when they entered. I thought we had this covered. How the hell did they get a search warrant for me?" A pause gave him a sense of well-being again. "Yes, call who you need to before it's too late. You're just as guilty as I am." He closed his phone, enraged by the slip-up, his heart now beating wildly as he watched the men, clearly without hesitation, dishevel his personal library.

"Any hunting knives or guns?" one uniformed officer shouted out.

"Well yes, of course. You've probably already found the row of rifles locked in the hallway." He choked a bit on his reply, not sure if his collection of knives might end up as some trophy for the precinct. He was glad Renee was away from the house and unable to make a scene at this dreadful manner of investigation. He was quickly calculating his version of the story he would tell and the miscalculation on the part of the police force. "I would be happy to answer any questions," he said to interrupt and, he hoped, suspend some of the search, "if you would stop this ransacking and sit down with me to talk."

"Sorry, sir," Gandy answered. "We are not here to interview; our team is strictly search and seizure."

"Dammit, Hughes!" he screamed as he redialed Ed. "Get a hold of that sorry ass of a captain and find out what's going on!" He slipped his phone into his pocket and tromped back downstairs, expecting to find his attorney at his door momentarily. He checked his watch and gazed off at the car entering his driveway. Ed was dependable, timely, and loyal. He was the one person Jack could pay to rely on.

Ed pulled up to the front of the house and jumped out quickly, waving a slip of paper high over his head as he brushed by Jack and hurried straight into the house. There in the foyer, amid marble and stonework, he called out loudly, his voice echoing in the nearly vacant, two-story landing. "Cease and desist!" Gandy leaned over the staircase railing. Ed loudly announced that he had orders from the superintendent of the New Orleans Police to stop what they were doing.

Jack came up behind him and patted him on the shoulder. "Damn, you work fast, ole man." The two were the same ripe age of sixty-three and had been paired together in business for nearly thirty years.

"I get paid to do my best," Ed said.

"That's it, boys! Let's cut and run," the young detective called out to his crew. All the officers stopped what they were doing and filed downstairs and out the front door like a small platoon. Jack stood beside his longtime partner, smiling as he watched the police exit in a blur of blue. Renee was just coming in, balancing a number of bags and boxes from shopping as the men cleared out. She had a puzzled look on her face as she set her packages on a small table.

"Jack? What in the world is going on?"

"Oh, a sham, dear—complete bureaucratic bullshit." She did not respond to him when he used foul language; she just never understood the desire to substitute perfectly divine descriptive words with such harsh, vile ones. She moved into the bedroom to set her purse down and returned to the entryway with a gasp.

"Why is our bedroom strewn about?"

"Damned police. They think we have something to offer on this …" He didn't want to say "case" and remind Renee of the mess they were in because of Maddie. She finished his sentence for him.

"Case. Murder case, dear." Her insincerity was cold and biting, and her stance flippant. She held an indignant attitude as she returned to the bedroom. While Renee began to put their items back in order, slamming the occasional drawer or closet door when handy, Jack motioned to Ed to head upstairs.

The two climbed the staircase quickly to chew on what had just transpired. As he arrived at the doorway, Jack's anger flared again.

"Look at this. Christ, they have no respect for the finer things in life what-soever!" Jack's leather-drenched, club-like study looked like a cheap flea market. Together they gathered and replaced items, straightening up the disarray of the desk and bookcases.

"The whiskey wasn't touched," Ed offered as some small consolation.

"Good!" Jack snapped. "Start pouring."

"It's ten a.m.," he answered.

"Pour!"

Ed poured them each a highball, placed ice in one and not the other, and handed off the tepid one to Jack. Ed liked the sound of ice clinking in his glass, and he swirled his drink slightly before he took his first sip. Jack did not sip at his drink but gulped it down and handed the empty to Ed for a refill. With the second drink, he began to settle down. "So where was the screwup?" he asked.

"Don't know. Obviously, the homicide unit was not here."

"I still want an explanation from Hughes."

"Yes, yes. Well, the point is they didn't find anything, did they?"

"No. Those files are locked in my credenza. At least they knew better than to break anything or to try to break into anything, and I was not offering a key."

"Good. We have enough to worry about; we don't need to open any more veins."

"Yeah, well you just get that dick of yours to find out who is ignoring our arrangement with the police. See if he can cross paths with the super."

"Will do, but the super was quick in responding with a fax to this morning's activities."

"Then have him check out Hughes and his chief detective. Maybe Jamison finally grew a pair and is branching out on his own."

"Could be. I doubt it, but could be. Anyway, nothing was pulled, and that's the important thing." Ed paused and thought as he sipped. "In fact, it might behoove you to let me take those files back with me to my place for safekeeping."

"Sure. Yeah, why risk anything? Who knows who may return tomorrow with another damned warrant."

"Good. That's a smart move. Any copies elsewhere?" Jack shook his head indicating there were no more copies. "And give me your banking and accounting files. They may be at risk as well."

"Fine, but call the bank before lunch and tell them not to discuss or show my information to anyone! I don't care if the goddamned president wants to see 'em; those papers are confidential—client privilege only. Got it?"

"Yes. Let's just hope they didn't contact the bank first before they came here."

"If those pricks divulge anything, someone's going to be taking an uncomfortably long trip out of country. I'm not kidding! Jesus!"

CHAPTER 49

CHECKING

"Rass, in here," Jamison called out. Jamison and Raskins were usually the first two to work. Raskins was pouring herself a cup of coffee. It was going to take a few cups to restore her to normal after the length of the day they'd had yesterday.

"Wanna cup, Chief?" she called back. They were the only two so far.

"Yeah, black, thanks," Jamison responded. Raskins entered Jamison's office and handed him his cup of coffee. The two held their cups for a moment, transfixed on the steam, inhaling the brewed beans, letting the beginning of their day settle within them. They both took drinks and exhaled with pleasure at the jolt they both needed to start their day. Jamison neared his window. Looking out at the vacant desks of his team, he said, "The boy said the shooter was tall, lean, dark-haired, wore a hat, was dressed in a suit, and had a toothpick in his mouth." He took another swallow of his coffee and set the cup down, turning to face Raskins. "We know the shooter had to be a cop or someone impersonating a cop," he continued. "Look out there and tell me if you notice anything."

Raskins was dumbfounded. All she saw were the desks of her team members. "Chief?" she said, not understanding his question. Some of the other detectives were starting to file in, loitering around the coffee maker.

"Keep your friends close and your enemies closer," he said to her. Raskins still didn't comprehend what her chief was driving at. Her fellow detectives were arriving, sorting things out at their desks, grabbing their coffees. "Look again and tell me what you see. A suit, a hat?" Raskins looked again, carefully observing her teammates.

"Oh, shit," she slowly replied. "Reynolds is always playing with a toothpick in his mouth."

"How tall would you say he is?"

"I'd say he stands a few inches over six feet. God, he fits the description perfectly."

"Yeah," Jamison said, "my exact thoughts. Details either match him perfectly or too perfectly and he's being set up. And look at this." He pulled a page out from a file with Doussaint's name on it. It was a sketch—a drawing of a man's features and coloring. "This is what the sketch artist drew based on Tyler's description of the killer."

"It looks just like him," Raskins confirmed.

"Yeah, exactly like him. Too coincidental?" he asked.

"You don't believe Tyler? Think he's lying for someone?" she asked him.

"No, I believe that kid, which is why you and Matthews are going to check into Reynolds."

"Sir?"

"Quietly. Check his bank account and phone bills. I want to know why and how this guy ended up here—specifically here."

"That was the captain's doing," Matthews stated as he entered Jamison's office, startling them at first.

"Once again, nice knocking, Don," Jamison snipped.

"I'd say perfect timing, and you're welcome. Ahem, as I was stating, right on cue, the captain recruited Reynolds and Nolan."

"Yeah, he was bragging about snatching up one that excelled academically," Raskins added. "And one—"

Jamison cut her off. "One that was the best marksman in the South." The three of them stood together in silence, each looking at the other.

"Fine, you know what? I am tired of pussyfooting around with the cap'n. You two dig up whatever you can on Reynolds."

"Already have," Matthews insisted.

"What? I just gave you the order," Jamison scoffed.

"Yeah, but based on what Rass told me last night, you would have given that order to me earlier if you could've, but you were too busy yesterday with the Doussaints and the lockdown. I knew you'd see the similar character descriptions, so I checked it out already."

"Donna, I take back half of the nasty things I've said about you," Jamison said as he grinned. "What did you find out—anything?"

Raskins sat down, trying to get her bearings and wrap her mind around the conversation as all of it slowly sank in.

"He comes from McAllen, Texas, right on the border, not too far from Reynosa, Mexico, where gangs and the cartel control drug-trafficking routes, money laundering, and arms trafficking as well. And he just received a payment of one hundred thousand dollars."

"Same amount the cap'n received and then paid out," Jamison said.

"Think the captain is paying Reynolds?" Raskins asked.

"I think the cap'n is on the take from Jack Doussaint, and either one could have paid Reynolds," Jamison said, frustrated with his early-morning sluggishness and the sobering fact that the shooter might be one of his own. When the weight of the moment hit, it crushed him to think this killer might be part of his small team of detectives.

"Does this mean Senator Doussaint paid to have his own mistress killed?" Matthews asked.

"Right now, anything is up for grabs. Did you get any connections with that payment?"

"No, cash deposit," Matthews pointed out. "But his phone records are interesting." Raskins and Jamison perked up.

"He's been talking to a number originating in Mexico. Unlisted, but I contacted surveillance first thing this morning and they pinpointed the cell to a certain wealthy member of the Mexican Familia."

"Don't tell me; let me guess—Imon Durrell?" Matthews nodded. "All right, look; this is confidential; nobody says a thing. We're not going to corner Reynolds unless we have evidence that is indisputable, so just take it step-by-step, carefully. Forensics came up with nothing in Algiers. About twenty different shoe prints in the area. Tire tracks match the forest ranger's vehicle. The killer could be anyone. Could be political, but the one thing I'd bet on is some derelict for hire. Don't know if we'll ever catch up with the killer; no trace evidence whatsoever at the Park or by Ms. Chandres's car." These were solemn words for cops to hear because they were plausible. The possibility that an unknown killer was out and about without a hint of recognition was a bitter pill to take. "But if we link this to Breen's murder because of the senator, then we're closer to zeroing in on Durrell for orchestrating both hits. We will have to concentrate on him, so don't rush this; we'll cinch the noose tight soon enough on Reynolds, then Durrell. Meanwhile, get Cap'n Hughes in room one for questioning. Gandy took a warrant and a crew of cops to call on the senator bright and early this morning. We'll see what he comes up with." He paused. "We are going to find some links on this case today," he said, trying to persuade himself of real possibilities.

"Yeah, well hey, good morning to us," Raskins noted as she left Jamison's office and headed into what would probably be another long and busy day.

CHAPTER 50

THE BIG QUESTION

"You wanted me present while you question someone?" Captain Hughes asked as Jamison entered room one.

"Actually, no. I need to ask you some questions, sir."

"Me? Now hold on, Chief, what in tarnation are you trying to pull here?"

"Please, Cap'n, just sit down." Hughes sat down and placed his hat on the table in front of him. Jamison squeezed in across from him and told him about the information that had just come to him, looking for a reaction.

"Money coming and going, and I hear you've got property worth quite a lot," Jamison said, insinuating something underhanded.

"Six point two million, to be exact," Hughes corrected him.

"So you get a cool hundred thousand from Jack every year and put it toward this offshore property?" Jamison said, egging him on. "Why *you*, down here? Why not officials in the capital?"

"Well, first, Mick, Jack deposits money into my account, and I withdraw it in cash and have it sent back to him. Nobody buys this badge. And he probably pays plenty of people in Baton Rouge, but New Orleans is a major port for the US. I'm sure he has business in this city that we haven't even uncovered yet."

"Oh, well that sounds nice, Cap'n, giving the money back. Except the money kept coming."

"And I kept giving it back," Hughes insisted.

"And the property? You expect me to believe you can afford this kind of property on some far-off island on your salary?"

"No, I expect you to believe the truth in black and white. If your detectives would investigate a little deeper, they'd discover that I inherited the property from my brother who died two months ago. It's all conspicuously clear; the information is there if they'd like to check it out."

"Still, you have quite a nest egg."

"Well, I'm not a player of the markets. With a meager income at first, you begin investing in a small way. Forty years later, those blue chips I held onto are worth a considerable amount of money. They split and split again, allowing me to add modestly to my portfolio. Then, after forty years of buying and hanging on, I've turned into a practical ole geezer worth three million."

"But you were intent on steering us clear of Jack; how do you explain that?"

"I do what I am told to do. I follow orders, Chief; you should try it sometime."

"And you just go along with dirty officials, no problem?" Jamison was determined for something to stick.

"Politicians and high-ranking police administrators don't get to their places of power without playing in the game. That's why I never put in to be superintendent," Hughes said with confidence. He felt better about this awkward questioning and relaxed a bit, sliding back into his chair. "I'm fine staying put as a captain; don't want any part of that bullshit that gets in the way of good police work."

"We think Reynolds might be on the take—might even be involved in the killing. You brought him here; what are we to make of that, Cap'n?"

"I brought the two best rookies in here I could find. One, top of his class academically, and one an outstanding marksman."

"Yeah, so much so he might be our shooter."

"That has nothing to do with me. I recruit the best I can find. I recall recruiting you to this precinct, Mick. You were a damn good rookie. A hotshot and a bit of a hothead as I recall. And look at you; you've succeeded, as I suspected you would. And you're still a bit of a hothead, but that's passion—good to have every now and then."

"Good to have! You're always busting my butt to be cool-headed," Jamison complained.

"That's part of my job too, Chief." Jamison looked up to Raskins and Matthews. No one knew what to ask next. They thought they had him, but his answers somehow rang true.

Then Jamison recalled a recent conversation. "Okay, Cap'n, then why the threat to me about being replaced? Remember the comment 'We never know why we're in a particular place'?"

"That was no threat," Hughes clarified.

"No? Sure about that? It sounded like one to me."

"The sound that hit you, Chief, was the sound of the truth. We don't know why we're called to a particular place or time or event. Maybe I'm here to be the cop in the upper echelon that won't kowtow to corruption. Maybe this one stubborn captain can make a difference; maybe not."

"Yeah, but you said—"

"Maybe you, Mick, and your damned passion and temper were meant to be here to defy my orders and refuse to look the other way. Maybe your purpose right now is to be the hurdle corruption has to jump. Maybe you are too high of a hurdle. One never knows; isn't that right? Isn't that what I said?"

Jamison was feeling confused. "You implied, sir, that I—"

"I told you the truth, Mick."

"Why didn't you just come out and tell me what you were getting at?"

"It's not my job."

"What? What the hell kind of answer is that? You're not going to shove that same bureaucratic bullshit my way."

"It's life, Mick."

"Wha?"

"It's not my job or anyone else's to find your purpose for you. We each have to discover our purpose for the here and now for ourselves."

"Oh man, really? You're going to kick my ass with some yin-yang wisdom shit?"

"It's true, and I found mine, which is why I'm retiring. You can discover yours or go ahead and keep banging your hot head against the wall if you like." Again, Matthews, Raskins, and Jamison all looked at each other, clueless as to how to combat the captain's rather profound comments.

"Then why so closed-mouthed all these years?" Jamison asked.

"Did you want to know any of this sooner? Advice is only taken when asked for. I did my job, lived my life. If you wanted to know more about me, all you had to do was ask."

Jamison tried to defend himself. "But—"

"But you were busy—in over your head solving New Orleans murder cases. You were doing exactly what I brought you here to do—a damned fine job of it." Jamison looked helplessly at his partners. All these years he and his crew had thought the captain's hat might have been screwed on too tight. Most cops worked their twenty years, took their pensions, then went on to second jobs as guards somewhere. But Hughes stayed on; he didn't have the usual aches and pains that plagued aging detectives, that plagued Jamison, and his hearing and eyesight were pretty good. His children were grown and off in other parts of the world. One was a machinist working with power grids; the other, a literary consultant. His wife had been a good companion, but she had passed before her time.

"I … I thought you'd be angry about all this," Jamison said.

"I'd be disappointed in you, Mick, if you hadn't questioned me. I wondered how much longer you were going to overlook my account as you collected data."

"Okay, I expected you to put up a fight, not become the Dalai Lama. Shit, Cap'n."

Captain Hughes began to laugh a hearty laugh. "Life can be funny, can't it? I slipped by in your life because I didn't mean much to anyone. Just an old man keeping his nose clean and doing his job. That's not exciting; that's not going to cause anybody to notice me. Hell, I was as good as invisible, except for keeping you on your toes. You weren't interested enough to really look at me until you suspected me of wrongdoing."

"Yeah, well," Jamison said softly as he scratched his head, feeling bad and a little embarrassed. He motioned for his two detectives to leave as he began to chuckle a bit himself. "You surprised me, sir," Jamison said humbly.

"Yeah, well, you'd be surprised to know this strict old fart looks forward to spending Christmas with my niece and her brood of children every year too, but I do. I enjoy those kids; they're something else," he said as he smiled. Jamison felt a burden lift from his shoulders. He didn't want to have to accuse his superior but was following leads. He felt a surge of calmness wash over him, pounds of stress and guilt melting away from him.

"I have to tell you, I'm a bit relieved you're not involved and won't be riding me on this case anymore."

"Nonsense," Hughes said sharply. "I expect this wrapped up and the final report on my desk in the next couple of days, Chief." Hughes stood up, adjusted his uniform, straightening out the button-down jacket, and tapped Jamison on the shoulder with his palm as he exited.

CHAPTER 51

REYNOLDS

They parked on St. Thomas and assessed that the neighborhood there in the lower garden district was nice—too nice for a cop. They knew he was living on something more than a cop's salary. After stepping past the hallway to where his apartment opened up, the detectives stood for a moment, perplexed by what they saw. The rooms were disheveled and filthy, full of discarded take-home food containers and strewn bottles. Water rings and food stains were on the furniture, dishes piled up in the sink, and drawers open, bulging with wadded-up clothing. It was not at all what they expected, considering Reynolds was always so well dressed.

"Appearances," Raskins said. "There're always layers to uncover."

"Dwindling habits," Webb offered.

"Man, when I was first on the force and floundering, I still tried to hold it together," Matthews added.

"Oh, but you had it easy, just holding down one job," Webb sneered.

"Yeah, not killing people on the side," Matthews replied. He looked around at the disarray and debris. "I don't understand complacency, even for a criminal. It's like a complete surrender behind closed doors. Kill, eat, bury—"

"Shut up, Matthews," Webb said, cutting him off.

"Hey, I'm just saying maybe it *is* just too much for him handling two jobs: one at the precinct and one as a killer for hire," Matthews responded in a sarcastic tone.

"Yeah, well don't *say*; start finding something tangible to take back to the chief," Raskins urged. A hush swallowed the room, and an irresistible force of resentment took over as the three prowled to unearth evidence that could destroy this young detective who had betrayed them.

After canvassing the room, they checked the closets and came upon their first solid lead. Inside one of Reynolds's suit coat pockets, they found a small piece of paper with a phone number written on it.

"Look at all these hats. He's always wearing a hat; think he's hiding a tattoo or bald spot?" Webb asked.

"Horns," Raskins replied as Matthews opened his cell and called the unusual number. A man with a heavy Spanish accent answered. Matthews said nothing, waiting to hear what might be said to him. The guttural voice cursed, and then the sound of a dial tone ended the call.

Raskins called headquarters to get a listing for the prefix. While waiting, she instructed her colleagues to see if they could get a tracer for the location of the phone right then. Matthews redialed, but no one answered.

"Surveillance has got to link with satellite coverage before this guy has time to think and ditch the phone," Webb said.

"Okay," Raskins said hurriedly. "Just grab what we've pulled, and let's get back to the station. We've got to get Reynolds's cell from him before his connection tips him off."

"I'm sure his phone log will give us a treasure trove of evidence," Webb said.

"If we can get it," Raskins replied as she was scooting them out the door to the car.

"Well, we've got it right here—our link, our discovery that indicates direct contact," Matthews stated as he opened his door.

"Not until we get back," Raskins said with desperate urgency. She dived in behind the wheel and flew back to the station house with full lights and sirens blaring.

Jamison was going over the first set of notes on the case when his sergeants blew in.

"Chief, your office!" Raskins called out, sputtering as if she were unable to catch her breath. Matthews and Webb came tumbling in after her as they raced to Jamison's office. Clearly out of breath and frantic, Jamison pulled his desk chair around to the front so the three could all sit down.

"Okay, okay," he said, trying to calm them. "What's up?"

"Reynolds," Matthews gasped.

"Jeez, Matthews, did you run all the way back here?"

"Got something on Reynolds, sir," Raskins said. "A phone number, and the guy on the other end? Spanish-speaking. But he's going to tip off Reynolds. We've got to get to him and get his cell. Where is he?"

"Oh, I've got him and Nolan doing some great rookie detective work," he snickered. "They're combing through Jack's and Maddie's phone records from the last few years, down the hall."

"We've got to get his cell," Raskins urged. "Webb, you go down and ask to use Nolan's phone first. Tell him you left yours in the car or something. Then ... um, then tell him his phone is too fancy and toss it back and ask Reynolds for his before either of them has time to think about it."

"Hey, not bad, Rass. You're pretty good on your feet," Matthews commented sarcastically.

"Shut up," she said, calming down. She pointed to Webb, "Go. Go get the phone." She shooed him out the door. As soon as Webb left, she felt terribly exhausted. "Wish it was quitting time; I could go for a mojito right about now."

"If he comes back with Reynolds's phone, I'll buy you two, Antionette," Matthews said with a grin.

"Hey, nobody calls me that 'cept my momma, Donald! And you're on," Raskins dipped her head down at him, indicating he was about to have to cough up some drinking money. "I have complete confidence in Webb."

Jamison enjoyed the playful jabs and enthusiasm his crew was displaying in his office as they waited. Only moments later, Webb was back from the hallway. He had both hands in his front pant pockets and was walking rather slowly. His poker face gave them no signs of success or failure until he peeled into Jamison's office, closed the door, and pulled a cell phone from his pocket with a smile.

"Ah!" Raskins jumped up and hugged him. She was filled with delight that their little impromptu scheme had worked. Matthews gave him a high five as Jamison skirted around them and pulled his chair back behind his desk to sit down. He motioned for Webb to give him the phone. He did, and the three sergeants stood excitedly before Jamison, waiting to hear about what they'd discovered.

"You don't think I'm going to share this man's personal calls with all of you, do you?" Jamison said in his usual chiefly way.

"Well, yeah, it's our discovery," Raskins said, still grinning.

"Well, you're wrong. No one is looking at or listening to this other than me."

"What do I tell Reynolds? He's going to want his phone back ASAP." Webb asked.

"Tell him I saw you with it and asked you to give it to me. We'll see what kind of reaction that brings."

"You're the boss," Webb replied reluctantly as he shrugged and stepped back from the desk.

"Yes, I am, thank you very much. Now, while I attend to boss work with his phone log, you can make some calls of your own. Rass, call Sara and Eric Doussaint to get Tyler back in here. All we need is for him to glimpse Reynolds and we've got a solid ID."

"Okay," Raskins replied, not too happily.

"Matthews, call Wynton Ellery and ask him to come back in. There's got to be a connection with this Imon Durrell. Early in the case, he said he met the Doussaints because some guy"—he looked down at pages of notes scattered on his desk—"Palerno, was trying to place something in their luggage. I want to find out what he came across."

Matthews nodded. "Yeah, that's right."

"Wanna bet Palerno is working for Durrell and that was just another attempt to create a Jack Doussaint scandal?"

"Beautiful, Chief, but no bets; I already owe someone two drinks."

"Just get him back in here to tell us about the incident. Webb, I want you to call and find out what happened to Palerno after he left customs. Was he arrested? Who paid his bail? Et cetera. Meanwhile we'll start tracking Reynolds's car via his GPS. If he is AWOL from work or has off-hours meetings, we'll know about it."

"Got it," Webb said as he left the office. The other two sergeants followed suit and headed back to their desks.

Reynolds had not been on anyone's radar; nevertheless, they would catch up with him. Jamison had a good feeling about this. "It's all coming together," he said aloud as he leaned back in his rickety chair and reached down to pull open the lower right drawer.

CHAPTER 52

THE FAMILY DIRECTION

Sara was glad to see Eric unboxing and fingering through some of his old philosophy books. She wondered if he was plunging into "matter" to escape the spiraling layers of complexities from the murder case. Nothing about the murders, Jack's business, her emotional past, or this new twist with Tyler offered sure footing. They were in the thick of it all, having to surrender to fate and the inadequacy of human endeavor. She felt sure Eric needed a reprieve from the loop for a bit; they all did.

Sara loved his earlier desire to pursue philosophy. Eric was simplistic in his approach, understanding philosophy as the study of everything that counts. He was also well aware that because the physicists had walked off with matter, and theologians with God, graduates of philosophy either went on pondering or became teachers, accountants, and computer programmers, regarding the field as overly poetic and prescientific.

Nevertheless, this was one subject Eric had so often and easily discussed with her. He had explained how Nietzsche specialized in short spurts and pulled no punches. Eric liked that, but Nietzsche had also stated God was dead. So, Eric had instead studied Whitehead, a mathematician-turned -metaphysician who had worked out the most comprehensive system: The Philosophy of Organisms, Occasions, and Becomings.

She saw Eric come to life when he talked about Whitehead. The process theory he so loved explained absolutely everything and was a theory that would make it okay for God to exist in the modern world. Whitehead had been universally admired for the pure scope of his understanding, his balanced intelligence, his ability to incorporate dualities, and his unwavering faith in the possibilities of total understanding. That was back in the 1940s, and with no subsequent philosopher sharing his faith, and with so few believing in God at all, his work quickly became obsolete.

This intrigued Eric. He wondered if he could be the one to excavate and restore Whitehead's theories and bring them up to speed in this age of technology, when so many gadgets had become miniature gods. Sara supported him wholeheartedly because she saw how much it filled the ache; he had to find his place in the world. He had always been a sincere, sweet young man with a drive to work amid an unknown. But his father had argued that philosophical mind games were beneath Eric and were certainly a waste of Jack's connections. Eric succumbed to the notion that his interest was just daydreaming. He knew he had to dive into a career that could allow him to afford him a home, his own family, and perhaps a hobby of pondering. And yes, it would be a shame to let Jack's contacts wither away. Instead she watched as philosophy was neatly folded and tucked away inside him as he studied business, law, and political science.

Eric groomed and patterned his mannerisms, his speech, his body language, and his actions by observing the many great mentors around him. As it turned out, he had become a fine, resourceful, polished man capable of charming politicians and holding his own with the cerebral brutes of the high court, all while still retaining the possibilities of the philosopher deep inside him.

She too was rummaging, clearing her head as she cleared out drawers and bags tucked into the backs of closets. She assessed it was impossible to know one's direction and the stability beneath one's feet. It seemed to her that feeling lost this time around had turned into a significant state of awakening. She felt light. Her confession had lifted her from her frail past to a new consciousness and a new path.

It was a gift, she thought, to have the averted mind, the harsh boundaries, dissolved. But as she sorted the piles of paperwork and old clothing, she considered that if they were going to amble about in uncertainty, they could at least be as neat as a pin while doing so.

She discovered quickly that almost every bag stored away had money tucked in it—a ten- or twenty-dollar bill, depending on the size of the bag. What for? Was this a way of holding on to items, like saving a patch of snow in the freezer to enjoy later as relief from summer's heat, or was this reimbursement for what was to be given away? She hadn't placed the bills here. She called out, "Eric, there's money in these bags. Did you do this?"

Eric was entrenched in reading the notes he had scribbled in the margins of his books. Sara carried a heavy black yard bag in one hand, handing it over to him, and holding a twenty-dollar bill in the other, interrupting his thoughts.

"Honey, there's money in these bags. Do you know anything about this?"

"Huh?" he replied as he switched his thoughts of the metaphysical back to his daily life. "What, dear?"

"I said there's money in these bags. It's weird. Did you put money in the bags in the closet?"

"No, no, but ..." He paused, closed his book upon his stomach, and grinned. "I think I know who did. Mom."

"Renee has been rummaging through our closets?" She was both curious and indignant that someone had been nosing into their things.

"She used to put a five or ten in my collection of things for the thrift stores and her charities when I was young. Whenever she asked me to sort through old clothes and toys and bundle them up to give away, she would add money."

"That's odd, Eric."

"Well, she said it would help me get used to giving some of what I had to others. Charity has always been a big part of Mom's agenda. Gram was a philanthropist and a volunteer who rolled up her sleeves and worked every day for the benefit of others. Mom grew up under her influence and has tried to emulate Gram all these years."

"Yeah, but money in a pile of old clothes?"

"She said it would help me let go. If I struggled to give away items I no longer used because of monetary value, then I should just see some actual money go with them. If I could see a ten-dollar bill go with my toys, I'd learn to view parting with my money down the road as a natural occurrence."

"Wow, that's actually kind of an amazing approach."

"Yeah, Renee has her good points; she's not exactly all about stuffed shirts and proper etiquette."

Renee was bony and fair, and she lived awash in the sin of abundant lobster and stale gin, but she had grown up amid "Negro" women who pressed her pleats and called her "baby," and who shouldered her upward into high society with their smiles and yawns through painfully public nights. She often told Eric about her upbringing and how she came to know God not in the lemon-colored church dress her mother bought her, not by the golden-rimmed offering plates that passed by each Sunday, but in the soft, full, brown voice of compassionate Cassie, whose lap held a great resting place, whose eyes were as dark and wide as any pool of thought, and who loved her dearly and completely.

It was the power and products of white men that taught Renee and the children of that era not to love themselves—not the Mammies or Cassies or Clarices—whom society deemed as lower class. The grotesque, self-anointing voice of Jim Crow invented the lies that damaged hearts both black and white.

Renee had found her emerging sun in the form of a round, uneducated woman who smelled of Crisco. Cassie's plump midnight skin was, to her, as beautiful as the satin sheets Cassie tucked beneath their mattresses. Her thick, saintly hands, yeasty and sensuous, calmed the storms as easily as Jesus did, and dried tears from the eyes of "chil'en" despite the sadness in her own solitary and despondent life.

Her father had died on the road. His heart had pushed from its chest into his neck as an embolism and had flattened his skin out like seawater. The sheriff had found his white hanky signaling from the car window. But it was Cassie's sweet song, her bird-mouth utterances, that sent him off to his grave, the last dreamy voice of reason that cut through the blur of death and the fear surrounding color lines. Renee never forgot Cassie's quiet strength and her face, as calm as the moon; nor did she forget her kind charity despite the injustices that undressed her.

From early childhood, Eric had listened intently to his mother's glowing descriptions of the beauty and elegance of her old home and landmarks. Every summer, they tended to the corner of the cemetery where so many generations of her family slept, enclosed by strong iron railing, exclusive in death as in life. They would sit in utter quiet in that graveyard as though they were under some kind of spell. Then Renee would brush her hands and say what a shame it was that they'd spent all that money to isolate them when they could have put their money to good use helping others.

"I really don't understand why Renee stays with Jack," Sara said softly, not wanting to bruise Eric's depiction of his parents.

"I actually asked her once. She said my father received her charity most of all. He had been good and kind—courageous early on. It was the corrosive nature of politics that changed him. She didn't want to leave him and let him sink into cynicism. It was important to her to smile and hold on. She said she didn't have the gift of prophecy, but she let her heart speak out a time or two, saying that Jack was either going to come alive in the eleventh hour and be absolved in the waking, or die from the wolf biding its time deep inside him. Either way, she would be there to forgive him or to bury him."

"Well, that generation didn't throw things away—especially not marriages."

"Yeah," Eric continued in a sarcastic tone, "and she said she had antidepressants to help dissolve the angst in their relationship. Not to worry."

"Ha, God that sounds like her!"

Eric had told Sara before about Renee's upbringing and her great empathy and charitable heart, but it was still a shock to her that her mother-in-law had secretly been going through their things and she didn't want to let the conversation go just yet.

"I hear you, Eric; I get it," she said, "but still, it's kind of weird her snooping in the backs of my closets!"

"I said Renee had some good points; not everything about her is normal or completely sane. She's probably just repeating what her mother did. Maybe Gram snooped in their closets and left money with them the first few years of their marriage. I don't know."

"Still, it's unnerving to think of her secretly going through our things. I don't like it."

"Gotta take the weird with the endearing, I guess."

"No. Next time you get a chance, tell her you learned the early lessons of generosity and she doesn't need to keep reminding you, okay?"

"If the subject comes up, I'll mention it."

"No, how about just bringing up the subject on your own?"

"Okay, okay. Next time we see her."

"Thanks." Sara turned and went back to the hallway near the entrance feeling a bit shaken that her mother-in-law had been rummaging through her things. She glanced over at Eric, who looked completely comfortable flopped along the length of the sofa cushions with his feet in white sweat socks dangling over one end as he disappeared back into philosophy.

Tyler came galloping down the stairwell. "Got my schoolwork done," he said, and he turned the corner past her, making a direct path for Eric. Sara was happy he was back in school and catching up.

"Lunch soon!" she called after him. He was already airborne. Eric was too delightful a target, and Tyler came crashing down on him, books and all.

"Ooof!" Eric called out as he doubled over under the weight of Tyler's surprise attack in his midsection.

"Almost lunchtime," Tyler told him.

"Ugh, how about switching to a dinner bell next time."

Tyler laughed at Eric's sweet sense of humor. He had neither displayed any resentment toward Tyler for being playful, nor for Tyler treating him like a bigger kid and a punching bag at times. Eric flung his books behind the couch and grabbed Tyler in a bear hug, rolling off his comfortable spot onto the floor. Tickling ensued followed by yelps of laughter calling out for help. Sara, caught up in their playfulness, left her things heading for them on the floor when the phone rang. She paused, then made a beeline for the kitchen portable. It was Raskins on the other end.

"Sorry to disturb you on the weekend," she said.

"Oh, no problem, Sergeant."

Tyler and Eric paused and sat up when they heard her say "Sergeant." So far, the police had meant a great deal of inconvenience and concern. Eric looked at Tyler and put his finger to his lips as he stood easing toward the kitchen to listen to the one-sided conversation.

"Yeah, uh, sure," he heard Sara reply. Then she moved through the dining room and into the living room, where she stood just a few feet away from Eric. "Let me check," she said, and she covered the speaker of the phone with her free hand. "It's Sergeant Raskins," she told him. "They want us to come back in on Monday. They think Tyler can ID the shooter. Can you get time off again?"

"Not in the morning. Full schedule before midterms," he said, surprised at the information coming from the station. "But Monday afternoon could work." She nodded, and as she began to tell Raskins, Eric interjected, saying, "We can be at the station about 3:30, then take Tyler out for an early dinner down in the French Quarter afterward."

She nodded to Eric and then replied on the phone, "We can be there about three-thirty. Will that work?" She waited. "Good. See you then."

Tyler was still sitting on the floor when Sara slipped back into the kitchen to set the phone down. When she came back in the room, Eric and Sara turned to Tyler, gave him a smile, and then moved near him on the floor.

"Was that about me?" he asked.

"Sort of," Sara answered him. "I think this whole thing is about to be over."

"How?"

"The police said they think they have the guy who shot those two men, but they need you to look at him and tell them if he is or is not the man you saw that day in the stadium and at the station."

"And that's all?"

"Yes. That will be the end of it."

Tyler smiled a little bit as he reflected. "Will I miss school?"

"Well, we'll just pick you up an hour early."

"Can I have my snack in the car on the way?"

"You can have your snack. And not only that; Eric is going to take us out for a nice dinner together afterward." He looked to Eric for affirmation. Eric was nodding.

"Can I order anything I want?" His eyes were growing with excitement.

"Anything you want, sweetie. It'll be a celebration dinner."

"All right!" he exclaimed, approving of the day's schedule.

"Now, little mister," Sara said, "Are your hands clean for lunch?" He shook his head. "Why don't you clean up and meet us in the kitchen."

He agreed and scurried off to the hall's half bath to wash up. Eric and Sara walked into the kitchen's midday light. Sara took a deep breath and looked around her. She loved the spaciousness and warmth of her kitchen. Eric paused at the island.

"Need some help?" he asked her, wondering what they would be fixing for lunch.

"Yes, on Monday," she said. "I will need your help on Monday as we finish this escapade."

CHAPTER 53

BEST LAID PLANS

Later that night, Eric watched Sara at the vanity. She was brushing her hair and checking her hands, her nails, her teeth. She opened a jar that smelled like a murky river and began to spread what looked like mud across her forehead, around her eyes, up and down the brim of her nose, and onto her cheeks and chin. He was thinking about her experience with her mom and how she lit up when she was with Tyler. He thought she had enough love in her for a whole community, and how that amazing, enthusiastic love had first enveloped him.

"You know," she said, gazing at him from her mirror, aware he was watching her, "I used to dream of making my fortune a la Sara Serenity, offering exotic mud facials and mineral baths at exorbitant fees." The cream on her face began to thicken and dry, paling slightly. "There's a real market now for men," she offered.

"Yes, and meditation, or brisk walks and deep, deep breathing," Eric quipped. "Powerful."

"You'd be surprised how calm you'd feel," she reproached him.

"Oh, I believe you; just thinking about it puts me to sleep."

Sara tossed a nearby cushion at him as he lay on the bed, smirking at her. "You're just suppressing your feminine side," she stated.

"Thank God for that," he touted, and he tucked the cushion under his arm and head. Sara got up and entered the adjacent bathroom to wash the clay from her face. "Why put that stuff on just to wash it off?" he asked rhetorically. He watched her hands steady in the cooling water, the carriage of her head, the grace of her neck, her body attentive and sure.

Looking at all that beauty, he was now pondering the sweet sounds a woman made when she was making love, and he began to hum a low, earthy hum, readying himself for her return.

"I'm sorry; did you say something?" Sara asked as she reached into the second drawer. Out came a tampon, the shining plastic symbol of disappointment. He saw it briefly whisked away but could hear the crinkle of the wrapper coming off. How he hated that sound.

"Timing," he whispered as Sara clicked off the nightstand lamp and pounced at him under the sheets.

"I love you so much," she said as she snuggled up beside him.

"Just lie here beside me, my love." He flung his words out like warm flames. "Just lie here and be content." He rolled toward her and kissed her head, his fingers filtering delicately through her hair as he took slow, deep breaths, reclaiming his absolute, willful, self-assured soul. "Listen; I've been thinking today. Can I share some thoughts with you?" he asked.

"Of course; I'm all ears," Sara replied as she closed her eyes and snuggled into the warmth of Eric's body.

"Well, you know everything has an element of laws, dynamics, and balances. With energy, we're learning to base our needs not on death and waste, but on renewal. Maybe we can learn at last to shape civilization in harmony with the earth. I mean, air, water, life—does it require humankind? No, but each drop of water, each form of life, we use, and we don't use anything wisely." She wrinkled her nose, trying to figure out his thoughts, but was content to listen.

In the old days, our minds, our spirits, and our bodies were part of the natural world. Men used to talk and fill the air with dreams of glory, great philosophical and theological plans, great scientific and technological advances. Achievements of epic proportions were planned and executed with strength and courage and daring with respect to humankind in the world. Now, instead of conquering death, enterprises cause it. Toxic substances and laws of economics prevail over research; we have turned on Mother Nature."

"Uhm ... yes," she slurred, thinking Eric had concluded his train of thought.

"Achievement is viewed as a line moving forward or a graph moving upward ... but life is cyclical," he continued. "The change we are required to make is radical, Sara; it has to happen within us and around us in the action we take. You know, I've come to realize in my work with Dad and politics that power warps because there is some sort of joy in domination. The powerful forget that they can become weak, that they too can break. And our whole society is on a power trip; we want more, we want it now, and we want it better than before no matter the cost. We're all walking around with little electric fences around us that spark at the slightest touch. We poison the beetle and the slug so we can grow superfoods, but we are dying from the poison we use. We don't need superfoods or chemically improved food; we just need food. I swear, Sara, society has got to come back to common, living dirt."

"So where is this going?" Sara asked, in a sleepy state.

"I don't see how anyone can live without a place of enchantment, so I want to use what I can legally to help preserve the treasures of life we are losing. Maybe it's Dad, and maybe it's this underlying current of struggle we're experiencing right now; I don't know, but something is stirring in me. You're the religious one; doesn't the Bible say to be good stewards?"

"It does," Sara remarked softly with her eyes still closed. "It also says to love each other, but we don't do that either."

"And just what does loving each other look like?"

Sara opened her eyes; she didn't enjoy being awakened but wanted to answer him with thought and truth. "Well, it doesn't mean we hug and kiss each other all the time." She rolled her head back so it was upright, looking at the ceiling. "It means tending to each other's needs, serving, putting others before yourself. Like feeding the hungry, sheltering the homeless, clothing the poor, visiting prisoners, giving others hope. You know, extending a part of yourself to another out of love."

"What about hell? Guess Dad's a good candidate for that."

"Well, if you mean a fiery eternal residence, I'm not sure if I believe that. I think hell is a result of sin, and I believe sin is when you separate yourself from God. So he might be living a kind of hell right now."

Sara was intrigued by the conversation. She wanted Eric to pursue something he loved and didn't always know what was rolling around in his head. Hearing him, she knew he wasn't regretful and that he didn't feel he'd missed his chance, but she felt he had grasped a notion that gave him insight and inspiration. The philosopher and lawyer was reinventing himself, conscious of life's conditions but motivated to slow the flood of materialism, waste, and power that could one day sweep us all into the last impossible storm. He had finally accepted that the traditional foundation of greed in business was provocative, blinding, and ultimately destructive.

"Dad's going to hit the ceiling; he will resent investing in me and consider this a betrayal."

"Oh please," Sara replied. "What kind of father drags his son into corruption anyway? He will just push past you and climb deeper into that cesspool of power."

Eric couldn't answer. His dad was not a decent man, and it was sort of heroic, he guessed, to move on, uncertain and searching, rather than stay as some symbolic gesture that would place him amid destruction and wreckage, forcing him to live like a guard dog.

Sara was so proud of him and welled up with tears. "Honey, what's wrong?" Eric asked, concerned that he might have frightened her with his idealistic notions.

"You know." She squeaked a bit as she tried to gather her emotions. "Most people determine the best day in their life by an experience or overwhelming incident. The best day of my life is every morning that I get to wake up by your side." Her voice was wet and soft, and her green eyes glistened when Eric rolled over to look her squarely in the face.

"You amaze me, Sara. I love you," he said simply before he kissed her and laid his head at her heart.

CHAPTER 54

FAIRY TALES AND FEAR

"Once upon a time, there was a princess who married a commoner," Raymond read aloud. "The king set aside his own wishes for his daughter, and allowed her to wed the young man she chose." He paused as he thumbed through the pink binder to reach the end of the story. On the last page, he read aloud again. "The tears ran down the princess's cheeks," he continued to read. "The king reached out and wiped her tears away with his hand. It was not the first time in his life he had been moved to do something for somebody else, and so he died quite happy."

"Quite a story!" Wynton called from inside the guest bedroom. He was pulling the last of Belinda's keepsakes and books, laying them on the bed to bag or box up for charity as he listened to his brother read. Raymond was in the next room, Keisha's room, looking through her things as he packed them into a deep rectangular box.

"What the hell kinda fairy tale is that?" Raymond called back. Wynton appeared in his daughter's doorway to see Raymond sitting atop the bed with the book in his hands. Keisha's room was all girl, with crowns and tutus hanging on ballet hooks. There was the simple small dot of roses in the pattern of the pink fabric that covered the pillow top for her window seat, and there was white shelving stuffed to the brim with books, CDs, and dolls.

"Keisha wrote that. Do *not* throw that in with anything we're giving away!" he said sternly.

"How you brainwash her so early on?" Raymond asked. Wynton pulled a plush pink throw pillow from behind Raymond and swatted him on the head.

"No brainwashing, she was an intuitive girl with brilliant grace and sensitivity," he responded.

"She be bright; that's for sure!" Raymond knew she was in fact a prodigy with a genius IQ. "Don' know no eight-year-olds who adapt fairy tales to modern life." Wynton nodded. He didn't know any either. He and Belinda had nurtured Keisha in the faith, in the breadth and depth of Christ's love. Her genius was one thing, but he knew it also took a special ingenuity for her to carve out her own circle of spirituality without distraction. Her writings were reflective of an understanding of beauty and tranquility even amid the cries and crankiness of childhood. Wynton was proud. He had a loving family life, a peaceful household—a sanctuary away from the haste and hostility out in the world.

"His majesty became a lame ole man," Wynton mentioned. "She did not shy away from illness or dying." He returned to the guest bedroom, leaving Raymond in thought about his precious little Einstein.

Back in the master bedroom with Belinda's things, he was reliving their trip to Paris, where Keisha had been conceived. They had exhausted themselves touring. The last day and night focused on relaxing, living slow and easy, enjoying the moments just being in Paris. Belinda had loved the Musée d'Orsay, and he thought about how it provided a romantic view of Paris and the Seine through the black arms of the giant clock window. The museum provided a romantic notion as well, first in the way the city had transformed a beautifully structured train station into an art museum, and then in the choice of displayed art, mostly impressionistic, which complemented each nuance of the building. He felt he had fallen in love with Belinda all over again because of their time there. It seemed as though they had been drifting in and out of a dream as they lingered in front of each frame, feeling unrestrained from gravity, sailing into the blue and golden shores, their thoughts cloudy among the red and pink spray of flowers, the karma of purple hues in the blur of a far-flung world of brushstrokes.

He freed a dozen or so hangers from the closet and ordered Belinda's clothes into neat piles on the bed. Accessories like belts and scarves were gently arranged in shopping bags like precious artifacts. He palmed his hands across the open, smooth, barren dresser drawers, feeling as if he had returned them to a natural wild state, as though freeing a wild animal from its trap. The white oak finish could reclaim its secret living.

Shoes, boots, and sandals were taped into a deep box. He glanced at the bed, recalling her form beneath its cover. Her beauty had been startling; her ease of form as simple and inviting as the lines of a Matisse painting.

He tried to simply breathe. His shallow inhalations instead hurt. It was as though he could not grasp the air around him. He felt helpless for a moment, as if packing her up prevented her spirit from taking its likely direction forward. He knew Belinda's spirit could never come back. He knew she couldn't splinter from her realm and touch him as he carried on. Still, he despised the callousness of packing, with the toxic fumes of boxes and plastic bags acting as vaults.

He walked to the window and, gazing down into the yard, mumbled, "The day I learned to be alone, I planted those azaleas for you." He paused, looking down to where he knew the baseline of his house was awash in color every spring. "I had wished for barbed wire, or a moat, but your and Keisha's sweet spirits pushed me on."

Raymond looked around Keisha's beautiful room. The sashes were still tied up, and the valance of material hung in a long sweep of pleats. She was a whirlwind in here, and he thought back to his easy boredom as a boy who doubted the permanence of anything. He closed his eyes and could hear her joyously humming and singing as she skipped around her room, longing to discover the sound of horse hooves and carriage wheels beneath her bedroom window. A tear came to his eye.

"She shudda never had to leave the palace," he said aloud.

"Maybe she never did," Wynton remarked as he came back in. "Maybe she had her eyes on the big palace and a kingdom not too far away."

Raymond snapped to, aware he could be on the threshold of another lecture. He quickly changed the subject. "Let's take a ball with us, and after we drop off them things, maybe go down to the park an pick up a game. Ain' done that in long time."

"Yeah, maybe. We'll see how the weather holds up. Meanwhile, are you about done?"

"Uh huh."

"Let's grab some lunch then."

"Great. You knows I like eating with you best of all."

"You mean you like eating and me paying best of all."

"Nah, man, is not like that. Well, not completely." They headed for the stairs as the phone began to ring. "You needa lose that land line, bruh," Raymond said as he hit the bottom stair. But Wynton had already picked up the phone.

"Uh huh. Well yeah, okay." He paused as Raymond listened. "No, definitely not. I can't take off Monday morning. Couldn't I just speak to you by phone? Do I absolutely need to come back in?" Raymond's ears perked up; he knew who was on the other end. "Well, if I have to, I can make it there about 3:45, something like that." There was a long pause before Wynton finished. "Fine. Thanks, Sergeant."

"Damn, I knew it. Was the N'awlins five-oh again, wasn't it?"

"Yeah, they want me to come in and talk to them about my first meeting with Eric and Sara. Sergeant Matthews said there might be a link with the guy we picked up at the airport and the guy who gave the orders to kill Madeleine Breen."

"So tell 'em what you know long distance. Don't go back over there, E."

"Evidently some new information has come in, and they want me to help sort the pieces for a connection."

"Right. We not falling for that again; right, E?" Wynton scrambled to find his keys. As he headed to the front door, he asked Raymond what he wanted for lunch. Raymond, following him out the door to the car, restated his comment. "We not falling for that again; right, E?"

"Well, it looks like the conclusion is coming around. The sergeant said they have an eyewitness to the shooter, so that'll pretty much be it."

"Good. Great. So let 'em finish while you stay home and talk to 'em long distance."

"I'm going to go," Wynton commented in a low, firm voice.

"E, that's crazy. Nothing good happen in that place. You already gave 'em plenty."

"Hey, Ray, not only am I going; you are going with me."

"Nah. Uh-uh," Raymond refuted as he slammed the car door shut.

"You need to reconcile your feelings about the police, Ray."

Looking from his angle in the car at Wynton's house, he said, "Nah, I needs to reconcile with that roof of yours, not the po-lice." He pulled up his shirt to remind Wynton of the scar on his back that he had received as he fell because his big brother had convinced him to help clear gutters from on top of the house. "A tall ladder wudda work just as well."

"I didn't have anything but a dinky little eight-foot ladder," Wynton said, trying to defend himself again.

"The edge of your roof was a challenge, but at least I done hadda chance. The po-lice take every opportunity away."

"I thought we'd been over this enough times; it was a setup, not intended for us."

Raymond thought about that day he was rounding the chimney, taking that completely unprotected step toward the edge and pivoting on his left foot as he lost control. Looking back, it seemed like a huge risk for an infinitely small benefit. He was also thinking about fear. What was he so afraid of? Something as simple as gravity had overcome his ability to hold on and had drawn him against his will through the air to the ground. He could have broken bones, even his neck, but he was not afraid of heights or falling because of that accident. Nothing was likely to happen at the station, but something inside him convinced him he would lose his power, his ability to land in a safe place, if he went with Wynton to New Orleans.

"You know, a therapist would have a good time with you," Wynton chuckled. Raymond mimicked him angrily.

"Ha ha, you a scream."

"Seriously, fear is closely related to hope. Both are responses to an unknown future. How has your upbringing worn so thin over the years?"

"Oh, no, here we go," Raymond sniped. "No lecture or sermon, E. Please don't get started on hope based on confidence in divine love. I knows the drill. Don't go there, 'kay? And I knows we all might fall and hit the ground hard sometime. Look, I ain' on the roof no more. They is worse things than falling off a roof."

"Well said. You *have* been listening. So how difficult is it to ride into N'awlins with your big brother and spend some time talking and, afterward, doing a little eating and drinking?"

"You didn't say nothing 'bouts food and drinks. I can go for that, bruh," he said in a higher singsong pitch while grinning that awesome, wicked smile. He turned to Wynton and said, "Preacher man, you be very persuasive."

Wynton laughed hard as they drove into town. His brother was so predictable and easily motivated by free food.

CHAPTER 55

ALMOST TIME

No life traveled by itself. Life stories dipped at times into one another like a mathematical intersection, circles flushing in and out at pivotal moments. Sometimes they crashed abruptly into one another at corners, and at other times they covered one another completely, like stones weighted and smoothed over beneath the rinse of a rolling river. Jamison was reflecting rather poetically on his case, thinking about how Nolan and Reynolds had made their way into his unit, and how the Ellerys and Doussaints crossed paths like a figure eight— like the symbol for infinity in this investigation. He guessed at the career track Hughes had carved out over the years, and the sort of grease needed to oil the tracks the senator had been pursuing.

Many times, he found himself longing to leave this place and build another kind of life. He was graying and growing weary. He was no longer the youthful dark-haired young man who burst into love; nor was he the professional whose nimble focus kept him on top of the game. It seemed this case, like life, was a series of loops twisting, elongating, and swooping through one another.

The immediate knot churning in his stomach was, of course, caused by the notion that one of his own men was likely the shooter his unit had been hunting for. His consciousness ached as any cop's would as he was hurtling faster and faster to the unimaginable and surreal emergence of betrayal. He was not nervous by nature, but he was nervous for this afternoon, which would unfold with Tyler identifying his young detective as the elusive killer.

The Doussaints were due in the station any minute, and he wondered if Reynolds even had any idea of his own suspicion or the evidence mounting against him. Had this young sharpshooter reluctantly resigned himself to a plot to make an extraordinary amount of money, or was he a dark force that had skidded along the perimeter of the law, gathering strength like the hurricanes that so often pounded the city? Could he be so callous and destructive? Jamison had no idea one way or the other, but the explosive moment of truth was about to present itself.

Matthews reached inside Jamison's office and knocked on his open door. "Mick, what's the procedure with the Doussaints?" Jamison shut down his questions and perspective and squared his body as if bracing for a fight.

"We'll get the whole team up here. I'll be out to greet them; you get them signed in and bring them back, and I'll talk with them with the whole team present."

"Yeah, okay."

"Okay what? Bring them back here, and I'll be out to greet them in front of the unit."

"Gotcha." Matthews had just turned to head back to his desk when he bumped into Gandy.

"Chief, both Ellerys are coming in; where do you want them?" Gandy asked. Matthews stopped, and both detectives looked at Jamison, waiting for an assessment and orders.

"Well ..." He took a deep breath. "Bring them back to my office, I guess." He hadn't really thought through the afternoon's timeline of events. Both detectives left, and Jamison grabbed a cigarette and placed it behind his left ear, making sure to take his own lighter this time to ensure he could have his smoke when he wanted it. He knew it would not be long before he needed it. He stepped out into the open floor. It held a stale, briny smell, and it certainly lacked the aesthetic furniture they enjoyed over in Vice. His unit was encased in the awful shade of caramel to cover blemishes in the walls. Considering the carnage they dealt with, he found it suiting.

He glanced around the room. The reality of setting up one of his own, the sheer weight of the day, and the anticipation of the shattering evidence were pressing heavy upon him. He noticed Webb fidgeting in his chair, pretending to catalogue facts. *Johnson and the rest,* he thought, *just might be plotting to boil someone amid the humdrum veil of the squad room.* Irrational thoughts surged momentarily, with fear blowing down his throat, rendering him unable to speak. His grim plan was causing him to move in pantomime, as he envisioned miscues leaking like a faucet until the shock of mistakes flooded the station.

His thoughts about Tyler suddenly rang true. He now understood the longing to be invisible, as transparent as glass, as thin as air, weightless and blue with no pity for his own flesh—a simple loss in the mirror, like a stream into unconsciousness. He was starting to feel a bit green as he tried to empty his thoughts. His palms were wet; he felt his heart knocking at his ribs, anxious to be let out; and it seemed as though he had a boulder for a tongue. He would have to catch his breath and show no evidence of ruin.

He glanced at Raskins before he spoke. She was monitoring the chase of blood from her arteries to her veins, certain for the moment that her heart must be radioactive. She was drumming her white nails on the safe boundary of her desk like a soft drummer's snare, waiting for the moments to unfold. She thought about how deception had snaked its way into the precinct, and she wished for deliverance from this sinister edge.

"All right, I want everyone on my team over here," Jamison said loudly. The detectives left their desks and moved closer to him. "We have some folks coming in to speak with us. They will not be here for questioning," he emphasized. "They have bits of information that might help us plug the holes in our murder case."

"Who?" Nolan asked.

"Well, the Ellery brothers are coming in. We think there's a direct link between that Palerno guy first arrested at customs and Imon Durrell, who seems to be calling all the shots. I want them to talk with us, and let's see what we can determine." He paused, breathing deeply for self-control. "Also, Eric and Sara Doussaint are coming in. They appear to have an eyewitness to the shooter. So heads up this afternoon." He was sending a clear signal to the handful of detectives aware of the implication.

Jamison looked at Reynolds to see whether there might be a change—a realization that they were closing in. Reynolds seemed calm but was shifting his weight back and forth from the balls of his feet to his heels and back again. He turned to Jamison, and the two made a sobering connection. Jamison thought about Reynolds's undefined loyalties. Reynolds couldn't imagine how anyone saw him tucked away among the elevated beams, and he decided to head to the parking garage for a chance to spy this so-called eyewitness before the arrival time. Jamison lit his cigarette as he watched Reynolds leave. He exhaled and then glanced at his watch. It was 3:40.

CHAPTER 56

THE ESCORT

Reynolds was scouting floors for open parking spaces, moving between the railing and the cars, crouching and peeking when he heard the echoing motor of a vehicle approaching. Two had traveled downward and exited, and a couple of cars were driving upward, toward where the most parking spaces were available. Doors slammed, and he spied Eric and Sara Doussaint and a kid. His mind raced back to that day of collecting gun parts; it was a child's voice that called out "broken" by the fountain. He thought about each gate, scanning, trying to jar his memory of everything he took in. The popcorn; he had just taken the bag and put some popcorn in his mouth, and he was moving forward. Yes, there was a boy across the ramp looking his way, and they had made eye contact.

His memory took him ahead quickly to his setup. He had shown his badge, moved some gawkers along, and pulled up the three barriers he had placed there the day before. He then moved up into the crossbeams unnoticed and set his scope and silencer. No one could see him as he waited. Was there a boy there? His mind was sifting through images frantically as the Doussaints made their way up the ramp toward the elevator. His shots were fired, he pocketed his hardware, climbed back down, slapped his hands to remove the dusty debris from the beams, dusted off his trousers, unrolled his sleeves, and put his jacket back on. He bent down to scoop up emptied cartridges and felt someone nearing but didn't look up to see so he could keep his face hidden. He just flashed his badge over his shoulder and stated, "Crime scene, move along." Was that someone a kid—this kid? There was only one way to find out.

Reynolds eased up from between cars and walked toward the threesome who were now about to enter the walkway to the elevator. He called out to stop them in their tracks. "Excuse me!" he yelled as he started to jog toward them. The Doussaints paused and turned to him, both adults holding hands with Tyler. Reynolds caught up and pretended to be catching his breath. "Sorry. Excuse me … you're here to see Chief Jamison about something rather important, yes?" he asked, nodding in a knowing fashion.

"Yes, we are," Eric replied.

"Whew, I almost missed you," he said jokingly. "My ass would be on night shifts." He loosened his tie. "I am supposed to escort you in. Can't be too cautious, you know." He smiled and extended his right hand.

Eric dropped Tyler's hand to grip the detective's hand and said, "Thanks. That makes me feel a whole lot better."

Seeing the moment for Tyler's free hand, he squatted down to say hi to the boy. "I'm Detective Reynolds; could I talk to you for a moment?" He looked up at Sara and Eric and smiled. "Just preliminary. Want to ensure he's all right with this; it's a pretty big step." He was already taking the boy's hand and stood up, placing his other hand on Eric's arm with a squeeze to comfort him, and he winked at him as he nodded.

"Well, uh, sure," Eric and Sara both said almost in unison.

"Good," Reynolds responded, and he walked Tyler several feet away from them. Eric and Sara looked at each other and then to Tyler's face. His eyes were huge, and he was shaking his head ever so slightly, indicating "no." It passed over them at first. They were just relieved to have an escort. Then Tyler's facial expression began to sink in. Their eyes widened, and they looked at each other realizing this was the same expression Tyler had had in Jamison's office. Tyler hadn't seen the killer as a suspect in the squad room; he had seen the killer as a detective on the case.

Horror gripped them as they tried to stay calm and think of a clever way out. The killer had Tyler, and there was no one else around. Eric inched over toward them and nervously stated, "We'd better get going then." Tyler had lost all color and looked frozen in fear. "I … I think he's ready," Eric stated in a cracking voice, and he held out a hand to Tyler.

Reynolds held firmly to both of Tyler's hands and said, "No, I think he needs more time," and he began to walk him farther away from the Doussaints. "In fact, he doesn't seem too certain after all."

Both Eric and Sara panicked. Sara blurted out, "Just let him go!"

The jig was up. Reynolds realized they were all on the same page now. He sneered at them. "No, can't really do that till we've had a chat."

Tyler yelled out, "It's him! it's him!"

"You don't know me! You can't come into a police station with wild accusations, boy," Reynolds told Tyler.

"I do know you," Tyler replied. "Remember the broken water fountain? You were pretending to drink from it and reached around the back to get something. I saw you. I told you it was broke."

Quickly, Reynolds had his gun at Tyler's head. His voice as steady as his hand, he tightened his grip around the boy. In a defiant tone, he spoke to Tyler. "There are millions of people in this city, kid; isn't it possible you were mistaken?" Reynolds felt confident that by applying the right pressure, he could get the young boy to recant his story.

Just then Jamison—along with Raskins, Matthews, and Gandy—barreled through the walkway from the elevator and stairwell area, guns drawn. All of them charged forward to Eric and Sara, and moved the Doussaints around the corner behind them as they kept their sidearms aimed at Reynolds.

Reynolds had already grabbed Tyler, turned him to face the detectives, thrown his arm around Tyler's waist and had placed the Glock against the right side of Tyler's head again. "Don't do something stupid," he sang out to the team of detectives and his boss. Jamison looked at Tyler for some recognition. His mouth was dry as he anticipated a standoff.

"Lay your guns down," Reynolds sternly insisted. The detectives stood firm. Webb, Davies, and Broussard arrived on the scene.

Jamison called out, "Reynolds, let the boy go."

Reynolds laughed and stood erect, picking Tyler up, holding him in front of his own body as a shield. He laughed again and repeated, "Put your guns down." The detectives knew by his laughter that this was a highly dangerous situation now. Reynolds had just told them he had nothing to live for.

Tyler started crying. Sara heard him from behind the corner and gasped, "Oh my Lord, no. Not now; not here," and she began to cry as well. Eric, frustrated at his inability to do anything, squeezed Sara's hands.

"Okay, okay, look," Jamison called out, "we will put our weapons down." He saw a couple of officers coming down from the top floor, circling in a bit from behind Reynolds as backup, so he slowly demonstrated his eagerness to lay down his gun. "C'mon, look; we're all putting our guns down." He gestured to his detectives nearest him to do the same. They did; their guns were lying there on the ground at parking deck level 4.

"Now kick them over to me," Reynolds yelled out. Jamison and the others did as he said. Reynolds turned left and right with Tyler in front of him. "The rest of them too," he stated, pointing his gun at the officers that had managed to circle in behind him.

"Stand down!" Jamison yelled out, and everyone heard the clattering and echo of guns against the concrete ramp.

"Please don't hurt him!" Sara screamed from behind the wall. She couldn't see anything that was going on; she only pictured the thin, young detective pointing his gun at Tyler.

"Now, everyone in front of me, face down!" Reynolds called out. He thought that as long as he threatened to kill the kid, they would have to comply and he'd be able to buy some time to get to his car and get away. The detectives moved in front of him, some getting down on their knees. "All the way down," Reynolds grunted. The detectives sprawled out on the ground in front of him and looked helplessly to Jamison, wondering whether they were going to lose either this confrontation, or Tyler, or both. Nolan and Johnson came running out and around the corner, but as they drew their weapons, they froze, stunned to see the entire team lying on the ground. "You too," Reynolds growled, "down!"

"Gene, what's going on? Don't do this, man," Nolan called out to his partner.

"Shut up and get down," Reynolds stated with newfound confidence, and he sneered outwardly at the threat of all these detectives and all their sidearms having been relinquished to his control. "No one make a move."

Jamison looked up. "You don't have to do this, son," he appealed to Reynolds. "Put your gun on me, Reynolds. He's a kid; let him leave." But Reynolds inched back and farther down the ramp. Tyler was frozen with fear and choked back tears.

The detectives were horrified, eyeing their fellow cop. All the team shared and meant to one another was evaporating right before their eyes. "Reynolds!" Jamison demanded, "Aim it at me. Let the kid go, and keep your gun on me." His voice was cracking with emotion as he could clearly see the dark resolve in Reynolds's face. He had never considered the possibility that Reynolds would be the one to make the demands today. His heart was racing as he desperately tried to appear calm and cool.

CHAPTER 57

THE SHOCK

Wynton and Raymond arrived in the parking garage and parked on level 3 on the ramp leading up to level 4, where Jamison's detectives were at a standoff. Standing up and stretching his back, Wynton casually walked over to Raymond's side of the car and shoved Raymond behind him, placing his finger on the front of his lips. He then gently and quietly closed Raymond's door, scrunched down, and pulled Raymond down beside him.

"What?" Raymond asked, disturbed at being pulled down.

"Shh, there's a guy with a gun to a kid's head up there."

"What?" Raymond peeked. "Shiieet, man, let's get outta here," he whispered.

"Can't walk away; the kid needs help." Wynton scooted toward the back bumper so he could see. Never taking his eyes off the shooter, Wynton said, "Get my gun from the glove compartment, and be quiet."

"E," Raymond whispered frantically, "you don't gotta be involved. Let's just escape down the ramp and call for more help. This is po-lice binness, not your binness."

"Most of the police are out clearing paths and running security drills for Obama's visit tomorrow. What's left of the police are up there," he said as he spied the situation. "They're running outta options. Get my gun," he said with authority.

"No," Raymond replied. "You ain' gotta be the one goes up there."

"Oh, that's it, huh? Everyone should walk away from situations when they have a choice to help?"

"Not everyone, just you."

"Ray, he's not going to suspect me. I can help change the situation, give him my car, maybe allow time for a sharpshooter to set up—something. Now please, give me my gun and be quiet about it."

Raymond retrieved the gun reluctantly and handed it to Wynton, shaking his head in disagreement with Wynton's intentions. Wynton tucked the gun into the back of his trousers and stepped out away from the cars. He put his hands up in the air and called out as he walked upward toward Reynolds, "Hey, buddy, maybe I can help. My car's right here."

Raymond, still hidden, whispered with rage, "Don't do it!"

Jamison looked at his detectives flanked to his right and then lifted his head and turned left toward Wynton, wondering what the hell he was doing.

Wynton called out again, "Obviously, if you have a gun on a child, you needa get away from something. Take me instead; I have a car right here." He walked closer and dropped his hands to his side.

"Stay back; stay where you are!" Reynolds called out to him. Wynton walked closer. "Keep your hands up," Reynolds told him. Wynton put his hands back up in the air.

"Hey, man, I'm just trying to help."

Raymond yelled out, "E!"

A detective, realizing it was Wynton Ellery, called out, "Ellery, stay back!"

Reynolds aimed his gun toward Wynton but continued to face Jamison, "Oh, he is another one of yours, is he?" Wynton pulled his gun to disarm Reynolds as he talked, while he was looking straight ahead at his chief. "Damn you!" Reynolds yelled at Jamison, and never turning to look, he fired his weapon at Wynton. As Wynton was hit, another shot rang out.

Wynton staggered momentarily and fell forward, struggling against the pain and searing heat in his midsection. His thoughts were a swirling tempest. He looked down and saw the bullet hole in his white linen shirt. It was framed by a circle of blood a few inches below his breastbone. The bullet had missed his heart but ripped through his stomach. He would survive for a few minutes as his stomach acids seeped into his chest cavity, slowly poisoning him from within.

The .45 slug caught Reynolds behind the ear, snapping his head sideways, choking his words in a bloody cough. His fingers released Tyler as he toppled forward, and his gun slipped through his hand as he clutched his throat, his life bleeding out at the top of his neck before he hit the pavement. A stunned silence lingered momentarily, and then there was a scurry of footsteps as officers flooded the ramp to retrieve their weapons.

Sara, upon hearing the gunfire, imagined Tyler being shot and jumped to her feet calling him as she rounded the corner. An officer nearest her told her to stay put, but she had already darted past him. Eric screamed after Sara, afraid she'd get caught in a line of fire. The detectives had already encircled the killer and were crouched in shooting stances with both hands on their weapons in case Reynolds came to and tried to put up one last fight.

Sara rushed to Tyler; Eric rushed to them both, embracing them and feeling overwhelmingly grateful. Jamison kicked Reynolds's gun away as he and Matthews jogged down to Wynton and Raymond. Jamison took Wynton's gun and checked the chamber; it was still fully loaded. "I saw him go down before he could shoot," Jamison stated anxiously. He then yelled back to his team of detectives to get the paramedics. He saw Raymond holding his brother and spun around to ask Matthews, "Where'd the other shot come from?"

Time slowed into a dreamlike state for everyone in the parking garage affected by the split-second decisions and reactions. Reynolds had squeezed the trigger and felt the kick of return fire. The pistol had discharged with a deafening roar, sending panic into the veins of the Doussaints, who feared Tyler's life was in jeopardy. Wynton's instinct to save a child had placed him in jeopardy.

Jamison turned to see his detectives and cops from the station's first floor scattered out midway between the fourth and fifth levels. Then, turning back, scanning down toward the darkened area by the curve up from level 3, he saw the captain step into the light. The police force, following Jamison's view, were stunned as their captain moved forward into the fluorescent lights and secured his firearm back in its holster.

Raymond was cradling his brother in his arms. Wynton had been opened up like a pomegranate, with blood collecting in the bowl of his stomach. The corridors of the ramp were still. Everyone was stunned by their captain's action, and their faces were transfixed, staring downhill toward Wynton. Raymond was whispering to him while his skin was warm and his eyes still blinking. Matthews rushed in between the two to lay Wynton flat on his back, and he lifted his legs up to Raymond and applied compression to the wound, where he was hemorrhaging.

Wynton motioned to Raymond with one finger to lean in. He felt light-headed and winced in pain, but he summoned all his faculties and strength to speak to his brother. His tone was light and breathy. "Strengthen your will" was all he could say.

"Got it, E, I really do, but you hold on. We gonna get you to the hospital and get you feeling better." Raymond shook with emotion. Wynton was cough-ing but determined to talk.

"Ray, I love you."

"E, you everything I love. Don't talk, man; just stay still."

Wynton's mouth opened and closed a couple of times without sound. It was sticky and dry, and he found it difficult to force words or swallow, but he tried to continue. "Make ..."

"He shouldn't talk," Matthews insisted. Raymond hushed his brother. The heavy fiber of death was sinking in on the bounty of flesh as Wynton drifted in and out of consciousness. Raymond held his breath at first, and then his composure broke and tears ran down his face. Even as he faced death, Wynton fearlessly reassured him. Wynton's body was becoming heavier as life was letting go.

"Don't, dogg; don't go, E," Raymond begged as he cried, still elevating his brother's legs. Then came the punishing, heavy-headed slobber of loss fattening in his throat, sputtering in teary strife from his gushing emotions searching for meaning. For a moment, he could not quiet himself. Storms were sweep-ing in, stripping him bare, whirling and scattering away every ounce of peace and freedom. He could see infinity in Wynton's paling skin and knew he was leaving. All that had rooted in Raymond was dying. His own body was useless as he held on to Wynton, holding tight to his bones, afraid they might split and splinter. Sara came up beside them and gasped, covering her mouth with both hands. Had Eric not been there to brace her, she would have fallen onto the pavement as well.

The shock hit everyone, leaving some too stricken to move, knowing an innocent bystander had surrendered his life in a volatile standoff. Others—struck by the cold, ruthless efficiency of Reynolds—moved away. It was over. He couldn't remain conscious. Wynton's hands fell lifeless to the garage floor, and he closed his eyes, never to open them again. His breathing stopped, his body weight slumped, and he was gone.

The paramedics came running with all their equipment and a board. They moved the surrounding officers away from Wynton and tried to revive him without success. A technician prodded his body with a stethoscope. No pulse. He quickly put a monitor on Wynton and ran a strip for the hospital. It showed asystole—no heartbeat. He looked over at Jamison and shook his head as he continued to work on Wynton. His partner, who was speaking on the phone with an ER doctor, motioned for him to stop and then came up beside him.

"The doc told us to call it," he softly said. The medic stopped with a sigh, looked at his watch, and pronounced Wynton Ellery dead at 4:12 p.m.

Raymond lost the best part of his world. He felt like a fish floundering on land, skinned and swollen, raw from the tug and reel. Where, he wondered, was the precious water that could save him, the blue weight that could wash away time and emotion, the elusive watery tomb that could consume him? Pain anchored his heart as he recalled Wynton's last words. Still, he let those last words seep deep into his being and soul, balancing the immediate loss of his brother with the impact of his message.

Even as Raymond tapped at the door of dark despair, restless, falling, disturbing memories pressing forward from within—words that could transform his thoughts, and answers that could surrender his mouth—that which had drummed his spirit began greening. It was as if something divine had laid hands on him—as if something had been passed from Wynton to Raymond after all, because there in that small space of loss and pain, in the place of death, without anyone noticing, he began to change. Strength radiated through him like a beam of light, clearing away all his misgivings. It kept him in the present moment, and in his grief at that moment, Raymond took this strength, this surreal presence, like a lightning rod.

His perception of Wynton's faithfulness, unrelenting optimism, and quiet, intuitive approach to life swept through his body, exploding in his mind. He could feel it and could sense a change; something he was encountering was altering him. Faith and courage—these were the hinges that opened and closed the world of Wynton, who offered no resistance. Emotionally, Raymond wanted to curl up into his brother and sob. Mentally, spiritually, he was filling with something greater than himself. An unexplainable surge was replacing a darkened center with some sort of perfect calm, restoring him, transforming loss with presence. In that miraculous moment, he was committing to change his brooding instability, to live moving forward for his brother with all the depth and integrity he could muster.

"I'm sorry; we're too late," one of the paramedics said to Raymond as he laid a hand on his shoulder.

Jamison pointed to the throng of detectives. "Got another body over there." The paramedics threw their instruments into their bags and rushed over to where Reynolds lay. The paramedics checked him, but it was already evident by Reynolds's fixed eyes that he was dead. Eric's and Sara's eyes were wet, and their faces were reddening from holding back their shock and sadness.

They, like the rest of the squad, felt defeated and drained, humbled by the risk Wynton had taken.

Raymond sat numbed, listening to the mumbling voices around him. Sara lifted Tyler up for Eric to hold, and she knelt to hug Raymond. As she held him in her arms, she wept. "He was a beautiful man," she said as she cried.

Raymond hugged her back, holding her tightly, whispering "Thank you" for her kind and correct words about his brother. They embraced in a long, loving hug.

"He sacrificed his life for my son," she stated, surprised at Wynton's unimaginable choice and that she had just called Tyler her son. She smiled through her tears, knowing expectations would rise in the wake of this man's death and the loss of a vibrant, engaging soul. It was one thing to understand the notion of sacrifice for another; it was quite something else to witness firsthand.

Wynton offered the belief in hope and possibilities to everyone he came across. In the end, amid the world's restlessness and madness, he gave the ultimate example of love, and how love can color one's life and change the nature and direction of one's reach.

Raymond's life had been flat, hollow. Sara's had been tirelessly retrospective, awash in pain. Though waning, Eric's need for reassurance kept him tediously searching for answers to missteps in his life and the lives of those around him. Tyler was frightened and wore his loss like a badge. This critical life-losing moment moved them all to more deeply appreciate the honesty in love, and its incredible and beautiful generosity. Having been jaded, they could now see love's limitless views. Each of them affected by this tragedy was sensing a shift in his or her level of feeling and thinking. They felt confident that whenever they might encounter dark times in their minds or hearts in the future, the image and memories of Wynton Ellery would sustain them.

CHAPTER 58

GOING ON

"Time don't bring no relief," Raymond said. "That line that time heal everything is a doggone lie. My brutha knew that too. Is change of attitude that melt the pain away." He was showing his new girlfriend the pictures of Belinda, Wynton, and Keisha that he kept out. "They keep me alive; they tells me it storms, but they is healing in love." He held up the pewter frame that protected his favorite photo of Wynton in white, fingered it lovingly, and then set it back down next to Wynton's dog-eared Bible. He was alone, the lone Ellery; he was not the enigma of theology Wynton embodied, but seeds had been planted. Seeds of reconciliation had been pushed deep inside, forgiveness had rooted, and love had begun to grow. Where darkness had overwhelmed his chance to strengthen, he was now blooming with restoration, true radiance, and authentic resilience as he found his footing and nourishment in a new, fertile soil. He was no longer the skeptical, arrogant young man suffering the weight of the human condition. Raymond concluded, "They is no absolute darkness; love is too transforming."

"Who is this?" she asked as she pointed to a frame which held the image of Sara and Eric Doussaint and Tyler. He thought about how love between a few had become his salvation.

"They part of my family," he said contently. "They over in Mandeville. I will take you to meet 'em someday soon." He extended his arm in a gentlemanly way, allowing her to move on in past the hallway. "Wanna see the rest of my house?" he asked her politely.

"Yes," she answered, and she moved into the great room. "I can see why this place is so special to you."

"Is the aura, is his spirit. I mean, my house now, and it lets in good amount of light, but E's spirit shining on in here," he claimed with a winning smile. "You hungry?" Before she could answer, Raymond was already ushering her to the couch. "You get comfortable while I fix us a little something for now." She sat down, and Raymond danced his way into the kitchen.

Farther northeast, across Lake Pontchartrain, the Doussaints were concluding a meeting. Every person seated at the conference table signed paperwork and shook hands. Sara turned from Eric and the social worker to bend down and hug Tyler. Her delicate, tender eyes gleamed at this young boy as though he were her firstborn. Where her lips had been parched, hiding gravestones in her mouth, they now smiled, sweet and sun-ripened, the mothy history released and replaced by fresh, berry-like laughter. The rattling bones of brokenness gave way to the skipping slip of a girl returning with curious gladness.

"That's it, kiddo," she said, tearing up joyfully at the notion that Tyler would forever be a part of their family. "You're stuck with us now, sweetie." She rubbed his back and straightened his shirt.

"Yay!" Tyler replied as he grinned first at Sara and then at Eric.

Eric caught Tyler's eye and said "Yay!" just as Tyler had. He then moved closer, leaning across the table to give Tyler a high five. Tyler slapped his hand enthusiastically, and Eric shook his hand wildly, blowing on it, pretending the high five from Tyler was so powerful that it hurt and burned. That made Tyler grin all the more. "Come on, partner," Eric said as he put out his other hand. "Let's go home." Tyler clasped his hand and reached with his free hand to find Sara. She was thanking all the proprietors but quickly stepped up to fold into Tyler's grip, which had been motioning her to his side. It was a grand moment of heading to the elevators as a threesome—as a family.

Back in New Orleans, where so much violence and confusion sliced into the lives of many, Jamison was hounding his detectives to get their paperwork to him by the close of the day. The captain came by, rounding the corner in his dress blues as usual. "Cap'n," Jamison addressed him as he lit a cigarette.

"Mick," Hughes replied.

Jamison exhaled a flurry of smoke. "Heard you're not going to wait it out."

"Nah, what's the point. Leaving now feels right considering the change in here."

"Yeah, it's been a shake-up all right. You going straight to the island?"

Hughes chuckled as Jamison took another deep drag. His shoulders moved up and down from his thinning frame as he laughed. Jamison thought it made him look like a marionette, and he wondered which was worse: picturing the captain sneering his usual racist, misogynist, homophobic sneer, or this frighteningly awkward laugh.

"Do I look like an island guy?" Hughes asked as he pushed his coat sleeve and shirt cuff up his arm a bit to reveal his aging, ghostly-pale skin. "Just because I inherited property doesn't mean I have to keep it." He nudged Jamison as if they'd been longtime buddies. "My brother was the sun nut, not me. I'll sell it, invest, maybe donate the money to charity in my brother's name. Where I live now is fine with me." Jamison nodded, considering what the captain had just said and knowing how stubbornly he held on to his habitual ways. "You?" Hughes asked.

"Yeah, hey, same ole same ole. We got a new recruit coming in this week to pair up with Nolan. Cassidy's his name. Nolan knows him from the academy, says he's a good guy." Jamison paused, putting the cigarette to his lips and pressing them around the clean white filter. He inhaled and exhaled. "Pretty much the same crew," he continued, smoke spewing out from his nose as he talked. "Webb and Davies moved over to Vice; gonna miss their insight. But still got Johnson, Gandy, Rass, Broussard, Nolan, and Donna hanging around."

"Johnson, still?" Hughes said. "He's got to be nearing retirement soon."

"Yeah, maybe another year," Jamison replied. "Hate to see him leave; he's a solid detective ... but Christ, can't wait for that damned old typewriter to be thrown out."

———————— • ————————

Up in Baton Rouge in his office on Third Street, Jack Doussaint was meeting with Ed and a couple of Louisiana congressmen. "I tell you," he exaggerated, "the Mexicans aren't just affecting Arizona and Texas. They're moving in on us as well."

"Money and power being gobbled up by the cartel as we speak," Ed reiterated.

"So what does that mean for us?" one of the two young congressmen asked.

"It means you need to commit your money and energy to shoring up loose ends," Jack said sternly. "We've got multimillion-dollar realty and computer buyouts going on. These guys are ruthless, well-trained; hell, we trained them ourselves here in the US, and they are spreading beyond drugs to bank accounts. They're spilling incestuously into our state." Jack was flushed as his temper grew. "We don't have time to wait, fellas," he pressed.

"What can we do?" asked the second congressman.

"Well, first I've got a name, Imon Durrell, and a location along the coast in Matamoros. Consider him your enemy and a link to more of your thieving, murdering enemies," he offered.

The congressmen looked at each other, "Yes," one said.

"We can look into this," the second congressman said convincingly to the first.

"You take Durrell out first, and the other cockroaches will reveal themselves as they scatter to take his place," Ed suggested, and he looked to Jack, who was winking and smiling. He held up his drink as if to toast Ed for a job well done.

"Yeah, they can do this," Jack stated. He then gulped at his liquor, placed the glass down on his custom cabinetry, and reached out to shake hands with the new congressmen. "A pleasure doing business with you," he said, patting them each on the back as he showed them the door. He stopped to reach inside his jacket pocket and pull out two cigars, each with a hundred-dollar bill wrapped around it. He handed over the money-wrapped cigars and said, "They're the finest Cuba has to offer, and there're plenty more where these came from—a lot more!"

Raymond returned to the couch with two plates of chicken and rice. He set the steaming plates onto the coffee table and then reached into one pocket to pull out two forks, and into another pocket for the paper napkins. His date snickered a bit. "Sweet tea?" he asked her.

"Yes, please," she responded with a smile. Raymond made some crashing noises in the kitchen and then came back to the couch with two glasses of tea clinking with ice. After setting them down, he reached for the remote and flopped onto the couch.

"Let's see, Discovery?" he asked as the power clicked on.

She scrunched her face a bit. "Um, no."

"BET?" he asked.

"Okay," she complied with a smile.

"Yes!" Raymond exclaimed, thrusting his arms up in the air in victory. There was a blessing in the midst of utter loss, in the profound moment when blindness turned into insight, modest connection into communion, narratives into sacred stories. Here was the gentle irony of standing in the place of another and finding that the unexpected transformation of his family, his own existence, which had been good, had now become nearly perfect.

NEW ORLEANS

We looked not for cheerful change,
No blankets, or tents, or cots thrown,
No rations cold and raw,
No water,
Not even sleep.

The dome amassed,
Burst open at the seams
With individual storms raging,
Elemental issues like shrapnel
Scattering the living,
The dead, untouched, as witness
For those who were battle-weary,
Riddled by age or grief or illness.

This was the collective legacy,
Streets teeming with people
That were silenced,
Desperation, the old grief-stricken friend
That came to thousands,
For those who drowned
Or those who survived
But lost everything.

Life floated facedown,
Anguish replaced homes
And entire neighborhoods
As the rest of the world
Watched in horror,
The human drama on TV,
The destruction so vast,
So complete.

Fierce orders came,
Munitions and men
Who would steady the human plight
Amid the apocalyptic floodwaters,
Who would restore order
And retrieve the poor,
Who would, without diversion,
Reduce the calamity created,
Assuring the public of "disaster relief."

Lifelines that hung from helicopters
As a last hope
Could not always fly,
And down came the storm beat,
To graveyard stones,
And down came the rooftop,
Grim-faced folk,
Despite enduring the flushing soil,
Despite hearts holding on,
The morning after, gave way.

When it was over,
Long after August 29,
Long after Katrina died,
Dull-brown waterlines
Cut across houses and buildings,
A brown haze hung above the city
Like a pestilent cloud,
Suffering people
Revved up impossible chants,
Ignited The Second Line,
Vying for validation.

Oh, but the press
And a "just" government
With sweeping wings of compassion
Dismissed the tyranny of poverty

And images that angered a nation,
Instead repeated the political rhetoric
That America's resolve had not weakened,
That we had learned the lessons of levees.

Rise, New Orleans,
Rise up.

(2005)

AUTHOR BIO

Janet Johnson Anderson has won numerous literary awards as a new author and has been an award-winning poet for several decades. She enjoyed a lengthy career in advertising and has remained a marketing consultant and freelance writer. She is an advocate for the special needs population and for women and girls worldwide where there is poverty and injustice.

Ms. Anderson visited New Orleans each year for seven years after Hurricane Katrina devastated the area. She was deeply moved by the destruction and lingering anguish felt by so many, and she wished to lend a voice to the emotional toll of people facing great personal loss.

The floodwaters are long gone, but Ms. Anderson's novel reveals signs of Katrina's lasting effects, comparing the hopeful repair from storm damage to the renewal we seek in our relationships and within the whole of humanity.

Born and raised along Chicago's North Shore, Ms. Anderson now lives in Huntsville, Alabama, is married, and has two grown daughters. Her books reflect community and global needs and are intended to inspire others to lend a hand and heart in the world.

jjabooks.com
facebook.com/jjabooks